What a journey it has been for E̶... she happened to see ITV's Lorraine Kelly announce the search for the next big thing in contemporary women's fiction. She sent in her 1,000 words and beat over 2,000 entries, winning the competition live on national TV on Valentine's Day. Her books have since gone on to be published in fifteen countries worldwide.

Away from the ITV sofa, she is currently surviving a hefty Victorian renovation in Staffordshire with husband Jim, their three boys and badly-behaved Hungarian Vizsla.

Perfect Strangers

Erin Knight

ONE PLACE. MANY STORIES

This novel is entirely a work of fiction. The names, characters and incidents portrayed in it are the work of the author's imagination. Any resemblance to actual persons, living or dead, events or localities is entirely coincidental.

HQ
An imprint of HarperCollins*Publishers* Ltd
1 London Bridge Street
London SE1 9GF

This paperback edition 2018

1
First published in Great Britain by
HQ, an imprint of HarperCollins*Publishers* Ltd 2018

ISBN: 978-0-00-817985-4

MIX
Paper from
responsible sources
FSC
www.fsc.org
FSC™ C007454

This book is produced from independently certified FSC paper
to ensure responsible forest management.

For more information visit: www.harpercollins.co.uk/green

Printed and bound in Great Britain by
CPI Group (UK) Ltd, Croydon, CR0 4YY

For Sarah, Emma, Kirsty and Steph, who loved our girl too.

I

The first lie Isobel told her parents was that she was going away to forget it all.

She lifted her face to the sun beating down on the armchair in which she'd stationed herself in the corner of the café window, the worn leather warm and hospitable beneath her forearms. The tourist board's website had promised *hospitality*. Other promises included *a flourishing cosmopolitan atmosphere* and *some of the best surf and lobster in the British Isles!* Fallenbay looked good in writing, but then Isobel knew better than to be suckered in by anything she read online. If she'd learnt nothing else, she'd learnt that much.

Fallenbay . . . *Bay of the Fallen*. Aptly named by the pirates who'd once besieged it. Now Isobel's holiday destination. Her time out. *A pretty distraction*. She'd pitched it to her parents with those very words. They'd tripped right off her tongue and into her mother's hopeful ears, easily as a damning rumour. Fallenbay was a just lucky hit. A random spot on the map Isobel had stuck her pin into. That was the second lie she told.

Isobel straightened her back and drained the last of the tea gone undrinkably cold while she'd been carefully observing the world passing by the windows of Coast, one of the harbour's many eateries jostling for position beneath an intense blue sky. It was almost too bright to look outside, but still she watched.

Come back refreshed, Isobel. Renewed! Uncle Keith's job offer will still be here waiting for you. You were wasted in teaching anyway, love. Her mum had jollied this encouraging prospect around a chewed lip while they'd all pretended that proofreading orders of services at Uncle Keith's printers wasn't a cataclysmic sidestep from Head of English at St Jude's secondary. The bottom line was, Uncle Keith wouldn't ask for references.

She took a breath and cleared her thoughts. A young mottled seagull bobbed along the pavement outside the café, eyes beady and accusatory. Isobel looked out over the ocean instead.

The aroma of newly warming pastries reached through the Coast. Metal kitchen equipment clanked and rattled in the background. The coming summer would be glorious here, and Isobel could stay that long if she wanted to; she had time and money to burn now. The universe's idea of a laugh. All that effort and hard work to save for their mortgage deposit. Months of overtime and cheap food. Nathan's motivational speeches when all Isobel wanted was a half-term in Mexico. *Renting is so temporary!* Turned out, so were they. Isobel scratched Nathan's name from her head and let her lungs fill and release. *Okey-doke, Isobel . . . you're here. Now what?*

She didn't have to go through with it. Home was only two hours away. Two hours and she could be back in her parents' semi, penning hopeless red circles around job adverts, or filling the spot left by Uncle Keith's last tea girl.

The growl of a flashy little coupé across the promenade knocked her thoughts nicely off course. The driver confidently nipped into the last parking space beside the ocean look-outs, interrupting the view she'd been sporadically enjoying of a lonely sailboat marooned from the world. The driver hopped out, rounding the meaty nose of his sports car, and Isobel watched the thirty-something casually stride towards the sandy, bleached decking running up to the café doors. Perhaps he was older. A youthful forty-something with a nice, stress-free existence and resulting unhaggard complexion. He might've held her attention in her former life – Nathan shared a similar blend of chiselled features and casual corporate composure – but she'd already lost interest, her pen retracing the same letters over the notepad lying expectantly on the table in front of her.

BASE CAMP 1

Her hands felt clammy. She could do this. She *would* do it. She just had to take her time, decide on her next step. Just like Jenny said.

Baby steps, Isobel. One at a time. You feel you've a moun-tain to climb, let's break that big, horrible bugger down into base camps, shall we? Now, Isobel . . . what are your goals? What's waiting for you at Base Camp 1?

Therapists loved analogies. Isobel could've pulled a great lesson plan together for her Year 7s just borrowing from Jenny's endless repertoire of similes and metaphors, only she didn't have any Year 7s now. *Baby steps.* Anything was possible long term – getting back to work was absolutely realistic. Isobel hadn't believed that any more than Jenny had.

A sharp voice shattered her thoughts. 'Evie! Put down that mobile phone and tell me what I've done to this nightmarish till again, it's spitting receipts!'

The pretty teenager hovering behind the counter had the same sunkissed curls as her mother. They both smiled a greeting as the man with the coupé made it to the welcoming display of pastries and vintage-style coffee-grinding equipment at the counter. The woman who'd served Isobel, with the wide smile and violently swinging earrings, pulled a pencil from her own piled up curls. She jabbed at the till with it as if poking a dead animal for signs of life. 'Morning, Jon! Give us a sec, I've flummoxed the only thing back here I absolutely can*not* manage without.'

'Thanks a lot, Mum.'

'Sorry, Evie, but my mental arithmetic really is hideous. This flipping till!'

Isobel tuned out their conversation. She rubbed clammy hands over her jeans and tried blowing the tension away, the way Sophie had shown her two nights ago while she'd packed her holdall and committed to climbing that mountain. *Listen to me, Is, I know what I'm talking about. I delivered Ella in the back of Mum's Nissan, I'm the master of steady breathing. If you feel panicky, blow!* Sophie had finished demonstrating the Lamaze technique before reverting to chewing her nails, recapping all the reasons Isobel shouldn't leave.

Soph hated all this, but she'd like Coast at least. Sophie was into industrial light fittings and the beach-house look. She'd tried something similar at their parents' semi. *I want Sophie to feel at home, love*, their mum had argued with Dad. *Let her decorate the conservatory, this is our daughter and granddaughter's home now too.* Just while she worked off the store card balances that had seen her default on enough rent payments to trigger the eviction notice. Sophie would learn one day. Impulse cost.

Isobel traced the view stretching over the endless Atlantic and back down over the intimate clusters of gallerias and boutique bistros nearly enclaving the lobstermen working away on the trawlers. So far Fallenbay was living up to its online reputation. Like Sophie, their folks would love Coast too, would love Fallenbay. They would love it, but they would never know. Not that Ella could buy a four-scooper from the beach's ice-cream hut or that Coast felt more like a cosy lookout point than an eatery (the universe having another laugh). They would never know because when the time came for truths, there would be nothing to tempt the Hedleys to visit this place, the bay of the fallen. Which was good. Because Fallenbay wasn't a place to make memories. It was the place to bury them.

'Ladies! Beautiful morning, isn't it? Americano please. Woah, flapjack's looking good, Cleo. Can I get a slice, for Sarah and Max too?'

Cleo hoped he didn't mistake the flush in her cheeks for schoolgirl blushing. She always blushed a little for Jonathan Hildred. It was completely involuntary, like one of those hiccupping fits she sometimes suffered, or a flickery eyelid. She definitely didn't fancy Jon – or no more than was acceptable for your best friend's fiancé anyway. Jon just had that Daniel Craig thing going on, and a grin that could send grown women back to their teenage selves with little more than a compliment about a flapjack. He was going to look phenomenal in his wedding suit; Cleo could see him now, adjusting his cuffs at the altar, Bond style.

'Sarah and Max on the beach?' she trilled. *Fancy schmancy.* Of course she didn't fancy Jon. Half the time she wondered if she was more excited about Sarah marrying Jon next summer than Sarah herself.

'Nope, meeting them in half an hour at the . . .' Jon dramatically fanned his hands, '. . . Marine Dinosaur Exhibition!'

'Where?'

'The aquarium. Max's running an obsession with Godzilla.

Sarah's hoping to find something green and scaly in there to float his boat.'

'I'll get Mr Hildred's Americano, Mum.' Evie's eyes were wide and lovely, and caked in too much bloody make-up again.

'No! Don't move from that spot until I can ring up an order, Eves. Kids are so techno-savvy nowadays, aren't they, Jon?' She banged the coffee grinds from the filter and a baby startled at the noise. Sam was always telling her she was too heavy-handed. This from an ex-boxer with knuckles like knees.

Evie made something bleep. 'There,' she declared. 'I came, I saw, I conquered.'

'Julius Caesar,' nodded Jon. Cleo fought not to mirror his smile.

Evie offered her smile freely. She looked like Cleo's little girl again when she smiled like that. Cleo felt a burst of pride then resumed mourning the daughter who'd moved aside so this tempestuous, sulky, make-up-abusing pain-in-the-bum could steal her spot at the dinner table. She gave Evie a quick shoulder squeeze. 'Well done, trouble. Heading for a B in maths too next month, aren't you, my brilliant girl? There you go, Jon. Americano. Godzilla, did you say? You know, if Max wants to meet a grouchy green reptilian, I have a lounge-lizard with a snotty nose at home he can try shifting off my sofa.'

'Mum,' Evie groaned. 'Dad can't help getting ill when he's laying bricks in the rain.'

'Oh, Evie, I'm only playing.' She wasn't. 'But I could've done with him looking at that microwave before he caught the lurgy. Keep your eye on it today, I think the timer's on the blink.'

Jon handed Evie his money. 'Makes for a nice change hearing one of our young adults defending their parent, Cleo. Usually it's the parents who won't hear a bad word. Loyalty's admirable, right, Evie? Shows maturity.'

'Right, Mr Hildred,' beamed Evie.

'And a B in GCSE maths? Great stuff. You know there are extra evening revision classes if you fancied really stretching yourself? Maybe see about pushing for an A if you're up for a challenge? Elodie Inman-Holt's enrolled; you two are pals aren't you, you could buddy-up?'

Cleo felt a mild stab of competition. On Evie's behalf, obviously. Why would Elodie even need extra classes? She was fluent in everything already. Languages . . . music . . . Elodie was like her God-awful mother Juliette, fluent in bloody life. And just to make things worse – okay, probably the part that really got up Cleo's nose – Juliette's daughter was one of the few teenage girls at that high school who didn't feel compelled to daub herself with those horrendous eyebrows Evie couldn't slather on garishly enough. Harry had recently made the mistake of comparing his twin sister to Sam the Eagle from *The Muppets*. Evie had given him a dead leg for it.

'Are you running revision classes, Mr H?'

Jon patted his hard, flat stomach. 'Not a chance, Evie. I need my evenings to keep the middle-aged spread at bay.' Cleo could vaguely remember Sam's washboard stomach. Vaguely.

'You look fine to me, Mr Hildred.' Was Evie blushing?

'Evie and some of the girls saw you surfing down at The Village a few weeks ago, Jon. I think you have a fan club,' teased Cleo.

'Muum, shut *up*!'

'What was it again? *Gorgeous . . . well fit . . .*'

'Oh my God, Mum, that was Cassie, not me! You are *so* embarrassing.'

Jon scratched his nose. '*Well fit,* huh? Good to know, Evie.'

Cleo chuckled under her breath. *Crap.* Lorna Brooks was heading for the counter wielding something green and organic-looking in a Tupperware tub, Marnie crying that hungry baby cry from her hip. The school mothers all adored Jonathan Hildred, and Lorna would stand here all day gushing over him while Marnie screamed the place down.

Cleo swung into action. 'Your change, Jon. Say hi to Godzilla! Ooh, and tell Sarah I'll call her later. I've seen some am-az-ing canapés in *Beautiful Bride* mag. Lorna! What can I get for you?'

Lorna jiggled in that way fraught new mothers on three hours' sleep jiggle their babies. Except Marnie was closer to nine months and already sturdy enough that she made Lorna, with her skinny arms and delicate pale chest, look like a waify big sister. Lorna readjusted her floaty neck scarf and Cleo braced herself. The woman always seemed to be on the brink of asking something profound but difficult to follow about global warming or, worse, the exact ingredients of Coast's 'organic' biscuits. (The oats were organic, the butter was not. It had given Cleo sleepless nights.)

'Cleo, help! Any chance you could throw Marnie's lunch in your microwave? She's so hungry at the mo, I can't fill her up.'

Marnie gnawed on her mother's shoulder. *Lunch? At 10am?* 'Have you tried steak and chips?' She was joking, obviously. Lorna's clearly wasn't a meat and deep-fried-anything kind of household.

'I daren't try her on anything too challenging, Cleo. Is that brie and cranberry baguette vegetarian? No bacony bits or surprises?' Lorna reached a pale freckled hand over the counter and presented Marnie's pot.

Evie had already been sucked back into the beam of her smartphone. 'Evie?' Cleo jabbed her with Marnie's lunch. 'Completely meat-free, Lorna. Would you like it toasted?'

Lorna glanced towards Jon, talking to the blonde girl still sitting on her own near the window. 'No thanks, Cleo. It's a real sun trap in that window, don't think I could manage a hot sandwich.'

Blinds. There was another job Sam hadn't gotten around to. Marnie cooed at the sight of Lorna's baguette. The little girl shared her mother's pale skin, and it was hot in that window; maybe they'd be more comfortable if they sat over by—

A loud bang exploded behind them.

'Evie! I told you to watch that thing today!'

'I did! I only put it on for twenty seconds! Hotspots and babies . . . I know the twenty-second rule, Mum.'

Cleo launched towards the microwave. 'If you would just stop goggling that flipping phone and concentrate!'

'The timer counted up instead of down, Mum. I swear, look . . . '

A green crime scene waited inside the microwave. Customers were craning necks. 'Lorna, I'm so sorry. Marnie's lunch . . .'

Lorna grimaced. 'It's fine, Cleo. That was the last of

Mummy's homemade pesto pasta, wasn't it, Marnie-Moo? But it's fine. I have milk, she can have milk, until we get home.'

'I'm so sorry, but the microwave . . . I won't be able to warm a bottle.'

Lorna was already weaving through the tables back to her own spot in the window. 'We have it covered, Cleo.' She settled herself into her chair and began fumbling at her blouse.

'Oh. Sure.' Cleo's eyes left Lorna's pale bosom and clocked a couple of the kids on the terrace outside stop inhaling their food just long enough to grin at each other. She glared through the glass. 'Keep that up, you little sods, and you can clear off.' Getting Harry and Evie to feed from her had been all kinds of awful. Hell hath no fury like a nipple with mastitis.

Evie tensed. 'Uh-oh, geriatric storm brewing, table four.'

Cleo recognised something in the posture of the man at the table neighbouring Lorna's. That incensed-embarrassed-unreasonable look that Cleo had once seen in a lunching corporate's face just before she'd been dispatched from the department store's restaurant to the ladies' changing rooms. *The manager thinks you'll be more comfortable somewhere private, madam.* Her neck burned at the memory. Harry and Evie's need for sustenance had got in the way of a grown man's need to finish his jacket potato without having to wrestle any of life's big questions, such as whether or not boobs really were just for groping.

The woman at table 4, face grey and puckered, twisted in her chair to face Lorna. 'My brother doesn't know where to look!'

'Sorry?' blinked Lorna.

Cleo bristled. 'Right.'

Evie caught Cleo's elbow 'Mum! What are you doing?'

'I'm going to offer Lorna a free drink and a seat out of that blazing sun. Then I'm going to inform table four that Coast welcomes breast-feeding mothers, even if they are members of Juliette Inman-Holt's PFA cult.'

She stalked around the counter, her bottom accidentally clipping two chairs on the way, but she didn't care. 'Lorna? Sorry to interrupt, I was just wondering, would you and Marnie like to use the new sofas? It's cooler over there, with no customers who—'

Lorna reared like a snake, eyes wide and wild. 'No customers to watch my baby feeding, is that it? Consuming the food Mother Nature intended for her?' Lorna's breast yanked free of Marnie's lips, Marnie's protestation immediate.

Cleo opened her mouth but her voice abandoned her, Lorna's boob staring straight at her, the gypsy blouse risen defiantly over the top of its fullness.

Lorna stood. 'It's alright my five-year-old son has to look at filthy girly mags every time I take him to the newsagents, isn't it? Absolutely fine when he flicks a music channel on that hordes of disco bimbos shake their thonged backsides at him? But . . .' Lorna cupped a hand to her mouth . . . 'Good God! Someone call the modesty police if a mother nurses her child. Well I've got news for you, Cleo Roberts.' Lorna's face had gone quite red. 'My daughter has a right to feed freely! I have a right to use my breasts!'

3

Isobel startled at the sound of the woman behind the counter banging away at the coffee machine. A baby began to cry over near the other window. She felt a wave of purpose wash through her, then noted the *Free Wifi* sign framed and hanging on the far brick wall like a gift waiting to be stolen. All those thoughts swelled somewhere at the bottom of her like a rising threat. The doubt. The ridiculousness of her goals.

She clasped her writing pad like a religious scripture.

Base Camp 1. Simple enough. *Home.* Home was Base Camp 1.

She scribbled the next few lines of writing as if indenting them into the page made them more achievable somehow.

2 - Job
3 - Friends
4 - Partner/Family
5 - Reputation
6 -

The pen flicked free of her grasp, skittering to the floor.

'Whoops, nearly.' A pair of expensive deck shoes arrived where Isobel reached. Their owner scooped up her biro and offered it back to her with a smile. She noticed it now, his boyish handsomeness, but still it didn't matter. She mustered a polite smile in return.

'Thanks.'

'No problem. A woman after my own heart.'

'Sorry?' He was older than Isobel but only a decade or so, and in that way that seemed to benefit the male sex and leave the females worrying about crows' feet and dermal fillers.

He nodded at her notepad. 'A list-maker. The world is divided into us and them, you know. The list-makers and the billionaires, according to Forbes.'

Isobel grimaced. She would definitely be worrying about crows' feet one day. Probably very soon. 'Sorry, I don't follow.'

'Forbes. According to them, the ultra-successful tend not to make lists. I can't function without them myself. Good luck with yours, maybe you'll buck the trend?' Isobel watched his eyes travel to the tabletop. Oh no, was he? Bugger, he was, he was skim-reading her list. She fought against slapping a hand over her pad like a child hiding the answers to a test and glugged another mouthful of tepid tea instead. 'Looks pretty aspirational. Hope you get to tick it all off soon.'

'Thanks.'

'I moved to Fallenbay with similar goals. It's a great place.' Isobel went with another smile. 'See you then.'

'Bye.' Her breathing relaxed as soon as he turned. She studied her list, the blank spot waiting next to Base Camp 6. Was it a base camp? Or was it the summit? What was it she was hoping to achieve here in Fallenbay exactly? A Happily Ever After? She was thinking on this point very carefully when something blew up in the kitchen.

'Evie! I told you to watch that thing today!'

Isobel stopped listening to the crisis over the exploding microwave. She was zoned out. Focused. Determined again.

Home. Job. Friends. Partner/Family. Reputation.

It was an aspirational list, he was right. It was just missing one final and integral point. Item 6. She penned it in without hesitation and a wave of calmness washed over her. If Sophie was going to watch her go down this route, then this would be Isobel's consolation prize. The best she could shoot for. The second summit. This would be what she wouldn't leave this shiny, clean, brochure-ready town without having first crossed off her list.

She clamped her pen between her fingers.

~~Base Camp 6.~~
SUMMIT: Criminal record.

4

'Muuum? I can't see, this water is dirty, I can't see!'

'You're breathing all over the glass, Maxy. Look,' Sarah grinned and pointed Max's rolled-up activity sheet, 'there's your nose print.'

Max drummed his finger against the tank. 'How is Pete the Pleth-io-thaur going to fit into this tank though, Mummy? When they are bigger than our house?'

Sarah's heart leapt for the occasional lisp Max had adopted. It only caught here and there, she would be robbed of it altogether once his big teeth came through. She swept the blonde hair from Max's eyes. He could be a poster child for Fallenbay's surf culture. People were always mistaking him for Jon's child. Unlike Will, Max looked nothing like their father. Yet. Will had been blonder at five too though. In a heartbeat he'd become a teenager, Patrick's dark waves steadily trampling Sarah's genes into submission. Will had inherited most of his dad's brooding features now; they were all Patrick Harrison had bothered leaving of himself for his children to hang on to.

'I wish Will came to the aquarium,' sighed Max. 'I need a piggyback so I can see in this tank.'

'You know, you're pretty lucky having your very own

fifteen-year-old, Maxy.' Max was the centre of the Harrison-Hildred household, everything seemed to orbit him like a crudely evolved planetary system. Football tournaments, swimming lessons, Sarah, Jon, Will – each spinning about Max at differing rates of significance. Max's footings were solid; it was Will always on the periphery. Why was it so tricky? Fathoming out a rhythm that worked equally for the four of them? It felt like bobbing for apples sometimes: the closer Sarah tried moving Jon and the boys towards a common centre, the further away Will bobbed.

You'll get him back, darling! her mother had reassured. *He's a teenager, let him get his angst out of his system.* Only, Will wasn't showing any angst. She'd quite like for Will to have a blow out, break something, slam a few doors. Instead of always being on the other side of one.

You're looking a gift horse in the mush! Cleo had snorted over their breakfast at Coast last week. *Be glad Will's not into skimpy clothes and warpaint. Have you seen Evie's eyebrows lately? I'm not kidding, Sar, I'm thinking of hiding her stash. Why can't I have a normal teenager? Who does alco-pops or ciggies? Why does mine have to do kohl?*

Sarah felt a tug on her sleeve. Max steered her to the next exhibit. Maybe she should be more grateful for Will's nonchalance instead of analysing it like a mad scientist, pinning it on all the change she was inflicting on him. The house move. The wedding. The intricacies of a second marriage.

Her stomach lurched. It did that rather a lot lately. *You are not pregnant*, she reassured herself. *You're just a liar.*

'Mummy, you're ringing.'

'Careful, Max, you'll pull my arm off.' She fumbled through

her bag, 'Maybe it's Will, changing his mind about meeting us?' It would be nice knowing where Will was spending any of his free time nowadays. She glanced at the caller ID, flicked off the volume and slid the phone into her jacket pocket.

'Was it Will?' Great orbs of light and shadow slid from the aquarium walls over Max's hopeful face.

'Nope. Only the estate agents, kiddo. Today's a family day, they can wait.'

A new vibration thrummed over her chest. Resistance was futile. 'Just a second, Max. They probably want to organise the For Sale sign. Hello?'

'Hello, Mrs Hildred?'

She forgave him his mistake. Mothers in their mid-to late-thirties normally were married, weren't they? Normally. It was all she'd ever wanted for the boys, a bit of normality. Positive role models. Love. Honesty. 'Speaking.'

'Hello, Tom here, Thacker and Daughters estate agents. I'm delighted to be ringing you with great news! We've received an offer on Milling Street.'

'An offer?' She could hear that almost-laughter thing her voice did when something ominous was coming and she needed to buy time before it hit. Like Ofsted declaring they were about to spring an inspection on Hornbeam. 'But . . . but we've only just gone on the market, we've had *one* viewing!'

'Impressive, isn't it?'

'Yes . . . But I'm afraid we're not taking anything less than the asking price.'

'More good news, Mrs Hildred! The purchasers have offered the full asking price.'

Sarah winced. 'But we haven't even got our For Sale board

up!' *Think*. 'Were they in a chain? We don't want to be in a chain. Not even a short one.' She felt sweaty. She was useless at bluffing.

'Cash buyer, Mrs Hildred. Super, hey?'

Acceptance settled swiftly. She'd always been the accepting sort. 'Can I get Jonathan to call you back, I'm just in the middle of something important with my son?'

Max buried his finger in his ear and began twisting it back and forth. She made a mental note to check if that crusty old bottle of hand sanitiser was still lurking in the bottom of her bag.

'I'll look forward to his call, Mrs Hildred. Cheerio.'

She shut off the phone. 'Stupid estate agents, working on bank holidays.' Max looked a question at her. They weren't allowed to say *stupid*. 'Sorry, kiddo. Come on, let's see if we can find any of Godzilla's cousins anywhere in the other tanks. Oh, look, Cretaceous Asia. Godzilla's a Japanese dinosaur, right?'

Max looked up at her. 'Godzilla isn't a normal dinosaur, Mummy.'

'Isn't he?'

'No. He's made up from different bits of different dinosaurs.'

'I see.' She hadn't got boxes. Sarah and the boys hadn't even viewed any of the properties on the flashy cliffside development Jon had all the glossy brochures for. *Compass Point. Navigate your family to a better lifestyle.* Sarah cringed inwardly every time Jon pulled one out. Now he'd put an eye-watering deposit down. It was happening. Already. When everyone, *everyone*, said house sales dragged out, how they'd be on the market for months. Will's GCSEs were starting soon, they couldn't move now. *Should've made more of a stand then, shouldn't you? Now it's too late.*

'What's do you think my favourite bit is, Mummy?'

'Hmm?'

'My favourite Godzilla bit? Guess, Mummy.'

Sarah rubbed her forehead. 'Tail?' How was she going to break it to Will? He loved Milling Street. He loved his room, school ten minutes away by bike, the beach and harbour shops not even that.

'Teeth!'

'Hmm? Oh, his teeth. I see.'

'No, look Mummy, teeth!'

She looked through the water. Something grimaced back at them. Max squealed with delight. 'Jon! I know it's you, Jon, I touched a shrimp with my actual finger!' Max ran around the water tube, slamming into Jon's legs.

'Hey, big fella! Having fun? What did I miss? Where have you been? What did you see? Ready for flapjack?'

Jon had caught the sun over the weekend. Sarah had stifled a giggle last night when he'd shown her his new wetsuit-shaped paler parts. Her body still reacted to him of course. It was her brain currently finding its role uncertain. Jon was handsome, charismatic, kind. Just because her mind was cautious didn't mean her eyes didn't enjoy what they could feast on. It was no different to Cleo tempting her with a fat slice of tiramisu when she was watching her calories. *See how delicious it looks, Sarah, any sane woman would fancy a slice of that!* Jon inspected Max's crumpled activity sheet attentively, head furrowed in concentration, eyes bright and serious. *Yes. Any sane woman would.*

Did it really matter that the butterflies never fully arrived? She wasn't a teenager any more for goodness sake, she and Jon were still compatible. Conversationally. Physically. Just, no butterflies. No big deal. Okay, so there had very definitely been butterflies when Patrick first burst into her life. Great big swarming butterflies of epic proportions, like Mothra, Godzilla's giant winged adversary. But then Patrick was a bit of a shit, and so a bit of a shitty yardstick. If it weren't for Max and Will, she'd regret ever clapping eyes on him. Their one-time adorable how-we-met story made her shudder now. Patrick swanning into the Students' Union, shiny new camera swinging from his neck, bracing his hands at her table declaring Sarah's to be the most perfect profile on campus and he'd know, he'd been staring through his lens at beautiful girls all day. *I'm not a pervert*, he'd assured her. *Well, maybe one part pervert to four parts decent chap.* She should've taken that swinging camera and garrotted him with it. Instead, she'd made love to Patrick Harrison all afternoon and fallen hopelessly in love, becoming Mrs Harrison by the following summer.

She glanced at Jon, Max still talking him through the creatures they'd already spotted. Jon was not a Patrick. And even though she didn't feel butterflies, she still felt something every morning when Jon walked out suited and booted for work, and even more so now, while he was at his absolute best in casual weekend T-shirt and jeans mode. With Max, who adored him. She was lucky to get another shot at this. A family for the boys. At times she wondered if there'd been some silly mix-up. As if she was the wrong suitcase Jon had mistakenly plucked off the airport conveyor belt and was now too embarrassed to return to its rightful owner because of his own sheer stupidity at getting something so utterly obvious so utterly wrong. But only dimwits like her did things like that – although in her defence, a surprise trip to Portugal with a ten-year-old and a colicky newborn had turned out to be a particularly disorientating experience.

Now here she was. Four years into her second chance and Jon still hadn't decided he'd made a terrible mistake. He just kept on driving her and the boys towards a hopeful horizon. It was the strangest thing.

'Whoa, Maxy . . . Who's this beautiful creature you've found in the aquarium? Can we take her home and keep her?'

Sarah's shoulders relaxed again. 'You looked like one of those gurners through the water,' she smiled. 'Reminded me a little of my Aunt Linda.' None of Sarah's father's side were much for smiling, too busy in-fighting over big egos and small inheritances.

Jon slipped his hand under the hem of her jacket. 'And you looked like a siren.' He pulled her into him. He was wearing the terrible Spiderman aftershave Max had bought him for Father's Day last year. Sarah let him kiss her, hoping it might be enough to chase away the fresh doubt. 'What do you think, Maxy, is Mum hiding a mermaid tail under this long dress, do you think?'

Max shrugged. He didn't care for mermaids. Sarah took a deep breath. 'The estate agent just called.'

'I know, he left me a voicemail. So, what do you think?'

Seventeen years she'd lived in that house. Will and Max's only home. 'Bit scary, I guess.'

'And a *little* bit exciting?'

'Sure. It's just . . .'

'A big change?' Jon kissed her on the head and gave the back of her neck a gentle, reassuring squeeze. 'It'll be okay, Sarah. I promise. This is going to be a great move for us. All of us. Especially Will.' He nuzzled into her. 'This is mine and Will's chance to start a new chapter together. Not as a confused young boy and his school counsellor, or wary son and the guy who moved in, but as equals, Sarah. This is our chance to start from zero, as equals. A solid family unit.'

5

There was two of everything in Curlew Cottage. Two sauce-pans, two plump little sofas, each with nautically inspired cushions, two bistro chairs sitting on the shady path out front. Isobel was disjointing the cottage's ethos, a conspicuously single entity in a setting made for two. It didn't strike her as a much-used holiday let. Holidaying couples looking for a peaceful bolthole from which to explore Fallenbay were welcome, the ad said. Dogs and young children, friendly or otherwise, were not.

'All settled then? Is it still quiet?' Sophie's voice crackled down the line. Isobel pressed the phone against her ear and heard her dad and Ella roaring with laughter in the background.

'Quieter than there.' She flexed her achy calf muscles. The hill that wound its way up here was a killer. Snaking and rising all the way up to where the cottage sat like a lost shoe under a gloomy canopy of evergreens. Isobel had smelled her clutch burning on her first crawl up the private road, but the price had been right and the particulars had promised privacy. Obscurity. Curlew Cottage had pretty much delivered.

Sophie shut a door and the laughter died. 'Weather improved?'

'Yeah, today was hot.'

Isobel had driven through sheeting rain to Fallenbay, the air inside the cottage musty when she'd first arrived. Bright, white plastered walls cold and cave-like to the touch. It didn't feel lived in at all, but then she'd sussed how to light the log burner and eaten her first meal-for-one looking out towards the harbour in the distance.

One-bed cottage . . . Fronted by private woodland . . . Open aspect to the rear . . . Sea view . . . Yes there was, but to see it she'd eaten her dinner standing up, leaning against the frame of the bathroom door, the distant boats bringing welcome specks of colour through the little square window over the bathtub.

Sophie fell quiet again. Isobel checked her reception while Sophie thought of something to say. 'So what are you thinking to your new digs? Now you've been there a couple of days? Did you ask about a landline?'

'There's a landline here, in the cottage. But I'm not sure how they'd charge for any calls I make so I'm just gonna stick with my mobile.'

'Great. A mobile with no reception. Here's hoping you keep it charged, at least. What about the rest of it?'

Of course it was charged, she wasn't stupid. She looked around the clean, compact cottage kitchen. 'It's okay. It's cosy.'

'Looked pokey on the photographs.'

'No, not pokey. Just . . . enough. Plenty of space actually, for a loner.'

'You're not a loner. Well, you're not alone, anyway. Agh, I hate thinking of you there by yourself, Isobel.'

'I'll probably be back next week.'

'No you won't,' Sophie said certainly. 'You looked different when you left here, Is. Determined. And just as I was getting used to stealing your clothes again.' Sophie was trying for upbeat. 'Come back. Please? I'll bunk with Ella, you can have the big room. We can come up with a brilliant plan – a bucket list! Everything you want to do with your life. I'll help you, however I can, which probably won't be much, granted. You're the smart one, but I got the bigger boobs so it's fine. Just . . . come home, Isobel. Please?'

She hovered next to the stable door, trying to catch another bar of signal. The sun was dying over the edge of the neighbouring woodland. *These sessions are to help you make your way out of the woods, Isobel.* Therapy speak. But it had been Sophie who'd led her through at the time, not Jenny and her analogies. If there had been any hint of a silver lining to the nightmare, Sophie had been it. They'd had a lifetime of lukewarm sisterhood, but then *the blip*, as their dad called it, had brought them together. The constant stream of unrelenting spite, the horrendous trail of filth and hate, it had somehow flowed out to something good right down at the core of them, forging their sisterhood into a solid, iron-like thing. They'd become a team Isobel could trust in, a message Sophie still hammered home at every given opportunity. And it was tempting. Despite everything Isobel knew now, Sophie's suggestion to go home and pretend was just so achingly tempting.

'I can't.'

'But what if you dip again, Is? You're so many miles away from us.'

'I'm not that far.'

'Have you taken anything there with you?'

'No.'

'Not even for emergencies?'

'No. That's what phones are for. I'll be fine.'

'I have a bad feeling about this.'

'You have a bad feeling about changing brands of shampoo, Soph. I can't just pop a pill every time I struggle with something. I need a better mechanism than that.'

'But . . .'

'Sophie, relax. Really, it's quite pleasant having a bit of thinking time. It's kind of lovely here actually. There's a sea view and everything. I walked down into the harbour this morning, had breakfast. It was good.'

'So . . . does it feel like you're kind of on holiday, sort of?'

Isobel's eyes followed a darting movement outside, a squirrel skittering up into the branches. Perhaps she should've found somewhere less treed. She wouldn't tell Sophie about the woodland just yet. She would keep that one in her pocket for now. Sophie's brain already worked overtime thanks to natural sisterly concern and too much *Most Evil* on Discovery HD. Knowing there was woodland next to the cottage would freak her out entirely. It had been Isobel's first thought when she'd seen the cottage ad. *What would Sophie think?* They both believed in big bad wolves.

Isobel held her cup of tea to her chest and breathed this new and foreign air. 'I guess it does. It's weird how quickly you get used to staying somewhere new.' It was the staying alone bit that felt alien, not the waking up beneath gnarled timber beams or the super-soft mattress or the different brands of cleaning products left for her in the cupboard under the sink.

She made a mental note to restock the cottage's provisions before she left, whenever that would be.

'I don't want you to get used to it. Spend a few more days down there in Freaksville if you have to, read some books, eat some seaside shit . . . and come home?'

'Everyone's been fairly normal so far, Soph. No webbed feet or anything.' Which wouldn't have been that odd really, given the whole town's thirst for watersports.

'Who have you met? Where have you been? Male or female?' There was a lilt of agitation to Sophie's tone.

'Sophie, relax. Just the old chap who owns this place, and a local coffee shop owner. She seemed quite nice, friendly.' Isobel felt for the woman in Coast. The spat she'd witnessed hadn't involved Isobel but her anxiety levels had still spiked. An actual real-life verbal altercation. Where people gesticulated and threw insults face-to-face, not hidden behind a computer keyboard. Or a username. A stupid username, like DEEP_DRILLERZ.

'Did you just say coffee shop?'

'Sophie, it's fine—'

'You promised you'd keep me in the loop!'

'I *am* keeping you in the loop.'

'No you aren't. You went *there*. You went straight to Coast without telling me!'

'Actually I walked past three times first. What a wimp, huh?'

Sophie made an exasperated sound. 'You're not a wimp, Isobel. Definitely not that. You're just a bit . . . mental.'

Sophie had no idea. 'Jenny thinks *mental* isn't constructive terminology, Soph.'

'She thought this little holiday idea of yours was legit, so let's not kid ourselves that Jenny's with the programme.' A silence stretched between them. Across the yard the owner of the cottages loaded his wolf-dog into his battered Land Rover. 'So you've met the owner of Coast. Fine. What about the old chap? The landlord?'

'Arthur? He lives in the smallholding, sort of next door. The two cottages share the track, he lives in the bigger one with his massive dog. You should see it, Soph.' The dog both scared and reassured Isobel. Anyone coming up that hill was announced by deep warning barks. Anyone who walked through the wrong boundary fence when they got up here was probably going to lose a leg. It wasn't young kids and dogs Arthur didn't want, it was a lawsuit.

'So is he an "old chap" as in silver-fox? Or dentures-next-to-the-bed?'

'Because I'm here to pull, Soph?'

'I was only asking.'

Isobel rolled her eyes. Sophie, always the sucker for a good-looker. *Start batting those eyelashes at the nice, decent boys for a change, Sophie Hedley, instead of all the slick-looking wild ones,* their mum had yelled up the stairs many, many times. *You won't bring half the trouble back to this house!*

'Well?'

'Somewhere between the two, I guess? He has grey bristles, wears a neckerchief and shouts a lot.'

'Who to? The dog?'

'I'm not sure, maybe. "Danny Boy", he calls. I haven't seen anyone else up here though. Maybe it is to the dog? Or to himself. Maybe he's a touch—'

'Mental too?'

'Here's hoping. It would be nice to be the normal one again.'

'You are normal.'

'Inconspicuous, then.' Another silence. 'I like him. He's old-fashioned. Chops his own logs, mends his own gate . . . slowly . . . bit like dad.' Arthur probably fed his dog the old-fashioned diet of postmen, too.

'Good he's just next door then.' Sophie exhaled, long and slow. 'So how was it in the café? Were you okay in there by yourself?'

That first trip into Coast had been a bit of a non-experience other than the eruption about the breast-feeding mother. Isobel had known roughly what to expect though before even setting foot inside the door. She'd done her homework and Googled it. To death. It was the people who'd thrown her. A steady stream of normal, everyday people enjoying the warm drinks and atmosphere. Not a monster in sight.

Isobel sighed. 'Yeah, of course. All good, all good.'

'So what did you do in there? I have a picture in my head of you sitting behind a newspaper, two eyeholes cut out of it.' Sophie waited for a laugh.

'Nothing really. Ordered a few pots of tea, a really good flapjack and just . . . thought about everything. About what I'm aiming for. One step at a time, like Jenny said.'

Name-dropping her therapist was a poorly veiled attempt to pretend any of this was a good idea. Jenny didn't matter, only Sophie mattered. Sophie being on board was integral. This was all about them, Isobel and Sophie, sisters with their secrets.

'And have they changed any? Those things you're aiming for?'

Isobel let a strand of text run through her mind like the credits of a disturbing film. Clear as reading it onscreen again, his words crisp and sharp and penetrative.

Filthy little bitch. Dirty, filthy little bitch. Didn't think of the consequences did you, bitch?

Consequences. Now there was a word. Isobel swallowed. 'You think I'm on a wild goose chase, don't you?'

Sophie hesitated. 'No. I think you're on a journey, Isobel. I'm just not sure it'll lead you anywhere you really want to go.'

6

'Then she says, "*I have a right to use my breasts! My daughter has a right to be fed!*" '

Cleo stopped for air. It was exhausting sounding like Lorna. Sarah seized her chance to speak. 'This is the same Lorna we're talking about here, isn't it? Pretty head scarves, porcelain skin? Lovely but hyper son in Max's class?'

Cleo nodded into the phone, resuming her Lorna impersonation full-fury. ' "*First I'm harassed by that battleaxe*" – that was when Lorna turned her baguette on me, Sarah – "*and now YOU are discriminating against me too! Against my baby! You, Cleo Roberts . . . a mother!*" '

Lorna had launched into an impressive tirade about 'women like Cleo', busy types too self-centred to fully appreciate the nutritional needs of their own babies, cheeky mare! But it had been hard enough for Cleo to hear all that guff; she wasn't about to inflict it on Sarah too. Sarah's battle with the boob had been worse than Cleo's after Patrick ditched Sarah and the boys. She'd tormented herself over the whole horrendous thing, of course. Poor girl.

'Do you know what she said then, Sar? "*You're supposed to support other women, not knock us down when we're vulnerable!*" '

Sarah was about to play devil's advocate, Cleo could smell it. Sarah always so annoyingly fair-handed, Cleo a raving madwoman by comparison.

'Maybe she was feeling just a bit vulnerable? Gosh, I remember what I was like after Max was born. I don't think I stopped crying for the first six months. I was a snotty, tired, milky mess. Poor Will. Stuck with a mum like that.'

'Vulnerable? Lorna? Ha! I could see the whites of her eyes, Sarah. I braced myself for a sandwich-related injury. I'd have been splashed all over that hideous Fallenbay Dartboard page . . . *BAGUETTE RAGE! Local businesswoman floored by fake brie!* And anyway, your situation was unique. You had every reason to cry for six months, and more. Awful man.'

'I think it's Fallenbay Pinboard.'

'I know. But it's more like a dartboard. Who even takes part in those awful anonymous Facebook pages? Complaining about the street lighting, ripping the high school to shreds, negative, negative, negative. People are hideous. No wonder kids misbehave online, the parents are just as antisocial.' Sam wandered into the kitchen, silently prodding at the leftovers. Max began yelling in Sarah's background, something about a bloody finger. 'The brie's not fake, by the way.'

'I have to go, Cle. Max's trying to pull another tooth out, the tyrant. Sebastian Brightman has told him baby teeth are for babies. Seb only wants to be friends with boys who are growing their big teeth.'

'Sounds like something Olivia Brightman's offspring would say. Anyway, ew. I hate blood. Makes my buttocks go funny. I'll leave you to it. Catch you in the week. Oh! And tell the school crazies not to boycott me, would you?'

'Like they'd listen to me, Cle. A lowly teacher. See you.'

Cleo put the phone down. Sam was still foraging. Leave him long enough and the dishes wouldn't need scraping at all. This was how their paths crossed now, Cleo at some mundane task, Sam quietly rooting nearby. They were like a night-vision segment on *Countryfile*. Two nocturnal creatures fumbling around the same hidden camera, occupying the same insignificant part of the ecosystem independently of one another. Except when they were fighting. Or feeding.

Sam popped something into his mouth and flicked on the kitchen TV. 'Good quiche, Cle.' She caught herself observing him like a farm vet again, looking for evidence of the middle-aged spread certain to sneak up on him while he wasn't looking and cut short his life like his poor father's. Builders had terrible diets. It was all bacon baps and flasks of syrupy tea. Ploughmen . . . apparently they knew how to eat.

Sam burst briefly to life. 'That clipped the wicket!'

'The microwave blew up today,' Cleo said idly. *I did tell you.*

Sam made a non-committal noise and propped himself over the back of one of the dining chairs, reverently checking the scores he'd missed. His neck was sunburnt. Was he working outside again now? He'd been tiling en-suites the last time they'd spoken about his job. Sam had been working on the Compass Point development site, the latest target of the Hornbeam school mothers and their petitions. Juliette had soon rallied the troops when she realised her super-home would have to share the coastline.

Cleo began aggressively scraping plates. 'I've been told to expect a boycott by the school mothers.' Juliette's PFA members hunted together in a well-orchestrated pack. *You'll be sorry, Cleo!* Lorna had warned. Cleo already felt a bit sorry and she hadn't actually done anything wrong. 'All thanks to a silly misunderstanding about a breast.' Sam wasn't listening. 'About a nipple, Sam . . . a great big nipple.'

'Humph?' he grunted, eyes fixed on the TV.

'Lorna was sitting in the café window with both bangers out, Sam.'

Finally, a flicker of interest. 'Fair play!'

Cleo smiled. *Bangers* was Sam's favourite boob word. Quite possibly because it doubled up for *sausages*, another of his favourite things.

Sam yelled at the TV. 'Fair play, my man, fair play! One-hundred-and-eight not out.'

Cleo scowled. *Heathen.* She wrung out the dishcloth and imagined Jonathan pouring Sarah a lovely glass of wine, listening attentively while she reflected on their day together at the marine dinosaur thingy.

'There'll be no end of nipples on the loose if we start hosting private functions like they do at the French place in town. Parties always get a bit rowdy; a bit of drunken debauchery might be just what the till needs.'

'We?' Sam laughed. 'Coast is your party, Cleo. Always has been. I would be up for a bit of debauchery though, love. Shout up anytime.'

She ignored him. 'Coast would be *our* party if you got involved. Convert the stores for me. Customers could watch the sunset over the ocean if we knocked through.'

'I offered to help out at weekends, Cleo. You weren't interested.'

35

'Yes, but that was behind the counter. You're a builder, Sam! Come *builder* this extension so we can expand . . .'

'I'm not talking shop now,' Sam said firmly. 'I've been at it all day.'

Cleo's scowled at the array of kitchen appliances awaiting her next move. 'Evie Roberts, get down here and load this dishwasher or I'm confiscating that bloody iPhone!'

Sam jumped. 'Bit louder, eh, Cleo?' He ran dry, cracked hands back and forth through his hair. A cloud of plaster dust rose into the air above him. Cleo had fallen in love with that hair once. Kevin Costner hair. Before Sam's had started to thin and hers started sprouting in new places.

'Go and have a cuppa, Cleo, I'll do it.'

'No, no, you've been on site all day, Sam, you just said so yourself. On a bank holiday. This is supposed to be a perk of having teenagers, remember? Them occasionally helping with the menial tasks.'

There was a dribble of balsamic down Sam's work fleece. More plaster dust clinging to the side of his eyebrow. He was such a child.

'Evie's been loading dishwashers all day, Cle. Let the kid have five minutes, hey? It's her bank holiday too.'

'She has not! I've been emptying the bloody dishwasher, thanks very much. Evie likes to look pretty and collect tips while I deal with exploding microwaves and hysterical mothers.' Thoughts of Lorna made her stomach twist again. She'd never known such an awful bunch of parents, not in all the time the twins were at Hornbeam. Mothers used to be civil back then. All in it together. Cleo blamed the arrival of social media. 'Monsters, they are,' she hissed over the sink.

'*Momsters*. I don't know how Sarah can bear dealing with them on a daily basis.'

'No one likes their job all the time, Cleo. I know I damn well don't.' He looked out onto the garden, the muscles in his cheek tensed.

'Evie!' Cleo barked. 'Evie should like her job, Sam, she gets paid enough for doing bugger all.' Cleo always sounded like a difficult teenager when bickering with Sam about their difficult teenager.

'She's fifteen.'

'Yes, thank you, Sam. I was there, I do remember it vividly. Lots of screaming, lots of babies. Not so many husbands to hand.'

'For crying out loud, Cle, let it go. Why do women have to drag stuff out? I was working, not dribbling over a barmaid somewhere. At least I'm still here. I bet Sarah doesn't think I'm such a useless git.'

Cleo ignored him again. It had all worked out for Sarah in the end. Her prince charming rode in and trampled down any bumpy ground left by Patrick Harrison, the selfish shit. Cleo eased off thoughts of Sarah's ex-husband and felt herself involuntarily forgiving Sam for that trail of balsamic dressing down his front. 'Evie! I'm not yelling for you all night, you know.'

'Sounds like you're yelling for her all night, darling.' Sam kissed her on the forehead. Cleo was sure he only did that nowadays just to piss her off.

'Are you having a shower or are you going to keep coating the kitchen with a fine layer of dust?'

'I love you too, darling wife. Thanks for the warmth.

Think maybe tomorrow I'll stay on site, cuddle up to a scaffold pole instead.'

'Well if you didn't always take Evie's side,' she spat irritably.

'I take my side, Cleo. The side where emptying the dishwasher myself is going to cut less time out of my evening than arguing with you and the kids over it.'

'Kid. Harry does his chores.'

'Excellent! We must be parenting half-right then.' He squeezed Cleo's shoulder. There was movement in the kitchen doorway.

'Afternoon, parents.' Harry stretched his arms above his head, his lean, muscled midriff peeping out below his Beastie Boys T-shirt.

'Hey Harry. Good day, son? What did you do with yourself, beach was it?' Sam could flit seemlessly from sparring partner to relaxed father mode, just like that. *Infuriating*.

'Nah, just hung out with the guys. The Village was dead so we played the courts mostly. Good day at work?'

Surfers' Village was the name given to the area where the locals congregated for the best surf, away from tourists and holidaying politicians. Evie would've headed straight for The Village today too, but Harry won the coin flip and Evie got the extra shift at Coast. She was probably still sulking now.

Sam rubbed the back of Harry's head, pulling him playfully into his chest. 'Work's work, kid. You make sure you come good on those exams. I don't want to see your hands looking like these in a few years, okay?'

Cleo stole a sideways glance. 'You need some cream on those, Sam. Harry, did you bring your washing down? I'm about to put a load on.'

'It's already in, I need my sports kit for the morning. I separated the whites and stuff.'

'My marvellous son.' She planted a kiss on Harry's cheek as he passed her for the fridge. He pulled a carton of milk out of the door and began glugging from the spout. 'Harry, get a glass.' He stopped guzzling and grinned from behind a milk moustache. Her beautiful long-eyelashed little boy was rolling over for this tall, gangly, fridge-raiding youth.

'What's up with Evie?' asked Harry.

'Other than a severe allergy to chores, I don't know, why?'

Sam walked into the sun room and slumped into one of the chairs, groaning as his body clocked off for the day.

'I think she's been crying. She came out of the bathroom like Alice Cooper and bit my head off for staring.'

Cleo rolled her eyes. 'Justin Bieber's probably going to be a father. Youth of today, I despair, I really do. I'll go up in a minute, thanks love. Have you got any homework, H?'

'I'll check after I've texted Ingred.'

'Just watch the network charges, okay, son? Denmark's a long way away.'

That woke you up, Sam. International texting charges. Ingred had only been in the UK for three weeks, and Harry's 'girlfriend' for just five days before the exchange trip ended and she'd returned to her Nordic homeland. 'Have you tried Skyping, Harry? It's free. Bloke at work uses it when his kid wants to talk to his mum.'

Cleo sniffed a scandal. 'Why, where's his mum?'

'Rich got custody.'

'Oh.' Single fathers were like exotic beings to Cleo. She never could fully grasp how any mother coped without knowing every little detail about her children's lives. It would drive her batty.

Harry shrugged. 'Ingred's Skype is glitchy or something. She said it's the new phone she's using. We haven't hooked up online at all yet. No calls either, which sucks. Texts only.'

'You sure she hasn't given you the wrong number, Romeo?' Sam teased.

Harry smiled to himself. 'No, Dad. We've been texting… like, *a lot.*'

Sam grinned. 'That's good, son. And probably a good thing your calls aren't getting through. No enormous bills hitting the doormat, right? You don't want to overload her with charm anyway, I mean, sending you her new number you the day she arrived home, she's keen enough. Must be the Roberts effect.' Sam winked at Cleo. He'd no idea about that trail of balsamic vinegar, no idea at all. 'Keep an eye on the texting costs, okay though, H? Your mother needs a new microwave. And a baguette-proof vest.'

Cleo scowled and stalked towards the stairs. 'It's rude to earwig phone calls.' Sam wouldn't be laughing for long. Cleo's sights were set on more than just a new microwave. That little French place in the harbour had started themed food nights. They were doing a roaring trade with the locals. No more relying on seasonal tourism. Who wanted to be prepping food day *and* night, though? Music. That was the key. Give the local lot an open-mic night, live music and light bites only.

She clasped the newel post and took a lungful of air to shout Evie again. Sam would just have to get his head around it. She planted a foot on the bottom step and looked up. 'Jeez, Evie! You scared me to death. What's the matter with you?'

Evie stood dishevelled at the top of the stairs, long brown hair straggled and weed-like around her red and flustered face. Cleo hesitated. Evie was a stomper. A door slammer. A pain in the bottom. She wasn't a crier. 'Evie? What is it?' Evie couldn't form her words, her chest spasming as she tried to speak. Cleo's own chest tightened. 'Evie? For goodness sake, tell me what's happened!'

'Someone . . . someone . . .'

Cleo felt a panic rising. 'Someone what?'

Evie burst into achy sobs. 'Someone called me *fat* on Facebook. *Everyone*'s seen!'

7

Isobel peered into the window of West Coast Ink. She'd only planned to walk along the footpaths around the cottage but her feet had kept going, Forrest Gumpish. The town was quiet now, the bank holiday given up to preparations for the working week ahead. Shutters were closed or closing, car spaces vacant. One or two shops, like The Organic Pantry up ahead, replenishing stock in peace.

It was quite enjoyable, this meandering, nosing in windows, looking at the objects inside without first scanning the faces. It felt like taking a sneaky look behind the scenes of a set, standing on the stage of a pretend town after the performance had finished, the crowds gone home. She twisted the bracelet over her wrist and allowed her eyes to dart around the gloom through the glass. There weren't any obvious signs that West Coast Ink offered laser removal, though it was hard to tell with the lights off. It didn't look like a tattoo shop in there, she could see that much. At least not like the one she'd stood outside with Sophie two years ago, clammy and nervous and a little bit buzzy after too many cocktails, Sophie talking her through the door with fibs: *It's a nice pain! Trust me, you'll ease into it!*

It had not been a nice pain. She'd almost buckled, almost

yelped, *Enough! I don't want any more! Leave it like that!* But Sophie had smiled at her from the other chair, and Isobel, not wanting to let the side down, had given her a weak thumbs-up. Sophie was hardcore. More hard-headed. More hard-hearted. They shared their dad's straight nose and mum's dark hair (before the bleach) and now a tattoo on the wrist apiece, but there the similarities ended.

She carried on along the kerb just as a young girl strode out from behind a truck, straight into Isobel's path. Isobel glimpsed two startled eyes over the top of the crate in the girl's arms, then watched her launch the lot across the pavement.

'Sorry, I didn't see you!' yelped the girl. She wore pumps and khaki shorts that made her look even more girlish as she began scrambling for the apples skittering across the kerb.

'Let me help, I was in a world of my own too.' Isobel made a grab for the crate first, righting it before any more rosy red orbs were lost. She lunged around the street, collecting the strays the girl hadn't reached yet. They regrouped on the pavement, an armful each.

'Thanks,' smiled the girl. 'Last week I dropped two watermelons. Have you ever seen one of those explode? My boss was *not* happy.' She had the same healthy complexion as the other locals, pretty without make-up, just the hint of decoration where a small clip pinned her hair off her face.

Isobel piled the apples into the box. 'Sometimes there just aren't enough hands.' The girl held an apple up for inspection. Isobel spotted just one or two dinks, then the girl's neon-pink nail polish, then . . .

Isobel glanced away.

'These are destined for the discount bin,' the girl sighed.

Isobel smiled mechanically. The girl was missing the tip of her middle finger and nearly half of her index, neat little nubs where her fingers should be. 'No, I'll buy them,' blurted Isobel. 'I have a fiver on me I think, I'll . . . make a crumble or something.'

'Elodie! Ever heard of switching your phone on?'

A teenage boy in a checked shirt and a pair of those funky Clark Kent glasses all the kids seemed to like walked hands-in-pockets across the street towards them. Isobel cringed. She used to tell the boys at St Jude's not to do that, after one tripped down the art block steps and couldn't free his hands in time. Ruined his teeth.

'Hey, I thought you were conquering alien worlds with your gamer buddies,' said the girl.

He slowed on his approach, giving Isobel a fleeting look. 'I was, but Mum's freakin' out. The cleaner's just found a letter crumpled inside the letterbox or something. She wants you to go home straight after your shift.'

The girl stiffened. 'What sort of letter? Did she open it?'

'No. Dad said it was an invasion of privacy. She thinks it's from the conservatoire. You'd better be turning up, Elodie. If she finds out I haven't been taking you, you'll get a slap on the wrist and I'll be grounded forever . . . without privileges.'

The girl glanced at Isobel standing there like a right wally waiting for her apples. 'Your hardware's safe, Milo. I haven't missed a single Saturday class, okay?'

'Sweet, 'cos I'm about to start season seven of *Sons of Anarchy* on Netflix, I need my laptop.'

Isobel rocked back on her heels trying not to look like a spare part. 'It's good . . . definitely hang on to your laptop.'

The girl chortled, 'He's never off it! You need to get out more, Milo.'

Isobel hoped Elodie's prettiness had been enough to save her from the taunts. She also felt for Milo who, like Isobel, was afflicted with a sassy sister. 'A computer's a bicycle for the mind, right? Can take you to a lot of places, I guess,' she smiled.

'He has that exact Steve Jobs quote! Milo's training up to take over Apple. He's just got to stop getting caught at school with iffy money-making schemes before Mum confiscates his laptop.'

'Not everyone's a child genius,' Milo said. He gave Isobel a furtive glance.

'Steve Jobs wasn't a child genius. A billionaire school dropout, actually.' She'd just danced on the grave of her teaching career. 'I just mean, you know, why shouldn't you take over Apple one day?'

Milo eyed her suspiciously. 'Yeah . . . Anyway, so Elodie, you nearly done?'

'Nearly,' she beamed. 'Let me just get a bag for these. I'll try not to give you the really bashed ones.' She nodded at Isobel and disappeared into the grocer's. Her brother set his hands back into his pockets. He peered into the crate on the pavement and tapped it with his foot. Isobel thought about starting a weather conversation. Or a surf conversation; she could do with learning some lingo.

'She's not selling you these, is she? They're knackered.'

'Oh, they're just a bit bruised. They'll be fine.'

Elodie strode back outside into the evening sun.

'Are all of these going cheap now then, Elodie?' Milo asked.

'Why? Do you want some? Don't eat them around Dad, you'll start him off on acid erosion again.'

Isobel ran her tongue over her molars, the sensitivity she always felt at the back there flaring in response.

'Not for me. Hobo Bob's digging around in the bins behind the French place again. I might take him some if they're going.'

Isobel took the bulging paper bag from the girl.

'They're not going for free, Milo.'

'Not even for a good cause?'

'Cough up. I know you're flush, I've seen you stuffing cash into your speakers.' Milo looked rumbled. Isobel looked at her shoes but the girl started talking to her again. 'Bob's our resident homeless person. Kind of a fixture.'

'That's a shame,' said Isobel. 'Why's he homeless?' It was an affluent enough town.

Elodie shrugged. 'Didn't he used to be a big banker or something, Milo? How do people go from high-flyer to eating from bins? It's crazy.'

'People fall from grace,' offered Isobel. Others were pushed.

Milo's hair flopped over his eyes. 'Hobo Bob fell a long way. His wife spread rumours about him hurting little girls. Never proved he was a perv, though.'

An unpleasantness stirred in Isobel's memory. A towering heap of captions. *Little tart, Romio's being too soft with her. Go on, hurt her mate. I'd hurt her. I'd hurt her till she squealed.*

Isobel's eyes flitted from shop front to shop front. *French place?* She found it: Pomme du Port.

'Bob's not a perv,' laughed Elodie. 'Stacey tried to buy him a latte again last week, he wouldn't go near her!'

'Was he ever convicted?' Isobel's neck was pulsing, her eyes fixed on the French restaurant. A banker would be good with computers, wouldn't he? But then so was her gran. And most bankers could spell *Romeo*.

'No evidence,' said Milo. 'Mud sticks, though. Like our Dad says, lose your name, lose everything.'

8

'Sticks and stones, Eves, sticks and stones. No fella really wants a bag of bones as a girlfriend, you know. It's a myth. All these young girls, starving themselves to look like magazine covers, they've all been touched up, they're not *real*, Eves!'

Cleo stopped herself from pointing out to Sam that girls as sharp as their daughter didn't sit around all day in the modern-day equivalent of embroidery circles, pondering all the ways in which they could become irresistible to testosterone-crazed teenage boys. A second thought chased the first. *Oh God. Of course they did.*

She carried on rubbing small circles on Evie's back, her fingers snagging on her daughter's hair. Why did they all like this matted, frizzy look? Most of the girls in the bay looked like they'd slept rough on the beach. It jarred with the obscene amount of time they all spent perfecting those awful pencilled eyebrows. 'Are you alright now, darling?' Evie seemed to have shrunk, looking more like her ten-year-old self with all her make-up smeared away, huddled into the sofa against her dad. Evie nodded and sipped her hot chocolate. There'd been no talking her into squirty cream or marshmallows. They'd be off the shopping list for a while now thanks to that little shit. Harry's mug of hot chocolate had been fully laden, marshmallows tumbling all over the place. He'd made himself scarce in that way men did when confronted with a crying female. Gone to spend his evening texting a cheerier female in Ingred.

Cleo cast an eye over her daughter, pretty plum nail polish on her toes, the navy pedal pushers she'd bought to go with the broderie anglaise top Evie had called 'a bit church'. It wormed its way in again.

Fat.

Evie was not fat. She had a lovely figure. She just didn't resemble a stick insect. She looked healthy. Bronzed and bright-eyed and fresh, the way all the coastal kids were. Okay, perhaps she had a touch of Sam's mother's full cheeks, but it only made her more beautiful when she grinned, not that she grinned often nowadays, but that was only because pouting was the new smiling, wasn't it? That funny way the girls (and boys) all drew their mouths up into tight little duckbills and glared beseechingly into the camera. Or was something really getting Evie down? Was Evie being bullied? Had Cleo missed a trick here?

A mother's rage stirred in the pit of her stomach. Evie drove her nuts; most days Cleo really could drive her into the middle of nowhere and leave her, but that was her right! A mother of twins earned all sorts of rights like that, it was the ultimate reward for surviving the raising of a tag team without Valium or social service intervention.

Cleo stopped rubbing circles. 'So who was it?' His Facebook name was Aeron Mycock. *Funny little shit.* Sam had nearly laughed.

'Dunno. Just some idiot.'

49

'From school?'

'Probably.'

'Probably? Surely you know who you're Facebook friends with, Evie?'

Evie paused. 'Not everyone.'

'What? Then why did you accept them on to your friends list?' Cleo could taste *You silly girl!* teetering on the tip of her tongue.

Evie blinked up at her. 'Because they asked me! And we have mutual friends!'

'That's your criteria? So if your *friends* befriended an axe-murderer— Don't roll your eyes, Evie.'

'It doesn't matter who it is! I don't even care what he called me. It's just . . . everyone seeing it and stuff. I didn't know until Cassie texted me and it had been on there for nearly *five* minutes.' Evie's voice wobbled again.

'Five minutes?' sputtered Sam. 'An hour's upset for five minutes?'

Cleo threw him a look. Five minutes was a lifetime when it came to public humiliation, especially when you were fifteen, didn't he get it? Evie had been in the stocks for a full five minutes before she'd deleted the peasant who'd been wanging rotten veg at her head.

Sam took the hint. 'Look. Whoever has upset you, Evie, they're not worth all this, love, that's all I'm saying. You're better than them, don't let them get you down.'

That's right, Sam. Don't worry about finding out who this kid is and marching over to his house, having it out with his father. You just sit there. There was a time when Sam would've banged on their door the way he'd once banged on Cleo's father's door; Cleo's mother had thought her bruised cheek would go unnoticed in a place like Wrecker's gym, but Sam had noticed alright.

Sam caught her watching him now. She looked away. She hadn't thought about those days in a long time. Sam's hands hadn't been so rough back then. Building sites had ruined his hands, not the boxing ring.

'Your dad's right, Evie. Ignore them. Rise above it. People who hide behind computers saying spiteful things aren't worth caring about. Cut them out of your world.'

Evie nodded. She had a smudge of hot chocolate on the bridge of her nose from the rim of her mug. 'One good thing . . .'

'What's that, Eves?'

'You just agreed on something. For a change.'

Cleo frowned. 'What do you mean?'

'You and Dad, you never agree on anything any more. You were arguing again. In the kitchen. The floors in this house are thin, remember. At least me being fat—'

'*Called* fat,' corrected Sam.

'At least me being *called* fat stopped you two snapping at each other for an hour.'

Cleo blinked at Sam. It was only bickering, wasn't it? There was never any malice. Not like that horrible *fat* comment. 'Your dad and I . . . they're only words, Evie.'

'I know. But the sticks and stones thing's a load of crap. Words can be like weapons, Mum. They do damage.'

9

Sarah tapped her mobile phone to her mouth. She eyed the clock again on the far wall of her classroom, flanked by a sea of the children's impressionist self-portraits. Another ten minutes and the hordes would be back, newly grazed knees, jumpers needing to be retrieved from the playground, friendships broken and rebuilt.

Staff phones confined to staff rooms had been one of her own rule proposals and now she was flouting it. Because she needed to get in touch with Will and couldn't bear being stuck in the staff room with Juliette while she made a personal call. She stole another look at Jon's message.

Hey beautiful, thought we could take the boys out to dinner tonight? Tell them the good news in style!

Italian's still Will's favourite, right? Think we should cover all bases ;)

She lay her phone screen-down on the desk, hung back over her chair until she was almost horizontal and stared up at the ceiling mobiles, swinging herself in a semi-circle the way some of the boys did when she left the classroom. The lines of the ceiling tiles twisted dizzily as she turned. How were they going to make this go smoothly? If Will didn't get upset about the house sale he was emotionally dead. Jon was good with the pep talks but he wasn't *that* good.

She slapped her hands over her eyes in defeat, something cold and unpleasant touched her cheek. Fantastic. Bright blue poster paint, all along the cuff of her cream cashmere cardi. Hooray. Sarah had never been a cashmere kind of girl, but Jon's style had just sort of permeated their home. They all seemed so much more polished nowadays: outfits matched, salon appointments were not only made but kept. Everything ticked along instead of stopping and starting in jerky, uncertain motions; they were all cogs in a well-maintained machine. All except for one, very subtle five-foot-eight squeak.

Will. How would he react? Flip out or keep it all in?

Sarah pulled a baby wipe from the top drawer of her desk and did what she could for the cardigan. Yes, she would text Will now, before his lunch hour was up. He could think about the house sale over the afternoon, hopefully mellow on it before they went to dinner, before Jon started popping corks.

Oh God. She couldn't text him. *Hi son, your family home's just been sold out from under you . . .* The driveway he'd learned to ride his bike on. The landing where they'd huddled, crying quietly together so as not to wake the baby, trying to make sense of Patrick's actions. Sarah's heart was thudding. It was going to take more than a bowlful of salmon tagliolini to help Will swallow this one.

'Miss Harrison?' Two little girls strode purposefully into

Class 2, Molly with her painful-looking plaits, and Darcey, black ringlets tumbling over her grey pinafore. Wide, brown eyes on the verge of spilling over.

'What is it, Darcey?'

Molly ushered Darcey to Sarah's desk, presenting her the way the hopeful presented afflicted loved ones to the Pope. They looked like a GAP ad, one black child, one white, each lovelier than they could know.

'Darcey's got poo up her legs, Miss Harrison. The dinner ladies told me to bring her up.'

Sarah threw her blue baby wipe at the waste paper basket and cast a look over Darcey's skinny legs. Darcey looked a treat, her little patent shoes shiny and smart. Sarah couldn't see anything sinister at all. Darcey spun, revealing a mustard-coloured streak up the insides of both ankles. *Crap.*

'Darcey, how's this happened?'

It was too much. One sniff of interrogation tipped Darcey over the edge. Her little shoulders began bobbing up and down, her body wracked with growing sobs and the shame of pooey tights. Molly smiled knowingly. 'It's okay, Darcey.'

How the bloody hell had she got that on her tights? Was someone lobbing dog doo over the school fence again?

Sarah set her hands on Darcey's shoulders. 'Molly's right, it really is okay, Darcey. Don't worry, we'll get you fixed up before any of the others return from lunch, okay? Look here, I keep a stash of baby wipes in my drawer for exactly these sorts of emergencies. You're not the only one who gets into a pickle, you know, look at my cardigan!' Sarah held up her ruined sleeve. 'Come on, let's see if I can get the worst of it, then we'll come up with a plan for your tights and my cardi, alrighty?'

Darcey rubbed the tears from her cheeks and nodded. 'Why have you got paint all over your clothes, Miss Harrison?'

Sarah swabbed clumsily at Darcey's ankles. There was every chance she was making it worse. 'I thought your portraits were all dry when I stapled them up during break. I should've done a better job of checking, shouldn't I?'

Molly gasped. 'Miss Harrison, you've smudged Tabitha's impressionist self-portrait. Her school shirt is rubbed over her mouth. Look, Miss!'

Sarah glanced up from Darcey's legs to the far wall, at Tabitha Brightman's face now blurry and smurf-like. *Shit*. Tabitha's mother was one of the PFA lot. And tomorrow was open-door Wednesday. There'd be calls of sabotage and job losses.

'Right, Darcey. I'm not sure we're going to get away with just wiping these tights off. I think we're going to have to whip them off instead. Molly? Could you go to the office and ask Mrs Broome to arrange for someone to take afternoon register please when the bell goes. I'm just going to help Darcey find some socks from the emergency box.' Molly nodded obediently and disappeared. Sarah led Darcey stiff-legged to the children's toilets.

Mr Church, the caretaker, was jostling a mop and bucket into the infant girls' loos when Sarah rounded Library Corner. 'You'll have to give me a minute, Mrs Harrison, someone's stuck paper towels in the plugholes again, we've a minor flood. I could open that one up for you?' Mr Church nodded to the disabled/visitors toilet.

'Thank you, Mr Church. Come on, Darcey, we can pop in here, just this once.'

Mr Church unlocked the room for them then returned to his flood. Sarah stood aside ushering Darcey in, pulling the door to between them. How was this going to work then? A six-year-old pulling those tights off without further disaster? Tights were a bugger at the best of times; it was one of the biggest perks of being a mother to boys, no tights.

Sarah called around the door. 'Darcey? Can you manage? Or would you like some help?'

It wouldn't be ideal, just the two of them in a single toilet. This was the way you had to think as a teacher now, Jon was constantly reminding her of this fact. *Don't leave yourself open to accusation. Ever.* Jon wasn't a mother, though.

'Darcey? How about you pull your tights down at the top, then I'll pull them over the yucky bit? So it doesn't go anywhere else?'

'Yes please, Miss Harrison,' Darcey whispered. Sarah nudged around the toilet door. Darcey's mum would rather Sarah helped, wouldn't she? Heidi Thurston had seemed lovely when they'd met at parents evening in February. She'd come straight from court and listened so attentively to Sarah's feedback on Darcey's progress that Sarah had felt like a flaky witness, her testimony about to be picked apart for scrutiny. There was an air of celebrity about Heidi Thurston, the PFA mums were desperate to bag a barrister.

'Let's get your shoes unbuckled first, shall we, sweetheart?'

'*No*. It's all Jonathan's.'

It came from the other side of the cubicle wall. Sarah stilled. Everyone knew about the disabled loo's acoustics. *Don't slag anyone off in the staff room. If someone's taking a whazz next door you're toast.* There had been an unfortunate incident involving a parent volunteer overhearing a damning rumour about her husband after popping into Hornbeam one morning to listen to the reception kids read. A written apology from the head had followed, and later a divorce. Now the key to the disabled toilet was stationed on a hook in the staff room. Just so everyone could be 'aware' of its use. The only other key hung on Mr Church's key chain.

'Jonathan's, really? But I thought . . . well, she's always lived there, hasn't she?'

There was more than one Jonathan in the world. And it was rude to eavesdrop. 'That's it, Darcey, just lift your leg a sec . . .'

More voices muffled through the wall. 'I just assumed the house would've rocketed in value and she'd be stumping up a good whack herself.' Olivia Brightman had a distinct, honeyed voice. She'd come into school to speak to Mr Pethers about running pony rides at the summer fair. And to Juliette about Sarah's private life.

'Sarah can't stump up seven hundred thousand, Olivia.'

'Good God, seven hundred thou? Is that how much they're going for up on the bluff? They're not even bespoke!'

'They do have stunning ocean views.'

'Yes, but Compass Point, have you ever heard anything so pretentious? She'll pop a baby out soon, you watch. New house, new husband, new ankle-biter.'

Sarah swallowed. Jon had suggested a five bed, so there was a guest room for the boys' friends. Or for grandparents, so they could stay over when babysitting . . . once a baby arrived. She felt her head whoosh. Darcey blinked up at her, barefoot on the toilet floor, her inside-out tights dangling from Sarah's hand. 'Come on, poppet, let's go find you some socks.'

'What was his name? Her first husband?'

Sarah's hand froze on the door handle. *First Husband*. Sarah, the femme fatale.

'Patrick Harrison. Incredibly talented photographer, got lucky when some sports giant liked one of his action shots. Started off as a wedding snapper.'

Olivia sniggered. Sarah flinched. She'd met a lovely wedding photographer last month. Her mother had sprung a surprise consultation. He'd had a kind, tired face and worked too hard for his money. Sarah had booked him in under twenty minutes because she felt sorry for him. And because she didn't want to talk weddings.

'So where's husband number one now, do you think?'

Juliette paused. 'Patio, probably. Patrick was the selfish sort, in fairness to her.' Juliette's reasonable deduction landed like a slap on the cheek.

'Maybe she cashed in his policies? Seven hundred thousand starting price? Hardly manageable on two teachers' salaries,' scoffed Olivia.

'Jonathan's sitting on a small fortune. He's loaded.'

'How do you know?'

Yes, how did she? There was a pulse thumping over Sarah's temple. They lived well, but not ostentatiously. Jon was subtle about it. 'Miss Harrison?' squeaked Darcey.

Sarah held her hand up, her 'silent signal' when she wanted the class to hush down.

Juliette hesitated. Probably checking the toilet key was definitely on the staff room wall. 'Karl read about it. In one of the nationals, right there in the surgery waiting room.

Hopeless receptionist hadn't recycled them for weeks, I can't abide clutter in Karl's waiting room.'

It was inevitable, talk was inevitable, Sarah knew this. It was silly and she'd never really worried about it much; it was Jon who'd said she would need to be prepared for tittle-tattle at some point, and she was. She just wasn't prepared for Juliette to be the one gathering the juicy cuts and processing them into a toxic gossip sausage.

'Spill, Juliette! What did Karl read? What have you got on Sarah Harrison's gorgeous fiancé?' Sarah imagined Olivia frothing at the mouth like one of her horses.

'It's yesterday's news, Olivia. Years old. The article was retrospective, looking at precedents for obscene payouts in education. Apparently, Jonathan Hildred had something of an ordeal a few years back at a very respected private school, Gloucester way. Left a lot better off than he started.'

There was another pause. Olivia was connecting the dots. 'Hot-stuff Hildred won some sort of payout?'

'More of a golden farewell, with a hint of "sorry, please don't sue us" thrown in. I wouldn't even be discussing it at all had it not been there in a national paper. I'm not really one for gossip, Olivia. I find it all a bit . . . *tacky* if I'm honest.'

Juliette knew. At least she thought she did.

The bell crackled through the corridor towards the disabled toilet. Sarah startled. 'Miss Harrison?'

'Yes, sorry, Darcey.' She had that awful, hot, adrenal feeling. She'd felt it before, standing like a complete and utter reject in the middle of a photography exhibition in a posh Portuguese hotel, a tired ten-year-old Will at her side in his dickie bow, Max asleep in her arms.

'Miss Harrison?'

'Yes, Darcey, what is it?'

Darcey's lip wobbled. 'You're dangling my tights in the toilet.'

10

Cleo was in a foul mood.

Why couldn't she feel more feisty, like one of those fiery women she'd watched on *Mob Wives* last night, snuggled up with Evie on her bed like sisters? She was supposed to wake up this morning and crack on. But here she was, a little bit teary and disjointed.

'Early menopause?' her mum had suggested down the phone line.

'Early dementia, Mother?' Cleo had replied.

She'd felt it as soon as she'd woken up this morning, before she'd even realised Sam hadn't made it up from the sofa all night again. At first, it had been Evie who'd popped into her head, making sense of the unsettled feeling brewing in her stomach. In the shower, it had been Sam. The angry cracks in his knuckles, bleeding and sore and never afforded the chance to heal. The resignation in his shoulders as he made his flask each morning.

Cleo had swallowed two aspirin and her mother's advice and counted her blessings. Sam was a pain in the neck. Fact. But he loved his family. Bigger fact. Evie needed to think more, but she was open and honest when she got it wrong. And Harry. Harry had finished his paper round then made

Evie breakfast this morning, which she'd left because she was off carbs now, but still, they must be doing something right in Harry at least, mustn't they? He was still easy. Easy H.

'Whatever's bothering you, Ma, bet it won't matter next week,' Harry had offered, ducking through the door with Evie's toast in his mouth.

He was right, it probably wouldn't. It was silly, this sense of foreboding Cleo was experiencing. Children were going hungry in other countries. In this country! There were worse things than *name-calling*. She'd told herself these things on the drive along the harbour into work this morning. And still her worries hadn't thinned any. And then the gulls had crapped all over the Mini right there in front of her as she'd opened up. And the bread delivery guy had forgotten her ciabattas. Then there'd been the hideous invoice waiting on Coast's doormat, this quarter's rates due again already.

She sighed, tied a clean blue barista's apron behind her back and pressed her nose to the inside of the store window. In the distance, beyond the last whitewashed cottages of the harbour and The Village, where a tribe of surfers already convened, sand dunes rolled down to the edge of the bay, marking the last spot on the horizon where the sun bled out each night. This view would be the envy of the town at dusk. She could picture it so vividly. Warm evening air, lanterns hanging over the terrace, gentle music against a backdrop of breaking surf. Why couldn't Sam see it too?

She rolled her cheeks against the cold glass, peering up the high street. Pomme du Port had new outside furniture. Minimalist, beautiful, expensive. Cleo scowled. What was French for *bollocks*? Maybe Evie knew. Elodie Inman-Holt definitely would. Elodie was on for an A* in French, Juliette had been boasting about it last week over a skinny latte and brand new Birkenstock handbag.

She pushed herself past the boxes cluttering up her route, yanked her hair back into a tighter ponytail and followed the smell of baking almond croissants back into the café. She hated that the bread was a cheat, another reason to extend: more oven space. She reached the back of the sweeping wooden counter, yanked on a few shiny chrome levers and began running the filters through on the coffee station. She tapped a finger on the machine while it gargled and bleeped. Bloody momsters. Boycott? Seriously? Lorna was bat-shit crazy.

Someone cleared their throat behind her. A full load of coffee grounds dropped from her hands exploding across the floor. 'Shit!'

'*Sorry!*'

The fidgety young woman on the other side of the counter winced. Cleo gritted her teeth 'Sorry. Pardon my French . . .'

The woman blinked at her. 'I didn't mean to make you jump, look at the mess I've caused. Here, I'll pay for that.'

Cleo batted a hand at the air while the girl fished for her purse. 'It's fine . . . just don't boycott the place for my filthy language.' The girl stopped fishing and tucked loose blonde curls behind one ear. There was something timid about her, like a little bird startled.

'Don't worry, really, I've heard plenty of filthy language in the workplace, and that wasn't filthy.'

Cleo fumbled with the coffee filters. 'Where do you work? Building site? Footy stadium?'

'*Did* work . . . just a high school. These ears are pretty much immune now.'

'You worked in a high school? Ugh, poor you. I have two teenagers. Sometimes I literally have to put my fingers inside my ears. Right inside,' she said, jabbing her fingers towards her ears. That was half true; only Evie's mouth had ever been threatened with a bar of soap.

'The staff were worse than the students.' The girl smiled and held out a long, slender arm. Her sleeve buttons clattered against one of the serviette dispensers. 'I'm Isobel.'

Customers didn't usually offer handshakes. She was about to ask for a job. 'Hi. I'm Cleo.' Isobel's hand felt ever-so-slightly smaller than Evie's, which Cleo had sneakily held for much of *Mob Wives* last night, trying to channel her inner lioness directly into her daughter. 'Welcome to Fallenbay, famed for pirate legends, Paralympians and potty-mouthed women. First visit?'

'Thanks. How did you know I'm just visiting?'

Cleo nodded to the leather armchairs in the window. 'Tourists tend to find a place they like fairly quickly and stick with it. Settlers shop around, get to know the area. Who are you holidaying with?'

Isobel repositioned her bag strap. 'More of a break-for-one type situation.'

'Good for you! I've always fancied that. Buggering off somewhere, *finding* myself.' Her interest spiked, she could smell a broken heart. There was a man in this picture somewhere, probably being punished for not trying hard enough. She was going to punish Sam one day too. Shake him up a bit. Wake up the sexy, red-blooded Alpha she'd fallen in love

64

with. But not before he'd fixed the plumbing in Evie's en-suite. 'Are you here for long?'

Isobel's jaw tensed. 'I don't suppose you've got any flapjack left? It was insanely good yesterday. I'm sure you've sold out.'

Definitely a broken heart. 'Sure. Can I get you a coffee with that? First customer of the day who lets a "shit" fly over their head gets their first cup on the house. Shop rules.'

'Thanks. Could I be really cheeky and make it a tea? Sorry, I get morning headaches; limiting caffeine's supposed to help.'

'No problem, pot of tea coming up.' Cleo set to work. Isobel slipped her bag over her head and perched on one of the wooden bar stools. 'Sleep, that's what kicks my headaches off,' said Cleo. 'A dreadful night's sleep.' Specifically, lying awake, thinking of ways to throttle nasty little Facebookers and neurotic earth mothers without the feds finding out. *The feds?* The bloody *feds?* Good God, one episode of *Mob Wives* and she was turning into a moll.

Isobel sat straight as a bookend at the counter. She reminded Cleo of Evie a little. Pretty round face, wide intelligent eyes. Something vulnerable in there too.

'Sleep? That would make sense. There's a dog, next door to my holiday cottage. A big one. Started barking at the milkman at five-thirty this morning. He was still going strong when I left.'

A yapping dog Cleo could cope with. It was a yapping mother she'd had to suffer. Well, she hoped Lorna felt better after her little outburst. One day she might not have the luxury of someone to fire off at, one day she might be stacked against a virtual menace, an *Aeron Mycock*, hurting her little girl over the internet where she couldn't wring his scrawny neck.

Isobel smiled at the wrong moment, and it was as if a defunct switch was thrown inside Cleo's emotional control centre, the feelings rushing from nowhere. *Oh God*, was she about to . . . no . . . *Oh God, no . . .*

Too late.

The first release of tears eked from Cleo's face. Isobel, bemused, was already rising to her feet. *Stop sobbing, you fool!* What was wrong with her? No wonder Evie was such a drama queen. Cleo had passed it on like a defective gene, and there she was blaming Sam's lot for Evie's puppy fat.

Isobel stood hands flattened on the counter. 'Do you need anything?'

It was such an odd response, it threw Cleo off track. Was she a counsellor? Or maybe she meant drugs? Yes, Isobel thought she was a complete fruit-loop, the sort of woman who needed to drop a Diazepam to see a pot of tea through to fruition without a meltdown. Isobel pulled at the serviette dispenser. 'Tissue?'

Cleo stole a few breaths. She took the serviette with the little slate blue C for Coast printed subtly in each corner and wiped her face. She'd agonised over how many Cs to have on the serviettes, the sizing, the shade of blue . . .

'Rough morning?' Isobel asked.

Rough? It had been a little rough, now it was officially bottom-clenchingly bad. 'Sorry. Not what you wanted for breakfast, profanity *and* crying. How embarrassing!' Phew, no wobble in her voice. 'I'm not usually a crier.' Why was she crying again? Was it Lorna's newly burning hatred for her? The furniture outside Pomme du Port? No, it was an amalgamation of things, a pile of silliness topped off by some horrid little snot calling her daughter names. A foul, hurtful, utterly uncalled-for name. Evie had shown her a screen-shot of the comment left beneath one of her million pouty selfies. *Fat cow*, he'd called her – not just *fat*, although that was obviously the part Evie found most offensive, the *fat* part. Personally Cleo would rather be called a *fat cow* than a *stupid woman*, for argument's sake, but Evie was fifteen so Cleo went with it, cheerily playing the whole thing down while inside her guts had twisted for both the *fat* and the *cow* that little shit had labelled her baby girl.

She tucked her tissue into her apron and straightened her shoulders. 'Aren't people rotten, Isobel?' she smiled. 'Cruel, just for the thrill of it?' Just for the sport. She set a pot of milk beside the cup and saucer. Isobel looked away. She suddenly seemed older than Cleo had first pegged her. A good ten years older than Evie, maybe.

'Yes, Cleo,' said Isobel. 'People can be very cruel indeed. Usually when they think there'll be no consequences.'

11

Sarah hovered outside Year 2's classroom door, heat creeping up her neck. Darcey skipped in ahead of her.

'I don't know what on earth's happened to your lovely self-portrait, Tabitha, I'm usually with the Year One children, aren't I? You know this because last year you were in Year One, weren't you, Tabitha? Now, I'm sure when Mrs Harrison finally arrives for class she'll have a perfectly good explan— Ah, here she is now. Stop crying, Tabitha, or you'll have two smudged faces.'

Juliette's brunette business bob had grown longer over the years she'd been working at Hornbeam Primary. Her fringe swept over to one side nowadays, softening the severe lines of her cheekbones and the tailored tops she always wore, cutting a threatening edge along her collarbone.

Sarah tried to keep her work wardrobe as casual as *smart* allowed. Juliette still dressed for the city finance career she'd curtailed to become mother extraordinaire to Elodie and Milo some sixteen and fourteen years ago respectively. What the banking world lost in a formidable career woman, Hornbeam's Year 1 class, the board of governors, and the PFA had since inherited in a no-nonsense higher level teaching assistant who liked to organise people the way Sarah imagined she used to organise numbers. Remotely. Methodically. And if the occasion called for it, ruthlessly.

Sarah cleared her throat quietly. She made a conscious effort not to slouch as she walked into her own classroom. 'Sit up, Sarah!' her father used to implore her at the dinner table, 'you look like a letter S. We should've named you something beginning with I, or L, or E. Maybe we could've improved your posture.' Her father had been a headmaster. Inside the home and out.

Sarah waited politely for Juliette to step out from behind the desk. Juliette had good posture. Nothing in the way she held herself betrayed how she'd been autopsying Sarah's private life in the staff room not ten minutes ago.

'Thank you, Mrs Inman-Holt. I can take it from here.' She'd become adept at avoiding all eye contact with Juliette. They'd been friends once. Bizarre to think it now. They'd laughed over their husbands' barbecuing skills, their children had played together, Will and Elodie's mutual affection for Play Doh at toddler group igniting a friendship lasting nearly seven years between their once-compatible families. Patrick and Karl had bonded over international basketball and Heidi Klum, Sarah and Juliette over the pursuit of the best kid-friendly careers and herb-infused cocktails. And then Sarah went and left the summerhouse door unlocked.

'Tabitha was hoping to have her portrait all fixed up in time for open-door Wednesday, weren't you, Tabitha? So your mother can see it?' Tabitha nodded. Thank goodness Olivia hadn't peeped her head around to wave at Tabitha on her way out of school. 'Perhaps whoever spoiled your lovely picture might offer to help you fix it?' Juliette didn't look at Sarah very often either. The simple act probably enough to transport Juliette back to that horrendous afternoon, the terrible discovery after the screaming had begun.

'We'll take a look at it at break, okay Tabitha?' soothed Sarah.

Juliette snapped her head around, her fringe obediently realigning itself. She walked between the front of the whiteboard and the two perfectly formed lines of children sitting cross-legged on the carpet. Sarah never had them all sitting so uniformly, like little druids waiting for the moon to do something significant.

'Before I go, Mr Pethers is expecting us to run through the new e-safety strategies at break, Mrs Harrison.'

Bugger. Sarah had forgotten Mr Pethers' last-minute meeting request. The internet had become a double-edged machete in school after one of the Year 3s had looked up a numeracy game and inadvertently found their way on to a website entitled *Let's Do METH!*

'Thank you, Mrs Inman-Holt. Tabitha, take a deep breath, we'll get it sorted before your mum comes in, alright?'

Juliette hesitated in the doorway. 'Speaking of e-safety, I've shut your mobile phone in the stationery cupboard, Mrs Harrison. You'd left it unattended on your desk. It's been vibrating.'

A lesser demon would've smirked, but Juliette was more of a subtle soul. A sideways glance was enough. *If I tell Mr Pethers on you, Sarah Harrison, you're going to be in BIG trouble.* This was how it was now Juliette worked at Hornbeam too. Sarah wasn't just at school five days a week, she was *back at school* five days a week. With her very own, impeccably dressed black cloud ready to rain down on her.

And Juliette had every right.

12

Isobel caught herself chewing slowly as Cleo chattered on about Fallenbay's natives.

'Totally true story, Jon literally clonked her with his surfboard. That's how they met! Right out there on my terrace. Sarah was just minding her own business and, *wham*! By rights I should get maid of honour; Sarah wanted me to but she was overruled, her parents browbeat her into asking some unpleasant sociopathic cousin, on her father's side, I think. Sarah's allergic to confrontation so, you know, she usually just rolls with what the masses want, she'd tell you as much herself. They're getting married next year. Why doesn't that kind of romance happen to the rest of us? It's all we want, right?'

Isobel swallowed the last of the complimentary madeleines Cleo had plonked on the table and began carefully stacking her spent tea things in front of her. Cleo vigorously wiped down the next table. She'd cheered up as the morning progressed. Work could do that. Isobel used to love her work too. The challenges, the kids, the sense of doing something useful with her life. Imparting knowledge. Making some tiny difference.

'You do know what I mean, don't you, Isobel?'

'Romance that's like a bang to the head?' Cleo couldn't be more wrong if she tried.

'Yes! Startling and unexpected. The closest to romantic my Sam gets is smiling affectionately at his favourite cheese.'

Isobel glanced at the faces in clusters of two or more at the other tables. She was the only person in here sitting alone, again. No odd-bods. No lone wolves. Just Isobel.

'How do I use the free wifi?'

Cleo popped fresh tealights inside a jam jar. 'Just log on, password's "coast".'

No register, no allocated user accounts. The name *DEEP_DRILLERZ* wouldn't mean anything to Cleo.

'Cleo? Could I ask you a question?'

'Fire away . . .'

'Do you get many locals in here? Or would you say it's mainly tourists passing through? Like me?'

Cleo frowned. 'Pomme du Port bag a lot of locals, but us, not so much after the lunch rush.' She set her hand on her hip. 'They're not even French in there, y'know, and they have the cheek to call themselves the apple of the harbour. Bloody charlatans.'

'But what about here? Free wifi must bring the locals in? Students? Workers?' *Psychological deviants*. Isobel's hands felt clammy, sickly thoughts pressing in. He could've sat in this chair, drunk from this cup.

Cleo huffed. 'It's a mix, really. We do get the locals in, but they stick to the morning, mainly, while the tourists are eating breakfast in their holiday lets. And we get the kids in through the summer holidays. Hordes of the buggers, hang around all day, but, y'know, if they're here they're not getting into any trouble.'

The onslaught had stopped by the summer. No more emails. No more links appearing on the Facebook walls of Isobel's friends and family. Had the school children invaded his turf for milkshakes and free wifi, is that what finally slowed him? Terrorising women online must be tricky with a café full of kids looking over your shoulder.

Cleo's eyes narrowed. It put Isobel on edge. Her therapist used to do that in their CBT sessions, Jenny's *analysing* face. Cleo slipped her hands into her apron. 'You know, if you're on *that* kind of holiday, Isobel, and are thinking about maybe . . . I don't know, meeting a local chap to have a flutter of holiday romance . . . you could try The Village.'

'The Village?' People in local hangouts knew other local people. Knew behaviours. Knew nicknames. Usernames.

Cleo's eyebrows lifted. 'Uhuh, plenty of eye-fodder down there!'

'You mean . . . *men*?'

Isobel's folks had been desperate for her to go away, to fall in love again and fix everything that was broken with a stranger and a proper good snog. They still thought she was fourteen. That everything would blow over as if it was an unfortunate, but not insurmountable, humiliation at the youth club disco. Sophie would be hoping for the same, of course, for Isobel to forget about 'the blip', forget about Nathan and everything he represented, everything that had gone. *See this as a silver lining, darling. A chance to open yourself up to new things. You might meet someone wonderful, feel that special spark again! Soon enough you'll be back on track with the*

*really important things, new home . . . new job . . . new circle
of friends, even!* Isobel's Base Camp list had found its footings
in the hopes her mother held for her. Those *really important
things.* Things a person didn't want to lose if they had them.

Cleo was staring. Her eyes round and knowing, she thought
she was on to something. 'Sure! If it is locals you're after
Surfers' Village is one of the unofficial zones, where outsiders
don't usually infiltrate.' Cleo tapped her finger to the side of
her nose. 'Unless they've got inside info, or they're Oli Adams
or some other board hero. But you're so lovely and blonde
and youthful, you'd fit right into the scene down there. It's
not surf season yet, but there are still plenty of boards to
bang your head on!'

Isobel resisted the urge to put her fingers to where root
regrowth would betray her natural brunette soon enough.
'Thanks, Cleo. But I think I'll stick to having a quiet one
with my book and that view.' She nodded towards the wall
of glass separating them from the busy harbour, distant surf
and endless horizon.

Cleo set about wiping the same table again. 'You're probably best. Men are hassle, all except for my Harry, so laid
back he's practically horizontal. He's gone and fallen for
an exchange student, *Ingred.* They're trying to do the long-
distance thing now she's gone back to Denmark, which means
I don't have to worry about what they're getting up to, if
you catch my drift. He won't admit it but he's besotted.
Absolutely besotted. Never off his phone since she sent him
her new number.'

'The perfect girlfriend,' agreed Isobel. She pulled her
jacket on and spotted a rabble of surfers rinsing off under

the beachside showers. The big buff one was pulling his wetsuit down to his middle, a raging swordfish tattoo thrashed across his ribs. He'd be just the type her sister would go for: gym-lover, probably trouble. Sophie attracted trouble, happily. The boy racer who hadn't bothered with seatbelts . . . the one who'd reeked of cannabis and kept eating their dad's chocolate Hobnobs . . . the guy with the flashy clothes who'd left her for dust after generously donating the other twenty-three chromosomes needed to make an Ella. Nathan had been a safe bet by contrast. Strait-laced, career-focused, the kind of guy you took home to meet your father. The kind of man Isobel thought she wanted to marry.

She blotted him out, freed the hair from the collar of her jacket and checked her watch instead. 'Sorry I stayed so long, Cleo, I meant to buy more food but . . .'

A gaggle of school kids bustled through Coast's main door, wooden blinds clattering against the glass. Isobel tucked her purse and book into her bag and slipped out of the window chair she'd been commandeering all morning. Not one base camp ticked off her list yet, not even close.

'But you've been too busy people-watching, I noticed! Well, it's a good spot.' Cleo grinned at something across the cobbled street. A young woman with an immaculate ponytail and tight trousers was trying to discreetly fish a wedgy from her bum. 'How differently we would all behave, hey, Isobel, if we thought someone was watching?'

Isobel exhaled slowly.

Two high school girls with matching back-combed hair and shortened school ties arrived at Cleo's shoulder. 'Mum, can me and Cassie just grab a sandwich and run? The school canteen's rammed and everything's fried as usual.'

'I told Evie she doesn't need to diet, Mrs R,' sighed the other girl.

'Hello girls,' beamed Cleo. 'No, you can't, you can queue like everyone else.'

Cleo's daughter rolled her eyes. She had pretty eyes; too much make-up, but that was teenage girls for you, and quite a few teenage boys too.

Isobel gathered her things. 'I'll probably see you tomorrow, Cleo, early again, unless next-door's dog decides to let me lie in.'

'You should complain. I probably know them. I could complain for you, if you like? I'm already ticking locals off. Are you staying in the harbour?'

Sophie had been explicitly clear on this point. *Do not tell anyone where you're staying.*

'No, it's just a small place, past the dunes. A cottage, I forget the name.'

'Not Curlew Cottage? Arthur Oakes' place? At the top of the lung-busting hill?'

Isobel hesitated. 'Ah . . . yep.' She wouldn't tell Sophie.

'Oh, *that* dog. You must have nerves of steel staying up there. Nearly had my husband's head off when he went to quote for guttering last autumn. Sam wouldn't even get out of his van, said it had gone rogue!'

'Didn't Mr Oakes feed his wife to that dog?' Evie grinned.

'Evie, don't be so dramatic. They didn't even have the dog when Mrs Oakes moved away. Teenage girls' overactive imaginations, honestly!'

'You wouldn't go up there on a dark night, would you, Mum? Even his wife doesn't want to be up there. If she's still alive, that is.'

'Oh, Evie. Sometimes people just . . . grow apart.'

'Chill, Mother. I'm only playing.' Evie glanced at Isobel. 'That dog won't hurt you. It just doesn't like men, that's all. Bet he doesn't bark at you, am I right?' Isobel hadn't really thought about it. Evie shrugged. 'Just don't take any strange men up there.'

'Thanks. Wasn't planning on it.'

'Have you met his sons yet, Isobel?' asked Cleo. 'You're in for a treat. Gorgeous, the both of them.'

'OMG, that *bangle* is gorgeous. Can I see?' Evie reached for Isobel's wrist without warning.

'Evie! Stop haranguing my customers!'

It had been a get-well gift from Sophie and Ella. Isobel lifted her arm for Evie to take a quick look, but she'd already caught Isobel gently by the elbow. 'Mum, look! You wanted birthday ideas, something like this would be perfect.' Evie turned to Isobel. 'Could I try it on?'

'Evie!'

'What? I won't run out of the door with it, Mum, jeez.' Isobel was nothing to do with this conversation. She undid the clasp, obediently slipping off the silver cuff.

'Sorry, Isobel. Oh, it really is lovely,' agreed Cleo, admiring the bracelet shuffling on to Evie's tanned wrist. 'It looks expensive though, Evie.'

'Harry's asked for a drum kit, they're not cheap.'

Cleo threw Isobel an exasperated look. 'My accountant

keeps telling me it won't be my business bankrupting me . . . it'll be those twins!'

Isobel shrugged. 'Sorry, I have no idea what it cost. It was a birthday present.' She tucked her hair behind her ear. Evie's focus shifted.

'How about something that costs less than jewellery and lasts a lifetime, Mum?'

Cleo looked at Isobel's wrist too. 'Oh no, lady. You have got absolutely no chance.'

'But everyone else has them, look!' Evie was nodding at Isobel. *Exhibit A*. 'It's different now, tattoos aren't just for thugs and sailors!'

Evie's friend guffawed. 'My dad's got loads, but he is actually a sailor and a bit of a thug. Mum's just got the divorce through, Mrs R.'

'Shh, Cassie. Look, Mum, it's really cute and girly. Little Red Riding Hood!'

Isobel pulled her jacket sleeve down to her knuckles and waited for the bangle to come back. She'd told Sophie all the reasons she wanted rid of the tattoo. Sophie had swung into fix-it mode and the bracelet had been on Isobel's wrist that night. Dealt with. Covered up. Sophie-style.

'No. Way. End of conversation, Evie.'

'Mum, I look way older than fifteen, I could just go anyway . . .'

'Evie!' Cleo sang. 'I strongly advise you do no such thing. Now, I won't be swayed so zip it. Tattoos are just . . . just . . .' She looked another apology at Isobel.

'Tacky? Common?' Isobel offered light-heartedly. 'It's fine, Cleo, really.' She'd never been a tattoo fan either, but Sophie had talked her into their sisterly pact, and they'd done so little as sisters that it had seemed worthwhile and overdue to do something lasting and memorable together. *Stupid.*

Cleo gritted her teeth. 'I was going to say, easy to regret. They're just so easy to regret.'

'Do you regret yours?' fired Evie. She was staring at Isobel now. Isobel rubbed her wrist. It was fairly boring as tattoos went. Sophie had challenged her to shock their parents for a change and do something out of character. Isobel had talked her on to a middle ground: she'd go through with it but they had to have similar designs, and they had to be literary-based, so Isobel could at least impress her English students who up until then suspected she was chronically strait-laced. It had been an easy choice, the favourite book they'd listened to a hundred times snuggled on their dad's lap. Red Riding Hood had made it on to Isobel's wrist, the Big Bad Wolf on to Soph's.

Evie was waiting for an answer. 'Honestly?' Isobel asked. 'Yes.'

'Yes?' frowned Evie.

'Yes. I regret it every day. It was fun at first. Now it's just a reminder.'

Evie cocked her head. 'A reminder of what?'

Don't be led. Don't be distinguishable. Protect your anonymity.

'To make better choices, Evie. It reminds me to make better choices.'

13

Cleo skipped out of Coast, earrings glinting in the sun. 'Isobel! Hang on!' she yelled over the heads of the diners sitting on the terrace, every one of them enjoying the view from behind dark sunglasses of either the coastline or their mobile phone. Mostly the latter. 'Goodness, it's like the cast of *The Matrix* out here,' she said, flip-flopping her way across the decking.

It was becoming increasingly difficult not to warm to Cleo. Not exactly ideal, Isobel realised, but then it wouldn't be the worst thing either, would it? Cleo would know everyone in this town. Every last crazy.

'Did I forget something?' asked Isobel. Had she paid? Cleo was waving something too small to decipher.

'Only your key! It was underneath your saucer. You should be careful with that. Arthur will have your deposit if he has to get a locksmith out.' Isobel was on a roll. First advertising where she was living, now leaving a key to the door. Soph would have a seizure.

'Thanks, Cleo.' Isobel took the key. She'd overlooked it because it wasn't a part of this new routine yet; the act was still new and she was still getting used to the props.

Cleo squinted under the sun. 'Where are you off to? Anywhere nice?'

Isobel took a look past the fishermen working in the harbour, the tavernas nestled between chic wine bars and eateries. Fallenbay's revered golden postbox couldn't be too hard to find; the war memorial had been in the distance, Isobel had committed the photograph to memory. Golden postbox, war memorial, ocean backdrop. A three-point constellation mapping Fallenbay as the only town in the UK in which that photo could've been taken, and he'd been generous enough to use it as his profile picture. 'I'm not sure, thought I might just go for a mooch. Take in the sights.'

Cleo nodded but was looking straight over Isobel's shoulder. The beefcake who'd been showering off his bulging physique was strapping his surfboard to the roof of his truck.

'Cleo serves good coffee,' croaked a customer from her table behind them, 'but it's the view I come for. No offence, Cleo.'

'None taken, Elsie,' sighed Cleo. 'I too am a sucker for a good pair of buttocks in a wetsuit.'

Isobel glanced at the second surfer. Darker hair, better proportioned body, way bigger board. 'The other guy's is so much bigger, isn't it?' She really did need to brush up on the surf lingo. Was it even a surfboard?

Cleo snorted. 'I wouldn't like to speculate, but given the size of his feet, probably.'

'Cleo Roberts,' cackled the old girl. 'Don't let your Sam catch you talking like that.'

Cleo shook the stray curls from her face. 'Elsie, Sam wouldn't notice if I took that delicious specimen home, sat him on the sofa and parked myself on his lap. Not unless I gave him Sam's TV remote.'

'Ouch,' said Isobel. 'He's just stood on something.'

'Who?' asked Cleo.

'The guy with the bigger surfboard.'

'*Paddle-board*, Isobel. You'll need to know this stuff to infiltrate The Village.'

'What's he doing?'

'It looks like he's hopping. Should've put his shoes on, silly sod. They're always up here bugging me for bandages and sympathy.'

The darker of the surfers leaned his paddle-board against his pal's truck and looked towards them all, one arm flat against his thigh, the other frantically waving overhead. Isobel fought a frown. Was that some kind of semaphore? He looked like a primary school child bursting with the correct answer.

Cleo leaned in towards Isobel's ear. 'That's Ben, one of the local instructors, demonstrating an internationally recognised distress signal. He's saying, *Cleo Roberts, I want to feel your hands . . . right now . . . all over my—*'

Elsie sniggered and looked at Isobel. 'She's always got the local fellas up here, dipping into her First Aid box.'

Cleo grinned. 'What can I say, girls? My milkshake brings all the boys to the yard.'

'Well it's bringing Benjamin and his buttocks,' rasped Elsie.

The less bulky surfer hobbled his way across the cobbled street towards them. 'Cleo! I need you!' he winced, grabbing at his leg as if he'd just severed it in a terrible accident.

'Told you,' Cleo whispered. 'If whatever it is you've just trodden in originated in a dog's bottom, Ben, be a darling and take it down the road to Pomme du Poop, use their facilities instead.'

He stopped just the other side of the rope barrier running up to the terrace and rubbed the wetness from the top of his cropped dark hair. Water droplets clung to his skin where his wetsuit stopped at the elbows. He gave Isobel a quick smile as if they were both in on something, then presented a bloody foot to Cleo.

'For goodness sake, Ben. My fifteen-year-old has more sense, put some shoes on. Wait there, you'll bleed all over my terrace. I'm going to start charging you for triage supplies, you know.'

Cleo turned away. Isobel sensed the danger of having to make awkward small talk. 'I'd better be going,' she blurted. She waved her key. 'Thanks for this, Cleo.'

Cleo threw a hand over her head. 'No problem! Keep an eye out for those Oakes boys I was telling you about.'

Isobel jogged her brain. 'Two gorgeous brothers. Got it.' As if face-values would ever matter again.

'You're halfway there already!' Cleo called as she ducked beneath an olive tree.

'What do you mean?' called Isobel.

'Those gorgeous Oakes boys, you've already met Arthur's eldest!' Isobel glanced at the bleeding surfer. 'And I can tell you now, Isobel, you're yet to meet the better looking of the two!'

Ben was smiling at his feet. Cleo gone already. Isobel reached out automatically for a stiff handshake. 'Mr Oakes' son?'

He grinned at the handshake. He had a friendly face that looked to have seen plenty of sun. And laughter. He was probably a very nice person too, maybe even genuine. Or maybe he was a nice-looking sociopath who took twisted pleasure in destroying the lives of strangers.

'Ben Oakes.'

'Isobel. Oliver.'

'I know. The girl who's moved into a cottage on a hill in the middle of nowhere, all by herself.'

Isobel gritted her teeth. 'Guess so. Nice to meet you.'

'Nice to meet you too, Isobel Oliver. Sorry about the blood.'

14

'Buona sera, signora, table for three this evening?'

'Grrr, raahhh . . . I'm going to eat everybody in this whole place, grrrr!'

'Maxy, could you keep a lid on the Godzilla bit until we're all sitting down? Or this nice man might not want to find us a spot. Table for four please. My . . .' Sarah stalled. *Fiancé* always felt alien on her tongue. *Boyfriend* just as misshapen. She was a divorced, stretch-marked mother of two. 'We're waiting on one more,' she smiled.

Hurry up, Jon. One waft of warm herby air and she was suddenly famished. She'd survived a whole day on a ration of Tic Tacs, just so she could avoid Juliette in the staff room.

'Very good, *signora*, this way.'

Will led the way. He'd done a quick change at home, swapping school uniform for his signature hoody and jeans. Sarah reached over Max, gently pulling Will's hood off his head. Will's head was always buried beneath something nowadays: Hoody . . . headphones . . . Sarah missed that head. She missed the days Will used to curl up on her lap, her fingers teasing through the deep brown curls she also missed kissing goodnight.

Will rubbed his hand over his hair and took the menus

offered to him. He had a couple of inches on the waiter. 'Thanks, we'll shout when we're ready.' The waiter nodded at Will and left. Will shuffled into the booth, pulling Max in after him. Will had been a scrawny eleven-year-old when they'd first met Jon. All elbows and knees. In a blink, he was almost a man, towering over Sarah for at least a year now. Broad shoulders, harder set to his jaw. He would be taller than his father one day. A bigger man. It was what Sarah wanted most, for Will and Max, that they would be bigger men than Patrick Harrison.

Will patted Max's head with a menu. 'Come on, shorty, let's get ready to order.'

Sarah took a seat opposite. She let go of the deep breath she'd been holding since the disabled loo and broke into a packet of breadsticks. 'So guys, have we had a good day? What have you been doing? Worst bits and best bits?'

Max began attacking a colouring sheet with the crayons the waiter had left. Will shrugged and leaned back into the booth, filling the space.

'Maxy? Best bit?' asked Sarah.

Max kept scribbling. 'Chloe's mummy brunged her new puppy to school. It's got long ears and is different colours and is called Fritz.'

'A new puppy? What a shame I missed him.'

Sarah missed everyone at school pickup; it was great. Max went into after-school club three nights a week while she finished up, usually with his nose pressed to the classroom window, watching his pals scooting up and down the yard while the 'normal mummies' chatted over fundraising initiatives and nit outbreaks. Those conversational circles Sarah never managed to navigate without feeling clumsy and disjointed.

'But you don't like dogs, Mummy.'

'I do . . . it's just . . .'

Max sighed. 'I know, Mr Fogharty's got long claws.' Mr Fogharty was a furred menace parading as a King Charles spaniel. Jon's mother preferred painting Mr Fogharty's nails to clipping them and Sarah's clothes usually paid the price. Max gasped with a new thought. 'Can we have a puppy, Mummy? I'll cut his nails with my art scissors, I'll be careful!'

Will grinned and shook his head. Since his braces came off it was almost criminal that he didn't smile more often. Will hadn't brought a single girl home yet, not one. There'd be a queue lining the street if he flashed those beautifully aligned teeth a little more.

'Sorry, Max, no one's home all day, it wouldn't be fair. And we do get to look after Mr Fogharty for Jon's mummy lots, don't we? So we don't really need a dog of our own, do we?'

'What about when we move house?' pressed Max. The muscle in Will's jaw tensed. 'Nanny Judy could stay at home with our puppy while we go to school. Or you could teach me at our house!'

'We'll talk about it later, Max. When things have settled down.'

If she thought a puppy would swing it for Will, she wouldn't hesitate. *What would swing it?* She needed a golden carrot, something to incentivise him. A reason to move. She just didn't have one right now. All afternoon she'd been in the grips of a mild panic at the prospect of Will going home to find not only a newly planted For Sale board in their driveway, but a big fat impatient SOLD slapped across it, too.

Will was watching her thinking it all out. 'So, what's the occasion?' he asked.

Sarah looked for Jon through the windows. 'Just thought we'd eat out tonight,' she lied.

'Mummy? I haven't told you my worst bit.'

'Sorry, Max. Go on.' Will pulled his phone from his pocket. Conversation over.

'Seb said I'm not allowed to like Chloe's new puppy.' Max changed crayons, eyes still fixed on the happy-faced pizza he'd been colouring ferociously.

Will's eyes remained fixed on his phone screen. 'Seb's not allowed to tell you what you're allowed to like or not.'

Max frowned, face serious while he picked through his big brother's words.

'I'm sure Seb meant something else, Max. I wonder where Jon's got to? He said six p.m.'

Will did a double-take at the restaurant doors. A smart-casual man with the beginnings of grey hair where his stylish rectangular glasses met his temples led his family inside. Sarah champed into a breadstick. Karl Inman-Holt had the only set of teeth in Fallenbay that could out-dazzle Will's. *Karl the Millionaire Mouth Magician*, Patrick used to call him. Patrick had been borderline jealous of Karl's success; Jon couldn't care less. Jon used the Horizon dental practice like everyone else in the bay. Everyone bar Sarah and the boys.

'What are we eating then?' She could hear the forced joviality in her voice.

Will was hawk-like, watching the Inman-Holts take their

table up by the pizza ovens. Sarah stole a quick look at the children who'd once played in Will's sand pit. She hadn't seen Elodie for at least a year now. She was still lovely, still a fan of floral tea dresses and retro pumps, just taller now, more willowy. More womanly. Milo had lost his baby face too. Goodness, he looked like Karl. *Did Elodie just smile at them?* Juliette looked over. Will muttered something under his breath.

'Are you okay, Mummy? Your neck's is going red.'

'Oh, it's just a bit hot in here, darling. I'm fine.' Jon had been in their lives for nearly four years and still Sarah couldn't sit in the same vicinity as the Inman-Holts without feeling out on a limb. An undesirable. A must-try-harder-er.

'I don't like Mrs Inman-Holt very much, Mummy,' whispered Max.

'No one does,' huffed Will, 'don't worry about it.'

Max leaned over the table, cupping a hand to his mouth. 'She makes me stay at the lunch table until I've eaten my crusts.'

Juliette was looking over again. Max was going to expose them both, whispering conspirators. 'Sit down, Maxy, like a big boy. I'm sure Mrs Inman-Holt just wants to make sure you're eating all the goodness you need. Don't you want to grow big and strong like Will?'

Will was stealing glances across the room too. He was on edge. The air had changed. Sarah felt defensive, even though Will would now stand nose to nose with Karl. She tried to read Will's expression. Max slumped back into his seat, catching one of the empty wine glasses with his elbow. Sarah watched it rattle from the table, exploding on the flagstones before she could stop it. Max's eyes widened.

'It's okay, Max. It was just an accident.' Sarah bent down out of Juliette's sight, reaching for the shards nearest her feet first.

'Mum, just leave it. The waiters will get it,' instructed Will, his voice tight. They should've gone somewhere else tonight. Out of town, fly-tip their 'wonderful news' about the house, then drive home again in unburdened silence. She lifted another spike of glass.

'I run ten minutes late and you start wrecking the joint!'

'Jon, I just smashed a glass! And my teacher is over there, look.'

'Stop pointing, Max,' groaned Will.

Relief flooded through Sarah like a warm drug. Jon bent down and kissed her on the cheek. He took the glass from her fingers. 'Let me get that, beautiful. You'll cut yourself. How's it going, fellas?'

Will nodded.

'Chloe has a puppy called Fritz!' said Max.

Jon held up a hand to the Inman-Holts. Elodie waved back without hesitation. Jon slipped his suit jacket on to the back of his chair. 'I am bloomin' Hank Marvin. What are we having, gang? Will? Are we thinking pizza, or that pasta you like? Come on, guys, let's go to town. Whatever you like.' Jon raised a hand into the air, as if about to burst into something operatic. 'A-think am-a gonna-have-a tha spicy meat-a-boll-az!'

Something lifted inside Sarah. 'Your Italian's really coming on.' Jon winked at her.

'What are these comics about, Jon?' asked Max.

Sarah scanned the covers of the magazines Jon had set

down. *Boys' Toys,* and something she couldn't read upside down. Both featured pool tables on their covers.

'Just a few ideas, young Maximus. Want to take a peek? I was thinking, if we stick together we might talk Mum into a home cinema. Or a man cave!'

'Our house is too small for a cinema inside it,' Max lisped.

'I guess we could use a bigger house then, huh?' Jon squeezed Sarah's knee under the table. He'd brought a whole bunch of carrots. Home cinemas . . . games rooms . . . golden incentives to lure Will from the only home he'd ever known.

'Will, reckon you could be talked into a home cinema? Little music studio, maybe? If you could choose anything, what would you go for?'

Will shrugged, but he'd only just prised his eyes from the magazine covers. For a second Sarah thought it might be easier than she'd thought. Will lobbed his menu on to the table and pulled his hood back up. 'The pizza.'

15

Harry dumped his bike on the front drive and wandered breathless into the garage. 'What are you up to, Ma?'

Cleo lumped another box of Sam's wall tiles on to the trolley she'd brought home from Coast. 'Hi, son. Just clearing a few things.'

Harry moved his sunglasses to his forehead. 'Need a hand?'

'Sure, could you load them into the back of my car? Your dad's using this place as a dumping ground, I want it all cleared. I need a new splashback at Coast anyway.'

'Y'know, a few egg boxes stapled to the walls in here could be a sweet place to, I dunno, keep a drum kit?' Harry grinned.

'Don't get your hopes up, H. I've got enough grand designs to organise with those back store rooms.'

'We're converting the stores?'

She rooted around her feet for the next box. 'Only if I can convince your father to do the work for me.' Cleo straightened up and thumped her head on Sam's punchbag again. It swung pointlessly from the garage ceiling. 'That's next to go, bloody thing. I told your father it would never get used.'

Harry tilted the trolley, pushing for the garage doors. 'We used it, Mum. Dad was pretty good until he knocked it out of the ceiling. Reckons it's like riding a bike.'

'What is?'

'Boxing.'

Ha! Sam hadn't boxed for over twenty years. All that time ago, when Cleo would help her mother deliver hot sandwiches to the gym offices, just so she could watch Sam Roberts' taught body twist and flex, lean and powerful. The only boxing Sam did these days was goggleboxing. 'Yes, but how long did it take him to fix it back to the ceiling joist again, Harry? A bloody age. And even then he said not to touch it, just in case. He probably used Blu-tac . . . a temporary fix just to stop me moaning.'

'Actually, I used a plate and bolt system, but those timbers are going to need replacing soon. Damp's getting through somewhere, I'll have to have a weekend at it.' Sam stood in the doorway between the kitchen utility and the garage, hair wet from the shower, wearing one of last year's best holiday shirts. Cleo gave him a point for getting out of his work clothes at least.

'Whenever you next get one of those, Sam. So, damp rafters? Brilliant. Are they dangerous?'

He wiggled his eyebrows. 'Not unless we start swinging from them, baby.' Cleo scowled. Sam held out a cup of tea. She struggled to take it, Sam's enormous industrial gloves like rubber buckets on her hands.

'Why didn't you say we had a leak?'

'Because I didn't need you adding anything else to that nagging – I mean, snagging – list you keep in your head for me, my love.'

She did not keep a snagging or a nagging list at all. 'I wouldn't moan if you took a bit more interest in what I say. Tell me the last time I moaned about something new? Go on!'

Sam sighed. 'Extending Coast . . . the school mothers . . . Pomme du Port's hygiene rating . . . the Inman-Holts' new Mercedes . . . Jonathan Hildred being a snappier dresser than me . . . No! Wait! That's an old complaint, forget that one, darling.'

He pecked her on the head before she could speak. She felt an instant fury. A silly part of her wanted to cry again, like she had to that poor young girl in Coast this morning. She shrugged off Sam's gloves, letting them fall to the floor the way Sam used to let his boxing gloves fall just before leaping over the ropes to kiss Cleo passionately before her mother saw.

'I didn't do anything to deserve what I got from Loopy Lorna Brooks, Sam. She was oversensitive and bloody horrible to me. But thanks.'

'She's not the only one who's oversensitive, Cleo.'

'What's that supposed to mean?'

'Heads-up, Mum's hands are on her hips . . . again. You two argue more than me and Harry now.' Evie stood in the doorway behind her father, clad head-to-toe in graphite grey gym gear that Cleo had never clapped eyes on before in her life.

'What is that?'

Evie blanched. 'They're old, I haven't worn them in ages.'

'Don't give me that, I do the bloody washing. And the label's sticking out of your neck! How have you paid for that lot? Trainers too!' Cleo yelped. 'Where have you found the cash for—' Even beneath the generous bronzer Evie's cheeks were reddening. 'Oh no, you better bloody well not have.'

Evie flattened herself against the utility door so Cleo could rampage through.

'Cleo . . .' Sam tried. He could smell an imminent explosion at a thousand paces. That and a sausage sandwich.

Cleo dragged a chair out from beneath the kitchen table that Sam had crafted for her out of old scaffold boards, and jumped up so she could reach the two terramundi jars sandwiched between her Nigella Lawson cook book collection and the twisted lump of driftwood she and Sam had found on their first dawn walk together along Mooner's beach.

It was supposed to be a joke! Keeping the clay jars out of reach, as if the notes she'd been feeding equally into the two pots were chocolate chip cookies the kids couldn't be trusted around. Harry's jar was nearest, and Cleo didn't bother giving it a shake; normally she'd feel a twinge of guilt but she was far too enraged right now for guilt. She hadn't been feeding the two jars all that equally, but Harry was never going to need as much extra tuition as Evie. Cleo grabbed Evie's jar and checked for signs of infiltration. Terramundi jars had to be smashed before surrendering their contents.

'You sneaky little—'

'You said it was for emergency purposes, Mum!'

'Dressing up as a sodding ninja? Tuition, Evie! That money was for extra tuition! So you don't end up flipping burgers for a sodding living!'

'You flip pancakes.'

Sam shook his head. 'Evie,' he groaned.

'I don't need the tuition! Not if I do the extra classes Mr Hildred suggested,' Evie bumbled. Evie always bumbled when she was lying through her teeth.

'Oh, that's your plan is it, Evie? So how come that's the

first you've said about extra classes? I'll just ring Sarah now then, shall I? Ask Jon to confirm you've signed yourself up?'

Sam pinched the skin above his nose.

'Well?' said Cleo, balancing the jar Evie had deftly managed to chip the base from. 'How much?' Because, *damn it*, Cleo couldn't remember exactly how many twenty-pound notes she'd fed into Evie's pot.

Sam braced his arms against the countertop. 'Cleo, she'll work it off at Coast.'

'She will not. She spends half her time there on her phone. She can take those clothes back and get my money back.'

'But—'

'But nothing. You still have the labels in them. You're taking them back. Now how much?'

'About one hundred . . . and thirty . . . ish.'

'I want that cash back in this pot tomorrow. Or else.'

Evie looked open-mouthed from Cleo to Sam. 'But Dad . . .'

'Cleo, I'm sure we can work something out.'

She glared, stopping Sam dead. 'Do you know how long it takes me to earn a clear profit of one hundred and thirty pounds selling teacakes? Do you have any idea?'

Sam straightened. 'No. But before tax it's about nine hours of backbreaking work, digging footings in the pouring rain while some snot-nosed upstart foreman asks me from his Range Rover window how many tea breaks I've stopped digging for. How much did those fancy new cushions in the sun room cost us again, Cle? You never said.'

Was he backing Evie up? Again? Evie's face said she couldn't call it either. *What happened to being on the same team, Sam?* What happened to him being in Cleo's corner?

Cleo stood there on the kitchen chair and reached out her hand as far as possible without overbalancing. She let the terramundi jar fall from her palm. It made a dull cracking sound like a thick egg before spilling its remaining contents on the kitchen tiles. 'There you go, Sam. You two share what's left between you.'

Her hand fell back to her side again. Sam's eyes held something she hadn't seen in them for years: the hardened look of an opponent.

Harry appeared in the doorway. 'What's going on? And why is Evie dressed like a funky assassin?'

Sam was still watching Cleo, working out where her next blow might come from.

She lifted her chin and looked at her daughter again. Evie steeled herself, sniffing back tears. 'I just wanted to start jogging. Some boys at school . . .' She blinked at her mother and Cleo felt another horrible penny drop. 'They've started calling me *the fat tranny.*'

16

Be relaxed . . . walk confidently . . . even if it can't smell fear, it'll smell a sweaty armpit, so chill out . . .

Isobel had Googled the best way to get her rubbish across Arthur Oakes' yard to the bins he'd instructed her to use. No sudden movements or noises, no encroaching on its territory . . . The list of things to aggravate an unfriendly, nervous, protective dog was alarmingly extensive.

She lifted the rubber lid of the dustbin and slung her recycling inside, not even looking at Arthur's ramshackle cottage, or the spot Wolf-Dog exploded from whenever the postman gingerly clambered out of his van. She started back along the track but could already sense it, a dark mass sweeping across Arthur's lawn towards the wire fence between them. *Don't run!* screamed through her head. The dog flew at the fence with a couple of serious warning barks and finally, a disappointed huff. She froze in case the sound of panicky flip-flops tipped it over the edge.

'Petal! Get back in here!' Arthur's gravelly voice carried from inside his cottage. Isobel gave the dog a sideways glance. *Petal?* Petal snorted at her and trotted off.

'Ooo-*kay*,' she breathed, heart hammering like a piston. 'That's enough of that.'

She flip-flopped the last hundred yards of stony path to Curlew Cottage, skipped up the steps and threw the door shut behind her. Her mobile was buzzing on top of the cottage's stack of *Come Boating!* mags.

'Soph?'

'Isobel, you sound out of breath. You okay?' Sophie's new weirdly matriarchal tone again.

'Yep. Good. Everything okay there? How's Ells Bells?'

'She's fine. Anyway. *So?*'

'So what?'

'So it's been nearly a week. Any more thoughts on when you might be coming home?'

It did suddenly feel like a long time. She'd been confident Sophie would've made a move by now, found the right words to bring her home. 'What are your thoughts, Sophie?' Maybe Sophie had the right words now.

'You know what I think. Pack your stuff and get in your car.'

Of course that's what Sophie thought. So it looked like Isobel was staying in Fallenbay. Fine. She was a new person here at least. A faceless tourist.

'I'm ready, Soph.'

'I had a feeling you were going to say that. Shit, Isobel.'

She filled her lungs. 'It'll be fine. That's the whole point, isn't it? To start off bricking it, only to find out the Bogey Man isn't as scary as I've convinced myself?' There was laughter in her voice, but there really hadn't been anything to laugh about. Nathan had said sorry. He wished he'd never set up the camera. But it was still too late. Way, way too late for them.

'What if the Bogey Man *is* that scary, Isobel?'

Isobel lobbed a salmon-coloured cushion with a white boat motif out of her way and sank down on to the hard wooden window seat. Arthur's devil dog was rolling around in a patch of blue cornflowers like a puppy. A puppy that would find your jugular before you could scream for help. 'Then I really will be facing my demons, which is a good thing. Jenny said.'

'Jenny didn't mean it like that and you know it.'

'I need you on board, Soph. I don't have techy colleagues like you. You said you'd help.'

'I should never have told you about all this. Just because some IT boffin who couldn't take a joke managed to catch out one of our stupid interns doesn't mean we should start gallivanting around like Sherlock and Watson. This whole idea is totally fucking stupid . . . Sorry.'

'You're right, it is.'

'I should never have told you about it,' Sophie repeated. But her revelation had galvanised Isobel, just at the right moment. There was a way to track the monster.

'This *idea* dragged me out of the dark, Soph. The thought of wearing a deerstalker hat and puffing on a big old pipe was just too tempting.' Sophie wasn't in the mood for jokes. She hated it now, her own throwaway suggestion, every last part of it. And so she should. Any sister would. And yes, the landscape had changed since, but a fact was still a fact: Isobel would still be sitting in Jenny's therapy sessions if Sophie hadn't told her there were ways to hook a troll. 'For the first time in nearly two years I feel like I'm taking control again, Sophie. Like I might take something back from him.'

She'd stared at DEEP_DRILLERZ's profile picture until her eyes ached. It hadn't shown his face of course, just his arrogance. She'd committed the image to memory. Ocean in the distance, war memorial on the right. Guitar slung across his back while he peed up a postbox painted gold in honour of the town's resident Paralympian. He'd casually desecrated that monument the way he'd casually desecrated Isobel's life, just because he could.

'Okay, Isobel. Okay. Tell me what I can do to help this stupid idea along.'

Isobel returned the image of DEEP_DRILLERZ's profile to that dark place in her brain where she kept it tucked into a little forensic file. 'I was kinda hoping you had that side of things covered actually, Soph.'

'Yes. I thought you would be. Okay, Isobel, if we're going ahead with this, here's what I think we should do. First, I'm going to set you up on Facebook again.'

'Wait, I don't want—'

'I'll set up some fake friends for you, too. Play out a little interaction between accounts.'

'But won't other people see? People who know me, I mean? They'll think I'm online again.'

'No, they shouldn't do, because it's fake. Yes, it'll be your name and stuff, but there are millions of Facebook accounts and this one's not going to be linked to anyone we know, so no one will get a suggestion to hook up with you. It's just for background. Fake background.'

'Sounds so easy. Faking it.'

'I'll do the same with a few other networks, but it's the blog that's the critical bit. That's where we'll look out for him.'

Heat crept up Isobel's neck. This had all been hypothetical, until now. Now it had legs. She would have to log on again.

Tumble down the rabbit hole where all the dirt and darkness and crap had nearly suffocated her last time. 'How often will I have to go on all of these pages?' Tiny beads of sweat were pooling behind her knees. She jimmied the iron latch beside her and pushed the cottage window open. Cool air greeted her.

'Never by yourself. That's the deal. I'll man the accounts, buffer anything unpleasant if it comes. You are not doing anything that could undo any of the progress you've made since last summer, understood? Or I'm out.'

The coolness blowing through the cottage and Sophie's no-nonsense stance were strangely calming. 'Understood.'

'So we need to catch his attention. It's not like he's going to spot you hanging around and ask if he can join you for brunch.'

'Wasn't actually planning on letting him get that close, Soph.'

'Good. That's good. So we need to draw him out. First online, then . . .'

'Then?'

'We'll think about that if we get to it. So I'll set everything up, get Isobel Hedley back out there again, living, breathing, doing normal stuff. Enjoying life. See if it's enough to prick his interest. Chances are he's not going to just stumble across Isobel Hedley, not unless he's still looking you up. Which is a pretty freaking creepy prospect. My guess is he's moved on to his next target. Scrotbag.'

The thought of him 'looking her up' made Isobel want to heave. 'Then what? Either way, I mean? What if he's not looking out for me? What if he is?'

'Either way, we bait the hook. See what bites.'

17

Cleo thought she could taste a hint of blood at the back of her throat. Any second now she'd cough up a lung. 'Good God, Evie, people do this for *fun*?'

'Doesn't Sarah do it for fun?' panted Evie.

'Sarah? Will and Max's mum Sarah? Not likely!' One of the reasons Cleo had quickly become drawn to Sarah (aside from Harry and Will's mutual love of karate-chopping Evie's Barbie lunchbox on their very first day at Hornbeam) was their shared hatred for exercise. Cleo actually went one further and harboured a quiet loathing for exercisers themselves, specifically those women who spent their mornings in gym gear, transforming themselves like little keep-fit butterflies into full make-up and Uggs by afternoon pickup.

'Mr Hildred's always telling the Year Eleven boys how men flirt with her. Does she go running over the bluff with him? She is quite trim . . . for an older woman.'

'Who, Sarah? She's thirty-nine, Evie.' God, it was too hard to speak. She was going to collapse on the sand in a minute, give herself to the shore like a resigned whale. The thought alone weakened her. She held a hand up in defeat. 'I think I'm dying, Eves.'

Evie slowed and planted both hands on her knees. 'Come on, Mum, just down to the jetty and back. One last push.'

Push? *Push?* Cleo had pushed two 6lb babies out of her body with only the midwives to scream at – *that* was pushing. This was plain horrific. 'I can't, Eves, I can't make it. I know I probably look like a runner, but this . . . this was never for me.' She batted a hand weakly at Evie. 'Go on without me, I'll watch.'

Evie straightened up and winced towards the ocean. Cleo caught a glimpse of the little girl she used to watch paddling along the shore, dipping her bottom in the water, shrieking with delight as the tide slid over her feet. She'd been going to save this for later. 'Eves, I was thinking, in bed last night . . .' Evie set her hands on her hips, Cleo's little girl gone again, a frowning teenager with boobs and dilemmas in her place. 'These remarks, on your Facebook account and things . . .'

Evie looked towards the ocean. 'I don't want to talk about it.'

Surprise, surprise. Teenage girls didn't want to nip nasty little social issues in the bud with help from the school shrink, they wanted to do it with alcopops and tremulous diary entries. Sam thought Cleo was overreacting of course, but what if it wasn't just a bit of name-calling? What if Evie really was teetering on the edge of some seismic social shift at school? What then? One mismanaged move and all this Facebook business could throw a great big jagged fault line right down the middle of her GCSEs.

'That's what I'm afraid of, Eves. So Dad and I were wondering if, just hear me out, if you wanted to . . .' How was she going to put this? ' . . . go and have a chat with Mr Hildred? If you've anything on your mind? You don't have to come to me or Dad, although that's obviously what we'd really like you to do, but if you don't want to there are other options, and Jon, *Mr Hildred*, is so easy to talk to and he's very discreet. He has to be, doesn't he? And he knows the laws of the school jungle and, well, I know you're good pals with Cassie and you talk to her but—'

'Fine.'

Cleo squinted into the hazy morning sun. 'Sorry?'

'I said *fine*. I'll speak to Mr Hildred.'

Cleo blinked. 'Oh. Okay then.'

Evie's face relaxed. 'So are we going for the pier or not?'

'Do we have to?'

Evie's attention shifted towards the harbour. 'Look, that's all you need, Mum. A motivational T-shirt.'

Cleo pushed sweaty curls back across her head. *Great.* Rachel Foley was power-walking along the beach in a snazzily patterned pair of Lycra leggings and a *This Girl Can* top.

'Cleo! Evie! Hiya!'

Rachel stepped up her hip-wiggling and sped along the sand. She was a big-boned girl with enviable glossy auburn hair and a perennially happy face that Cleo both liked and disliked, depending on the day. Cleo reminded herself not to hold Rachel's social circle against her; she couldn't help Chloe being in Year 1 at Hornbeam along with the offspring of baguette-fiend Lorna Brooks and Olivia-bigmouth-Brightman, Juliette's rabid bloody sidekick.

'I thought it was you! I didn't know you jogged. Mother-daughter time, how lovely!'

Was Rachel wearing full make-up? This early? Cleo

squinted. Yes, yes she was. Blusher, lippy, the lot. Even Evie had toned it down after dragging herself out of bed. The eyebrows had made the cut, mind. 'Hello, Rachel. Evie and I were just blowing away the cobwebs, weren't we?' And the odd lung.

'Of course! You open later on Wednesdays, I almost forgot. We're your Tuesday and Thursday girls, aren't we?'

'Indeed you are. Didn't see you girls in Coast yesterday though, Rachel. That's not like you Hornbeam mums.'

Rachel was grinning. It was her defence mechanism. Cleo preferred to smash things; she'd learned this in the kitchen last night. Cleo grinned back. This smacked of Lorna's hissy fit. 'Oh, you know how it is, Cleo. The school summer fair's coming up next month and, well, it's been absolutely hectic getting the stalls agreed and organised before Juliette tells us off!'

'Well, just let me know how many cupcakes Coast's providing for the cake stall. What was it last year? Three hundred? For free?' Hornbeam had made a killing off Cleo's donated cupcakes, and she'd enjoyed manning the stall, helping torrents of children to decorate their cakes while their svelte, summery mothers huddled around their Pimms.

'Well, erm, I think they've had a little rejig this year, Cleo.' *They?* Rachel was distancing herself from the pack.

'A rejig?'

Rachel chewed her lip. She had pink lipstick on her front tooth. 'The school is trying to educate the children on healthy eating, you see. We all agreed it's a good idea to, um, reduce their sugar intake, encourage them to try out healthier alternatives.'

'Oh?'

'Yes, so, they're, um . . . not having a cupcake stand as such this year . . .'

'As such?'

'No . . . well, we *are* having a cupcake stand, just . . . not *your* sort of cupcakes.' Rachel gritted her teeth. Evie stepped back.

'And what are *my* sort of cupcakes, Rachel?'

Rachel looked to Evie for help. 'Umm . . . the *sugary* ones?' Evie started drawing shapes in the sand with her new trainer. 'Lorna suggested they try fruit and veg muffins, or something. She's always going on about Isaac and Marnie preferring healthier, home-baked veggie muffins over the sickly sort . . .' Rachel's voice trailed off. 'Sorry, Cleo. Those were her words.'

'Oh were they now? Juliette's given me the elbow, after all these years, so Lorna can run my cake stall?'

'I'm really sorry, Cleo. Blummin' heck, you know how much I love everything you bake. But *please*, try to understand,' Rachel's voice dropped to a whisper, 'I have to stay on good terms with the other Year One mums. Chloe's got another five years to go at Hornbeam.'

'It's not a young offender's institution, Rachel,' snapped Cleo. She ignored the stitch biting into her side and stood up. 'Good luck with that bunch of vampires. Evie? Are we running to this goddamn pier or what?'

18

Isobel's image was still taking some getting used to. The woman reflected in the windows of Coast had regained some weight at least, but the hair, blonde and unstyled, would never stop catching her off-guard. She was a fake Isobel, an impression of herself, an actor. Even her clothes felt costume-like, long flowing skirts and modest vest tops replacing the strappier versions she used to slouch around in once school broke for summer. She ignored herself and pushed against Coast's door. It didn't budge. *Closed?*

A bubble of conversation took shape around the terrace. Isobel glanced towards the voices. A petite blonde was relaxing at a table, almost hidden behind a wall of olive trees.

'He's a brilliant bloke, jitters are natural, Sarah. *Doubt* is natural.' Isobel turned for the street. 'Isobel? Hello! Isobel!' Cleo's head popped into view, then a hand, enthusiastically beckoning. 'I thought I heard someone. Come meet my best friend, we were just talking about women taking chances. You're an adventure-seeker, come say hi!'

Isobel hesitated. She should've walked faster, now she had to pretend before breakfast.

'We don't open until eleven on Wednesdays, it's the only chance Sarah and I get to be friends, isn't it, Sar? Sarah pretends she's lesson-planning, and I pretend I'm balancing my books. Isobel, Sarah, Sarah, Isobel. Isobel has wanderlust. Found herself in Fallenbay on a one-girl adventure like Julia Roberts in that *Eat, Pray, Something* film. You've come to find yourself, haven't you, Isobel?'

Isobel smiled. This was going to be excruciating.

Sarah tucked already sleek hair neatly behind her ear. 'Hi, Isobel.' Sarah extended a hand over a table affectionately laid with carafes of juice and folded napkins weighted with cutlery and too much choice for two. Brown knees peeped from under her blue shirt-dress; she looked like someone who went yachting at weekends. Isobel instantly regretted the lack of effort she'd made with her hair this morning.

'Sorry, I didn't mean to gatecrash.'

'Not at all!' beamed Cleo. 'We were just saying, not nearly enough interesting women in this town any more, they're all obsessed with finding new ways to innovate their skincare regimes and smothering, sorry, *mothering*, their children.'

'You were saying that, Cle. I was just thinking I need a new wrinkle cream.' Sarah shared a smile with Isobel. Cleo missed it.

'Sarah teaches at the town primary. Knows all the horror-parents.'

'Can we not talk about Juliette and co, Cle?'

'Sorry, you're absolutely right. I've already had one of that lot dent my morning. Isobel, you're still standing? Take a seat. Dig in.' Isobel obediently slipped into a rattan chair.

'I'm sure Rachel didn't mean to upset you,' tried Sarah.

Cleo swished her butter knife. 'She shouldn't have gone power-waddling all over my morning. Today started so well, too. Did I mention I was *jogging* when Rachel and her daft grin showed up?'

'Only twice.' Sarah's eyes creased at the edges when she smiled. Some women were just blessed with that universally approved beauty. Blonde – check. Good bone structure – check. Others had to work towards it the way Isobel had the night she'd borrowed Sophie's red cocktail dress to blow Nathan's socks off. She'd been aiming for beautiful, but she hadn't made it past *pig. Pig* by popular consensus. *Ugly pig. Pig on heat. Fat pig. Skinny Pig. Horny pig.* Several variations of *pig* peppering the hundreds of comments left beneath the footage of her in that beautiful dress. In their kitchen. Maybe they'd have gone easier if she'd been more aesthetically pleasing. Like Sarah.

Stop it.

'Let me boast! I can hardly walk, my buttocks are aching so diabolically. Do you work out, Isobel? Clearly you do, there's nothing to you. Why do I always make friends with gorgeous women? It's a bloody bad habit. Coffee?' Cleo was already poised with the cafetiere. 'Sorry, forgot . . . headaches. Tea then? Milk or lemon?'

Cleo talked so fast that listening was a bit like a workout. 'Lemon, thanks.'

'Have a muffin. Have two! I'm already eyeing up a third.' Cleo started loading a plate.

Sarah tapped her cup. 'You're a fox, Cleo. Sam still makes cow eyes at you after how many years of marriage?'

'Twenty-three.'

'Twenty-three?' marvelled Isobel. 'Wow.' She and Nathan hadn't even made it to an engagement ring.

'Sam tells Cleo she's beautiful all the time, Isobel. It's that hair. Women would kill for that natural curl.'

'Ha! Tell Evie that, she detests hers.' Cleo's smile faded. Isobel stirred her tea and tried to blend in.

'So, what's wrong with Evie?' asked Sarah, around a delicate mouthful of something.

Cleo sighed. 'My antennae are twitching.'

Sarah bit into another forkful and held her hand over her mouth. A diamond glinted in the sunlight. 'Go on.'

'She's having stick off some little shits at school. It's not cyber-bullying, not yet, just . . .' Cleo batted a hand. 'Childish stuff. Name-calling. Crappy comments about her looks. Unimaginative little weasels.' Isobel sipped quietly from her teacup. 'I was stunned she was so upset at first. You know Evie, perfectly capable of fighting her corner. So now I'm wondering . . . is something else going on?'

Isobel's voice came from nowhere. 'Something else?' Cleo might be missing something catastrophic on her daughter's horizon. The internet was good at delivering *catastrophic*.

'Well, she has these emotional outbursts, usually when she catches me and Sam arguing. Which admittedly is probably too often. I feel like we're setting her off, which is awful, but it's also the only time she actually tells us if something's bothering her.'

Sarah's fork hovered at the edge of her plate. 'Don't beat yourself up, Cleo. I'd hate to be a teenager today, everything documented and up for public viewing. Plus it's GCSE season. Evie probably just needs an outlet.'

'I know. And I am making an effort, to get along better with Sam, I mean. I sent him an uncharacteristically nice text just this morning so I'm not all bad.'

'A nice text?' winked Sarah. 'I see.'

'We don't *sext* each other, Sarah. Good God, could you imagine? I'd need a panoramic lens just to get everything in.'

'Evie and Harry brought that letter home too then? My mother read Will's out. He was mortified.'

Cleo looked at Isobel. 'The high school are concerned our children are moronic enough to photograph their genitals. Honestly, they think we're dragging them up. No, I just texted Sam to suggest we make an effort, for Evie really. Put on a united front. We're going to the cinema. We'll argue.'

'Everyone argues, Cle.'

'You two never argue! Honestly, Isobel, Sarah and Jon *never* argue. They're disgusting.'

'Only because he has his space and I have mine. I like it when he goes running every night. Is that bad? Am I ungrateful?' Sarah stabbed at a blueberry and popped it between her teeth. 'Do you have children, Isobel?'

'Just a niece. Ella. She's five.'

'Very wise,' piped Cleo. 'Kids are trouble. Especially teens. Although you haven't had a peep out of Will yet, have you Sar?'

'Nope,' sighed Sarah.

'Still no sign of a girlfriend then?'

'Not yet. Although he did shout at Max last month after he opened Will's text message without needing the code.'

'Girlfriend alert! Don't you think, Isobel?' Isobel smiled and sipped her tea.

'Not unless her name's *Edward*. Does Harry know him, Cle? I think he's new. Will's always dashing off to meet him.'

Cleo frowned. 'H hasn't mentioned an Edward, but then

he's all loved up with the lovely Ingred from Copenhagen. I keep catching him taking selfies with puppy-dog eyes. Dread to think what it's costing us getting them to her inbox. Anyway, I'm counting my blessings. The way I see it, if Harry's busy fantasising about a girl all the way over *there*, he can't be getting himself into much trouble with girls over *here*, can he? I don't want to have to do the condom talk, and Sam's useless.'

'You're putting me off my pancake, Cle.'

'Sorry. I can't believe how fast our little boys are growing into men.'

'I know, it's scary,' agreed Sarah. 'Doesn't seem five minutes since they were holding hands marching into pre-school together.'

Cleo grinned behind her cup. 'You'll be having the condom talk with Max before long, Sarah.'

'Don't!' yipped Sarah. She looked at Isobel. 'Max is five.'

'Oh. Is he at the school where you teach?'

'He is.'

'Handy for the school run,' smiled Isobel.

'Yup. Not so handy when you need to put your parent's hat on, though. I'm dreading sports day.'

'Hmph?' A fleck of muffin shot from Cleo's mouth.

'I told you, the whole school's running a vote on which child's pet should be Mr Pethers' co-umpire this year.'

'Whose brilliant idea was that? You're a pet-free home,' mumbled Cleo.

'Exactly.'

'Oh, just pop him a garden bug in a tub and let him name it what he likes.'

Sarah rubbed her forehead. 'Max was already crazy about

getting a puppy, this pet election is sending him into overdrive. On top of Sebastian Brightman pushing his buttons.'

'What's up with Max and Olivia's kid?'

'Oh, nothing really. Max won't eat brown bread sandwiches any more because Seb says brown bread is for ducks. He's stopped wearing his orange raincoat because Seb says orange is the colour of orangutan poo. Max hates breakfast club on Tuesdays now because Seb's told the other breakfast kids not to play with Max, the orangutan-poo-wearing, duck-food-eating kid.' Sarah pushed her pancake away. 'Sorry. You did ask.'

'Have you tried collaring Olivia? Too busy horse riding, I expect. All those dressage rosettes, you'd think she'd be able to train her offspring to behave.'

'Maybe you could try a play date?' suggested Isobel. 'They might have more chance finding a common ground away from the rest of the class?'

Sarah nodded towards her cup. 'I agree, Max and Seb probably would find common ground if they were given the chance. It's just a little complicated, and too boring to go into, but Olivia wouldn't be keen on a play date at our house.'

'No, because Olivia and the rest of the Hornbeam momsters swallow everything Juliette's got to say like chocolate-covered rabbit shits.' Cleo stiffened. 'Did you just hear that? Those bloody cats in my bins!' Cleo was on her feet. 'Back in a jiffy.'

They watched her go. She was making a detour via two schoolboys hovering by the terrace ramp, both pointing their phones towards the café windows.

'What are they doing?' asked Isobel.

'At a guess, piggybacking Cleo's wifi.'

The shorter schoolboy studied his phone while his bulkier friend tapped at a wooden post with his shoe. Isobel would've recognised the first boy more quickly, but he wasn't in the hipster glasses he'd worn outside the organic veg shop.

'Go on, you'll be late if you don't get a shuffle on,' shooed Cleo. 'And get your mother to top up your data, Milo!' she called.

'She won't!' he called back.

'Yeah,' the other boy snorted, 'his mum thinks too much internet will warp his little mind.'

'Get going, boys,' Cleo instructed, marching purposefully towards the back of Coast.

'So, wanderlust, Isobel? Sounds exciting.'

She felt her thoughts stall like those fainting goats Ella liked to watch on YouTube. She should've put more effort into her back story before making pretend friends with chatty locals.

'Not really. More of a flexible holiday.' It sounded like a lie.

'So why Fallenbay, of all the places?'

Because I'm a teacher too. With a lesson to teach. 'Um . . . the surf. I want to learn.'

'Yeah, the schools here are great, you should book in with the Blue Fin guys. They started my boys off.'

'Go on! Move it along! You can't just rummage through my things, even if they are the unwanted bits. Go on or I'll call the police.' Cleo emerged from behind the café, arms spread wide, herding a man looking at her in complete bewilderment. He had a thick matted beard and duct tape around his trainers.

'Poor guy,' said Sarah quietly. Cleo was trying to drive him towards the street, but their generously laden breakfast table had caught his attention. Isobel felt her breathing quicken. The fallen-from-grace banker. Who liked to hurt girls.

'We should give him something to eat,' Sarah decided. 'We'll have to be discreet though. Cleo bans customers for encouraging the gulls, she'll go berserk if we encourage that gentleman. Uh-oh, I think he's read my mind.'

Isobel's heart was pattering steadily.

'No, no, come away from there please, this way! Walk this way and I'll find you something to take with you.' But his eyes were already locked on the pastries and fruit. 'No! Don't bother my guests! I'm so sorry, girls . . .'

He kept on coming. The smell of stale clothes over something less pleasant reached Isobel first. His features were dark and furrowed. Pitiful. Wretched. A man who hurt girls deserved an existence like this, didn't he? He came close enough that he was staring down at her. She thought about standing, making herself taller, more formidable. The way you were supposed to when confronted by a bear . . . or was it a wolf you should stand your ground with?

'Isobel?' Sarah gently touched her hand. Isobel looked down, her knuckles were white, her fist clamped around a fork she couldn't recall grabbing.

A figure jogged across the terrace. 'He's harmless, Mrs R. Come on, Bob, I've got a box of sarnies here. I hate tuna but the old dear thinks it'll make me smarter. Step this way, Bob.'

'Milo, I don't think you should—' Sarah stopped herself.

'It's cool. Cheers for letting us bum off your wifi, Mrs R, you're a life-saver, serious. Bob likes the beach, don't you, Bob? And tuna sarnies. We're going that way anyway.'

Cleo stopped eying Isobel and the fork. 'Milo, hurry up and get yourselves to school.'

'It's cool, Mrs. R, just don't tell the mother you saw us.'

19

Sarah leant back on her chair and peered along the hallway. Max's orange raincoat lay abandoned at the bottom of the stairs. At the end of the corridor a familiar rump peeped into view around the kitchen doorway. 'Mum, stop rummaging through my pantry!' Her mother's greying Bardot style popped around the door instead.

'It'll take you months to eat this lot, darling. You'll be paying removal costs for . . .' her mother inspected another tin, ' . . . kidney beans.'

Sarah grimaced. She wasn't a fan of kidney beans. Patrick had called her boring for picking hers out of a chilli con carne once. Patrick had thought her boring for all sorts of reasons.

She lobbed her pen on to the *Healthy! Happy! Hooray!* paperwork Mr Pethers had dumped on her and abandoned the study. 'I think you're forgetting how much Will eats now, Mum,' she called ahead. She made the kitchen doorway, the boys' heights measured and remeasured up the frame. Soon a stranger would paint all over their milestones.

Disbelief glowered in Sarah's mother's eyes. 'Mulligatawny soup?'

'Think that came in last year's Harvest Festival basket.'

'Eat, pack or food bank?'

'Mum, we only received the offer two days ago. What even is Mulligatawny?' Sarah rinsed her cup under the tap and looked out on to the back garden. More than a decade of forgotten junk still needed clearing from Patrick's long-abandoned summerhouse. The rotting shed had been off limits for a long time now; even Jon avoided it, despite it being the only space big enough to house his treadmill. It had been a small mercy the children had been in there and not inside the main house when Elodie had been hurt. A place they could close the door on.

'Hello? Earth to Sarah?'

'Sorry. You were saying?'

Milo was growing up. His voice this morning had been deep and confident, just like Karl's. He'd still avoided eye contact though, the way Juliette had trained him.

'I said, I believe it's similar to a curried soup.'

'What is?'

'*Mulligatawny!*'

'Oh. Mulligatawny,' Sarah repeated absently. 'Sounds like an Irish cove . . . or rare owl maybe . . .'

Sarah's mother glared over her reading glasses. 'Are you on drugs, darling? I've been reading about M-Cat in the *Mail*. Your father thinks M-Cat and internet porn are going to be the downfall of at least the next two generations.'

Sarah was on drugs, as it happened. Just the one secret pill, every day, religiously.

'Goodness, that was a rather hefty sigh, darling. And there I was thinking that moving to a palatial new home overlooking the ocean was something to be upbeat about.'

'Tea, Mum?'

'Yes please. It is, though, isn't it, darling?'

'Is what?'

'Something to be upbeat about?'

'Of course. Where's your cup?'

'By the teapot. Your father's always saying you'd both be better off putting your cash into property. Savings just aren't worth the bother since interest rates died.'

'Must be right, then. If Dad says so. Chamomile or regular?'

'Regular is fine.'

She reached for the pot of teabags. Her mum's hand appeared over hers. 'Everyone deserves a happy ending, darling. Sometimes I wonder if you don't believe you're about due yours.'

'You worry too much, Mum.'

'Then what's the matter, darling? And don't say *nothing*, I can sense it. You're holding back.'

'I'm not. It's just . . .' What was wrong with her again? That formless thing her thoughts kept bumping into, having to reroute themselves around? Will's detachment? Max playing up before school? Or something else. 'The boys are settled and . . . it's just a lot of money to spend on one house and—'

'It's a huge amount of money, on a *house*. But a fresh start for you all? A family home? I can't think of anything more worthy of your hard-earned money.'

'It's not my money.'

'Some of it is.'

'And most of it isn't.'

'Sarah, you're a family! It's a golden nest egg for you all.'

She poured the tea. 'It doesn't feel like a nest egg. It feels like something that should be . . . kept to one side.' Something that didn't belong in their nest at all. A cuckoo's egg.

'You should be using that money for good. It's the very least Jon deserves after all that school put him through. I'm glad he did so well out of the rotters.'

'There were no winners in that situation, Mum.'

'You're the winner, darling! If Jon hadn't made a new start here, you'd never have met. It's fate!'

Sarah had Googled her once. The girl. Only once. She'd fallen pregnant the same year the school had expelled her and issued their grovelling apology to Jon. Expelled from school, then from her family home. Sixteen and alone. There had been a follow up article in a local paper, a picture of her sticking two fingers up at the camera, baby on her hip. *Thank goodness for those tests Jeremy Kyle can do*, Jon's mother had blurted over too many sherries, *or the little tramp would've tried pinning that on my boy too*. Sarah's father had artfully changed the subject. That was three Christmasses ago. There hadn't been a joint family gathering since.

Sarah's mum buffed the worktop with her thumb. 'I'm not implying for a second that any amount of compensation could've made that business worthwhile, darling. I just can't see why you aren't more enthusiastic about this place selling when Jon's clearly so eager to invest in a wonderful future with you all. He must be desperate to put that horrendous business behind him, wouldn't you say?'

'We don't really talk about it. We didn't know each other back then, so . . .'

'No, but we've all known girls like that. Silly, confused schoolgirls. They were around when I was at school, and rest assured they'll be around when young Max is too. Take it from me, and I've been married to a headmaster for more years than I care to remember, there will always be troubled young girls with active imaginations and silly, unreachable crushes on the people trying to help them.'

'Can we not talk about this now, Mum, I'm supposed to be finishing my homework.'

Mr Pethers wanted a healthy-eating pamphlet to gently coax the 'marshmallow children' away from the snacks their parents were sending in and on to something *Healthy! Happy! Hooray!* instead. 'Marshmallow children' was Juliette's term. She had swung into action after discovering Flumps in eleven (*Eleven, Mr Pethers!*) lunchboxes the week the supermarket ran a BOGOF. Sarah had suggested forgetting the pamphlets and running an energetic lunchtime class instead, like the Cardio Club Jon ran at the high school. But no. They were to educate, not entertain. Sarah had reluctantly accepted the poisoned chalice of 'educating' parents, with a few mornings of home-working to sweeten the deal.

'I'll shut up then, darling.' A line usually reserved for Sarah's father. She felt suitably tyrannical.

'Would you like a biscuit, Mum? Cleo sent some back for the boys this morning. Her usuals.'

'Triple choc and cashew?'

'Yep.'

'Lovely.' All was forgiven. Sarah reached into the very top of the pantry.

'Darling, you've a secret stash! I had a secret stash of gin and cigarettes, you know, my salvation when your father had the examiners in.'

'I wondered what your secret was.' Stiff drinks appealed hugely whenever Sarah's father was around. She'd had a stash of cigarettes too once, in the summerhouse, for the months after Patrick decided he didn't really want to have a family any more. Solitude, darkness and sweetly burning tobacco, her one-time reward at the end of each day she'd managed to hold it together for William.

'Lordy, Cleo bakes a mean cookie.'

'Suggestions for healthy snacks please,' Sarah mumbled, biting into hers.

Her mother's eyes flickered at her new task. 'I thought you were here to lesson-plan?'

'I've been lumbered with a healthy-snack initiative. Another cookie?'

'Please, darling.'

'The war on sugar, etc, etc.'

'Well, it's not a bad thing, I don't think. There's so much more awareness now, so many more links. Obesity and diabetes . . . age and infertility . . . Did you know that thirty-five is the new cut-off point, darling?'

'Cut-off for what?' Sarah caught a whiff of ambush. Too late.

'For having babies, darling! You and Jon need to get a wriggle on.'

'Are you still in that gin stash, Mother? I passed the thirty-five mark four years ago.'

'Exactly! Your eggs, darling. They're on the decline now, aren't they? I read it when I went for my flu jab.'

'Eggs . . . there's a healthy snack. Hard-boiled eggs. Like mine.'

'Sarcasm ages the face, darling. After thirty-five you're classed as high risk, that's all I wanted to say.'

'I'm not pregnant, Mum. So . . .'

'Not *yet*. But Jon mentioned you're hopeful. Sorry, I wasn't supposed to say anything.'

She stopped chewing. 'Jon said that? He said *hopeful*?' They weren't at the *hopeful* stage. They'd agreed they were at the *we'll talk about it once we've moved house* stage.

'Weeks ago, we had lunch at Squires. He said you're leaving it up to fate, no pressure.'

'When did you go for lunch?'

'Don't be surprised, darling. Your father and I have grown very close to Jonathan. Your father thinks he's marvellous and you know how hard it is to please some people. Speaking of which, when are you posting the wedding invitations? Your Aunt Mary's lot have been on the phone wanting to know when they can expect theirs.'

Sarah chomped down on another mouthful. 'It'll happen when it happens, Mum. Invitations, babies . . . all of it will just have to happen when it happens.' There was a crunch, then a searing pain along her jaw.

'What is it, darling?'

'Nothing. I'm fine,' she lied. *Excellent!* An eight-mile drive to Dewelsbury for an emergency appointment for a cracked tooth. She let her tongue examine the newly jagged ridge of her molar. Bloody cashews. *Healthy! Happy! Hooray!*

Her mother's hand was back over hers. 'Don't leave the important invitation too late, Sarah, darling.'

'Mum, I'll post them, okay? This week.'

'No, darling, I mean your invitation to the *stork*. Jonathan will make a wonderful father. He's relaxed, supportive, lets you do things your own way. You and I both know not all men are like that, are they?' Sarah had followed her father into teaching and still she hadn't measured up. She'd followed Patrick all the way to a photography exhibition in a Portuguese hotel, dragging their little boys along behind her. She hadn't measured up there either.

'No, Mum. They're not.'

'You've got a good'un now, darling. You remember that. Jonathan Hildred's a keeper. Alrighty?'

20

Cleo repositioned the cordless phone between her shoulder and ear and jump-reached for the shuttering. Bloody hell, she ached. Evie would have to go it alone if she wanted to run again in the next forty-eight hours.

'This line's really terrible, Isobel, stand somewhere else. Yes, I do know where he lives, it's the massive white showy house on the bluff, the one with all the glass and pretentious angles. You must've seen it from your cottage, it's visible from the international space station. But really, there's no need for you to go up there, Milo's always chatting to Hobo Bob.'

Had Isobel fretted all day about this?

'But Milo's only, what, fourteen? I just feel a bit uncomfortable they left together and . . .'

Cleo pushed a couple of seats back under their tables with her bum and collected up the last few menu holders from outside. It had gone cool; the air tasted saltier when the heat left it. 'Isobel, take it from me, Milo can handle himself. He's been raised by a Rottweiler. If you go up there to check Bob didn't eat him today, Juliette will collar Milo for loitering around the harbour when he should've been on his way to school. He won't thank you for it. Poor kid already has his work cut out living under that very long shadow of his sister's. You should see this girl - smart . . . beautiful . . .'

'Yeah, I met her briefly, at the veg shop. She was lovely.'

'That's right: lovely, eloquent, exceptional Elodie. To be fair, she's very likeable. Look, if it makes you feel better, I'll call Harry now and check he saw Milo at school, okay? They both do basketball at lunchtime. Usually I'd just suggest a little light Facebook stalking to check Milo's alive, but the Inman-Holt kids aren't even allowed accounts.'

'Thanks, Cleo. They seem like nice kids.'

She set the menus down behind the counter and switched the phone to her other ear. 'They are, I'll give Juliette that. I'm sure Elodie's part android though. She's in the same year as my two and nothing like them. Every Saturday, one of my kids will be down at The Village hanging out with their friends, dunking each other in the surf or on the skate ramps or whatever, and the other will be moaning like Billy-O about working a shift in Coast. Elodie Inman-Holt, on the other hand, will get on a bus and travel an hour into Dewelsbury to the Dewelsbury Junior Conservatoire and spend her whole day playing Bach, feeding her greatness. For fun. On a Saturday. At sixteen. As if being an A-grade student across the board and working part time at the organic veg shop didn't keep her enriched enough.'

'Wow,' breathed Isobel. 'And with the added challenge of . . .' Isobel's line was awful.

Cleo flicked the backlights off behind the counter. 'An unfortunate *injury*? Yes, well . . . Inman-Holts sure do like to rise to a challenge?'

'Conservatoire. Blimey. Good for her.'

'Guess what she plays… Only the bloody piano, Isobel. As I said, Elodie casts a *long* shadow.'

'Poor Milo.'

'Uh-uh.' Cleo bust a gut to treat the twins equally. Well, except for when she'd been piling more money into Evie's emergency tuition fund than her brother's. 'Milo's okay, he's just not cut out for being a diamond like his sister, that's the shame for him. I wish Juliette would get that and accept it's okay to only have *one* ten-carat kid, but then Juliette called Evie feral once so I'm sure she'd happily tell me where I was going wrong with mine, too.

'Maybe.' Juliette should be careful.' Isobel sounded distant again. 'Favouritism fractures a family.'

'Oh I know. You should dislike your children equally,' laughed Cleo. 'I'm just kidding. I could never do what Juliette does and shove one of my two into summer school every year, trying to bring them up to the other one's standard. Why she can't just let Milo be a surf bum for six weeks with the other local kids, I'll never know. What's the worst that could happen? He wastes a summer on his Xbox instead of inside another classroom?' She locked up and walked towards her car, glancing about the deserted terrace. Isobel had made her a bit jittery. It occurred to Cleo that no one really knew for sure whether Hobo Bob was a danger or not. Was that rust on her wheel arch? *For God's sake.* She looked towards the fancy homes on the bluff. 'I mean, Juliette's made it already, she has a nice life, a disgustingly gorgeous home, great kids . . . she's even got a circle of dimwits following her around, hanging on her every word, but she's always *striving*, she's always going for more. It's like, *hey, Juliette, save some room at the top of the food chain for someone else, wouldja?* Sarah really struggles sometimes, being stuck with her all day.'

'They don't get along?'

'Not exactly. But that crack's been widening for years. I really felt for Sar today, seeing Milo. She was desperate to say 'hello', I could feel it.'

'What do you mean?'

'Sarah's Milo's Godmother.' She unlocked her Mini, checking towards the bins again.

'And she couldn't speak to him?'

'Nope. Not worth the aggro. Too much water has thundered under the bridge between Sarah and Milo's folks. It's a shame. Sarah's so fond of Milo. Patrick, Sarah's first husband, didn't want any more children after Will, so when they became pally with Juliette and Karl, Milo became a borrowed little brother for Will. Of course, Will's got Max now, but things used to be very different seven or eight years ago when Sarah and Juliette were closer. Juliette wasn't quite so uptight back then. We used to walk our kids into school together, me and my twins, Sarah with Will, Juliette with Elodie. But even then I always felt a little for Milo, shuffling along behind. Elodie's always been two years and one almighty leap ahead of him, but that's just my opinion. And Evie was six when Juliette said she was feral, so I've had a long time to let our beef marinate. You probably shouldn't take on board a single thing I say about Juliette.'

'Are you in your car yet?'

'I'm not a teenage girl, Isobel.'

'Sorry. Just checking. You shouldn't walk to your car while you're on your phone, it's distracting.'

'Distracted? *Moi*? I'm like a keen-eyed eagle, Isobel. Nothing gets past these peepers. Oh . . . bugger.'

'What is it?'

'I've walked out with the shop phone.'

21

Isobel was starting to forgive Petal the devil dog for waking her so early. She couldn't remember a morning so beautiful. There was something special about watching a new sun climbing over the headland and touching a part of the ocean betrothed to sunsets. Nature's infidelity. How many of those mornings did a person get to bank in their lifetime?

She felt the cool sand under her palms and remembered yesterday's less brilliant start, the vivid, noisy dream that always woke her cold and clammy, leaving her with a banging headache and tight throat for breakfast. Same format, more or less. Taking assembly at St Jude's, school hall packed with students and staff, her inspired PowerPoint presentation playing out on the projector screen above the stage. Then the video cut in, same as always, followed by her fumbling uselessly with her clicker as the grunting, squealing, giggling boomed through the speaker system. They all laughed, students, parents, teachers, special guests. It was just so funny, until the caption rolled over the footage like the start of *Star Wars*.

Look at me,

Isobel Yvonne Hedley . . . too fucking good for anyone,

even my dull little boyfriend . . . but he'll come crawling back . . .

Last night's sleep had been better.

She pressed her toes into the sand and let the morning air fill her lungs. She pulled a banana from her bag and peeled into it. Four surfers sat in silhouette against a sparkling ocean, rising and falling with the pulse of the water. Were they waiting to catch a wave? Is that what they did? Wait for a big one, something of such scary proportions there was no telling if it would take them safely back to shore or crush them against the rocks?

Isobel was surfing. Sort of. Right here, sitting on the sand, waiting for Sophie to spot their wave, waiting for the big one to find them. Sink or swim. It could go either way. If – *if* – Sophie could find their wave.

She bit into her banana. The breeze whipped up a sprinkling of sand, flattening half of her hair across her face. *Sandy, banana-ry hair, lovely.* She checked a few strands. Too many days spent under a coastal sun had finished off what hastily bleaching it blonde had started. She was starting to look like Kurt Cobain. She missed her normal colour. She missed her normal everything. She missed her parents. She missed Ella.

She missed Sophie.

Bells in the distance counted the hour. Eight a.m. Milo had played on her mind since she woke. What if Cleo had forgotten to ask her son? That was how children slipped through the net. Milo's mother might not even notice him gone. She'd give it until nine; if this was his usual route to school, she could just casually check he was alive and well herself.

Isobel gathered her sandals and started barefooting it

back towards the promenade steps. She made the top just as a teenager with one of those floppy topped hairstyles left his group of school friends and walked towards the same bin Isobel was about to chuck her banana into. She scanned their faces. Milo wasn't among them. One of the school kids whistled. 'Nice arse.' Ignoring teenagers was a talent you honed during trainee teacher placement. 'Oi, blondie, I'm talking to you.' Isobel blanked him and made a beeline for the newsagents. Milo might be in there.

'Beautiful morning, isn't it?' A tanned Ben Oakes in a *High-Five-Me!* T-shirt and sunglasses waved from the back of his truck. A younger kid in full wetsuit rounded the pickup and passed him a bag of apples. Ben took a bite into one and patted the boy's shoulder. Laughter erupted between the schoolboys behind Isobel.

'Nice wetsuit, didn't know cabbages could float.' The schoolboy laughing hardest was gangly, a smattering of acne around his mouth.

Another voice followed the first. 'Freakoid.'

Bullies loved an easy target. Isobel thought of Melanie. Teachers shouldn't have favourites, but Melanie McLoughlin had been Isobel's soft spot at St Jude's. Superb artist, wickedly dry sense of humour. But a quiet red-head with an underactive thyroid, Melanie had been the Year 9 boys' Christmasses all rolled in to one.

Isobel waved over at Ben and his friend. She couldn't place the younger boy's age. Maybe fifteen? Maybe twenty. Like Melanie, an easy target for spiteful kids. One of the schoolboys shouldered his way through the laughers on the promenade. He lifted his chin. 'Alright, Dan?'

Dan gave an enigmatic thumbs-up. 'Hi Will! We've got a new board! Wanna come with us?'

'Can't, mate. School today. Maybe at the weekend.' Will returned a thumbs-up and walked for the street. He shoved the spotty kid hard in the back as he went. Isobel walked away too. Belittlers were empowered by their audience. No audience, no belittlement. She'd just say a quick hello to Ben and his friend on her way to the newsagents.

She came to a standstill by the truck. So this was the elusive *Danny Boy* she'd heard Arthur calling through the cottage. Ben nudged Daniel's arm. 'Go on, buddy. Say *hi*. I told you already, she's nice.'

'What's her name again?' whispered Dan. Isobel smiled at her sandals.

'Isobel,' Ben whispered back.

Nathan's cousin Gareth had Down's Syndrome. Gaz had started his university degree two months before Isobel flounced out of her and Nathan's flat for the last time. There'd been a feature on the local news, Gaz's Fresher's week. Gareth's parents had been furious with his old college for master-minding it. Gaz was working hard to tread the same path as anyone else, and there they all were, plonking him back on a different one again.

'Hi Daniel.'

'Hello. How do you know who I am?'

'Well, I don't. But I've heard about you.'

'What have you heard?'

'Oh, good things,' she smiled.

'What good things?' He was about to call her out. On a politeness. She should've thought ahead.

'Umm . . . just that . . .' What had Cleo said? 'You're the . . . better-looking Oakes brother,' she said truthfully.

Ben grinned. 'Isobel heard right, didn't she, Dan?'

'Yes she did,' beamed Daniel. 'I'm the best body-boarder, too.'

'Are not,' protested Ben. He began pulling bags of gear from the back of his pickup.

'You definitely look like a chap who's ready to go body-boarding, Dan,' agreed Isobel.

Daniel nodded purposefully and set to retrieving a body-board from the pickup with a look of intense concentration.

Ben dropped a few bags on the sand. He moved his shades to sit on top of his head. 'Settling in okay?' He had dark eyes like his brother and father, but Daniel's features were softer, rounder, with none of his brother's angles.

'Yep. Thanks.'

'Getting on alright with Petal?'

Isobel smiled at her feet again. Her toes were just peeping out in front of her skirt. 'Yeah . . . I'm really enjoying our time together. That fence will hold, right?'

Ben grinned. 'Don't take it to heart. I'm family and she hates me.'

'Only because Petal doesn't like it when you playfight with me,' Daniel argued. 'Petal doesn't like boys, only me, but she'll like you because you are a girl.'

'Phew,' smiled Isobel.

Ben busied himself untying something else from his truck. 'So, girls don't usually holiday alone. Should Petal expect any more friends to join you? Anyone she might bark at?'

He's only being friendly. But Isobel felt suddenly exposed.

Sophie had instructed her not to advertise that she was on her own. She couldn't exactly hide it from the landlord's son though. 'My sister. My sister might be joining me.' And she might not.

'Cool,' said Ben. The schoolboys were walking for the high street. Ben watched them go. 'Hey, Dan? Why don't you ask Isobel if she likes to body-board?'

One of the schoolboys threw a drinks carton at another. Ben's eyes didn't leave them. Isobel watched them too. The spotty one was gurning at Daniel again.

'No way,' blurted Ben, 'was that a dolphin?' Isobel glanced out to sea. Something green whizzed past her peripheral vision.

'I don't see any dolphins, Ben,' said Dan.

Ben shouted up towards the school kids. 'Sorry, pal. Sorry!' He was holding a hand up in apology. He flicked to a thumbs-up, then back to an open apologetic hand. The gurner rubbed the back of his head. 'Bad apple, mate. I was aiming for the bin. Sorry, bud.'

'Would you like to come and body-board with us today, Isobel? We might see dolphins,' asked Daniel.

'Thanks Dan, I would, but . . .' *But I think your brother just assaulted a schoolboy with one of his five-a-day.* Not that she was holding it against him. Dan blinked at her, waiting for an answer. She tried to think of an innocent fib, but being a fake Isobel all day was draining. She went with a good clean hit of honesty instead. 'I haven't shaved my legs for months, Dan. Pretty sure I'd scare your waves away.'

22

Cleo set another tray of Gruyère and poppyseed twists out to cool, and pondered the momsters' usual corner. So what if they hadn't been in since Lorna's hissy fit? It didn't mean anything, Coast wouldn't crumble. *Would it?*

She slipped a knife along one of the large delivery boxes she'd signed for this morning. It was silly really, the thrill she experienced tearing into one of the shop's deliveries, but she always felt eight years old again, role-playing at *Cleo's Café* in her mother's sandwich kitchen. She yanked at the box and delved through the plastic padding into the first mound of mini-loaf moulds and cupcake cases. She rummaged around, running a cursory count of the contents. *Not that I don't trust you, Evie,* but it was an easy mistake to make. Cleo had done it herself once, ordered six thousand instead of six hundred takeaway drinks cups. Her accountant thought she was trying to pull a fast one.

Fifty . . . one hundred . . . The numbers looked right, two hundred-ish per box. *You done good, Eves.* She began humming along to the Bob Marley track Harry had added to the playlist, and was halfway through a line with the Wailers when an ominous bob swooshed in through the door.

Juliette had been a noticeably absent force. Noticeable because Juliette was a creature of habit. She liked a double decaf, takeout, on her way home from Hornbeam every afternoon without fail. Until this week. Cleo tightened her barista's apron with a readying yank.

'Morning, Juliette.'

'Cleo.'

'Everything alright?' No talk of boycotts? Cake stalls? Coast's impending take-down?

'Everything's fine, thank you.'

God, she was so uptight. 'Good! I was starting to miss you,' Cleo teased. Juliette wasn't boycotting after all; here she was. 'Not in school this morning?'

Juliette flashed a flat smile. She cast a look over the fresh bakes beneath the display as if scrutinising a row of unfortunate school children for nits. 'Yes, actually. I'm just running a few errands on my way back.'

Booo. Juliette didn't want to play. Cleo got back to picking through her new cupcake cases. She didn't know why she hadn't thought of it before, branding the cases. People scrunched serviettes into their palms where no one could see them, but cupcakes were held aloft, in full view of gaping mouths and salivating children. Cleo had been missing a trick until Evie suggested it. So long as they were subtle, no garish lettering, of course. Evie had even found an online design service; she'd taken care of the lot.

'Double decaf, Juliette?' She pulled the plastic wrapping off the first tube of cupcake cases. *Shit.* She tore into another pack. Same as the first.

'Not today, thank you.' Juliette peered over the counter.

'Nice and low key, Cleo. You'll be able to read those from the other end of the beach.'

What the hell had Evie ordered? The word 'COAST' barely fit, the lettering way too big. She couldn't use these! They were unashamedly self-serving, they didn't *whisper* 'Coast' like she'd specifically instructed, they bloody screamed it. *For God's sake, Evie!* More money, straight down the pan.

'Something wrong, Cleo?'

Shut up, Juliette. Cleo forced a smile. 'No double decaf? What can I do for you then?' *Take you out back and poke you in the eye with a Gruyère and poppyseed twist?*

Juliette's beady eyes turned to her Chloé handbag. She pulled out a stack of flyers. 'You've always supported the school, Cleo. We were hoping you'd hand out a few posters for the summer fair, perhaps give one out with every cupcake?' *Cupcake* slipped from Juliette's expensive lipstick like a rusty spike. Cheeky mare. They both knew full well that Juliette and her PFA disciples had ousted Cleo from the fair.

Cleo gave her another forced smile. 'Always happy to do what I can for Hornbeam, Juliette.'

'You're a real Hornbeam friend, Cleo.'

Stuck-up cow. She couldn't resist. Sarah hated her doing it but it was an easy shot to fire and Cleo didn't have any other ammo. 'Say hi to Sarah when you get back to school for me, Juliette. Have you seen how fabulous she's looking at the mo? Body of a twenty-year-old, that one. She's going to look stunning at the wedding. Gwyneth Paltrow, eat your heart out.'

Juliette zipped her bag closed. Cleo knew a green-eyed monster when she saw one. Juliette never had regained pole position as school mum with the most fanciable husband since Jon Hildred had first ridden into town handing that baton straight to Sarah. Juliette couldn't stand coming in second at anything.

'I'm sure she will.' Juliette turned for the door. Cleo thought about pulling a face behind her but Harry was hoofing it up the walkway, school blazer flapping behind him. Juliette left before Harry blustered in.

'What are you doing here? Why aren't you in school?' Harry looked pale and sweaty and five years younger than he had this morning.

'Mum, I . . . I need . . .' Harry dropped his things at the counter and stood there, vacant. Cleo reached a hand to his forehead.

'You're all clammy, are you ill?' She never said *sick* in Coast. It wasn't a word her patrons wanted to hear, in any context.

Harry looked semi-catatonic. He'd run a fever of forty degrees once when he was little. His eyes reminded Cleo of that long night, when they'd thought he'd contracted meningitis or something just as horrifying. 'Harry? Do you want me to call Dad to run you home?'

'Mum? Can I work extra shifts after school? Lots, I mean? I could be here at three-thirty every day, and I could stay until closing and clean down. You could spend more time at home and not have to do it all yourself. I could tile the splashback for you – if Dad shows me I can do it . . . I can do lots of stuff . . .'

'Harry! Take a breath! I know I can be a mean mum but I wouldn't inflict *that* much on you.' She wouldn't even inflict it on Evie. Harry rubbed a hand up and down the back of his neck. 'Harry, do you need money for something?'

He looked at the ceiling fan whirring over the two of them. 'Yes.'

'How much? Don't tell me you've forgotten some over-priced school trip and now I've got to find it all by home time?' Harry shot a look at her. 'Oh, Harry, where are you going and how much?' She hit a button on the till and the drawer flung forth.

Harry rubbed at his temple. 'Three-fifty.'

'Three-fifty?' she laughed. 'You've come all the way here for three pounds fifty? Where are you going, the ice-cream man?'

'Three hundred and fifty, Mum. That's how much I need.'

'Three hundred and fifty quid! What, *now?*'

'I'm sorry, Mum. I didn't want to ask, but I need to take it in. Today. I'm sorry. I'll earn it back, I promise.'

'You don't have to pay for your own school trips. Since when . . . Let me ring the sch—'

'No, Mum, please. Look, it doesn't matter, I'll just say I'm not going.'

'You won't. I'm not very pleased about this and we *are* going to talk about this later. Where on earth are you supposed to be going?'

He didn't seem sure. 'Denmark.'

Something whimsical and romantic engaged in Cleo's mind. Harry might see his first love again! 'Denmark? I take it this trip is partnered up to a certain pretty exchange student's school then?' Harry paled. He looked like he might throw up. Was he actually love sick? 'Panic not, my child. I don't think I've got enough here in petty cash. Have you got your bank card with you?' Harry nodded. 'Right, I'll transfer it now, you'll have to walk past the cashpoint on your way back to school. Don't. Bloody. Lose. It.' More nodding. 'And bring back all the info, Harry. What about passports? Dates? Any of those little details mothers like to have?'

He still looked queasy. 'I'll sort it. I'll sort all of it. I promise.'

She was about to ask if he'd like to take a sandwich back to school, but Harry had just vomited all over the café floor.

Isobel had never seen a golden postbox in the flesh. She stood back and beheld it, the way she thought she should behold something that large and golden, like an ancient Egyptian monument, only more toilet-roll-shaped, and camply British.

It was all very British in Fallenbay. Even from here on the mount she could see sandalled day-trippers enjoying cream teas outside quaint skinny buildings painted in soft pastels. She twisted her bangle around and around her wrist. He was here. This was the only concrete thing she knew about him, that he'd unzipped himself in this exact spot, turned his back on the town raising Paralympians and literally pissed all over someone else's achievement. He'd even taken a photo of himself doing it. DEEP_DRILLERZ was here somewhere. Her senses were screaming it.

'Mr Fogharty, come baaack!'

Isobel turned to the other screams coming from further down the embankment. The paper bag she'd just been holding tugged free of her hand, the lunch she'd lost her appetite for subjected to a merciless shaking in the jaws of a skittish little spaniel. 'Hey, dog!' The falafel wrap was a goner.

A blonde-haired boy about the same age as Ella in a bright

blue school polo shirt arrived on the hill, attached to the other end of the snack-thief's retractable lead.

'Maxy, hang on!' called a woman. Isobel stood impotently watching her food disappear. The little lad reeled himself towards the dog, eyes widening the closer he came.

'Max!' A man this time. 'You forgot the invitations!'

Isobel recognised the first half of the couple walking into view immediately. His little boy, despite the saucer-like eyes, looked just like the chap with the coupé, the fellow list-maker she'd met in Coast.

The woman with him assessed the scene, flattening a hand to her forehead. She hurried over the grass towards Isobel and whipped off her sunglasses. 'I'm so sorry, has he been bothering you?' Isobel probably looked as surprised as she did.

'Hi again, no . . . it's fine. Really.'

Sarah gritted her teeth anyway. 'Max? What has Mr Fogharty got there?'

He pointed straight at Isobel. 'This lady's thing, Mummy. Mr Fogharty snatched it in his mouth and bit her hand.'

Isobel laughed. 'He didn't bite my hand. Just my sandwich. Sorry, I didn't give it to him, I hope he's okay. It's only falafel.' Was falafel okay for dogs? She didn't know, she'd never had one. She'd been a career girl until fourteen months ago.

'Oh my goodness, Isobel, I'm so sorry. I can't believe he's just stolen your lunch. Mr Fogharty, get down! Jon, we need to stop him scrambling up people, he keeps scratching us all to ribbons!'

Sarah's partner snapped his fingers and the dog skittered over to him. 'Hello again!' He was more tailored today, his shirt undone just enough for the end of a day's work. A school ID sat next to a memory stick on the strap hanging from his neck.

'Mr Fogharty just ran and *stoled* this lady's bag and bit her fingers off, Jon!'

'No fingers were bitten off,' insisted Isobel, wiggling her fingers.

'I'm so sorry, Isobel.' A light blush rose in Sarah's cheeks.

'So, you ladies know each other?' Jon fussed the dog into a frenzy with one hand, helping Max scramble up on to his shoulder with the other. Isobel felt like an alien, beamed down into the heart of an unsuspecting family.

'Cleo introduced us yesterday morning. Isobel and I had breakfast.'

'How very nice too,' said Jon.

Sarah smiled sheepishly and spoke from the corner of her mouth. 'Jon? Mr Fogharty's your mother's dog, so, erm . . . what does she do when he steals from strangers?'

The little boy began to giggle. Jon slipped into a grin. 'Well, thankfully, Mr Fogharty has impeccable taste and only steals from very nice and *hopefully* forgiving young ladies.' Sarah rolled her eyes and started to smile too. 'And technically, we're not strangers, we met at Cleo's too, when you two dashed off to the aquarium without me. We share a love of lists. Jon Hildred.' He extended an arm. Isobel took it automatically. 'Sarah's incredibly lucky and unfairly handsome fiancé.'

'I'm so sorry about your food, Isobel,' Sarah repeated. 'We could dash to one of the delis in the harbour and bring you something back if you could give us twenty minutes?'

'But Mummy, we're meeting Will.'

Sarah's shoulders dropped. 'Let me call him. Will's my – *our*

– eldest, he could swing by Coast and bring a replacement, Cleo can pull together anything, short notice. Falafel did you say?'

'Honestly, there's no need. I wasn't hungry anyway. It was a just-in-case snack.'

Jon ducked towards Sarah. 'And Will's already running late, honey. You guys aren't going to get Max to his footy tournament if Will has to detour first.'

'Honestly, I'm glad the sandwich went to an appreciative recipient,' Isobel interrupted.

Jon squeezed Sarah into him. 'We'll sort it out with Cleo, make sure there's something waiting next time Isobel goes in. Sounds like you're a valued customer already if Cleo's breaking out the private breakfast invitations. I've been hinting for years but the girls won't let me in their gang.'

'Absolutely not,' smiled Sarah.

'Cleo's been very welcoming,' agreed Isobel. Cleo didn't know her from Adam, she should be more cautious.

'Cleo's lovely. Please don't tell her I offered to go to one of the harbour delis,' winced Sarah.

Jon checked his watch. 'Righto, Maxy, my boy! Are we posting our stupendously golden invitations, as expertly chosen by Max the Great, into this gloriously golden postbox?'

Max giggled. Sarah fished in her bag, retrieving a stack of sealed envelopes. 'Can't we just give Will five more minutes, guys? It would be nice if he was here too.'

Isobel wished she'd made her excuses already. She never knew when to leave a party.

Jon pecked Sarah on the head. 'I'm really sorry, honey, but I've got to get back to school, a few of my Duke of Edinburgh kids are falling behind with their programmes, we've got to have this mentor meeting before we sit down with the Head next week.'

'Par for the course,' smiled Sarah.

Max set his hands either side of Jon's face and peered down from his shoulders. 'But aren't you coming to my football match?'

'Gonna do my best, kiddo.'

'But Mummy doesn't shout the right things like you do.'

'Good job Will's going then. He'll tell Mum what to shout.'

'Yess!' shouted Max.

'Here you go, Max.'

Max stretched for the envelopes, feeding them impatiently into the postbox. Sarah bothered at the diamond on her engagement finger.

'Good job, Maximus!' Come on then, Mr Fogharty, let's give you a proper run where you won't bother anyone. I think I'll just give him twenty minutes off the lead over Acorn Woods before I drop him back. Max, I've got to dash. So have you and Mum. Don't forget to mark up. And remember, when the other kid's marking you, fall back to where you want him to go. He'll have to follow you away from the penalty box, okay, son?' Max nodded as if that made complete sense. Jon set him down with a kiss. 'Isobel, lovely to meet you, sorry you were the victim of Mr Fogharty's brazen criminality. Sarah,' he kissed her tenderly on the mouth and patted the postbox, 'no backing out on me now, Mrs Hildred.'

24

Sebastian Brightman didn't play for the Fallenbay Falcons Under-6s, he played for the Cullet's Colts, the opposition. *The enemy*, as Will had put it while Sarah fumbled to get Max's shin pads over his ankles.

'Max! Watch number seven!' roared Will.

'Go on, Maxy,' Sarah uttered. *Don't let him push you around.*

She kept out of the cheering mother wars. It was all so tense, the swimming galas, sports days . . . even Under-6 football. *Too much argy-bargy,* her mum would say. *Too much aggression.* Her mother hated confrontation, maybe it was hereditary. Had they both been born that way? Or had they both learned?

Sarah eyed the spectators across the pitch. She couldn't call too loudly even if she wanted to. Even if she had been an Alpha-mother like Juliette or Olivia, half of the opposition parents would be sitting across the table from her at the next parents' evening. Olivia would already be crawling across it now she'd seen Tabitha's sabotaged self-portrait.

Someone scored. Will groaned. He shook his head at the ground and walked in a small circle.

'So, late back from school again. How come?' It was so

much easier when their conversations played out over a background of busyness. Cooking dinner, pottering around his room, watching Max's team go two-nil down.

Will shrugged beneath his hoody. 'You were only posting invitations. Didn't think you needed me there.'

She wanted to say that wasn't the point, but they had so few conversations these days that she didn't want to waste a go. Will had met them nearly an hour later than planned. No mention of where he'd been or who he'd been there with. Again. An echo was building in the back of her mind, her father's critique, reverberating through the years. *You've been too soft with that boy. If you'd been stricter with him he'd never have taken that girl in the shed in the first place. It was off limits!*

'So where did you go instead, Will? You haven't brought any friends home from school for weeks, I'm starting to wonder if I'm buying the wrong junk for you guys to eat.' She was trying for light-hearted, but something was off. Something had been off with Will for a while.

'Max! Lean into him, let him know you're there!'

Sarah studied Will's changing face. There was a vein that would pop out along his temple whenever he became fired up. There since he was a baby, when he'd scream blue murder if Sarah moved too far out of his sight. When he still needed her. Patrick had taken to sleeping in the spare room. Had she been too soft with Will back then? Should she have left him to cry in his cot, kept her husband closer instead? Will's vein didn't care where she was any more, but it popped now for Max, desperately dribbling the football towards the Colts' goal.

'So, is everything okay with your friends?'

Will had always had good friends. Will was a decent lad, he attracted decent pals. Which was why she'd thought it was the wedding at first, this change in him she couldn't put her finger on. She still thought it was the wedding, but there was more to it than that. She never saw Will's buddies any more, yet his phone never stopped buzzing. She heard it through the night sometimes. She'd told Jon it was notifications, silly updates coming through on her own phone downstairs, but she knew Will was talking to someone, late, when the rest of the house was sleeping. When the school friends Sarah knew were also probably sleeping.

'Everything's fine, Mum. That's it, Max . . . Max! Man on . . . *man on*!'

Sebastian kicked Max's legs out from under him, the parents dotted around the pitch giving a collective *ooh*, relieved it wasn't their little boy who'd just been nobbled.

Will roared to life. 'Ref! Ref! Are you watching this game?'

'Will! *Don't*.'

Max's blotchy little face looked etched with pain. Sarah stepped forwards. *Open your eyes, you plank!* A whistle blew. 'Max has to come off now?'

'He can't play if he can't walk, Mum. And it's nearly full-time anyway.'

Sebastian shrugged his remorseless bony shoulders and looked at his mother. Max was holding back the tears, but they would come, they were on the way, Sebastian had placed the order.

Should she go to him? Or would she make it worse? Will bolted on to the pitch while Sarah dithered. He scooped Max into his arms. Max rolled into his brother's chest and already his shoulders were moving in the telltale rhythm of silent sobbing. Sarah glanced across the astroturf. Olivia Brightman's mouth turned down at the edges in a fleeting show of regret, then she got back to clapping with Lorna Brooks and Alison and Kevin Brown at Max's scuppered run for goal. The Browns looked to Max, matching expressions of concern as they clapped.

Will set him down on his feet. 'Are you okay, Maxy?' Sarah couldn't help it, she put her hand protectively over Max's head and hugged him into her. Max was instantly undone.

'I . . . hate . . . Seb,' he sobbed around snatched breaths. 'He . . . always . . . kicks my legs. I don't . . . like it.'

'Kick him back, Max. As hard as you can. He won't do it again.'

Sarah shot Will a look. The final whistle blew. *Finally*. They'd started late because the Colts' manager had forgotten to bring the register. Sarah still had to finish drafting up her *Healthy! Happy! Holy Hell!* manifesto when she got home, after she'd fed the boys and got Max bathed and read *Godzilla Returns!* cover to cover.

'Did we win?' blinked Max.

Will rubbed his head. 'Not today, shorty.'

A huddle of twenty-somethings began jostling themselves out of their jackets over by the meshed fencing around the pitch. Some of them were pulling their feet up to their buttocks, stretching their legs out before play. One of them tapped his watch as he walked past Max's coach.

They'd been waiting in front of the new banners along the north side of the pitch. *Put a Brighter Smile on your Horizon*. More advertising for the Inman-Holts' dental practice. Karl's sponsorship of the sports centre had just paid for a complete refurbishment of the tennis courts. Juliette had been telling Mr Pethers about it. Karl really didn't want any advertising for Horizon, but the sports committee were just so grateful they went ahead and did their own thing anyway. Mr Pethers had listened attentively, then worded Juliette on new iPads for the library.

Max's coach waved his arms, ushering the Falcons and Colts over to one side so they could begin their post-match talk-down. Sarah checked her watch. Jon would still be tied up organising Duke of Edinburgh stragglers; he was worse than Sarah at breaking away from school meetings. She stepped forwards to follow Will and Max towards the other kids and walked into a tall, solid form. She apologised instinctively.

'Watch where you're going, sweetheart. Shouldn't still be on the pitch anyway, our slot started ten minutes ago.'

'Sorry,' she repeated.

She glanced over her shoulder at the group of men already firing their football around to one another. A few expletives floated on the warm evening air behind her. Couldn't they wait five minutes until the children were out of the way first? She skipped to catch up with the boys. A football sailed over her at speed, ricocheting noisily off the wire fencing where the Colts' parents still congregated. They all cowered as if a bomb had just gone off. Lorna spun her body away, shielding her front and the baby daughter in her arms.

A subdued flutter of laughter broke out behind Sarah. They'd kicked that ball hard enough to seriously hurt either a mother or her baby, and they thought it was funny?

'Problem?' one of them sneered.

The Falcons' coach called out, 'Let's carry this on in the sports centre reception, shall we, folks? Let these chaps get on with their game?'

Chaps? They weren't chaps, they were thugs. Sarah turned back to look for Will and Max. Will was bending down to Max's bootlaces. Everyone else was heading for the exit at the end of the enclosure, she wanted the boys out of here too.

'Will, time to get off the pitch.' She watched Will straighten up and hold Max's hand, then a violent stinging bang erupted in her face.

25

Isobel had been out of the cottage for nine hours straight. She'd visited the pirate museum, the shellfish hatchery, the golden postbox, the pier aquarium and the free part of the castle grounds. It was the done thing in the Hedley family: hit a holiday destination and explore. As kids it was Isobel and Sophie's job to stick together and see what was around. The Hedley girls were good at reconnaissance missions, just not the sticking together bit.

It was a good fifty-minute walk back to the cottage, she reckoned. She was knackered. By chance she'd picked up a card for Stevie's Cars in the aquarium gift shop, and she made the call on her last ten per cent of battery, asking to be collected from the last identifiable location her tired legs had walked her past. She was just making her way to the lobby of the leisure centre when the first ball clattered against the fence alongside her. It was the only reason she'd been looking in that direction when the second football slammed straight into that poor woman's face.

Isobel stopped. Was she alright? It had knocked her straight off her feet. Isobel hung back a few seconds. All those adults in there and no one was moving to help her. *Ah, no, there you go.* A lad in a hoody started running across the pitch, and then a familiar blonde boy in a too-big football strip followed the bigger lad to the fallen woman. Mark. No, *Max*. The woman on the ground tried to get up on to her elbows. Was that *Sarah*? Isobel backed up and slipped through the enclosure gate, circumnavigating a gathering of primary-school-aged footballers and their appropriate adults.

'Mum, are you alright? Mum?' The older boy was crouched down, trying to get Sarah to sit up. She looked dazed, a little bleeding starting from her mouth.

'Mummy?' Max was ashen.

Sarah flattened a hand to her cheek, eyes wide. 'I'm fine, I'm fine.' More blood streaked from her mouth. Why wasn't anyone helping her?

The boy in the hoody was suddenly on his feet, rigid with rage at the men dotted across the pitch, watching . . . waiting . . . 'What do you think you're doing? That's my mum, you stupid dick!' He pushed back the hood from his head, dark scruffy hair falling around his eyes. Isobel recognised him as the boy Daniel had invited to look at his new body-board that morning, just before Ben had thrown his apple at the gurner.

'Language, Will. There are kids here.' The man speaking had a whistle dangling from his neck and a paunch suggesting he whistled more than he footballed.

'You noticed?' snapped Will. 'Didn't tell *them* that though, did you, Coach? When they were swearing? Or booting foot-balls around little kids? But you'll tell me, 'cause I'm fifteen. My mum's bleeding, are you gonna tell them now?' His voice was getting higher. Max began to cry. Isobel stepped around the parents and crouched next to Max and his mum.

'Hey, Max. Do you remember me from earlier? Your dog

pinched my sandwich straight out of my hand, do you remember? What was he called again, Mr . . .' Max looked at Isobel bewildered, but he nodded.

'Mr Fogharty,' he whimpered. Will moved out of Isobel's eyeshot.

'Mr Fogharty! I remember now. Shall we help Mum get up, Max? Sarah, are you alright?'

Sarah's hand was covering her mouth, blood beginning to find its way through the joins of her fingers. She nodded. She let Isobel steady her by the elbow and planted her feet on the ground.

'You're brave for fifteen, aren't you, mate?' One of the footballers was biting. 'Hadn't you better wait for your dad before you start getting yourself into trouble, little man?'

Will drove his hands forwards into the bigger man's chest. It sent him backwards, but not much. And not enough to wipe the look off his face.

'Will!' More blood flowed over Sarah's chin, but she was up, Sarah was up. Isobel breathed a little easier. She couldn't see what was causing all that blood, though.

'Goodness, has anyone got a tissue?' asked someone.

'Sorry, Sarah, hang on . . .' Isobel went into her bag and fished out a wad of serviettes she'd kept from Coast yesterday. Sarah pressed them to her mouth. Her eyes were watering, fixed on Will.

'Don't bother, mate. You're not big enough to play just yet. If the daft cow got off the pitch when your time was up—'

Will reared up again.

The coach finally made a move. 'Will, relax . . . *relax!*' Isobel didn't think that making a grab for Will's hood was *that* good an idea. She'd seen boys Will's age kick their way through fire doors. They kind of hulked-out. No teacher she'd ever seen had been strong enough to stop any teen mid-hulk.

Thought so. Will shrugged straight out of the coach's grasp and squared up nose to nose with the idiot. Where was Jon? Isobel surveyed the perimeter.

'Oi! That's enough!'

A middle-aged man with designer glasses and a squash racket stalked across the pitch towards them. Will kicked a drinks bottle as hard as he could, sending it bouncing across the ground.

'Do you need more tissues, Sarah?' Isobel was trying to get a better look at her but Sarah was preoccupied with the new arrival.

'You lot, clear off,' he instructed the footballers.

'*Fuck off.*'

Parents gasped. Sarah reached for Will, pulling him to stand back with her and Max. Will's fists were trembling.

'These are the only floodlit pitches in Fallenbay, fellas.'

'And?'

'And I'm assuming at least *some* of you work and have to play at night? I'm a lucky bloke, I get to choose my hours, so I'm playing golf tomorrow morning with the chairman of the leisure trust. A few of you are big blokes. Use the gym here too? Addictive, isn't it?' There was a restlessness between some of them. 'Unless you want me to have your memberships revoked before I tee off tomorrow, I'd go and get yourselves a refund for tonight's pitch hire, lads. Go cool off.'

'Sarah, are you alright?' asked Isobel quietly. Sarah nodded. The footballers were weighing up their options. The one holding the ball sucked his teeth and looked at his friend. The friend picked up his drinks bottle and walked for the gate. Another followed. 'Clumsy bitch,' mumbled another.

Isobel's heart was pumping.

'Thank you,' murmured Sarah from behind the wad of tissues.

The guy in the squash gear took a deep breath. 'Are you okay, Sarah? Can I help? That's quite a bleed.'

'Can I help at all, Karl?' blurted one of the mothers. Isobel almost jumped; the woman with the caramel highlights and riding boots had been quietly watching Sarah bleed until now.

'No, I'm good, thank you, Olivia. Sarah? Mind if I take a look?'

Sarah nodded and opened her mouth. There was something intimate about the inside of a person's mouth. Isobel looked away. Will had walked to the fence, glaring at the men leaving. Max welded himself to Sarah's leg.

'Sorry, I haven't got my gloves, I can't use my hands. Your tongue . . . could you just . . . Ah, I see . . . you've broken a tooth. You may need a small stitch inside that cheek, Sarah.'

Sarah batted her hands. 'No, it's fine, I broke it yesterday. Think it just caught the sharp part, that's all.' She was still bleeding. Isobel passed her more serviettes and smiled at the dentist. *Please stop making her talk.*

'Why don't we pop over to the surgery now? I can have one of my nurses meet us there, get you fixed up in no time?' Isobel followed Karl's eyes to the clean white building across the street, *Horizon* in minimalist signage across the lawns.

'I could sit with the boys, Sarah,' offered Isobel.

'Oh, no, really, there's no need. It can wait until morning. Thanks.'

'Tomorrow then?' said Karl. 'I can give you an emergency appointment first thing. Golf can wait, he was going to beat me anyway.'

Sarah sounded more assertive. 'Thank you, Karl. Really. But I'm already booked in this week with my own dentist.' Isobel offered her last tissue.

Will stalked back towards them, scooping up a bag on his way, then a child's jacket, Karl's eyes following him like a threat.

'Would you like me to call someone for you, Mrs Harrison? Your fiancé?' Sarah looked at the woman in the riding boots and tried to smile. 'Thanks, Mrs Brightman, but he's in meetings. And honestly, I'm—'

'Can I drop you and the boys home, Sarah?' asked Karl.

Will took Max's hand in his. 'Mum, we're going. Come on.'

Karl stiffened. 'Your mother's had a bang to the head, William. Let me run you all home. Please?'

Will blanked him, his voice thick with something Isobel couldn't put her finger on. 'Your car's here, Mum. Let's go.'

'I'm fine, Karl, really. It's so embarrassing. Funny, really.' Sarah looked set to cry.

Karl's mouth formed a hard line. Sarah's eyes moved from Will to the man trying to help them.

'I could drive you,' blurted Isobel. 'In your car . . . so you don't have to leave it. I'd only be covered third party, but I've walked, so . . . I could drive you home, if it helps?'

What on earth was she doing? There she went again, blatantly breaking one of Sophie's solid-as-a-rock-don't-even-think-about-flexing-me rules. *Don't get involved*. Why would Sarah even want a woman she'd only just met driving her and her children around? She hadn't hit her head *that* hard.

'I'm not sure we've met. Karl Inman-Holt.' Isobel connected the dots. Milo's dad. Husband of the Rottweiler.

'Hello.'

'I used to be Sarah's dentist. Are you a new parent in town?'

Isobel got the feeling she was half a conversation away from being signed up to his patient list. Sarah started to look less pale and more hopeful. 'No, I . . . I just know Sarah and Max.' She was using the term 'know' *very* loosely.

'Thanks, Isobel,' interrupted Sarah. 'Boys, get your things. Quickly. Thank you, Karl. For helping just now. We appreciate it.' Sarah planted a set of car keys in Isobel's hand. 'All sorted.' Isobel wasn't sure who she was trying to convince.

26

'Sam, you can't eat *two* hotdogs, your poor arteries!' That reminded Cleo, Evie's en-suite sink needed unclogging. She dreaded to think what might be lurking in the U-bend; she had definitely gotten a whiff of ciggies when Cassie and Verity last stayed over.

A thought bolted into Cleo's consciousness. *Verity Faulkener.* She hadn't seen hide nor hair of Verity since that weekend. Had the girls fallen out? Cleo had survived school friends like Verity herself, beautiful and magnetic, adored by boys, feared and revered by the girls. The sort of *friend* who could talk you into a little light shoplifting and then hold it against you if you didn't see the funny side of a determined security guard chasing you down the street.

Sam took both hotdogs from the girl serving and held them up either side of his head. 'One for each ear,' he grimaced, bobbing his head towards Cleo. *Cheeky sod.* She was not a nag.

Cleo turned on her heels. She'd dusted off a cheeky pair of peep-toes for their date, nicked some of Evie's best nail polish too. Sam loved Cleo's feet, he thought them dainty. Pretty. It was no big achievement given the sweaty hooves Sam had shared a gym with when they'd first started getting serious, but still she'd found herself raiding Evie's stash of colours tonight, just for him.

She walked over to the ketchup and mustard dispensers near the pick'n'mix and felt the thrill of a memory, the times she'd done exactly this, teetering ahead of Sam in her best shoes pretending she didn't care about the other girls hanging around Wrecker's gym because Cleo with the curls was the only girl Samuel Roberts would ever step outside the ring for.

'How are you going to work those then, you've got your hands full.' She smugly popped another piece of popcorn in her mouth and waited for Sam to struggle with the mustard pump. Already tonight had been a change in rhythm, the two of them moving around each other in the bedroom, taking turns to shower and dress for their evening out. It had been nice. Easy. When had her fuse grown so short with him? Sam was a good husband, wasn't he? A good man. Sometimes she could feel herself about to explode; she wished she could stop but it was just so easy to fire off in his direction. Why was that? Because he took it? Because he still knew how to take a blow?

'You're doing your serious face thing, my love. What's up?'

'Nothing. I was just thinking.'

'About?'

'How you're going to ketchup those dogs with no spare hand.'

Sam held one of his hotdogs up and shoved it into his mouth. It hung there flaccidly. He waved his empty hand at her like a magician before pumping away on the mustard and ketchup dispensers.

'You are such a child.'

He slipped his hand around her waist. That thrill was rising in her again. The quiet eighteen-year-old with the deadly left hook and deadlier blue eyes who Cleo had fallen in love with was staring straight back at her. He took the hotdog out of his mouth and leant into her. 'You look good enough to eat tonight, Mrs Roberts. Crazy idea, I know, but why don't we forget the film and just go home?'

A dormant sensation was stirring. Sam's sweetly spiced aftershave in place of the normal whiff of building work, the intent in his eyes, the glass of wine he'd poured for her while she'd put on her make-up . . . Cleo was definitely somewhere on the periphery of being persuaded. Sam grinned. He knew he'd spotted a weakness. All those years, thousands of hours training in Wrecker's, pummelling his opponents, dancing around them, beating them down. *The boy moves like water! Don't be fooled by a calm surface, there's a deadly undercurrent rrrraging beneath Sammy the Rrrroughhouse Rrrroberts!*

'Why are you looking at me like that, Sam?'

He leant further in and kissed her, right there in the cinema lobby. Kissed her deeply and slowly, the way they used to. 'Because I'd like to take you home.' Cleo swallowed. 'But it's only seven-thirty. The kids . . .'

'Evie's out running with Cassie—'

'Again?' Hang on, wasn't it Cassie they'd driven past on the promenade? With the youths throwing chips at seagulls?

'And Harry's barricaded himself in his bedroom in a paddy.' Sam wiggled his eyebrows. 'So, Cleo with the curls, d'ya think your mum will let you come back to my place for a look at my new punchbag?'

Cleo giggled and lay a hand flat against his chest. 'Harry's not in a paddy, he's sick.'

'He's not sick, he's hurting.'

'Hurting? Why would Harry be hurting?'

He snuck another bite of his hotdog. Arousal over, there was ketchup at the corner of his mouth. 'It's all off.'

'What is? The trip to Denmark?'

'Trip to Denmark? No, the great love affair. Ingred's dumped him.'

'Already? How do you know? Don't talk with your mouth full.'

'I don't. But her photos were in the bin when I put the recycling out. He was all loved up yesterday so I don't think he was the one doing any elbowing.'

'Poor Harry.' Cleo felt her mood dampen. Harry didn't really do *sad*. And barricading himself in his bedroom was a little OTT. Poor lad. Ingred was so elfin and pretty and exotically foreign; H had never been on his phone so much. Now he'd been ditched. Discarded. Harry was unwanted. It was putting Cleo right off the idea of going home and having clumsy sex with his father, even if it would be the first time in flipping ages and just thinking about it had made her a tiny bit predatory because she knew full well even clumsy sex would do wonders to ease the tension building in her shoulders since Lorna got her knickers in a twist.

She grabbed Sam's wrist, tearing herself a mouthful of his hotdog. She'd bitten off more than she could chew; it was tricky talking around a giant Frankfurter. 'Can we go in and watch the movie first? We've paid already and it's got Daniel Craig in it.'

'Who's Daniel Craig? Not that fella in the budgie-smugglers on your laptop screensaver?'

Cleo dabbed her mouth. 'That's the one. Doesn't he remind you of Jon?'

'James Bond? They're both overrated, I suppose.'

'What's wrong with Jon?'

'Apart from being a pretty boy? Nothing.'

'What's wrong with James Bond then?'

'Chases too many women and ponces around in flashy motors. Prat.'

'Oh.'

'Why does he remind you of Jon?'

'Don't know really. Suppose it's the flashy car.'

27

'He was only trying to help, Will.'

'No one asked for his help. Psycho.'

Sarah returned to looking out of the passenger window.

Isobel's iPhone was cradled in the cup holder of Sarah's Volvo, blinking to life between them. She caught a glimpse of *SOPHIE* mid-screen before she had to concentrate on the road. She tried to steal another sideways glance before the preview of Sophie's text faded.

Facebook's all set. Fingers fucking crossed.

Isobel shot a look in the rearview mirror. Will's eyes met hers. He looked out of his window.

'You have a message, lady.' *Bugger*. Max was looking at her phone.

'*Isobel*, Max. This lady's name is *Isobel*.'

Had Max read Sophie's f-bomb? Was he old enough to read texts? Ella was old enough but not proficient enough to beat a four-second preview.

'I'm so sorry about all of this,' apologised Sarah. 'And Karl's not a psycho, Will.'

Max kicked the back of Isobel's chair when he spoke.

'What's a psycho?' Max had a lisp. *Psycho* had never sounded so adorable. If politicians used children like Max to deliver their speeches on education cuts, no one would rally.

'Idiot then, whatever. He's definitely an idiot. And his wife.'

'Mummy says we're not allowed to say *idiot*, Will.'

'Do you think Mrs Inman-Holt's an idiot, Max?'

Max looked at his mother then tried to sink down into his car seat where she couldn't see him nodding.

'You did say *right* on the corner, didn't you?' interrupted Isobel.

Sarah nodded. Her face looked perfectly fine now, there was just a little residual puffiness around her eyes, nothing more. 'Ours is the pale blue one. With the hanging baskets.'

'Not the blue one with the big tree at the front, or the pink house, or the white one . . .' kicked Max.

'The one with the Sold sign,' muttered Will.

'That's our house!' squealed Max. 'There's my blow-up Godzilla, look! In that window up there!'

Isobel crawled towards the pastel blue townhouse. Most of the other houses in the row of Georgian terraces looked like marshmallows with railings out front, but Sarah's imposing end terrace looked casually aspirational, like a *Homes & Gardens* spread showing the mere mortals in their readership what might be achieved with just a period property and the right family to breathe life into it. Easy peasy.

'Our off-road parking's just down here. Follow the hedgerow and . . . these are our garages.' More hanging baskets with understated blooms framed the two parking bays along the side of the property. Isobel pulled alongside the garages just as Jon's black car nipped in around them, music throbbing from behind closed windows. Will jumped out of the Volvo. He ducked through the carport before Max even started unclipping his belt. Isobel grabbed her phone. 'I'll let you guys get back to your evening.'

'Would you like to come in for a cup of tea? I've completely railroaded your day today, Isobel. Twice in fact. I'm so sorry.'

'Actually, I'm going to head back.' They'd just driven over the island with the scaled down galleon that all the seagulls liked to poop on. Isobel knew her way back from the poopy galleon, a twenty-five-minute walk, max.

'Jon? Could you give Isobel a lift back to . . .' Sarah blinked and looked at her. 'I'm sorry, I don't know where you're staying.'

Jon frowned at Isobel sitting in the driver's side. 'Hello again. Are you following me?'

'Hello.' She felt her face flush. 'Not intentionally.'

Jon looked at Sarah. 'Everything okay, baby?'

'Fine. Could you run Isobel back? Where are you staying, Isobel?'

'I'm at Curlew Cottage. The holiday let at the top of the private road with the *No Trespassers* sign, next to the woodland.'

'Mr Oakes' smallholding?' asked Sarah. Her eyes instantly focused. 'You wouldn't know if he's still having problems with teenagers up there? Trespassing, I mean. That's who the sign's for, the kids who keep using Mr Oakes' woodland to do who knows what in.'

There were teenagers skulking around in the woodland next to the cottage? That was all Isobel needed, strangers in dark corners. 'I haven't seen anything. Or heard. Mr Oakes' dog's a pretty effective warning system.'

Sarah looked vacantly towards her carport.

'So, are we recruiting a chauffeur now, or has Mummy been drinking again?' Jon grinned through the driver's window at Max in the back.

'Nothing quite as exciting, unfortunately. Are you happy to let Jon run you home, Isobel? I'd feel less awful if you'd accept a lift.'

Her legs were pretty achy now that she'd rested them. 'A lift would be great, thanks.'

Jon slapped his hands together. 'Okey-doke, do you want to hop in my car? Or scooch over? Let's take mine, it's more pretentious. Attractive girl in the front, the gossips will love it.' He opened Isobel's door and bowed. 'After you, m'lady. Let me just nip into the house and grab my trainers. These new loafers have been pinching the hell out of my big toe.' He tapped the roof of the car and skipped through the carport and into the garden.

'Are you sure you're alright?' Isobel asked Sarah.

Sarah nodded. 'Thanks for stepping in back there. And sorry about Will, he's not normally so . . .'

'Will's fine. Honestly.'

'I'm not making excuses for him, it's just, Will has a history, sort of . . . with the dentist's daughter. It would've been awkward had you not given me an out.'

'No need to explain.' Isobel was an old hand at bleak histories. She wasn't going to push Sarah for gory details on Will's.

Jon emerged from the carport shadows. Sarah took a note from her purse. 'Pick Isobel up a bottle of wine on the way. And could you get me a box of painkillers too, please?'

'Are you okay? What sort of painkillers? Headache or . . . don't say you're coming down with those stomach cramps all the kids have been infecting each other with at Hornbeam? Don't worry, Isobel, I've got some hand sanitiser in my glove-box.'

'No, not the dreaded stomach bug. We don't have it, Isobel, I promise. Toothache, Jon. Anything for toothache.'

'You got it.' Jon looked to Isobel. 'Are we fit?'

'Sure. Take care, Sarah.'

Jon did a comedy skip towards his car. Isobel smiled, despite Sophie's words smouldering in her head. *Don't. Befriend. Strangers.*

28

Cleo gave the car door a bloody good slam and stalked towards the porch.

'I suppose that bonk's out of the window then?' Sam called resignedly across the driveway.

She let herself in, looking daggers back at him as she stormed inside. A refund for the moron sitting behind them, were they serious? He was the one who'd jabbered through the whole sodding film! Idiotic cinema staff.

Cleo listened for signs of life as she stalked silently through the lounge. Dammit, tonight was supposed to put Eves at ease about their marriage, not stress her out entirely. Sam was just letting himself in behind her, the great useless lump. He followed her into the kitchen.

'Go on, get it off your chest.'

She ignored him for a moment. Then let rip. 'That usher was rude to me and you just stood there. First Lorna and her boob crusade, now some little jobsworth with a flashlight!' She swung around for the kettle and jammed on the tap.

'He wasn't rude, Cleo. He'd had complaints.'

'Yes! About me! *Me*! I can't believe it!' She snapped open the kettle lid and shoved the whole thing under the flow. 'Doing his job would've been frogmarching that Neanderthal from the screening and getting *him* to pay for everyone else's tickets. Instead, he flashes his stupid little penis extension in *my* face and asks *me* to stop disrupting the film. *Twerp.*' Sam tilted his chin into his chest and chuckled. Cleo thrust the kettle on to the side. 'It's not fucking funny.'

'You threw your popcorn in his face, darling.'

'Yes, I noticed how quickly you started reeling off the apologies. For God's sake, Sam. There was a time you would have punched his lights out!'

'Not unless he was in the bloody ring I wouldn't! That dipstick . . . he wasn't a *threat*, Cleo. He was just a bit pissed. In a *really* boring film. I wish I'd knocked a few beers back too.'

'It had *excellent* reviews,' she hissed.

'You're missing one tiny point here, Cle. That usher was shining his light on the only threatening person in there. A five-foot-six menace in a very nice blue dress.'

'I should've bought the jumbo popcorn and thrown that. Half of it was unpopped kernels anyway, people break teeth on those.'

'Jesus, Cleo, lighten *up*. People ruin films, popcorn doesn't always pop . . . children die of hunger. Every day. Pick your protests.'

'Don't do that, Sam. Don't take away my right to feel wronged because terrible things happen in far-off lands.'

'Terrible things happen every day all around us, Cleo. We're just lucky we don't have that sort of perspective.'

'I have perspective.'

'You think so? Here's one for you. Rich, my new van buddy? Before his missus left him after fourteen years, she told him two things. One, she wasn't sure she'd ever really loved the poor bloke, and two, she'd never been sure their kid was his.' Cleo's nostrils ceased flaring immediately. 'Imagine that, Cle? Finding out the child you love more than anything in this world might not be yours. After all that time. Thinking you knew your place in the world.'

Cleo swallowed. 'That's terrible.'

Sam nodded. 'And d'ya know what Rich did? When she told him? He took Charlie and that callous cow straight to Boots for a DNA kit.'

Cleo's heart started to patter for the little boy caught between angry, warring parents. She was also a tiny bit appalled that such things as DNA testing kits could be bought on the high street next to throat lozenges and verruca gel. 'That poor boy,' she said sombrely. 'Must've been so traumatic for him.'

'Not really, Charlie got three strikes and made himself a good bit of pocket money betting his old man he could out-bowl him.'

'I don't follow.'

'Rich couldn't do it. He knew his head was all over the place, said he stopped driving for the pharmacy and started looking for something to distract himself, before he made the biggest mistake of his life and changed the way he saw that kid. *His* kid, whatever his blood might turn up. Rich pulled into the first place he saw and took the kid bowling instead.'

'But . . . what about his ex?'

'She went bowling too. I guess she got to say something sharp in the middle of a fight and never pay the price for it. She must've just got it after that, that Rich was the better of them for Charlie. She gave him custody and she sees Charlie at weekends.'

He'd done it. Sam had disarmed her. Round 1 to Rrrroughhouse Rrrroberts. 'You should invite them round, Sam. Introduce Charlie to Harry. They could come for a proper dinner.'

'Cleo, they don't need saving, sweetheart. They just aren't a neat little nuclear family. The point I'm making is, people take knocks. Perspectives change. We're lucky, Cleo, ours has never had to. But you've got to lighten up. Or you're gonna miss the bigger stuff.'

She pulled her earrings out and set them on the side. 'I know we're lucky.'

'Then what's eating you? It's like you're borderline crazy all the time. Are you unhappy?'

Sam's frankness took her by surprise. *Cranky* wasn't unhappy. *Crazy* wasn't unhappy, either. 'Why would you ask that?'

Sam puffed out his cheeks. 'We have a nice life, Cle. It's not perfect, it's not always shiny, but it's not broken. What happened to Rich, I couldn't cope with that. Anything coming between me and those two kids upstairs, anything that might hurt us as a family . . . I'd crumble. Roughhouse Roberts, out for the count. Throw in the towel.'

'No you wouldn't,' she lied. He totally would, Sam would absolutely crumble if anything happened to Harry or Evie.

He crossed the kitchen, taking her hands from behind her. 'We've got two beautiful, healthy kids, a good home in a safe community, and we've got each other, warts and all. But if you're unhappy, Cle, despite everything we have, then we've got a real problem.'

'I'm not unhappy. I just . . .'

'Want more?'

'Yes. I just want more.'

'Okay, Cleo. Then what more do you want? Because I'm getting tired of tiptoeing around you when I get home at night. So you tell me now what it is you want, and we'll see what we can do about it. But Cleo, don't come to me in a year's time and say you want something else, because I'm getting too old, my bones ache. I'm running out of energy.'

Cleo rubbed at the ache starting in her forehead and tried to decipher the look on Sam's face. He was still handsome, still gave in to her when she pushed hard enough. Still happy enough just to be happy enough. But Cleo wanted that teeny bit more.

'I want to extend Coast. I want it to be a roaring success that doesn't wobble when the school mothers try to shake it down. I want you to back me up.'

'I'll always back you up. Even when you're being an arse, like tonight.'

'Then you'll help me?'

'I'll help you. I love you, Cleo. Always have.'

'I love you too.'

'So are we friends then?'

'Yes, Sam. We're friends.'

'Great stuff. So how about that bonk?'

29

Sarah lay awake, a hand sandwiched between her pillow and cheek. And not her good cheek. Her tongue bothered at the cut inside her mouth, then the jagged rim of her tooth. Still painful. Still jagged. Jon had stocked up on the paracetamol. He could only buy two boxes, in case he was feeling suicidal, the cashier said. By the time she saw the dentist on Saturday she'd be rattling with pills.

Her eyes flicked wide open. *Pills.*

She listened to the rhythm of Jon's breathing. *Asleep. Definitely.* Jon snored softly, like a cat. There was always a temptation to cuddle up to him, run a hand through his hair. It had started the first night she'd watched him sleeping, this otherworldly being with great post-sex hair and hilarious anecdotes, landed in her bed. *Her bed!*

She eased the duvet from her side. So began the cycle of reasoning, the justifications, ready in case he ever walked in on her mid-swallow.

I feel older than I thought I did . . . There's just so much going on . . . You think you wouldn't mind a pregnant bride, but . . .

Men had been spooked by less. This was her ritual. All for keeping one modicum of control safely hidden in a forgotten bath toy in the loo-roll cupboard. She left the bedroom and tiptoed silently towards the end of the hall. She had her own en-suite to hide things in, but Jon was a lover of showers and was always in there freshening up after his runs, dog walks, after-school clubs . . . The family bathroom was safer. And nobody ever changed the loo rolls but Sarah.

She stepped into the bathroom, leaving the door open behind her. The landing floorboards creaked like an old ship; anyone approaching would be too sleep-fuddled to avoid them. She reached into the tallboy, behind the stack of Andrex, and found the familiar form of a plastic toy tugboat. She pulled it from its hiding place and lifted the upper deck revealing the slip of pills inside.

Thursday. She popped it out, swallowed it, then replaced the boat with its contraband cargo. There was no excuse. She acknowledged this with every pill she popped. Jon deserved better. He'd given her so much. Given the boys so much. But how would she explain it? How the last time there'd been a baby in the house she'd let it all fall apart? Taken her eye off the ball.

She padded back along the landing, the last place she'd watched Patrick kiss their children before the airport taxi arrived. *See you next week, family!* he'd grinned up the stairs. Sarah had wished him luck for the big exhibition, giddily knowing they'd see him there in less than thirty-six hours. *Surprise!*

She should never have gone to Portugal. Her father was right. What mother dragged two little boys on to a plane to another country on a whimsical notion of, what, romance? Spontaneity? A stab at proving to her husband she wasn't so boring after all? The planning was exhilarating after months of maternity leave. She'd swung a family suite in the same hotel as the exhibition (check-in were going to put Patrick in there on arrival; the concierge had become Sarah's inside man after a flurry of clandestine emails), activities were in place for her and the kids when Patrick needed to schmooze. Sure he was going to be proud of them, coming all that way to support him, but wait until he saw the boys in those matching dickie bows!

She would never forgive herself for those matching dickie bows. Dressing the boys up for it, as if rejection was a gift. Something awarded.

She crept towards Max's bed. His spaceman pyjamas had ridden up over his tummy, hands balled either side of his head as if someone had knocked him out cold. Max had slept soundly like that in her arms while his family crumbled around him in a five-star hotel lobby. Will had not slept through it. Will had drunk it all in. The soaring foyer ceiling, the babble of European photography enthusiasts. Will had gazed at this upgraded version of his father in bewildered awe, they both had, Patrick with his slightly different posture and his slightly different laugh. Sarah and the boys had arrived there like lost property. A trio of assorted baggage misdirected to the wrong half of Patrick's life. One look and she knew. They didn't belong to him any more, Paddy Harrison, reinvented sports photographer. They had once, like a pair of fondly worn slippers. Now they were simply the wrong shoes for his shiny new outfit.

Sarah bent down and kissed the blond hair, sweet with the scent of No-More-Tears shampoo. There had never been any tears from Max; Patrick was long gone before Max had turned one. He hadn't had to listen like Will had.

There has to be more out there, Sarah. I'm sorry. This . . . it's just not enough.

She pulled the dinosaur covers over Max's compact little body and left him to his dreams. Patrick could never know what he'd given away. He didn't deserve them. Not Max, who thought if he swallowed an apple pip an apple tree would grow inside him until it burst from his nostrils, necessitating a trip to the tree surgeon. And not Will, who would take on a five-a-side football team because his mum was silly enough to save a goal with her face.

Anyway, Jon was here now. How many men took on the children of another? She deserved to choke on those pills.

Will's bedroom door was ajar, his legs hanging off either side of his bed, soft snores drifting through the darkness.

It was too rare an opportunity to give away. She moved silently across his bedroom and pressed a kiss gently into his curls. He smelled of No-More-Tears too. A thought turned to a whisper. 'I love you, Will.'

He stirred. Sarah took her cue. She was almost at the door, ready to slip back into bed with Jon like a cheating spouse, when a green glow filtered through the pocket of one of the jackets hanging from Will's door. She hesitated. Candy Crush notification? Software update? She glanced back at Will, almost completely dangling from his bed. It wasn't curiosity; E-safety was every parent's responsibility, that's what they taught at Hornbeam.

She unzipped the pocket of Will's Adidas jacket and lifted the phone from inside. *EDWARD.* One o'clock in the morning was a tad late for Will's elusive friend to be texting him. She touched the name. *Enter passcode.*

Sarah put the phone back and heard something rustle beneath it. It felt like fabric at first, clumps of fibres in a small plastic bag. The smell hit her almost immediately. Her head whooshed. What the hell was Will doing with pot in his pocket? Will couldn't do drugs! He couldn't bring drugs into this house!

'Sarah?' Jon's voice was slack with sleep. She heard his feet hit the floorboards. *Shit.* Where was she going to stash this? The bathtime boat? Her mouth? Jon would see this as a direct hit on the trust he'd been working so hard to build with Will. Jon abhorred secrets, he'd be more upset Will was *hiding* pot than smoking the bloody stuff. Did Will even smoke? He'd never, ever smelled of it.

Jon groaned with tiredness. She stuffed the hash back into Will's jacket pocket and nipped out on to the landing. Her bedroom door opened.

'Are you okay?' Jon whispered.

'I thought I heard Max, it's okay, go to bed.' Lies didn't usually come to her so easily. Living with Patrick for ten years must have had an effect.

Jon rubbed his eye like a tired child. 'Tooth okay? Still looks swollen. Shall I run downstairs for more painkillers?'

She shook her head. 'It looks worse than it feels.' Knowing Will had secrets felt worse than anything else.

'Come back to bed then, honey,' Jon yawned. 'It'll look better in the morning. Everything always looks better in the morning.'

30

Cleo mustered all the strength left in her upper body and prised Sam's gargantuan arm from where it pinned her to the bed. Sam grunted, mumbled something about bacon and drifted back into a deep sleep.

Cleo squinted at her bedside clock. *One-thirty-four.* A raging thirst had woken her. She was dehydrated from too much salty popcorn. Or too much excellent sex. She caught herself smiling into the darkness. The night had taken an unexpected turn. She hauled herself naked and pleasantly exhausted from Sam's side of the bed and fumbled around for her nightdress. Something had lifted in her. It was more than just the romp they'd enjoyed (and enjoyed again), it was *optimism*. Finally, Coast was going to be the hub of the harbour. Live music, evening events . . . *Yes.* Coast was on the move. She would be the engine, Sam would be the machine. The Inman-Holts wouldn't be the only ones around here with a solid family business and fabulous cars.

She stepped out on to the landing, craving water now. She'd eaten most of the popcorn just to pass the time. By God, what a boring film, what was Daniel Craig thinking? And he had far too many clothes on, *throughout*, which probably hadn't helped her mood any before the plonker in the row behind started getting on everybody's nerves.

She reached Harry's door and realised she hadn't checked in on the kids yet. Sam had distracted her with his impression of a raging elephant . . . utterly childish, pulling his trouser pockets out like that. Been pulling the same gag for years though, so it was kind of precious on the right days. Harry's door was shut tight. She turned the handle and peered inside. She did this, checked in on the kids religiously on her way to bed, ever since they really were her *babies* and she'd obsessed about them overheating, or rolling on to their faces, or having their fingertips nibbled off by some wild animal getting in through a window somewhere.

Harry's covers rose and fell with the silent rhythm of his breathing. *Poor H.* Cleo had never had to deal with the aching and bemusing pain of first love; she'd married hers.

She fought the urge to wake Harry up and give him a hug, tell him not to worry about silly Danish girls who clearly couldn't recognise a lovely, brilliant boy if their lives depended on it. She hugged at his door instead, taking in the microcosm of her son's bedroom. Lego had long since been replaced with surfboards. Posters of Teenage Mutant Ninja Turtles traded for NBA stars. She gave a parting glance to the homework books spread across his computer desk and hoped his first throes into heartbreak would be short-lived.

Sam wasn't worried. *Give him a week, tops, he'll be chasing girls around the bay before you know it. His heart won't be the part of his anatomy you'll worry about him protecting, I tell you now.*

Cleo pulled Harry's door to. *You'd better not cock up his*

GCSEs, you little strumpet. His exams started soon, and then there was the small issue of the twins' sixteenth birthdays less than a month from now to throw even more chaos into the pot.

She made a mental note to look up Ingred's Facebook account for signs of personality defects. She needed to finalise the kids' birthday presents while she was online too. There was that beautiful dress Evie kept gazing longingly at in the designer shop window, but what size would she risk ordering? Now Evie was crash-exercising?

She crossed the landing to Evie's room, feeling her after-sex glow start to slip away.

Evie had fallen asleep with her lamp on, full make-up, one headphone still wedged into her ear. Cleo studied her for a few moments before she killed the light. Why did Evie feel the need to cover over that beautiful face all the time? They'd watched a documentary together on Channel 4 last year: *Make-up – the masks we hide behind*, or some other psychobabble nonsense. Cleo had scoffed when one woman talked about make-up empowering her, the hour set aside to decorate herself each morning absolutely critical to her mental wellbeing. Cleo was doing well if she managed a bit of eyeshadow and a blob of anti-frizz serum between chucking the kids out for school and opening up at Coast. But Evie was different. There had been changes lately, Evie's circle of friends had shrunk, she was spending less time at The Village with the other kids, more time in here with that bloody phone glued to her hand, sometimes wired almost directly to her brain, like now. Cleo teased the earphone from Evie's ear. She wrapped the wires around the device allowing those horrible sods to torment her daughter at will. Throwing it out of the window wouldn't be such a terrible idea. But Evie had to learn when, and *how*, to shut off. Self-defence in the internet age.

Cleo set the phone down on the desk beside Evie's bed, right next to the Matryoshka dolls she had treasured since she was little. Was Evie wearing a mask? Was she like those dolls, hiding herself, the real Evie, inside layers of other, gobbier, trendier, make-upped Evies? Posters of skinny models and androgynous popstars looked down from her bedroom wall. Their hollow eyes and expressions made Cleo question herself. What sort of young woman was Evie growing into? Harry was about as hard to read as a *Run, Spot, Run!* book, but Evie? Evie was a mystery.

Cleo tucked her in. She reached for the lamp switch just as Evie stretched her hands above her head, revealing the angry, bloodied scratch-marks tracking the insides of her arms.

31

Isobel watched the thin cotton drape billowing in the bedroom window. She shouldn't have slept with it ajar, but last
night had been muggy. Like her thoughts.

Her arm lay outstretched on the pillow. She let her eyes
trail along it to the girl she'd had needled on to her wrist.
A fun nod to sisterhood, now a tag. A stamp. Her most
distinguishing feature. If she was ever hideously disfigured in
a freak accident, this would be her identifying mark. Forensics
would look at her lifeless, nameless body, see her tattoo and
declare, *She's no Jane Doe, fellas, she's that silly tart off the
internet. Isobel Hedley.*

'Can we see your tattoo, Miss?'

Isobel scrunched her eyes shut and let herself go back
there. She'd been swept up in her own potency. The kids had
gone crazy for Eminem, Adele, Arctic Monkeys . . . they were
getting it; poetry had started to take on a new tangible form
with the help of their favourite artists and a lesson jammed
with YouTube videos.

'Go on, Miss. Show us.'

She'd felt so *hip*. On a wavelength with the fourteen-year-
olds she knew she could pull up a level if they would just
remain engaged. But they were engaged already, Isobel just

didn't know it yet. Engaged, coordinated, and about to deliver a potent lesson of their own.

Isobel flopped her arm over her face and tried to blot out the rest, but the memory was already uncoiling itself.

She'd undone her cuff and obliged, a teacher with a tattoo *and* an English lesson on musical poetry, how cool was she? The kids were working together, Melanie McLoughlin sat huddled with the hockey girls rewriting a Beyoncé number with their own lyrics. Poetic techniques were making sense, Melanie was making friends. Isobel had been riding a high.

'Oh my God, it is though . . . it's actually, like, you though, Miss . . .' She hadn't even seen it coming.

'What's me?' So imbecilic! To be ambushed by a handful of children. They'd rounded on her the way some of them rounded on Melanie when she ate her lunch alone. A choreography of comments, herding their target to the final insult. The kill zone.

Another girl clamped her hand around Isobel's wrist for a better look. 'Get lost, you can't tell from that, you can't even see it unless you zoom right in.'

'I zoomed right in,' laughed one of them.

'It's Little Red Riding Wh— I mean Hood, Miss, innit? That tattoo?'

'It is her! Her name's on it anyway, where it said "share if you think she should be sent to the headmaster"!'

'And her address is on it. Can we come round for dinner? Number nineteen, innit, Miss?'

'What are you lot waffling about?' she'd asked.

'On Twitter, Miss. You're famous.'

They'd completely lost her. 'I'm not on Twitter!'

'You are now!'

'Is your boyfriend called Nathan, Miss? Yahoo says you live with Nathan someone. Is he a bit frisky, Miss?' The laughter had changed then. The faintest flutter of a red flag had called a warning in her head.

'You're an internet star now, Miss. My big brother wants your autograph.'

'Yeah, we all know where he wants it too!'

They'd become jackals. Pairs of eyes. Watching. Waiting on her next move.

'Shut up. All of you, *shut up*!' Melanie had stood bolt upright from her desk, fury rising in her cheeks.

'You shut up, McNugget muncher.'

'Knock it off, guys.' Isobel had used her firm-but-fair voice. But the balance had already shifted. Melanie looked combative. Isobel buttoned up her sleeve. 'Right, back to it. Who's next on the YouTube jukebox?'

One of the girls stood and calmly strode to the laptop at the front of the class. Her fingers rattled over the keyboard. Kids were so proficient these days. The whiteboard behind Isobel's desk came alight with colour and sound. No song played. No musical poetry. Just the generic soundtrack of two giggly twenty-somethings having drunken sex in their own kitchen.

Isobel froze in the middle of the classroom. She distinctly remembered not being able to move a millimetre. She was like one of those horror story patients, all but anaesthetised, everything paralysed bar her eyes and brain and the thing sending adrenalin to her heart.

'Yee-*haw*! He's got her on the chopping block!'

'Eugh, Miss! I hope you never made his sarnies on that in the morning.'

The class erupted around her with the jeers of children who knew the boundaries had just been blown to oblivion. Melanie McLoughlin charged past, swatted the laptop clean off Isobel's desk. The footage stalled on Nathan nipping at Isobel's breast.

'What the fuck, fatso? We were watching that.'

Isobel curled into a ball on the bed. *Stupid. Stupid. Stupid.*

She rubbed angrily at the tears streaking over her face. *Leaks*, celebrities called them. How could she have known there was a 'leak' when she hadn't even known there was still a video? He'd sworn there were no other copies.

'I'm going to try a spot of vlogging!' Nathan had declared. '*The secret life of a graphic designer.*' The camera was set up to catch him wandering around the flat at night being all creative genius-y while the world slept. Must've been a shock when he'd first come to edit everything together; he'd been too hammered at the time to remember the motion sensors, or what they might catch. They'd gasped and giggled and cringed together when he'd shown her the footage, a largely uneventful bonk by the toaster.

'It's not a bad quality picture for an Argos buy, is it? We could keep it somewhere . . . if you wanted?'

'Too clear, actually,' Isobel had snorted, 'but I won't ever want to watch us at it again. Home videos are not the "next level" I was getting at, Nath.'

She was very reasonable about the whole thing. It was easy

to be reasonable when you thought you had control. He'd deleted it in front of her. Straight off her laptop, the memory card too. So that was the end of it, see? No panic necessary.

Isobel wiped her eyes against her pillow. She should've panicked. Instead, she'd filled her head with pathetic ideas. Within a few months she'd strode from the flat with an overnight bag, ready to wait it out at her parents' house while Nathan decided how long he was going to remain a commitment-phobe. Christmas came and went. No ring appeared beneath the tree. She felt herself becoming more resentful. He was calling, of course, asking her to go home, but why wasn't he taking the opportunity to be romantic? To sweep her off her feet with a grand gesture like boyfriends were supposed to?

It was New Year's Day when he finally showed up on her parents' doorstep. Not to sweep her off her feet though, but to knock her straight off them. She'd been nursing an impressive hangover after a heavy night with Sophie's hardcore friends. Nathan's revelation had been rudely sobering.

'The video, Isobel . . . *the* video, it's on-fucking-line!'

Nathan had shared this unfortunate 'discovery' completely straight-faced. Ashen. She'd felt like vomiting on her mum's welcome mat but couldn't be sure that wasn't partly down to the cocktails.

'Take it down!'

'I can't – I didn't upload it!'

'Do you expect me to believe that?' Did he think she was stupid? 'What, it got there all by itself and you just *happened* to be the one to stumble across it? I'm a *teacher*, Nathan! Do you understand? *Take it down*!'

'I'm telling you, Isobel. I stumbled across it. You blocked me on Facebook and I was just trying to find out whose New Year photos you might be tagged in. It was driving me *crazy* not knowing who you were out with last night. I Googled your name a few times, then it came up on this website.'

He'd told her about PegOr2.com. Swore blind he hadn't uploaded anything as he'd sat home alone, miserable, while she'd successfully made him jealous.

It had swiftly dawned on her that Nathan hadn't gone to her parents' house to win her back, he'd gone to make sure she knew he'd uploaded the sex tape. Revenge porn only worked when the target knew it existed.

'*Take it down!*' she'd screeched. The hysteria had been rapid once she realised the video had been online for hours already. While she'd partied and slept off her bad head.

'I can't!'

Sophie had blinked around the doorway asking if everything was okay.

'I'll get the police to take it down if you don't, Nathan!' Isobel screamed.

'I didn't post the video! I swear!'

Nathan swore. Isobel swore.

She made the mistake of looking it up online the second the door was slammed.

Look at me, Isobel Yvonne Hedley . . . too fucking good for anyone, even my dull little boyfriend . . . The caption already striking a chord with an endless stream of strangers, united behind poor Nathan.

Skank. Dude's better off without her.

Hoes are all the same. Forget her, brother!

Bitch aint all that, small titties for a start.

Sophie had slammed shut the laptop. Isobel had gone back later for another hideous look but it was gone. Nathan had left, the video taken down shortly thereafter. Gone. No trace.

'Please stop crying, Is. They're just strangers trying to knock you down. Saddos in their mum's spare bedrooms.'

Isobel was the saddo in her mum's spare bedroom, but Soph was right. It was the very reason sites like PegOr2.com existed, so pond-feeders could gang up and use their collective weight to vilify a girl they didn't know for dumping a bloke they didn't know either . . . even though Isobel hadn't really *dumped* Nathan.

Sophie had paced the bedroom, fraught. 'You don't know these people, Isobel. They don't know you, don't let it touch you.'

They hadn't even sounded English, they'd sounded remote, in another land. They were awful, but inconsequential. Vast bodies of water separated them from her.

'That's it, then. The end of me and Nathan,' she'd said stoically. 'Probably best I found out before squandering any more years on him.'

She'd put a brave face on but it was surprisingly heart-breaking. And chronically disappointing. That their years together had ended in a tacky virtual slurry pit, where social amoebas festered and waited for something new and unfortunate to fall in for them to feed on.

The first three weeks of January had been spent checking and rechecking that the twenty-minute movie hadn't resurfaced somewhere. But it was gone. Definitely gone. So she'd stopped looking. Three more weeks of false security had passed before the YouTube takedown in her classroom.

Isobel rolled on to her other side and stared at the wall. DEEP_DRILLERZ hadn't sounded particularly sociopathic when his username had first started appearing next to Isobel and Nathan's home movie. Silly, really, that she would make assumptions. She'd covered Shakespeare enough times. *What's in a name?*

Six weeks. Six long, quiet weeks . . . then *bam*. The footage was everywhere. Had DEEP_DRILLERZ been planning it all that time? Had Isobel been a *project*? How had he got hold of it? Nathan? No. Nathan had offered up every gadget in the flat if they wanted to look for a smoking gun. 'Anyone could've downloaded it while it was first online,' he had pointed out. Then he'd told her he was going off social media, severing every connection linking him to her. Like hacking off a gangrenous toe.

It wasn't Nathan who'd spread the footage. Even at their lowest point, that was well beyond his limits. He hadn't exactly shone on that film himself, that he'd share it so close to home never made any sense. All those people knew Nathan too. No, this weirdo calling himself DEEP_DRILLERZ had downloaded it from PegOr2.com on New Year's Eve and saved it. A treat for later. He'd spent the following six weeks digging up what he could on the *Isobel Yvonne Hedley* named and shamed in the original video caption. He'd done his homework on her, and he'd found it all. Her home address, her work address, her teacher profile on the school website, her Facebook account (which he couldn't post on), her Facebook friends list (whose accounts he'd posted to instead).

That six-week interim had been his plotting time, his brainstorming. His chance to get his ducks all lined up so that when he finally decided, as a Valentine's Day *larf*, to upload the video exposing a slutty school teacher, regurgitating it on revenge site after revenge site, he'd know exactly where to leave his trail of hyperlinks for maximum impact on Isobel's safe little life.

Her heart raced as she remembered.

She *had* been a project. Unlike the first batch of strangers all flocking to Nathan's defence, this guy – DEEP_DRILLERZ – wasn't remote. He wasn't a vast body of water away from her life, he was all over it, all through it like a dirty infection. A virus. DEEP_DRILLERZ touched her home, her family, her colleagues, actively seeking them out. And on Valentine's Day, once he'd posted to the school Twitter feed, he'd touched Isobel's Year 9 English students too.

DEEP_DRILLERZ had booby-trapped her world. There was nowhere in her private or professional life that he hadn't been, planting links to *Little Red Riding Whore*, a soft porno starring Isobel Yvonne Hedley, the unwitting lead.

Newspapers portrayed trolls as dimwits. Thick and stupid. But he was thorough. Dedicated. Chilling. A *total psycho*, Sophie said. But it was easy for Sophie to point the pitchfork at the beastie. Easy to keep herself away from the sharp end.

Isobel startled, Petal's barks beating back the silence of the cottage. She hugged the pillow to her face and breathed shallow, hot breaths while she came back to the here and now. Her body felt taut, ready, as if she'd heard another noise in the emptiness. An imminent threat. Danger ahead.

32

'Is Max going to be an aeroplane for much longer, do we think? He'll tread mud in the Jag if he keeps wearing that path into the lawn. Tell him to stop now, Sarah. Or we'll have to put the park off for another day.'

Sarah craned her neck for a look on to the garden. Max flew another figure of eight around the pear tree and sundial, arms outstretched. She opened her mouth to call him just as her mum peered around the living room doorway.

'David, it's bone dry, stop fussing. Be glad he's not still being a puppy dog. Can't Jon's mother stop palming off that little dog of hers, just while Max is so . . .'

'Dog crazy? I think Mr Fogharty makes the no-to-the-dog thing a little easier for him actually, Mum.' Jon must've thought the same, he was running Mr Fogharty back and forth a lot lately. Not that Max was doing much of the running with them.

'*A little easier*? Just say *no*.' Sarah's father had one of those voices that filled every corner of a room. An orator's voice. He rocked forwards and back on his brown brogues as if waiting for Sarah to recount her European cities. 'That's where you go wrong, Sarah. You make excuses.'

Just count to ten . . . 1 . . . 2 . . .

'The easiest route is always a good firm *no*,' he boomed. 'Particularly with boys.'

Oh. Okay. She might try that. *No, Will! You will not smoke marijuana. No. No to class B drugs. No!*

Will's bedroom floor creaked overhead. She'd left him to lie in. She'd felt stiff and awkward around him since the jacket-pocket discovery. If he was lying in, he couldn't be doing anything he shouldn't, could he? With anyone he shouldn't. Like *Edward*, texting him through the night.

'Doesn't look like my other grandson is putting in an appearance this morning so I'll wait in the car,' blustered Sarah's father.

Her mother straightened the lounge curtains. 'Max and I will be out in a minute. You go and warm the air-conditioning up, David.'

Sarah smiled a goodbye. *Bye Dad!* always sounded forcibly chirpy. *Goodbye father* made him sound like Darth Vader. She felt her mother's eyes on her. 'Don't think I haven't noticed you wrapping up my ornaments, Mum.'

'Doesn't hurt to get ahead of yourself, sweetheart.'

'You're tempting fate, you know, packing. You'll jinx the sale. We'll end up putting everything back again to stage our perfect home.' What a whopper that was. She was in danger of becoming a prolific liar, like Patrick. Their druggy son had no chance.

'*Stage* it? You make yourself sound fraudulent!'

Sarah perched on the arm of one of the retro armchairs Jon had picked up at some designer auction and watched Max playing by himself outside. 'Max'll miss that rope swing.' There were no established trees up at Compass Point, everything squeaky-clean new.

'Max needs a little friend to play with, not a rope.'

'Mum, don't.'

'You're delaying, Sarah. You used to do that as a little girl, put a thing off hoping it would disappear completely.'

'I am not. I'm . . . proceeding with caution.'

'Towards what? You have a smart, educated, hardworking man who not only loves you, Sarah, and clearly wants to make a life with you, but is prepared to take on not one but *two* children sired by another man.'

'They're not farm animals, Mum.'

Max was investigating something on his finger outside. He gave it a sniff and grimaced.

'Jon's charming, polite, a non-smoker. He's also a bit of alright on the eye.'

'I know, Mum, I know. Stop flapping. Pack another ornament.'

Feet thudded down the stairs. Kitchen cupboards rattled noisily, moments later Will shot into the lounge.

'Mum, I'm *really* late, can you give me a lift? Please?' He stuffed a set of headphones and wallet into his backpack.

'And . . . *clothes*?'

Will glanced down and considered his pyjama bottoms. Lines divvied up the lean muscles of his growing body.

'My word, William. You are starting to fill out, aren't you? Is that a hickey, young man?'

Sarah snapped her head around. Will was already edging through the door. A hickey? *A love bite?* 'Lift where?' she asked. He hovered half-hidden behind the lounge door. 'Could you drop me by the theatre?'

The open-air theatre was near-derelict. She tried to dampen

the accusation in her voice. 'What's by the theatre? Other than the bus stop?' Will stalled. Was he off to meet his dealer? Was he going to score some pot off some sleazy delinquent a bus ride away? Her little boy who'd been flying his own aeroplanes around the pear tree in the back garden a blink ago? Will's phone started bleeping.

'Excuse me, young man. Before you put your mouth near that phone of yours . . .' Sarah's mother tapped her cheek.

'Sorry, Grandma. Are you okay?' Will kissed her obediently.

'Yes, I'm very well thank you, darling. Your grandfather and I will take you on the way to the park.'

'I really need to shower first, Gran.'

'Your grandfather's ready to go, William.'

'Two minutes. *Please*?'

It suddenly twigged. Sarah hadn't needed to bully Will into the shower for months. Some days he left the house smelling better than Jon. Will ferreted in his bag again. Sarah's mum mouthed *girl* over his head.

'You have two minutes. And leave your fancy contraption, please, I want to Google the weather before we leave. Max wouldn't take his orange mackintosh last time and got ruddy drenched.'

Will dithered but surrendered his phone without argument. There was a chance Sarah's mother possessed actual magical powers.

'Forget Google, Gran. There's an app. Look . . . touch the sunshine.'

'Yes, yes, I've got it. Go and do something with that mop of hair before your grandfather has a fit.'

Will dashed out leaving Sarah's mother marvelling at the

forecast. 'Have you two fallen out?' Max stopped circling the tree, shimmying up it instead.

'Not yet.' The pot conversation was off-limits. Sarah's mother was convinced two Lemsips in one hit would kill you dead. 'I think I embarrassed him at Max's football match the other night. Some men were being . . . *unhelpful*. Will tried to stand his ground. I think he felt Karl Inman-Holt stepped on his toes. Accidentally. That I let him.'

'Karl Inman-Holt? He'd better not have gone near William's toes. That boy was skittish around grown men for *months* thanks to that rough-handed, bullying . . . *shit*.'

'Mother!' *Shit* jarred with powdery make-up and immaculate French twists. *Shit* was something her mum saved for special occasions.

'He was trying to help.' Karl wasn't a bully. He was a father, who'd reacted once in the heat of the moment, which had been very hot as it happened. It was more than Patrick had ever done for his children.

'William's toes aren't his to tread on. They're ours.'

'I'm losing him, Mum. I can feel it.'

'Of course you are! He's fifteen, you're the last thing in the world he's interested in. He wants girls, his friends, loud music and mischief. Not teachers and parents. Unfortunately darling, you and Jon are both.'

'Jon's not a teacher.'

'He works at William's school, Sarah, he might as well be. Ah! Lovely. Would you look at that, plenty of sun all day.' She passed Will's phone over.

'Make the most of it. We're supposed to be getting the back end of a hurricane later in the month.'

'Good heavens! Max has just fallen out of that tree.' Sarah gave Max a quick onceover through the patio doors. The ground was only two feet beneath the branch he'd dangled from. He fell all the time. 'I'll go, you chase up William. Before your father starts papping his horn.'

Sarah's mum let herself out into the garden, navigating heeled court shoes around the micro cars Max had left strewn over the patio.

Will's phone buzzed against Sarah's palm.

Snapchat? Jon said the kids were all into these message thingies at the high school. Picture messages, but with a countdown or something, 10 . . . 9 . . . 8 . . . then on zero the picture vanished. The sender of Will's Snapchat message had a nonsensical username that Sarah didn't bother to reread.

SWIPE TO OPEN.

It was automatic. She hadn't meant to. The screen had commanded her to *swipe,* and true to form she'd done as instructed.

TAP TO VIEW

Her thumb hovered this time. It felt wrong, but was it? She was allowed, wasn't she? To check her son's activities? Cleo did.

Allowed? Sarah, I'm entitled! I have the kids' codes, that's the deal. I don't bother with Harry's, but Evie's phone? I'm in there like a ferret. Anyway, I pay the monthly tariffs. Technically, they're mine.

Sarah paid for Will's phone, too. She didn't know his code though. Only her mother's prudence about the weather had seen his unlocked phone anywhere near Sarah's hands.

Max and her mum were just reaching the French doors. Sarah tapped to view. An image appeared. The countdown began. 10 . . . 9 . . .

Her heart twisted. A scribbled message sat in bright green over the photo, carefully placed so as not to obscure the bits making the blood rush to Sarah's head.

Not long to wait now xx

5 . . . 4 . . .

She couldn't see the boy's face. Just the aroused parts. Full frontal. Torso similar to Will's. Another high-schooler. Not old enough. Not nearly old enough.

1 . . . 0 . . .

The message shut down. Sarah's head whooshed. Her mother pressed through the glass doors.

'Mummy! My tooth came out! On the floor! Granny helped me find it!' Sarah slapped Will's phone face down on the coffee table.

'It's a nice clean'un, Max. I should think the tooth fairy will be leaving you a shiny penny for this. What do you think, Mummy? Darling? Are you alright, you look peaky? It's only a tooth.'

Will thundered down the stairs again and swept into the living room. A wave of fruity shower gel hit Sarah's senses. 'Where's my phone, Gran?'

Sarah looked at the carpet. A naked teenage boy. A naked, aroused teenage boy, sending Will naked, aroused photographs of himself.

'There, look. On the table. It's going to be a hot one today, boys. Slip, slap, slop!'

Not long to wait now.

For what? Was this who Will was rushing off to see right now? Where he ducked off to every Saturday morning, now she thought about it.

Sarah found herself standing up without realising she'd moved. 'I'll take you.'

'Gran's taking me.'

'Come on then, my darlings. Boys, give your mother a kiss.'

'I'll take you.'

'Sarah, you've your dental appointment.'

'Bye, Mummy.' Max slammed into Sarah with an arsenal of wet kisses. 'Kiss Mummy, Will.'

'Max, come *on*!'

Was she losing Will? Or had she already lost him?

'Goodbye, my darling,' sang her mother. 'We'll meet you at twelve outside the Soda Shack. And cheer up! Anyone would think you were going to the gallows. It's only the dentist!'

33

Isobel stretched her legs across the other bistro chair. She'd seen darker snowflakes.

'Stevie Wonder or Mazza Monroe?'

'Stevie, please.'

Sophie sucked in a breath and began belting out 'Happy Birthday' down the line. It was a fairly decent Stevie cover.

Ella giggled in the background. 'That's not the happy birthday song, Mummy.' Ella cut in with the more traditional version, and Isobel lay back in her chair, face lifted to the sunshine, waiting for her to finish. She'd set herself up with the laptop as per Sophie's instructional texts this morning, headphones on so she had her hands free to surf the net. And because putting Sophie on speakerphone floated the risk of Arthur or Dan overhearing. 'That was beautiful, Ella,' she said finally.

'Are you having a nice birthday, Aunty Isobelly?'

'The best. I miss you though.' She'd been on edge since Sophie's first text came through.

'I miss you too. Nanny said we can make you a cake today and eat it for you here.'

'Yum. Can you make it chocolate, please?'

'Yes. We will,' said Ella, matter-of-factly. Isobel imagined

Ella in her usual Saturday get-up. Half-fastened Disney Princess costume, pair of wellies. It ached. 'Are you still feeling better, Aunty Isobelly?'

'I am. I feel very well, thank you. I'm going to bring you back a mermaid's tail from the aquarium here.'

Ella squealed. 'Bye, Aunty Isobelly-button, I love you.'

'I love you too, Ells-bells.'

Sophie waited for Ella to leave the room. Isobel waited with her. She heard a door close, all birthday jovialities lost on the other side. 'Are you online, Isobel?'

'Yes.' She could hardly see the screen for glare, but the cottage wifi was patchier than the phone reception.

'Type this.' Sophie reeled off a web address. Isobel's personal blog, apparently. Isobel typed obediently, ignoring the tightening in her throat. The search engine delivered. Her eyes greedily skimmed the content.

'Isobel Hedley' had been a busy girl since her last venture into social media. *My Year in Pictures!* called her latest blog post. She'd been skiing, thinking about a career change, partying with friends, pampering herself at the spa. A catalogue of blog posts dedicated to the fun-filled life she'd been living, all accompanied by archived photos borrowed from Isobel's old memory stick. Sophie had created a montage of images, evidencing how Isobel Hedley had bounced back.

Can't hold me down! captioned a side view of Isobel. She was throwing back a glass of champers, ski goggles covering most of her face, her old brunette hair hanging in the loose plaits all the chalet girls wore during Isobel's gap year adventure. It was the sort of thing she might've even said back then, jumping on to her snow-board again after nearly braining herself.

Now it was a challenge. To an invisible opponent. Sophie was goading DEEP_DRILLERZ. Daring him to come put Isobel Hedley back in her place.

Isobel whizzed through all of the photos. She saw a confident dark-haired girl she vaguely recognised, larking around, making fun of herself, flaunting her carelessness. These photos didn't even remind her of herself, they reminded her of Sophie. Sophie had always been the more vivacious sister, the sister these snapshots were more suited to, only Sophie hadn't gotten the chance to take gap years or go travelling. She'd had Ella.

'Some of these are years old,' said Isobel.

'I know. Doesn't matter.'

'You can't see my face properly on any of them.'

'No, I know. I thought you would be more comfortable with that. Just in case anyone you know stumbles across this stuff, maybe because they're wondering where you disappeared to or whatever and run a search on your name, this way they still wouldn't know it was you for sure. I've been careful.'

'But this *blog* . . . It's still showing my life, Sophie, I've still been to those places. I still,' Isobel reread her bio, 'work in education.' Actually, she didn't. Not any more.

'So do lots of people, Is. If we can lead him to this blog, there are enough markers there for him to think it's you, the same Isobel Hedley he had a thing for. But on the other hand, if one of your old colleagues stumbles across it there's nothing definitive there to say they've found the same Isobel Hedley. Do you follow?' Soph had thought of every angle. *Please let her have thought of every angle.* 'Is? Are you still there?'

She was still scrolling. It was difficult to stomach. So much showing off, posing for the camera. Sophie had tagged every photo ten different ways to widen their circulation. *#good-times #lovethis #yolo*

Likeminded snow-boarders, fun-havers, fashionistas were already lengthening a trail of visitor comments.

Love those vintage kicks!

Courchevel, our fave too x

Hey pretty lady, check out my travel blog? :)

There was a gently increasing patter in Isobel's chest. This had never been part of the plan. Facing the chatty masses again. 'I thought I wasn't going to look at this stuff. People are saying things . . .' People she didn't know, strangers, trying to communicate with her. But not with her, with the fake, no, the *original* Isobel Hedley. The confident, *can't hold me down!* Isobel Hedley, who still had dark hair and friends and other people's respect.

'It's okay, Isobel. Or I wouldn't have shown you. I've moderated every one of those comments, okay? I have to approve them before they're allowed on there.'

'Do we need them?' Her heart was already racing. Strangers. Reaching out to her. Commenting. It made her nauseous. This had all been her idea. Sophie had said *no* and Isobel had pushed against her until she gave way. Now her chest felt tight.

'He won't leave a comment if no one else has, Isobel. The blog needs to look authentic, comments from a cross-section of people will help that.'

She wiped her lip with a clammy hand. She tried cooling them on the glass of cordial sitting on top of the *Surfing 101* book left on the doorstep this morning.

'If anyone dodgy responds, Isobel, I'll know about it first. I'll tell you if I let anyone suspect post on there, okay? You won't have to see.'

There was a metallic taste in Isobel's mouth, but she was steeling herself. Bringing herself back from the edge. 'And as admin you can see their IP addresses? All of those people, leaving their comments?' It was all about the addresses, Sophie had explained. You could trace a person by their IP address. Everyone had them, well, every computer connecting to the internet did. They wouldn't show up on Facebook pages when someone commented on your wall, but they showed up on blogs, when comments were left there. If you had admin rights to the blog, you got to see the IP addresses.

'Every one. Are you okay? You sound weird.'

'I'm fine. So how do we get him here? To the blog?'

'I've posted links. He's just got to click.'

'Click where?'

'The Facebook page I've set up . . . Twitter . . .' Sophie paused. 'PegOr2.com.' Isobel's mouth was completely dry. Adrenalin junkies and foodies interacting positively with a blog was one thing. PegOr2.com wasn't populated by anyone wanting to interact positively with anything.

'It was where he first noticed you, Isobel. Where he got his copy of the video. Makes sense to leave a trail of breadcrumbs from there. I've linked on the other sites too.'

The other sites. Sophie meant the really dark places. Online gutters where hundreds of videos degraded people again and again with every viewer's hit. Places Isobel didn't want Sophie going on her behalf, not even now.

'Who's to say he still visits those websites, Sophie? It was a year ago.' Not quite a year though since he'd finally called the witch-hunt off. Five months of non-stop harassment, then nothing.

'He might not. But he interacted a lot with a few of the other degenerates on those sites, so there's a chance they still get together online. Let's face it, they won't have much else going on in their lives. You were his toy at the end of the day. The ball he finally kicked over. With any luck, now that it's just bounced back into his yard, if he doesn't spot it himself, one of his scrote buddies might and let him know.'

It was sick. People even knowing about those websites, let alone contributing to them. Isobel had apparently deserved to be knocked down a peg or two, and there had been a user-friendly website all set up and ready. An abuser-friendly website. Of course there had. There were websites for bored spouses to arrange affairs, websites mentoring fragile adolescents to starvation, websites encouraging desperate children to hang themselves from their bunkbeds. The world was a sick place. Of course there'd been a website like PegOr2.com. There were thousands, allowing toxic contributors to remain faceless, destructive cowards.

But of all the strangers scrambling to take their shots at Isobel, the 'slut in the video', they all paled beside DEEP_DRILLERZ. DEEP_DRILLERZ. The big man hiding behind a profile picture of himself urinating on the only golden postbox in the country within eyeshot of both a war memorial and the deep blue sea. DEEP_DRILLERZ. The troll who'd dwarfed them all. PegOr2 had read like a knitting forum once DEEP_DRILLERZ had shared the video with his shameth-atbitch.com buddies.

Isobel checked her headphones were still sitting snugly. There was a tremble in her hand. She swallowed. 'What did you write? About the blog links? To tempt him to click on them?'

This was the bait Sophie had been talking about. The blog was the hook, the place they might snag him, but the bait was whatever Sophie wrote about 'life-lovin' Isobel Hedley' and her 'blog'. The juicy worm they hoped would tempt DEEP_DRILLERZ to come back for another bite.

'Isobel . . . some of this . . . you don't need to worry yourself with it.'

'What did you write? I want to know.'

There was a pressure point on the wrist that could help calm an oncoming episode of anxiety. Jenny said it didn't work for everyone. Isobel pinched it on the off-chance.

'Isobel . . .'

'Just tell me. It's fine, I can handle it.'

'I wrote . . . I wrote what they all wrote . . . last time.' Sophie cleared her throat again.

'Go on.' Could Sophie even say it?

'I wrote, *Click here to see who's back in the saddle . . . Little Red Riding Whore.*'

Someone tapped Isobel's shoulder. Her body lurched upwards, headphones yanking free, phone clattering to the floor. She slammed shut her laptop.

'Whoa,' called Ben, his palms upturned as if he were corner-ing a skittish pony.

Petal threw herself snarling and wild against the wire fence over the way. Dan looked at the upturned bakery box on the floor, then worriedly at Isobel, the crazy woman.

'It's alright, mate. Just an accident. It's salvageable!' reassured Ben.

Dan looked back to the sticky mess at their feet. He and Ben were wearing matching Billabong beach shoes. Isobel was barefoot, save for a spattering of strawberry sauce. 'I'm sorry, I'm really sorry, I didn't hear you coming. Oh no, I've ruined your . . .' Ben lifted the lid away from an explosion of cream and strawberries. A candle slid off what would have been a nice Victoria sponge.

He started laughing. 'Don't worry. We didn't bake it. Daniel here just wanted you to have something sweet from the bakery. No one's allowed to let their birthday slip by around here.'

Arthur had taken her date of birth when he'd signed her in. Isobel could've said anything, she hadn't needed to show any ID. He'd asked Isobel's name and her mother's maiden name had tripped right out. *Isobel Oliver* didn't bring up explicit images on Google. *Isobel Oliver* didn't yield search engine results detailing a high school English teacher bringing her school into disrepute. She hadn't given anyone here her real name and she never would. Her phone buzzed angrily against the floor. *Sophie*. Probaby freaking out.

'Do you want to get that?' asked Ben.

'It's just . . . telesales.' She reached down and clicked off Sophie's call. Daniel cocked his head, studying Isobel like a bird studying a rotten berry. He could smell a rat. How hard would it be for DEEP_DRILLERZ? Or would Sophie out-sneak him?

'Happy birthday, Isobel. Sorry we frightened you,' said Daniel. 'Can we eat your cake now?'

34

'Harry, what on earth is wrong with you today? The caramel's *there* . . . same as always. That's the second banana split you've doused with Caesar dressing!' Cleo didn't really know how to broach it, the Ingred issue. Quite frankly, she had bigger problems with Evie right now, but Harry was turning into Miss Havisham. He'd hardly spoken since Thursday. And if he wasn't pushing cold dinner around his plate, Cleo was finding it scraped into the kitchen bin.

She looked over the counter at the steady activity of Saturday customers, eating, sipping from straws, wiping their children's mouths. They had a few seconds before anyone else approached the counter. She touched his elbow. 'Harry?' He looked awful. *Distraught*. Wasn't he sleeping? 'It will pass, son. The horrible aching feeling. You won't always feel so terrible about it.'

Harry stared at a piece of quiche under the counter as if it held all the answers. 'I don't want to talk about it, Mum.'

'There are plenty more fish—'

'I don't want to talk about it, Mum! Okay? Is that okay with you?' Harry's eyes were wild with emotion, his voice made Cleo flinch. A customer glanced up from her menu.

'Harry?'

Harry's expression suddenly transformed him into her little boy again, all wide eyes and hopelessness. He used to walk out past the other children and their parents after a rotten day at school looking like that, trying to hold it all inside until he reached Cleo and could bury his face in her thigh. Tears were coming. Any second now. She ushered him towards the stores. 'Sweetheart, if Ingred was worth—'

'Stop saying her name!' Harry pushed the tears off his cheeks with a closed fist. 'I don't want to talk about her ever again, okay?'

'Okay, Harry. Okay.' Sam hadn't said he was taking it *this* hard, crikey.

Great. One week away from the twins sitting their GCSEs and some fifteen-year-old girl hundreds of miles away had Harry thinking he was worthless, and Evie . . .

Cleo felt a swell of emotion rise up inside her. Evie's arms. The damage. What had she been *thinking*? How had she done it to herself? With her nails? A stick? *Why?* She swallowed down the tears she could suddenly feel rising. If only Evie's problems were the size of Harry's.

'Harry, I'm not going to mention her, okay? But just let me say this. We've all been there, son. And it's crap. And I know you don't want to hear it but I'm your mum so I have to say it. You have your exams coming up. The next six weeks are the culmination of five years at high school. Please, if you're feeling upset or you need to talk, get it off your chest, son, okay?'

Harry sniffed. 'I can't, Mum.'

'Why? Because I wouldn't understand? Your exams are important, H. You've worked too hard to cock them up now.

Go have a chat with one of the pastoral team at school if you don't want to talk to me or Dad or your mates about her, that's what they're there for Harry. Use them. If it makes you feel any better, Evie went for a chat with Mr Hildred yesterday.'

Harry blinked dampened eyelashes. 'Why would Evie go to the school shrink?'

'He's not a shrink. He's a pastoral officer.'

'So why's Evie speaking to him?'

Because she's not speaking to me, that's why! 'Because that's what Mr Hildred's there for, Harry. To help you kids get your heads around things you might not want to talk to anyone else about. Do you see much of her at school?'

'Who, Evie?' A tiny voice warned that she wasn't giving Harry's upset her full attention. Harry shrugged his shoulders. 'Sometimes.'

'What about Verity? Does she still see Verity?'

'Dunno. Evie hangs with Cassie sometimes. Cassie's with Verity more, though.'

'So who does Evie have lunch with? Who does she spend her breaks with?'

Harry sniffed, his eyes still puffy. 'Her phone, mostly. She hangs around the sports hall on it at lunch.' That was another thing on Evie's birthday list, a phone upgrade. A model that could suck twenty-five hours out of her day instead of the paltry twenty-four as standard.

'Cassie doesn't come home with her any more. Have you heard anything? Have they fallen out?'

More shrugging. 'Maybe she's blown them off for a lad.'

'A boyfriend?' It wasn't a *ridiculous* idea. No, she would know. There were signs heralding the first giddy rush of love.

Lots of telltale signs. Not one of them looked like the insides of Evie's arms.

'What did Mr Hildred say to her?' asked Harry.

'Evie will talk about that when she's ready, son.'

What a crock. Cleo had tried already and Evie wasn't spilling anything. *If you're gonna grill me about every little thing, you might as well come into the meetings with me.* Yes, well, she would, wouldn't she? Given half a chance. Find out exactly who was saying what about *fat trannies* and exactly who their parents were. How *dare* they push her daughter into . . .

She tried to clear her head. Sam would go berserk when he knew what their little girl had done to herself. Cleo had left Evie's bedroom and slipped back into bed with him, staring into the darkness, trying to think of innocent explanations for those awful bloodied marks.

'She's okay, though?' asked Harry. Evie drove Harry nuts too, but she was his twin, there were rules.

'Sorry, son. We didn't come back here to talk about Evie, did we? Are you sure there's nothing you want to talk through?'

'Customers,' said Harry. Two women with matching satchels were eyeing up the menu outside. The harbour behind them was alive with sun-seekers.

Cleo checked the café then looked back to Harry, propped against the wall. 'Look, it's a gorgeous day. I can man the sails here. Why don't you go and give Zack and Theo a call, head to the basketball courts or just go hang out, get some colour in your cheeks? There's a fridge full of food at home and Dad's working today if you wanted to get the guitars and stuff out? Make some noise. It'll do you good.'

Harry spoke towards the floor. 'Thanks. But I need my wages.'

'What for? Hang on, what are those women doing? Are they taking photographs of my sign?'

She made a beeline for the two women outside, trying to shake off the irritation she knew would be in her voice. 'Can I help you?'

They met her with smiles, one extended a hand. 'Hi! Great place, are you the owner?'

Cleo wasn't fooled. She'd opened enough humdingers with Sam in her time to know that a compliment could put your opponent completely on the back foot, even a seasoned semi-pro boxer.

'Thanks. Why are you taking photographs of my café?'

'Hello, Cleo. We're from the *Dewelsbury Gazette*, could we chat about your no-breast-feeding policy? We'd love to tell Coast's side of the story.'

35

Sarah stopped admiring the new summery display of bath bombs in the pamper shop window and wiped Max's chin. 'How's that ice lolly, Max? What does the red bit taste of?'

Max tapped a sticky finger to his chin, searching the cloudless sky for the answer. 'Watermelon! Can we have ice lollies for lunch tomorrow too?'

Sarah was rebelling. Her parents had returned from the park in her father's vintage Jaguar, sunglasses on, engine running, depositing Max outside the Soda Shack with the seamless exchange of an underworld transaction. Max had clambered from the car red-faced and sweaty. He'd asked Sarah for an ice pop and his grandfather answered for her. *No snacks before lunch*. Technically it was a frozen drink, but there was no point arguing.

Sarah bit into her Cornetto, careful not to chew on her new temporary crown. *Two hundred and forty pounds, Mrs Harrison. Plus the antibiotics*. She could've had Botox for that, a beautifully smooth face like the twenty-year-old dental receptionist. She wasn't completely sure how she felt about erasing laughter lines, though. She didn't share Jon's quiet preoccupation with remaining youthful. Not yet anyway.

'So did you have fun at the park? Were there lots of other children there this morning?'

Parenting was so much easier when they were still little and you already knew the answers to the questions you asked them. Sarah had ratcheted up a bleak list of questions for Will since opening his Snapchat this morning.

Who the hell is EDWARD?

Why is he texting you at night?

How old is he?

Is he your dealer?

Does he Snapchat explicit photographs too?

Are you being groomed, Will?

DO YOU UNDERSTAND THE DANGERS?

Max licked his ice lolly. 'Darcey was there with Cole and their daddy.'

Sarah pushed predatory paedophiles to one side of her mind. 'Oh? Did you play with Darcey?'

'Yes. And Chloe and Isaac.'

'Chloe and Isaac from your class?'

Max nodded, peering into the window of Tails 'n' Scales. They should've crossed the street well before this point. Max found it physically impossible to walk past without giving the creatures inside one full head count.

'That was nice then, Max? Seeing your school friends in the park. Is Chloe feeling better after her tummy bug? Did everyone play nicely?' Sarah could hear the hope in her voice. When Seb wasn't there the other kids stood half a chance.

'Yes,' yipped Max. 'Chloe was making burgers and pizza in the sand pit and Isaac was the customer and Darcey and me did the washering up.'

'Pizza *and* burgers? I'm surprised you had any room left for your ice lolly.'

Max sighed. 'They weren't real, Mummy. They were sand pizzas. Can I have a cow T-shirt, please? Can we get one from the T-shirt shop by the beach?'

There was a tank inside the window, cricket-like creatures co-habiting with some sort of lizard.

'A cow T-shirt?'

She watched the lizard's eye roll benignly down at the nearest oblivious bug. Patrick had called her benign once. *My wife's so benign, so easy to be around, isn't she?* Like a tumour. A non-threatening lump people learned to live with. Or had cut away. Patrick had delivered it like a compliment, so Sarah had accepted it as one. Boring, benign Sarah.

'Like the cow T-shirts Isaac and Chloe were wearing today.'

'Isaac and Chloe had matching T-shirts on?' If Lorna Brooks and Rachel Foley had been at the park with their kids, Darcey's family too, had she forgotten an event? The PFA was forever organising meet and greets in the park. Is that why the kids had been in matching T-shirts? An informal concert? A fundraiser? She took another bite of Cornetto. *School newsletter . . . school newsletter . . .* Balls, she couldn't think.

'What did the T-shirts say, Max?'

'NOT! A! COW!' Max thrust the last of his lolly in the air with each word.

'What on earth does that mean?' laughed Sarah.

'We were shouting it with Isaac's mummy in the park, but Grandad said it spoils it for everyone when children can't have fun without shouting and squealing. Can we go inside the pet shop?'

'No, you have an ice lolly.'

'Pleeease? Mrs Upton said it's last chance this week to tell her what our pets are called so Mr Pethers can let everyone pick their favourite one in assembly on Friday and that one will be the school mascot until the end of term! I need to get a pet so I can tell Mrs Upton what he's called!'

Sarah could happily throttle Mrs Upton for this stupid pet election.

'We aren't getting a pet today, Max. We're going to get some lunch from Cleo's and then we're sitting on the beach until Jon takes us to look at the new house.'

It was another betrayal. Nipping off to look at the new hillside development while Will was . . . where was Will again? Her stomach lurched. *Edward*. Drug dealer? Fifty-year-old pervert? Both! And potentially just a bus ride away from the safety of Fallenbay. Will could be with him right now, completely of his own volition.

'But Mummy—'

'No, Max. I'm not talking about this today,' she snapped.

See? She could say no, her father was wrong. Her phone bleeped. Max sulked while she opened the message from Cleo.

Get here quick! Bring anyone with a baby!! Anyone who'll b/feed on camera!! Lorna and co, they'll shut me down!!!! They've brought PLACARDS!!!!!!

36

Isobel knew Sophie's latest text by heart already.

Meant to say earlier, even if this doesn't work out, what you're doing still takes guts. Facing a thing head on. You're not his victim any more sis. Be proud of that xxxx

Sophie had been trying to talk Isobel into going home for from the moment she arrived. That last text nearly had her packing her things and jumping in the car. If she read it again she might call this whole ridiculous thing off, so here she was, walking into town looking for a distraction instead.

Isobel slowed, poised cameras catching her eye. Tourists in crisp shorts were watching something unfolding at Coast. Cleo was leaning behind a smiling woman with a large pair of hoop earrings who kept repositioning herself for the photographer. The photographer lowered her camera and Cleo's smile faded.

'She's some woman, Cleo Roberts.'

Ben Oakes slowed for a look too. He smiled beneath his shades, pointing his paper towards Cleo's terrace. A straggly group of mostly women with young children in matching T-shirts was dispersing. 'I think she's just shown her first ever mob of protesters why Sam never wins an argument.'

'Protesters? Think I'll come back when it's quieter.'

Ben pulled his glasses off. 'Or, as we're here already, you could let me buy you one of Cleo's legendary coffees? By way of apology.'

'For?'

'For dropping your cake.'

'Really, there's no need. If I hadn't reared up like a crazy person, Dan wouldn't have knocked you and . . . coffee doesn't like me, gives me headaches so . . .'

Ben nodded to himself. 'I'm in a tough spot then. I don't want to cause anyone any headaches. How about we forget the coffee, play it safe with a beer instead?'

She rubbed at the brittle blonde braid running through the front of her hair. A flimsy effort to limit the effects of sun on her bleach-ravaged barnet. 'I don't really drink, Ben, and—'

'Ever?'

Isobel shrugged. It was a precautionary thing. She'd been pleasantly drunk when she'd stumbled giggling and unaware back into the flat, into their kitchen, too drunk to notice Nathan's camera set-up. And she'd been out drinking with Sophie's friends that fateful New Year's Eve when she'd attempted to make Nathan jealous. Both ended in tears.

'So . . . no coffee, no alcohol?' Ben puffed out his cheeks. 'How do you feel about *water*?'

Isobel frowned. 'Water? It's . . . fine?'

'Okay then. See you later, Isobel.' He turned and walked away. Isobel's body was still angled for retreat as she watched him go. Weren't they just mid-conversation? She'd offended him. Hardly surprising really.

A sleek Mercedes cut between her and the tourists. Banter

broke out amongst a group of kids sitting at one of Cleo's bistro tables.

'Uh-oh, you're in trouble now, Milo.'

Isobel did a double-take at the group. One of Milo's pals was ruffling his hair. Another began standing menus up along the table. 'Hide behind here, mate!' Milo was the only one not laughing.

A woman stepped from the Merc, calling up to the terrace. 'Milo? You're supposed to have gone into Dewelsbury with your sister!'

'Milooo . . . Someone was supposed to be babysitting the child prodigy, not drinking milkshakes,' laughed his friend.

Milo stiffened. 'She didn't want me to go with her.'

'Of course she did,' snapped the woman, 'it's an hour on the bus. Not everyone's happy to converse with *vagrants*, Milo. What if she's been harassed? You're supposed to look after her.'

'Elodie's *my* big sister. She should be looking after me.'

Isobel walked away from the conversation nose-diving in front of her. She headed around Milo's mother's car for the pavement just as someone called down from the terrace. 'Isobel! Are you coming in for lunch? We're almost a full-house, *so* busy today.'

A camera swung in Isobel's direction, clicking aggressively. Cleo still had a baby on her hip, gesticulating to the woman with the notepad. She reminded Isobel of a celebrity visiting the third world, there with a camera crew and a message.

'Hi, yep, I guess. If you can squeeze me in?'

Milo's mother looked pointedly at Isobel then clamped a hand on the rim of her car door. 'Milo, let's go. You can put your Saturday to better use, the Summer holidays are coming up and you still haven't found yourself a Saturday job yet. Get your things.'

'Milo doesn't need a job, Mrs Inman-Holt, he's nearly as minted as you and Dr Karl,' laughed one of the other boys.

'Yeah, cheers for the milkshakes, Money-Bags,' said another.

'Are you harassing my customers, Juliette?' Cleo smiled conspiratorially at Isobel.

Juliette ignored her. 'Milo. Now.'

Cleo looked calm, like a cruising shark. Waiting for something meaty enough to bite into. 'I suppose the T-shirts were your brainchild were they, Juliette? Lorna couldn't organise a wet head in a downpour. This has *classroom assistant* written all over it.'

'Before you say anything silly, Cleo, I bottle-fed both of mine. So *obviously* I have no problem with babies and cow-based formula milk.'

'You're the rabble ringleader, Juliette. Everyone knows.'

'So where's my T-shirt, Cleo?'

Cleo raised her chin like a challenge. This was about to escalate. 'Not everyone can wear a T-shirt emblazoned with *Not A Cow!*, can they, Juliette? Not while keeping a straight face.' Milo's friends fidgeted with stifled laughter.

Isobel wished she'd walked faster. She could slide away, just go for it. Cleo wouldn't even notice.

'Go on! You tell your mother what you've damned well done!' A sturdy-looking man in battered work jeans frog-marched Evie along the pavement. Cleo's simmering fury went off-boil. She called to a sullen-looking boy serving at one of the tables behind her, 'Harry, take the baby back to Sarah's sister-in-law . . .'

The man with his hands on Evie's shoulders steered her along the ramp, his neck the same deep pink as his spattered polo shirt. 'Show her!' he demanded. 'Show your mother what you've done.'

'Sam! What are you *doing*?' hissed Cleo. 'Be *careful* with her, don't hold her arm like that, she's . . . she's hurt it already.'

Milo gave Evie and her dad a parting glance and got into the car with his mum.

'You're right, Cleo! She bloody well has hurt it! Look at this bloody mess! I only nipped into the newsagent's for a packet of plasters, and who do I spot? Next door? Sat in the bloody chair? *My daughter*. Fifteen years old . . . in a tattoo parlour!'

37

Misophonia. Sarah's father had it. Couldn't abide hearing anyone slurp, swallow, chew or chomp their food. He'd never exploded into a blood-boiling rage but his potential had always been palpable around the dinner table.

Sarah drummed her fingers on the steering wheel. The same flurry of wet noise sounded next to her. Jon's sister chewed gum like a sprinter ran. In short fast bursts.

'So Mum was like, I'll have the baby for you a couple of afternoons a week and you can go back to college, get some qualifications like Jonathan. I said to her, look, Mum, me and Jon just aren't built the same. I'm never going to be a teacher or have a big fancy house, you know? Like you lot live in.' If Caroline thought their house was big now, Jon was about to blow her mind with the next effort. Caroline swung her head towards Sarah from the passenger seat, giant earrings flopping against her cheeks. Sarah got another whiff of fruity fresh breath. *You don't have misophonia. You're just irritable.* Pre-menstrual, hopefully. She realised she hadn't even thanked Caroline.

'It was really good of you to come today, Caroline. You really helped Cleo out.'

Jon had finally given Sarah Caroline's new number. He

hadn't seemed too bothered that Sarah was postponing their visit to the Compass Point development because Cleo had a mini crisis to avert. Not bothered at all, until Caroline's name came up.

Caroline chewed and grinned over from her seat. 'No worries! I'm not completely useless. Jon thinks I'm useless, but we can't all have golden balls, can we? Anyway, it was nice to hear from you. I keep saying to our ma, Sarah's not *that* much older than me, we could go clubbing. Get to know each other properly before the wedding.'

Clubbing? What, seal pups? Surely not three a.m. dancing? Sarah's coordination was shocking.

Caroline peered down the neck of her shirt. 'Little monkey's got a tooth coming. I had no idea they were so ferocious! Oscar really nipped me back there, I nearly flung him across the café when that journo was taking all those pics!'

'I remember that feeling. The first bite.'

'Little buggers,' laughed Caroline.

Sarah tapped the steering wheel again. Why had Jon been so certain that enlisting Caroline would be such a waste of time? Sarah would've loved a sibling; Jon should make the effort to see his more. His mum didn't come over much either. In four years they'd only shared one Christmas together, and Jon had insisted on running Caroline and Elizabeth home as soon as Sarah cleared the table. Elizabeth's paper Christmas hat had fallen to the floor. She'd bent over to pick it up and broke wind. It had made both the boys' Christmas day.

'Do you think you'll feed him yourself for much longer, Caroline?'

'What do you mean?'

'Oscar. I couldn't get Max to breast-feed for as long as I'd hoped, it was so frustrating. Awful, actually. He became dehydrated, my milk dried up and . . .' And his father hadn't wanted him, or he hadn't wanted Sarah, with Max another casualty of his mother's not-enoughness.

Sarah glimpsed the mop of blond in the back seat, Max's eyes watching the horizon for signs of Godzilla or Sebastian Brightman, or any of the many marvellously important things her marvellously important boy thought about.

Caroline threw her head back and cackled. 'I don't breast-feed Oscar! He had formula before you picked us up. I've just started him on baby rice too, and yoghurt. He loves his yoghurt, don't you, babes?'

'You don't breast-feed him? But at Cleo's . . .'

'Yeah? You said you needed someone who wouldn't mind breast-feeding to be in the newspapers. I don't think he got anything outta me, I've never fed him that way before, but so long as the pics look good, right?'

Caroline's smile was framed by a pale pink lipgloss. Sarah locked eyes on the road. She was sitting beside a *complete* lunatic.

'I've always wanted to be interviewed,' chewed Caroline. 'Even when Jon was going through all that hassle with the girl, what was her name again? *Lucy the tartlet*. Even then, I was always waiting for a knock at the door or something, so I could say my bit to the newspapers, but of course,' Caroline paused to flick long coppery extensions over her shoulder, 'Jon banned us from saying anything. Said it'd jeopardise the compo for all of us if we breathed a word about him to anyone who might twist things. I was like, *Whoa, Jon!*

Par-a-noi-a! What would we say that was bad? Mum couldn't say anything bad about him if her life depended on it. It wasn't like he *shared* the compo anyway. I mean, he did get me my tumble dryer and paid off my catalogue account, and he did move Mum and me out here nearer the seaside, away from all them curtain-twitchers which was nice and I am grateful, but anyone would think he was José Simpson the way he was going on. It was José Simpson, wasn't it? That fella who was on trial?'

'OJ,' said Sarah.

'Oh, no thanks, I daren't. I forgot to nip to the loo before we left. Dunno why Jonathan was so paranoid though, look at him! Mr Nice Guy. He always was, you know. Even when he used to be a little shit at home, he always went off to school and had all the teachers telling Mum what a little angel he was. Honestly, I didn't ever know why he was so uptight, it was so obvious he was being stitched up by that Lucy, but then police dealings do that to a person, don't they? Make you feel guilty when you aren't.'

Sarah checked the children in her rearview mirror. She wondered whether Max was listening in that way five-year-olds sometimes did, absorbing every last word when you really didn't want them to.

Her name was Lucy Timmons, the girl. *Lucy the Liar*, an ex-school friend had been quoted. *Lucy the fantasist.* Or on the few occasions Jon had spoken about her, *Poor Lucy.*

'It's always the odd ones, don't you think?' asked Caroline.

'Odd ones?'

Caroline spun in her seat, checking the boys before carrying on. Sarah welled with dread. Caroline lowered her voice, overshaping her words so Sarah could still catch them. 'Acc-u-sers. They're always a bit rough around the edges, aren't they? Those girls that try pinning things on their teachers. How often do you see a well-dressed, well-spoken fifteen-year-old with nice parents and good grades throwing their accusations around?'

This wasn't somewhere Sarah and Jon went. Sarah had gotten the gist of things when Jon first told her, when he'd Googled himself right there in front of her, pointing out the best, and worst, the papers had reported at the time. He'd been open and honest, the court ruthless in their excavations of his character, his background; they'd even danced around the impact of his late father's crippling early onset dementia. Because of course, men reacted in all sorts of ways to, say, a suffering parent. They might even seek solace in the arms of a fifteen-year-old child. The courts went there, digging until satisfied there was nothing to find. Sarah and Jon didn't need to go there too. They'd agreed they both had pasts they'd rather not keep skinning their knees on.

'He needed counselling, you know? After nearly losing his job.' Sarah knew. Jon had remortgaged his house to pay his legal costs when the school suspended him without following a single one of their own procedures. He hid it remarkably well now but he'd been burned. By the teaching profession, by the legal system, by the student he was trying to help manage falling grades and indifferent parents.

Caroline folded her arms across her chest. 'Jon was guilty until proven innocent. Then when he became innocent again that toff school didn't know what to do with him. Good job our Jon's legal team knew exactly what to do with *them*.'

It slipped out before Sarah could stop it. 'Lucy Timmons was well spoken.'

She checked Max again in the rearview, opening and closing his hand an inch from his face, open and closed, open and closed, like one of the sea anemones he loved.

'Not well spoken enough, though, was she, Sar? They threw her story out the dorm-room window. That's the thing with expensive schools, the kids've got too much money. All those bad habits . . . we couldn't afford drugs when we were kids! As soon as they found that coke in her room, they were never going to listen to anything she had to say, were they? She was unreliable. And pregnant within months of it all blowing over; even her parents had had enough of her by then. Don't blame them. I was always expecting her to try and pin that on our Jon too. Like Mum says, our Jon's lucky you can go on Jeremy Kyle and get a test or that trollop might've pulled a fast one. Now look at her, she's a cliché. It is *cliché*, isn't it? *Cleesh . . . quiche . . .*'

The local press had devoured the girl's downward slide. Her privileged background, the best education money could buy. The one-bedroomed council flat she and the baby moved into after her elite parents cut her off.

'Our Jon should've had double what that school coughed up. It's not right, one person destroying someone else's life, just because they couldn't have things the way they wanted them. Silly little girl. She was looking for a father figure and Jon was the only one there to listen. The silly cow ruined it for herself when she went and confused her feelings, didn't she? Now where is she? Probably in a high-rise somewhere, ten kids under her feet, raking in the benefits and still no bloke to make up for the father who shoved her into boarding school.'

Sarah drove along the winding coastal road out of town, Compass Point's domineering billboard boasting its battalion of executive homes on the bluff, still just in her rearview. She wondered what sort of home Lucy Timmons and her child had now. There had been no winners in that situation, no winners at all. Jon's compensation only seemed to make the whole thing worse, even more unpalatable. It made Jon skittish too. Fifty thousand pounds of it had been deposited in the old coal chute in the cellar. Jon called it *just-in-case* money. There couldn't be many situations necessitating quick access to fifty grand in cash, but what did she know? Jon wanted it close, under lock and key. Not that he made any secret of where that key was kept.

'Jon's life wasn't ruined, Caroline. Just . . . rerouted.'

'Well I think people should pay for the wrong they do in this world. No matter who you are, or how old you are, or how rich or stupid or sorry you are, people should pay their dues. Should be held to account. Got anything I can spit this chewing gum in, hun?'

38

'You are fifteen years old, Evie. *Fifteen*! What the hell are you playing at?'

Sam couldn't contain his anger long enough to wait until closing time, so Harry was holding the fort at Coast while Cleo and Evie had been nigh on bundled into the cab of Sam's van. Now here they were parked at the lookout point on the bluff.

'Sixteen in three weeks.'

'I don't give a damn!' thundered Sam. Cleo jumped. She'd been silently watching the tide coming in, wondering how many momentous decisions had been made in this very spot, how many lovers, families, friends had driven up here to deliver ultimatums, share secrets, or in this case, give fifteen-year-old girls the mother of all bollockings.

'Sam . . .' tried Cleo.

'No! You wanted me to be stricter with her and you were right, okay, Cle? You were bloody right. I should've listened. Evie, you're banned from hanging around with Cassie.'

'What?' protested Evie.

'I don't think we can pin this on Cassie, Sam.'

Sam didn't know, didn't realise Evie was already shrinking

away from her friends. Cutting her last lifeline didn't sound like the greatest idea.

'You are banned from doing anything that isn't school, home, or helping your mother at Coast. Do you understand me?'

'But . . .' Evie looked like she'd just had her lifeblood sucked from her.

'Don't argue with me, young lady! You've pushed too bloody far. Just like your mother said you would.' Cleo rubbed her temples. It was annoying being right all the time. But Sam didn't know all the facts. He hadn't been reading up on what Cleo had been reading up on, he didn't know how thin the ice they were skating on really was. *Look for the signs*, the internet had prompted. Evie showed more than one. The withdrawing from her social group, the low self-esteem, the pounds she'd lost, at first attributed by Cleo to the jogging but now swiftly becoming part of a bigger, more sinister picture. And the scratches. Those awful angry lines lying hidden right there under Evie's sleeve, along with her first ever tattoo.

'It's just a little heart, Sam. You won't see it under her school shirt.'

'It's not even a heart now, thanks to Dad storming in like a nutter halfway through. Thanks a lot.' Evie was welling up again.

Sam turned, leaning back against the inside of his door. 'Am I missing something here? Suddenly this is something you're alright with then, is it, Cle? Have you hit your head?'

'No. But it's smaller than her thumbnail. Yes, I'm upset, but it's not the end of the world. No one needs to fly off the handle here.' *No one needs to hurt themselves over it.* Evie looked more astonished than Sam.

'Phone.'

Evie blinked at him. 'What?'

'Now.'

'*Mum*?' Evie was wedged between them, she had nowhere to go. Sam held out a hand. Cleo looked out of the window.

'You can have it back when I know exactly what you're up to. And not until.'

Evie dug into her pocket, angrily slapping her phone on to the dash. 'You always treat me like a child.'

'You are a child, Evie,' sighed Sam.

'You would say that, wouldn't you! But I'm sixteen in three weeks, I'll be old enough to marry, to join the army, *to leave home*!' She launched herself over Cleo's lap, scrambling through the passenger door.

'Evie!'

'Leave her, Sam. Let her cool off. Let's all just cool off.'

Sam rubbed a hand over his face then clasped both hands to the steering wheel. Evie stomped in the general direction of home. 'Old enough to marry or enlist? God help the poor bugger who signs that one up for either.' Cleo eyed Evie's relinquished mobile phone. 'I'm stunned, to be honest, Cle. Stunned at the trick she's pulled, stunned you haven't killed her. I haven't got a clue what's going on in our house some-times. Harry's turned into a zombie, and Evie?'

Cleo picked up the phone, allowing her fingers to take her straight to Evie's Facebook page. Memes of cats and captions, links to the latest boyband news, make-up tips, celebrity mar-riage crises expertly de-wrinkled by Cassie and Verity . . . these were the posts littering Evie's profile page last week, before one horrible boy called her one horrible name. She scrolled back to the most recent posts on Evie's wall.

'No one likes you Roberts. Or your muppet brother.'

'Revision tip for Evie – put your books on the doughnut shelf in your mum's café, you'll see them more often!'

'Says no dogs aloud in Coast, why does Evie get special treatment?'

Comment after comment, some tame, others less so. All of them by authors Cleo didn't recognise, accounts she couldn't look at because their privacy settings were more fit for purpose than Evie's.

She turned the screen so Sam could see and swallowed the burning swell of hurt and fury she felt for her daughter. 'That's why I haven't killed her, Sam. Because there are enough people hurting our little girl already.'

39

Bar the sounds of a light breeze fighting its way through the woodland outside, Curlew Cottage was silent. Isobel tapped her fingers against the cover of the magazine she hadn't been reading. She threw it on to the coffee table and sank back into the sofa. There was a pressure building in her head. It had been coming on all day, ever since Sophie showed her the fake Isobel Hedley blog. The real Isobel Hedley had felt herself drowning again pretty quickly after that. Thoughts could be like that. Like quicksand.

Right then. A distraction was what she needed. *Britain's Got Talent*? There wasn't much else on offer tonight. This year's series was already into the later rounds though, wasn't it? The real draw was earlier on, watching the masses, clumsy sword-swallowers and tone-deaf hopefuls murdering cheesy songs, the baying audience screaming *Off! Off! Off!* because it's okay to cut down and laugh at those people onstage; they were there voluntarily, in the spotlight, and therefore asking for it. Just like Isobel. And now she was asking for it again.

Isobel looked at her laptop, charging on the floor beside the log burner. Somewhere inside that laptop there was an active Isobel Hedley online again, baiting a troll named DEEP_DRILLERZ to follow the trail back to her. A version of her, anyway. A carefully crafted version she hadn't taken a very good look at yet.

She briefly considered it. *No.* An evening of obsession was not going to help. And Sophie had made her promise. No digging around in the fake blog or the fake Facebook account or the fake anything unless Sophie went into the dirt first.

She breathed deeply. *Distraction . . . distraction . . .*

The bottle of wine Sarah's fiancé had picked up for her on the way home the other night was still sitting unopened in the kitchen next to the bowl of eggs Daniel had appeared with this afternoon. There was a nice little arsenal of goodies building up at Curlew Cottage. Isobel could almost forget Fallenbay housed any unsavoury types at all.

Sod it. It was her birthday. She was twenty-eight, not ten. She could have a glass of wine if she wanted to on a Saturday evening, couldn't she? Soph thought she should've brought an emergency pack of Prozac for any 'quicksand' days. She didn't need Prozac. She didn't even need the glass of wine she was going to pour herself. She just needed to stop worrying what it all meant all the time.

She stood and walked to the kitchen. *I am having a glass of wine in my little cottage, because I can.* There, she felt better already. She pulled open the only utensil drawer and fished through the potato peeler, the apple corer, the egg slicer. 'So where's the bottle opener, Arthur?' Another rifle turned up nothing. Arthur would have one at his place, surely? Isobel slipped into her red pumps and skipped down the stone steps to the yard. Petal looked up from Arthur's lawn, a hunk of sinuous meat between her front legs. Isobel slowed and weighed up her odds. *Maybe not.*

It was still warm out in the sun, a balmy evening laced with the scent of forest and Arthur's sweet peas. She could walk into town, there was a mini-market at the top of the bay. This monster hill was making her fitter, she could enjoy the stroll, be back within the hour. Actually, she might even grab herself a few goodies, knock up a few cherry pancakes with the eggs from Daniel. There wouldn't even be any fighting Ella for them, she could share them with Simon Cowell instead. Why *shouldn't* she celebrate her birthday? Why should she give everything up so easily? Because a bunch of internet bullies knocked her legs out from under her? It was constant, this sitting around quietly waiting for something to happen. Wasn't turning twenty-eight years old worth celebrating?

She nipped back into the cottage and grabbed her keys. For all her faults, Sophie never shied away from her life. Sophie had got through being ignored, whispered about, shunned. The shame of falling pregnant in high school, the unforgivable selfishness of leaving Ella with their mum so Sophie could limp through the exams she was destined to fail, according to Mrs Conley at number seventy-six. They'd all had their turn on Sophie. Teachers, neighbours . . . those same neighbours going out of their way to call a *hello* to Isobel when she'd visited home. That was the funny thing about people, how quickly they turned. Berating grown women for having consensual sex with their boyfriends, pillorying sixteen-year-old girls caught out by their body clocks. It all carried the same penalty. Finger-wagging and judgement. Belittlement. Which was all fine and dandy for those who'd never had to chew on a consequence.

Sophie was right. You had to dust yourself off. Particularly on your birthday.

I've got air in my lungs and sun on my face, Petal, thought Isobel, stalking happily down the hill. Petal didn't look up from her portion of postman. Isobel would be stuffing herself stupid too by the time *Britain's Got Talent* came on.

40

Sarah gripped the phone to her ear. Nothing sounded suspect in Will's background. 'But you've been out all day. Come home for something to eat first. Max's in bed zonked already, thought I'd grab the chance to make us a curry. Something with a bit more kick.' Will's response was a foregone conclusion.

'I'm meeting a friend. I'll get something later.'

'Which friend?' She sounded like Cleo. Straight in with the questions, no dancing around.

'Just a friend, Mum. You don't know him.'

No. She didn't. *He's not necessarily a fifty-year-old pervert, Sarah.* Maybe not, but all of Will's friends had slept over here, eaten here, left their things lying around here. Why not the elusive *Edward*? Why was Will hiding him? Was it him Will was constantly texting? Angling his phone away for? Smiling at his screen for? Was Edward a funny, comedic friend? Or a perverse, predatory one?

'Will, you left first thing, I never know where you are any more. I'm worried about you.'

'Don't be.'

From where she was standing she could see straight through

the kitchen window, his surfboard still hanging in the carport. 'Where have you been all day?'

'The Village . . . then I went round to Charlie's.'

The Village? Without his board? 'Who's Charlie?'

'The new kid. His dad works with Sam Roberts. Check if you want.' Sarah felt caught out. Cleo wouldn't have given a hoot; she didn't really care about filtering accusations from her voice. But Cleo hadn't grown up hearing it. *Is that eyeshadow I see? Is that you eating too loudly? Are you sure you didn't miss clear signs your husband was unhappy?*

Sarah cleared her throat. 'Why would I need to check, Will?' A keg of questions exploded in her head.

Are you lying to me, William?

Are you smoking pot and looking at pictures of naked boys?

Is that why your phone pings all night long?

Was that sexually provocative photo a one-off? Or a regular fix?

Are you sharing those sorts of images too, Will?

Her heart climbed into her neck. She opened her mouth to let it crawl out, or at least let one of those questions out into the open.

'I'll see you later, Mum. Eat without me.' The line went dead.

She threw the phone across the marble worktop and winced at the noise. She listened out for a second but Max had been limp with sleep before she'd slipped her arm out from under him and tucked him in.

She wanted to scream. She'd been here before, accepting

half-truths down the phone because she wasn't brave enough to ask a straight and reasonable question.

Across the lawn, the summerhouse offered an old invitation. She listened again for Max. It was stupid, but she was already walking through the back of the kitchen to let herself out into the garden. She ducked under the low boughs of the pear tree, following Max's bike tracks around the lawn past the trampoline. No one had used the summerhouse properly since their barbecue with Juliette and Karl, but when Patrick left, for a time it had become Sarah's secret sanctuary. A precious half-hour of seclusion behind a closed door when the boys were all tucked up. Just the baby monitor, an emergency cigarette and the darkness.

Sarah nudged open the summerhouse door and pressed herself inside. There was still enough evening light to be reminded of the junk stacked in here, and the melancholy atmosphere of abandonment. It hadn't always been so unloved. Bedecked in bright blankets and cushions, this had been the kids' favourite spot for summer evening storytelling. Sarah had shared countless sunsets and G&Ts with Juliette in here too, Karl and Patrick usually disappearing inside to find the sports channel. It was never the place to leave dangerous things lying around. She should've made sure she'd locked up properly, but she'd relaxed. Let the complacency set in.

She stumbled through the gloom around tennis rackets, folded parasols, the stack of children's bikes she should've eBayed for a few pounds before the rust had claimed them. *Yes*, there it was. Her old faithful, the vintage oil tin Patrick had bought for a photography prop, still hanging from the eave. She felt a tiny burst of anticipation. It was a long shot. She hadn't puffed on a cigarette for a very long time. Not since she'd been whacked on the head by a wayward surfboard and the man on the other end had been so concerned about delayed concussion he'd insisted on shadowing her for the rest of the day, and the next four years.

Sarah didn't want to smoke a cigarette. Just pretend. Feel something of that precious alone time again. She clambered over the growing bulk of junk towards the oil tin and pictured Jon hovering over the bed, beating his chest. *Me Tarzan, you Jane. Clearing summerhouse, man's job!* Chivalrous Jon. Even when he'd nearly knocked her out with a surfboard. Will had introduced him as his school counsellor. Jon had asked Will if it was okay to take them all for lunch. He'd ordered feta and watermelon for the boys before showing Will the merits of his new surfboard while Max toddled on the sand. Then he'd asked for Sarah's permission too, to gently feel his way through her hair and assess the progress of her lump. He'd complimented her on her shampoo, then seven-thirty secret cigarette time had come and gone while Max had snoozed on Jon's chest and they'd watched the last boats coming in with Will. Jon had slotted in so seamlessly, the perfectly shaped piece to their puzzle, there hadn't been any space or need left for secret smoking in summerhouses.

She moved a couple of paint pots, balanced on one and reached for the oil tin. Her fingers fished for the feeling of . . . yes, sure enough, a dusty pack of Marlboro Lights, almost forgotten. She shook the pack instinctively, a promise rattled inside. She placed the tip of a cigarette between her lips, sucked at the unlit stick and blew imaginary smoke into the air. It was tempting. Boy, it was tempting.

Jon pounded through the carport into the garden. She shoved the cigarette back into its box. Jon hated smoking. He hated anything that aged or desecrated the body. *Shit*, he was looking over at the open door. He changed direction. *Oh God, he's coming in.* Sarah watched him, panting from his run. He reached the door as she lobbed the cigarette pack towards the shadows. It bounced somewhere near the Victorian chimney pot she'd never gotten to planting. Jon ducked his head around the door, surveying the gloom, Sarah standing in the belly of it.

'Hey?'

'Hey.'

'What are you up to?' he panted.

'Just . . . seeing what needs taking to the tip.' *Not bad.*

He glanced down at her legs. 'In a little cotton skirt? Not exactly shed-clearing clothes.' He edged into the summer-house. 'Where are the kids?'

'Will's out, obviously. Max is sleeping already.'

Sarah made a mental note. *Tooth fairy. Get pound coin from car. Don't forget.*

Jon pushed the door closed behind him with zero effort. His chest jarred with snatched breaths. Sarah could see the sweat beading on his shoulders the closer he came. He'd been pushing himself. Running hard. The way he did after a bad day, when exercise seemed less about enhancing his body and more about punishing it. Making it sorry.

'I like the skirt.' Jon's eyes were wide and alert, adrenalin still pumping. He moved closer, close enough so she could smell the sweat and cologne mingled on his skin. He could probably smell Keralan fish curry on hers. 'You have great legs, Sarah. Show me what's between them.'

'Hmm?' Well this was new. She felt laughter form in her throat. They usually had giggly sex, enjoyed a good sex life, rigorous, regular, at least one of them rolling away with a jubilant, *Fuck! That was so great* ... Usually Jon. Sarah liked to listen out for signs of disappointment lest she miss them a second time.

She looked to see if he were about to giggle too; bossy lover wasn't Jon's usual style.

He stepped towards her and she laid her hands on his chest. His heart was thudding, too fast. Panicky and erratic. Was he alright? His eyes were glazed, fiercely blue, looking straight at her, but not seeing her. Was he somewhere else? She'd asked herself many times whether the answer to that same question had been in Patrick's eyes, if only she'd been astute enough to look for it.

Jon was not about to giggle. Sarah felt an odd seriousness steal her laughter away. 'Max might—'

Jon's finger was suddenly over her mouth. He ran it along her lower lip, pressing without permission into her mouth. She felt her feet cement her to the spot. His run on the bluff, the air, or maybe just the sweat, had left his skin with a saltiness. She hadn't anticipated the pushing and withdrawing of his finger between her lips. In and out. Salty throughout. Her heart rate hitched. This was definitely new. She wasn't completely sure a sweaty finger in the mouth was all that erotic. Maybe it was? Maybe she should stop being so boring and embrace a finger in the mouth like she should have embraced kidney beans in her chilli con carne, but the mother in her was thinking about hand sanitisers and other people's germs on the handrail Jon always stretched out on. Also, what about her temporary crown? *Be careful,* her dentist had said.

She might've gone so far as to let her thoughts trail off completely then, to the growing epidemic of Norovirus sweeping the local schools and how many of those kids liked to swing on the same handrail Jon used, but then Jon retrieved his finger and pressed his hand between her legs instead.

He forced a whisper right into her ear. 'I'm going to fuck you now, Sarah. In the dark and the dirt where no one can hear us. I'm going to lift up your skirt, I'm going to fuck you, and you're going to say, *thank you, Jonathan.*'

41

Isobel rocked on her heels while the cashier whipped her items over the scanner. Maybe she'd gone just a bit crazy? She'd worked up an appetite walking into the harbour, and it was fatal going food shopping on an empty stomach. She hadn't been able to decide between chocolate sauce for the pancakes or the canned squirty cream Ella loved. She'd picked up both.

The cashier handed her a bag of indulgence. Isobel paid. How was she going to get all this back up the hill?

'Excuse me?'

A young woman with a smattering of freckles cocked her head, birdlike, at Isobel. There were three bumper bags of chewy sweets in her basket. Isobel felt a kindred sweet-toothed spirit. 'Hi?'

'That was you today, wasn't it? In Coast? You were the lady with Cleo and Juliette, when they were having their *little chat* out front.' The brunette ducked her head towards Isobel. Were they sharing a secret? 'You were the woman who didn't want her photograph taken, weren't you?'

Isobel frowned. 'Ah, probably not the only one.'

'Did I see you in there last week, too? When I was ousted for breast-feeding my baby by that Cleo Roberts.' *That* Cleo Roberts rang a little alarm bell.

Isobel gave her best non-committal shake of the head. 'I'm not sure.'

'There's a great coffee shop next to the old-fashioned sweet shop by the pier. You should try it, less teenagers hanging around, all trying to jump on to the free wifi. The quality of the food's better too. Cleo slathers butter on everything, I'm not convinced she's one hundred per cent honest about the ingredients she lists, either. She ought to be careful. People like her end up giving allergic children anaphylactic shock.'

Isobel was being lobbied. In the exit of a mini-mart, between a tower of handbaskets and on-offer fabric softener. She was being lobbied by a woman with a chip on her shoulder, subtly obscured by nice hair and a pretty scarf, to withhold future custom from *that* Cleo Roberts. Cleo. Isobel's almost friend.

'You know that's defamation?'

The woman blinked at her. Isobel caught a whiff of the Isobel she used to be. 'Slander, actually. Did you know, if Cleo caught wind of anyone suggesting she wasn't fit to run her café business responsibly, she'd have grounds to seek damages? She wouldn't even need to prove financial loss first, just prove something defamatory was said. With a witness statement, let's say. By someone who just happened to be there at the time the defamatory comment was made. In a supermarket, for example . . .'

The other woman drew her chin back into her lovely scarf. Isobel clenched her teeth. She felt her heart flutter to life. This could go either way. *Screw it*. She knew all about defamation. She knew the laws of slander centred on very specific accusations against a person. Saying somebody had HIV or was promiscuous, a *slag* for example, all fell within the parameters of slander in the eyes of the law, which was all fine and dandy and prosecutable in the real world, the world Isobel was standing in right now. The world of unpleasant face-to-face conversations at checkouts. But it didn't fly online. Isobel knew this first-hand. Despite a person being 'outed' online as a *slag*, a *Little Red Riding Whore*, an alleged *HIV carrying fleabag*, there wasn't an awfully brilliant chance of those responsible ever coming close to prosecution. Online slanderers tended to get away with it. They were rarely confronted. Rarely held accountable. Rarely made to think twice before saying another nasty word, unlike the woman standing gobsmacked in front of Isobel right now.

Isobel shrugged. 'I'll tell you what, I'll forget I even heard the word *anaphylactic* today, and you go give Cleo's flapjack a fair trial sometime. It's really very good. Deliciously buttery.'

42

Sarah sat on her bed, towelling her hair. Jon pulled himself into his lounge pants and checked his teeth in the dresser mirror.

'You ready to eat, Sar?'

No. She wasn't hungry. She was thinking. About silly things. 'Sure, give me a second and I'll put it out.' She hadn't factored in being held up in the summerhouse. The curry had had too much time in the oven, the fish would be dry but Jon would still eat it enthusiastically and tell her how delicious it was. Or would he? He might throw her another curveball, *sorry but I can't eat this crap, darling.* He'd thrown her one in the summerhouse. *I didn't tell you to kick those panties off, Sarah. Slip them back on, that's it, just over your ankles.*

Her phone bleeped on the bedside table. Some distant hope of Will asking if there was any tea left for him began to take shape.

Jon was checking for non-existent signs of thinning hair. 'You finish up. I'll set dinner out. Are we having red or white? You said fish, right? Oh, Cleo's after you . . .' He passed her phone over and returned to the mirror. 'We should get her and Sam up here, have a bite together some time. Sam's good company, isn't he?'

'Yep. That would be nice. I think they're having a few issues with the kids, though. Maybe in a few weeks. When their GCSEs are out of the way and we know what we're doing too.' Where they were living, for example. Whether Will was grappling with his sexuality. Why their own sexual style had suddenly changed. Little things like that.

'Yeah, I know. Evie Roberts came to see me on Friday.'

'Evie did?'

Jon turned his head side to side, checking one side of his face against the other. 'Evie's struggling. Exams, other kids. It's tough in the fifth year.'

'Does Cleo know?'

'It was Cleo's idea. Help Evie work through things. Get her back on track before exams start.'

Cleo hadn't said. She'd told Sarah about the Facebook bullies, her worries about the knock-on effects of too many arguments with Sam, but she hadn't mentioned Evie needing Jon's help.

'Is she okay?'

Jon shrugged. 'You know how girls can be. Small things become big things. Reality gets lost behind emotional responses.' Sarah stopped herself from asking anything that might break Jon and Evie's confidences. 'Put it this way, I'm glad we have boys. I wouldn't want to be in charge of a volatile teenage girl, that's a fact.'

Sarah ran a brush through her hair. Was Evie volatile? Feisty, Sarah would've said. Spirited. But volatile? She opened Cleo's text message.

*Have alcohol. And sea view. Will be here all night unless
my arse of a husband grounds me too xxx*

Evie probably did have a volatile side. She was genetically
predisposed. Cleo would've been a nightmare teen. 'Actually,
do you mind if I nip out? Cleo's just doing a few bits at Coast
and I said I'd give her a hand, I completely forgot.'

Jon padded across the bedroom carpet. He set his hands
on her shoulders, gently rubbing them along her neck. 'What
about dinner? You must be hungry. I know I worked up an
appetite out there.' He patted her shoulder. She smiled with
him.

'I won't be long. Max shouldn't wake now.'

'Max'll be fine. So long as he doesn't try to come between
me and whatever's in that oven.' Jon wiggled his eyebrows,
'I'll save some for Will, kid's probably been working up an
appetite too.'

43

Isobel stepped out of the mini-mart and gave a fleeting thought to finding a taxi. She glanced down towards the harbour on the off-chance one would be parked up. She almost didn't spot Cleo at all, sitting on the terrace steps.

Cleo gave a lazy wave in Isobel's direction, licked her ice lolly and carried on gazing out towards the ocean. Isobel changed course.

'No home to go to?' she called.

Cleo bit the end off her lollipop. 'Isobel, hello. Fancy a liqueur? I've got Cointreau, Kahlua-ha-ha, Tiaaa Mariaaah ...'

Cleo was slurring, some deliberate, some not. Isobel peered down at the tray of homemade ice pops in varying shades of brown. 'I can smell those from here, what are they? Irish coffee?'

'Yeee-ep.' Cleo had another lick. 'But without the coffee. They're just . . . Irishes. Little frozen Irishes.'

'Are you okay, Cleo?'

'Yeee-ep. Sam accuses me of wasting money all the time so I'm putting my liqueur stock to good use. I can't sell it, you see, Isobel, until I've got an alcohol licence. Which is a bit unlikely now Sam's spat his big old dummy out. Of *course* I was going to involve the papers. *Duh*! What did he expect? It was a golden marketing opportunity!'

Isobel set her shopping bag down and sat beside Cleo. 'You mean about Coast being baby-friendly?'

'No . . . about the open-mic night. It was a brilliant chance to spread the word!' Cleo rolled her eyes and put on a whiny voice. '*There's no way we can have those back rooms cleaned up in time for an open-mic night, Cleo. What if they bring in too much custom, Cleo? I work five days a week already, are you trying to kill me, Cleo?*' Cleo's alcohol-tinged voice returned. 'He's really pissed off. Evie didn't bloody help. So I'm probably not going to be having my extension or my open-mic night after all. So I won't need my alcohol licence.' Cleo lifted an almost completely melted tray of iced liqueurs. 'Oh, poo. Have an Irish ice pop with me, Isobel. Don't make me watch my investments drip away into a sticky puddle.' Cleo slurped straight from the tray.

Isobel hadn't eaten yet. Neat liqueurs probably weren't—

Too late. Cleo thrust a lolly towards her. 'Go on, have a bite.'

Isobel's stomach reacted. 'Baileys. Not bad.'

She recalled Cleo's husband frogmarching Evie over these very steps earlier. Evie had been floating around in her thoughts ever since Cleo had first told her about the Facebook issues. The girl had looked so embarrassed today, Isobel had really felt for her. 'Cleo? Tell me to mind my own business, but is Evie alright?'

'No. Not really. We had a differing of opinions on her *maturity*. Sam tried to ground her but she stormed off. She's only just turned up at the house. You know, she tries telling us she's old enough for this and that, then she disappears to sulk for hours like a naughty toddler, leaving me and Sam to squabble it out between us.'

'But she is home safe?' Kids did silly things when they were highly strung. Adults did silly things, too.

'She's safe. I came back here and sent Will home, Sam drove all over the place looking for her. One minute she was up on the bluff and the next he'd lost sight of her. He was probably too busy gawping at those beautiful new houses up there, convincing himself he wouldn't love one as much as the next person.' Cleo sighed. 'I think Evie might be going off the rails. You worked in a school, didn't you? How do you deal with a derailing teenager?'

Isobel needed to finish this ice pop before the whole lot dripped all over her pumps. She took another bite. 'Just keep the dialogue open, I suppose. Make sure Evie's got someone to talk to. Someone she trusts.' Isobel had been that person to Melanie McLoughlin. Mel had listened to her preaching the importance of standing up to bullies, standing your ground, facing your demons . . . And then watched Isobel run straight out of that poetry lesson and never come back.

She finished her slushy shot of liqueur. Cleo had another ready for her. 'Cointreau?'

'Thanks.'

'She won't talk to us, not now we've embarrassed her in front of "the whole stupid world". Sam didn't stop at the tattoo. You left before he went full-bore into the too much make-up, too little help around the house, too much junk food arguments.'

'Does she have anyone else?' Evie needed someone to do

for her what Sophie was breaking her back to do for Isobel, to straighten things out as best she could.

'She had a chat with one of the school pastoral officers last week. You know Jon Hildred? Sarah's Jon?' Isobel nodded with a mouthful of frozen Cointreau. 'Jon was brilliant with Will when he was first working through Sarah and Patrick's divorce. Which was why Sarah was stunned that Jon was even *remotely* interested in her, being Will's mum. Most blokes would run a mile knowing all the murky bits about a woman's broken marriage. Patrick left Sarah so flat. She had no self-esteem. It was awful. Jon picked her up and changed all that. He rescued her. Now I just need him to rescue Evie a little bit too.'

Cleo was either slurring again or Isobel was starting to feel the effects of these Irishes. 'You're glad Evie's talking to him then?'

'Absolutely. Evie needs to get whatever's bothering her out of her system. Before she ruins her exams. Before Sam throttles her. She can't let a bunch of divs calling her a "fat tranny" change who she is and how she behaves. She just can't!' Cleo picked up one of the bottles she had in the box beside her. She unscrewed the top and took a glug of rum. Isobel remembered this was pirate territory. Cleo was probably descended. 'It's only a bit of name-calling. She needs to shake it off. *Don't feed the trolls*!' Cleo took another glug and passed the bottle.

Isobel took a hit. Yes, it was just name-calling. DEEP_DRILLERZ was nothing but a name-caller. But that wasn't going to save him. She let the sweet fieriness of rum warm her through. Life could have been worse over the last year. She could've been a person like DEEP_DRILLERZ. But she wasn't, she was a person like her. An idiot, granted. But not a bad person, not a cruel person. She bumped shoulders with Cleo. 'Evie will be fine, Cleo. And all of those horrible people will still be horrible people, and Evie won't care about them any more because she's decent and they're nothing . . . just voiceless words drifting away on the internet somewhere, where no one really exists.'

A car horn papped. 'Is this the party?' Sarah looked like a teenager with her hair all wet behind a girly headband. She rested an arm along the window ledge of her car. 'Are we all alright?'

Cleo stood and almost overbalanced. 'Not really, Sar.' She hiccupped. 'You heard Sam blowing off. He's accused me of only caring about world domination. Which of course I do, but it's not *all* I think about. Fancy an Irish?'

'Um, *no*. I have the car.'

Cleo blew a raspberry. 'Why did you drive, Sar, I said I had alcohol!'

Isobel chuckled. Was she tipsy already?

'I came to check you were okay. And to take you home if you need a lift?'

'Actually, I do! Isobel? Are you coming?' Cleo pulled her up by the arm.

'Coming where?'

'Yes, where are we going?' frowned Sarah.

Cleo knocked back another rum hit. 'West Coast Ink, please, driver! I'm going to show my fat-head husband how you stand up to fat-head tattooists who think it's alright to scar people's children.'

44

Sarah slowed and cut off the engine. 'Are you sure this is a good idea?'

Cleo roughed her curls so they pouffed out like a multi-coloured crest. A curly chaos of blondes and browns. Her eyes were bright and steadfast.

'Probably not.' She jumped out of Sarah's Volvo and straightened her bra strap. Sarah unclicked her belt. Were they all going in?

'If Sam thinks I'm scared of some meat-head with teardrops on his cheeks, he's forgotten the girl he married.'

Cleo trounced off along the pavement, shoulders back, bottom strutting purposefully, Sarah in steady pursuit like a worried daughter, glancing back for something – *reassurance?* – from Isobel. Isobel still felt giggly. She really wanted to laugh. No wonder Fallenbay had a history for skirmishing pirates. Rum sent you mental.

Cleo swung open the door, sending it clattering against the wall inside. Isobel admired dramatic pendant lights and ornate mirrors while several faces turned to watch them file into West Coast Ink like ducklings behind their mother. Hands hesitated, buzzing equipment quieted. A mellow song played out on the radio. Cleo had the floor. She set a hand on her hip and raised her chin.

'I'd like to speak to the manager,' she said to no one in particular.

A guy sporting one of those hula-hoop holes in his earlobe was outlining an anchor on a bald chap's head. Another kid, not far out of his teens, sat hunched over a chair while a big guy with cornrows and very nice arms worked a skull between his shoulder blades.

'Oh, wow, flowers . . .' Sarah prattled, '. . . peeping through skeletal eye-sockets. Pretty.'

Isobel giggled under her breath. A slender brunette with petite features and clothes clinging to her honed body slipped the reading glasses off her nose. She braced her hands over the counter. She had tattoo sleeves from wrist to shoulder, hair braided high, mohawk-style, the rest falling around her face. 'I'm the owner, can I help?'

Cleo shifted her weight on to her other foot. She was turning red. They all probably were. This felt like being back at school, finding yourself in the presence of the coolest fifth-year girl, quite a few bad boys and a lot of sharp implements. Cleo cleared her throat. She was about to let rip. She wasn't fazed by Lara-Croft-type edgy young women with very cool hair.

'I would like to know . . .' She trailed off.

'Yes?' smiled the owner.

'I would like . . .'

'*Yes?*' squinted the brunette.

'I'm here for . . .'

'Uh-uh?'

'A tattoo,' blurted Cleo. 'A small one.'

'She doesn't want a tattoo,' Sarah laughed nervously.

'No, no . . . actually I do. Why shouldn't I? If Sam wants to be an old fart waiting for retirement to creep around, fine!'

'But you came here to—'

Cleo spoke through a grin. 'That's right. To *show* Sam . . . I'm only bloody forty-two. Let's do it!'

'You sure you ladies came in here for a tattoo?'

'Yes. Absolutely. My friend recommended you,' Cleo blathered.

'Which friend?'

Isobel held her breath and waited for the words *fifteen-year-old* and *daughter* to make an appearance. Cleo blinked. Her eyes lit up. 'Ben Oakes, he's got a tiddler.'

The brunette chortled. 'Ben wouldn't appreciate you saying that, but you're right, he has. Little goldfish. Did it myself. Ben's a good guy, my sister loved paddle-boarding with him. Do you remember me saying, Mart? How much Ruby got out of those three days with him last summer? It's great what he's doing down in the cove.' The brunette drummed her fingers on the counter. 'Well, alrighty then. Seeing as Ben's recommended us, if you're not wanting anything drastic we can fit you in now, no problem. So what are you thinking?'

Sarah looked like a primary school teacher poised at the edge of the Christmas play, ready to intervene if anyone said the wrong words.

'Umm . . . well . . . the skulls are very nice and . . . umm . . . ooh! *Snakes* . . .' Cleo's eyes looked glassy. Isobel grinned, it was a wonder she could focus on anything.

'Can we have a minute?' Sarah ushered Cleo into a huddle. Isobel tried to look serious. 'What the hell are you doing?'

'Showing my husband that my balls are probably . . .' Cleo scrunched one eye shut and held up her finger and thumb, '. . . a *leedle* bit bigger than his.'

'Maybe we should come back another time, Cleo?' tried Isobel. It had felt good to be out in the company of other women, not women babysitting her the way her mother and sister did, just women. She'd been having a nice detour on her way to cherry pancakes in front of *Britain's Got Talent* but there was something around the edges now. Something on the periphery starting to fray the fun. Maybe it was the smell, the subtle tang of antiseptic. The reality of tattooing yourself on a whim. Or the dying taste of alcohol on her tongue. Dutch courage. She'd knocked back two Bacardis before Sophie had got her into Moody's Tattoos and Piercings. *Little Red Riding Hood? You're such a daddy's girl! One day, Is, that halo's going to fall around your ankles.* Isobel twisted her bangle around her wrist.

'Does it hurt?' Cleo whispered. Isobel shook her head. 'Do you think I should have one?' She shook her head again. Cleo leant back into their huddle, her whispering growing louder. 'Can't one of us just have a small tattoo? So we're not being rude?' Cleo swung her head to face Isobel. 'Isobel!' she blurted. 'You've done this before! Would you like another? I'll pay!'

Someone laughed. A tattooist stopped buzzing and pivoted on his chair. Isobel swallowed. 'I don't really want the one I've got.' She was speaking too quietly. It made Cleo louder.

'Don't you? Excuse me! Could you take my friend's tattoo off? Or can you only put them on?'

An explosion of adrenalin shot through Isobel's body.

'Mart's your man for laser removal.' The brunette jabbed a biro at Mart working on the anchor.

Mart tipped an imaginary cap. 'At your service.'

Cleo was holding court again. 'My friend Isobel doesn't like her tattoo. Do you, Isobel?'

Isobel flushed. 'Cleo, it's fine.'

'I can take a look,' said Mart politely.

'No. I'm fine. Thanks,' Isobel repeated.

'She's shy,' nodded Cleo.

The guy working the flowery eye-sockets looked over. 'Guaranteed we've seen worse.' Her neck was getting hotter. Everyone in the world suddenly wanted a look. 'It's not an ex's name, is it?' he said lightly.

Mart laughed at her. 'Don't be embarrassed. We get loads of exes. Exes are to be expected. Get a cover-up, way cheaper than the laser route.'

The owner jabbed her pen in the opposite direction. 'Luke's your man for cover-ups.'

Luke stood. 'So can we see what you've got?' Isobel's hands grew clammy. 'Please be something I haven't seen before. I never forget a tat, they're, like, tattooed on to my brain or something.'

'Yeah, I get that too. *Tattoo recognition*. We should get paid to ID villains!' said one of the others.

They might've seen Isobel's already. They might've watched her and Nathan in the kitchen like hundreds of others. They could've commented. He could be in here right now. Luke or the other one. DEEP_DRILLERZ. Who'd zoomed in on her tattoo, her identifying mark. He'd know it was her, *maybe why she'd come*. Something unpleasant was happening in her chest. A tickly, panicky, runaway feeling, faster and faster, gathering momentum.

'Isobel? Are you okay? Is your bracelet bothering you?'

'It's hot in here.' She dabbed the beads of sweat starting at the back of her neck. Her face felt hot, her chest tight.

'Isobel? Do you need a glass of water?' Sarah's eyes were wide, which only made it worse.

Calm down. For God's sake, calm yourself down. He doesn't know you're here. 'Where's the bathroom?' she managed.

The woman pointed her pen. Isobel made it to the back of the shop. She locked the toilet door after her, throwing on the cold tap. A soothing shock of water cooled her neck. She splashed her chest. *Think about your breathing . . . nice and slow . . . you are not in any danger, you don't have to do anything you don't want to. Breathe in, breathe out.* It was simple really. *Breathe in, breathe out. Nothing bad is going to happen.*

A knock. 'Isobel? Are you okay?'

The girl in the mirror looked pale, eyes too dark, chest wet, breathing too deeply. 'Coming,' she called.

'Sorry, can you come quickly? We need to leave. Cleo feels sick.'

She tucked wet hair behind her ears and opened the door.

'Are you okay?' Sarah hovered in the doorway like a fretful mother.

The shakiness would wear off in a few minutes. She took a steady breath and smiled. 'Sure. 'I'm absolutely fine.'

45

'This is ridiculous. Look, I teach at the primary school. I'm a responsible person. I have not touched a drop of alcohol,' protested Sarah.

Isobel was losing the gentle fuzziness of the liqueurs, her flighty jaunt to the staff toilet sobering her up. That and Cleo making good on her threat to be ill. They'd just made it outside in time.

Sarah paced the pavement. 'Why does a *man* always have to ride in and save the day? We're perfectly capable. All the hard work the suffragettes did for us and we still call the men in.' Sarah glared back at West Coast Ink's window, the owner standing guard over the till, Sarah's car keys locked inside. 'Even the ones who look like they could take a tiger out with their eyelash curlers.' They'd confiscated Sarah's car keys and called Ben Oakes, seeing as he'd recommended them to the woman who'd just spewed all over their section of pavement. The owner found it difficult to believe a sober primary school teacher would drive drunk friends into town for body art. They were doing Sarah a favour having a mutual friend come and check all was well.

Cleo slumped against the promenade bench. A blue pickup

with Blue Fin Surf School along the doors pulled in alongside them.

'This is so ridiculous,' snapped Sarah. Her phone rang as Ben got out of his truck.

'Before you get that, could you just walk in a straight line for me please, Mrs Harrison?' grinned Ben.

Sarah rolled her eyes and walked back towards West Coast Ink. She answered her phone at the door, waiting for Ben to catch her up, verify her sobriety. They were back outside within the minute. 'Isobel, I've got to get home, Max is up crying for me. Can I drop you home on the way to Cleo's?'

'It's in the opposite direction. I'll walk. You get home to Max.'

'No, you can't walk. I'll run you back first. Max is fine. He does this every Sunday night before school starts for the week. Obviously he doesn't realise he's a night early.' She rubbed her eyes and looked suddenly tired out.

Ben stood quietly behind her, waiting to be discharged. 'I can run Isobel home, I was going to drop in on my pa anyway. Check he's not blowing all his pension on tele-voting for a street-dancing dog on that show. Daniel goes crazy for it. The one with the buzzers.'

Sarah fidgeted. 'Thanks, Ben, but I'll take Isobel home first, then Cleo.' Cleo heaved again. 'No, I'll take Cleo first, give my car seats a chance of survival.'

Ben buried his hands in his pocket. 'Sarah, I'm going that way. If Isobel's happy for a lift . . .'

Sarah shook her head firmly. 'Really, I'd rather—'

'Sarah! Keep talking like this and Isobel's gonna think I'm

an oddball who can't be trusted. She'll be fine. I'll even drive extra carefully. Scout's honour.'

Isobel let the conversation ping-pong around her. Sarah fiddled with her ring again. 'Maybe it's your safety I'm looking out for, Ben. Maybe it's you who could be in danger of being taken advantage of.' Sarah looked at her. 'I don't really think that, I'm just making the point. Men get accused all the time of all sorts by women they hardly know, Ben. No offence, Isobel.'

Isobel shrugged. 'None taken. I like your stance on equality. Look, I'm perfectly fine. You go. Ben's promised to be a perfect gentleman and I promise not to accuse him of anything awful.'

Cleo made another retching noise from the bench. Sarah glanced from Isobel to Cleo. 'Jon's only just had my car valeted,' she grimaced. 'Ben, would you mind helping me get her into the car? Sam can help at the other end. I just need to get her strapped in.'

Ben helped Sarah get Cleo to her feet. A few awkward nudges and Cleo was staggering quite well towards Sarah's Volvo.

'Can I call you later, Isobel?' asked Sarah. 'Cleo will have your number in her phone, won't she?' Isobel nodded. Sarah pulled off as Isobel remembered her shopping on Sarah's back seat, her cherries and chocolate sauce, and the fact she hadn't given her mobile number to anyone in Fallenbay.

Ben held a hand towards his truck. 'Ready?'

She looked across the bay towards the dunes on the other side. It wasn't that far.

'Y'know, I think I'll be okay. Thanks, though. You get off, you might catch the last of *Britain's Got Talent*.'

Ben scratched his head. 'I'm going that way, it seems silly for you to walk.'

It wasn't silly to not get into a truck with somebody you didn't know. 'Look, I appreciate the offer. And you seem very nice, and I'm sure you are, but I don't really know you from Adam. And you don't know me, so I think I'm just going to walk . . . then everyone knows where they are.'

There. Perfect sense.

'So, you're going to walk for half an hour, at dusk, on your own, up a deserted track, past barren sand dunes and private woodland, where any local weirdo could be lurking . . . rather than take a lift from a guy you see from your window every day?'

Isobel shrugged. 'Pretty much.'

46

The inky blue of another night sky bled down over the bay. Ben was right about the sand dunes, they were barren; sorry tufts of yellow grasses silently trembling as Isobel walked alongside them. The truck had been less conspicuous while she'd still been within the limits of the harbour, pulling into spaces between stationary cars ahead of her, waiting for her to catch up on foot before pulling off again. Now she'd made it past the dunes and to the first leafy welcome of the woodlands, there was no denying the truck creeping along up ahead was all for her.

He hadn't spoken the whole way. Neither had she. Yet he'd driven so close that she'd caught every song he'd listened to for the last twenty-five minutes. A Radiohead fan. Mostly.

Isobel reached the gated entrance to Acorn Woods and leant against the fencing. She fished a small, sharp stone from her pump. The truck slowed right down and waited a few yards ahead. She'd watched dog-walkers coming and going over the footpath here, but the adjoining woodland blanketed with bluebells right at the top of the track was Arthur Oakes' alone. Arthur cut in front of Isobel's cottage every night to let Petal run free in there. Those teenagers

Sarah thought were hopping over the boundary into Arthur's woods would have to be kamikaze with Petal running patrols.

Isobel slipped on her shoe and finally waved at the truck and acknowledged Ben. Red brake lights flared in the gloom of the lane.

'Think I'll be okay from here!'

Ben popped his head out of the driver's window. 'You look like you're having a technical problem with your shoe. Are you sure you don't want to jump in? This hill's a toughie.'

She'd got a bit bored of walking to be honest, but Ben was chaperoning her home like a ten-year-old and a ten-year-old's stubbornness had set in. 'Kerb-crawling can't be very efficient for gas-guzzlers. You might as well have walked with me.'

He smiled and drummed his fingers on the ledge of his door. 'No thank you. I feel much safer in here.'

She was catching him up again. The air was cooler the further up into the trees the lane took her. 'Safer?' There was a hint of breathlessness in her voice now.

'Absolutely. Sarah's right, you know. It's not just women who have to watch the company they keep. To coin a phrase I heard recently, Miss Oliver, I don't really know you from Adam.'

She caught him grinning in the wing mirror. He was the opposite of Nathan. Nathan liked to put the mileage in with moisturisers and nose trimmers. Ben Oakes was rough around the edges. Sophie would love him of course. Isobel braced her hands on her knees pushing herself on against the gradient. She remembered her shopping, left in Sarah's car.

Ben was still grinning.

Isobel tried to talk without sounding wheezy. 'No, you're right. You can never be too careful.'

He let her catch him up. 'Exactly. Just because you look very nice and smile a lot when you talk, you could be hiding all sorts of troubling realities . . .'

'Troubling realities?'

'Sure. You might like red sauce on your bacon sandwiches instead of brown or, I don't know, socks and Crocs, which is a very hot look right now amongst the older Fallenbay community but a troubling reality nonetheless.'

Isobel smiled at her aching feet. Socks and Crocs sounded amazing right now.

'You might not even be who you say you are.' Her stomach flipped. 'You might have a whole other identity . . . like Cat Woman. A guy can't be too careful.'

The same anxiety she'd felt in West Coast Ink spiked again. That feeling of being hung out to dry by people who knew more about her than they should. Was Ben accusing her? Did he know she'd lied? Withheld her real surname? Where had she slipped up? *Jesus.*

Petal had heard them coming and was already stationed at the nearest point of Arthur's fence. 'Hey beautiful!' called Ben. 'Come to welcome me home?' Petal launched into a frenzy of barking. 'Petal! I love you, you're so mean to me!'

Petal ramped up her protest. Daniel appeared on the doorstep to his cottage.

'Thanks for the lift,' Isobel babbled. 'Bye.'

'I didn't give you a lift! Thanks for not endangering me!' But she was already striding towards her cottage, door key ready.

47

Any appetite for cherry pancakes and laughing at the TV had been left somewhere on the walk home. Ben's truck was still outside Arthur's as Isobel double-checked the locks. She padded through to the bathroom, checking her phone on the wash stand. Sophie still hadn't messaged back. She perched on the edge of the bath and checked the water temperature instead.

Someone knocked at the cottage door and she was on her feet again, listening. Petal was as good as a fanfare but there was no barking to go with that knock. She stepped silently down the cottage stairs, ducking her head for a look through the lounge window. Petal was there behind Arthur's wire fence, standing to attention, snout pointed straight towards Curlew's front door. It wasn't quite dark yet, but close enough. Another knock.

'Isobel? Are you in? It's Sarah.'

She let out a breath, giving her heart a few seconds to settle before crossing the hallway for the door. Sarah's headband was replaced by a damp knot now at the back of her head, showing off high cheekbones and big brown worried eyes. 'Can I come in?'

'Sure.' Isobel pulled the door all the way open. Sarah stepped into the hallway. 'You didn't have to come up here, it's only a bit of shopping.'

Sarah frowned. There was a small gift bag in her hand where Isobel had expected a plastic supermarket carrier to be.

I just wanted to give you these. Actually, I bought them yesterday but the day got away from me. I was hoping to drop them off at some point to say thanks for driving me and the boys home last week, rather than just barking at Jon to grab you a bottle of wine. It's nothing much, just—'

'Bath bombs.' The air in the hallway filled with the scent of citrusy flowers and talc. She closed the front door and led Sarah off the hall. 'I only packed a few basics before coming to Fallenbay, these will be really great. Thank you. How's Max now?'

Sarah followed her into the lounge, taking a seat stiffly, like a visitor. Isobel perched on the facing sofa. 'He's fine now. Jon called as I was leaving Cleo's. Will was lying on the bed watching Godzilla with him. Max, not Jon. Max definitely does not want me home now, he knows I'll spoil the fun. You got back okay then?'

'Yes. You didn't need to come all the way up here to check, though. You must feel like everybody's mum tonight.'

Sarah bothered at the edge of a cushion. 'Not really. My fifteen-year-old's hardly spoken to me all week.' A small silence uncoiled itself. 'Actually, Isobel, I did need to check on you. Back in the tattooist's, before you went to the bathroom . . .'

Isobel repositioned herself on the sofa. Sarah had duped her with a gift bag. 'Yeah, sorry about that. Think it must've been those slushy shot things of Cleo's. Went straight to my

head! I hadn't really eaten, and I don't like needles and . . .'
It was a sterling performance for an on-the-hop effort.

Sarah blinked at her. 'Who doesn't know you're here?'

'Sorry?'

'In the tattooist's, you said you felt hot, then you said, "He doesn't know I'm here", then you went to the bathroom and splashed water on your face.'

Her face was getting warmer again now. 'I said what?' There was a silly yip in her voice. She had no recollection of saying anything like that. She couldn't have said that. Not out loud.

Sarah set the cushion aside. 'Look, Isobel. You don't have to tell me anything. We hardly know each other, even though you've been very kind to me already, helping me at the football, and not asking us to put Mr Fogharty down for being a complete menace, and . . . well, you're really nice and I'm glad Cleo introduced us, which is why I'm surprised I'm even here saying this because I don't want to make you feel awkward . . . I don't want to make myself feel awkward either, but . . .' Sarah needed to splash her face too. 'It's just that, I do know what it's like to deal with what I suppose you might call a . . . a panic attack. And what I saw tonight, what I think I saw tonight, well, was you possibly having a similar sort of problem. If you don't mind me saying so.'

Crikey, she was good. Isobel hadn't considered finding herself in the company of others who might know what they were looking at if they saw it. What was the appropriate response to being called out? Laugh it off? Total truth? Lie?

'Who can't know you're here, Isobel?'

Sarah was like a softly spoken pitbull, jaws gently locked on. Isobel was trying to think of something acceptable to say but her mouth had stopped working. The same thing had happened in the Head's office. She'd just sat there, nodding remotely while the governors outlined all the ways Isobel's not-so-private life impaired her ability to teach successfully. As if she hadn't already fathomed that she could never stand up in front of those students ever again.

'Isobel, Cleo's my friend. After tonight she's going to be all over you because Cleo thinks you're lovely too, and you are lovely, I can tell already, and now she'll consider your friendship as good as bonded over a minor incident in a tattoo parlour, because Cleo values a person who'll ride into battle with her, so to speak, because she would absolutely ride into battle for any one of her friends, no matter how silly or serious the situation. So you can just tell me to keep my nose out, but I still have to ask . . . why are you in Fallenbay?'

Laugh. Truth. Lie. Why had she come to Fallenbay? To teach one last lesson? About consequence? To the person who'd wrecked it all for her? All she'd done so far was make friends.

'I came to take some time out.' There. Neither a lie nor a truth.

Sarah nodded softly and looked away. 'I'm not suggesting you're in any sort of trouble, Isobel. It's just . . . if you were worried . . . about anything . . . or anyone . . . I don't know, *following you here . . .*'

'No,' Isobel said flatly. There was no danger. There was no danger in what she and Sophie were doing. It was all virtual. All online. Sophie's hands tightly on the reins.

'No?'

'No, Sarah, there's no danger.'

'Danger?'

Hadn't Sarah said danger? Or did she say *trouble*? Sarah had stopped fidgeting now, looking dead straight at Isobel, unflinching, direct. 'I meant *trouble*,' tried Isobel.

Sarah had gone quite still. 'Good. I'm just making sure you know you wouldn't have to deal with that sort of thing on your own, Isobel. You know, if there was something, or someone, you needed to avoid.'

Sarah was still locked on. A lump formed in Isobel's throat. A stupid lump about to give her away. *Give it away yourself then! For once!* Every day it was like carrying a boulder on her back. Sarah was offering a place for her to set it down awhile.

Isobel's voice sounded floaty and far off when she spoke, as if none of this unfortunate business had ever been that big a deal. 'I'm not avoiding anyone. It's a bit late for all that. He caused maximum damage every way he could already.' She smiled then, knowing it wouldn't make her eyes.

Sarah's eyes didn't leave Isobel's. 'I'm sorry, Isobel. Cleo said she thought you might have broken up with someone before you came to Fallenbay. I know how awful that can be.'

Isobel nodded. 'Cleo has a good nose. I thought we'd be planning our wedding by now.'

'I'm sorry, he obviously hurt you.'

'Yes, well . . . I hurt him too. But it wasn't Nathan who did the most damage.'

Sarah could probably smell another woman in the picture. A leggy lovely who'd turned Nathan's head. Sarah settled her hands in her lap. 'Who did cause the most damage, Isobel?'

275

Jenny and Sophie had been the only people who'd ever heard the sorry tale straight from Isobel's mouth. Everyone else knew about the video courtesy of DEEP_DRILLERZ himself. Now it was Isobel's to share again, her grubby little secret to do with as she wished. What would it matter to tell Sarah some of it? Sarah was nothing to do with Isobel's real life. There was a strange freedom in the realisation that she was about to let some of it go. Of her own volition. To a person who could grasp what it would mean to be a teacher and an internet whore all at once. Sarah would appreciate the ramifications of living in a house with a young child, constantly worrying about any more balding *fans* turning up on the doorstep with bunches of flowers, condoms and gooey eyes.

'The most damage? I suppose that would be the man who spread a video of me having sex with my boyfriend all over the internet, dug up as many of my contact details as he could, and connected the dots.'

'Isobel, that's . . . that's *horrendous*. Worse than horrendous, it's . . .'

'All over with,' Isobel said firmly.

Sarah put her hand over her mouth. Isobel felt suddenly compelled to open hers wide. To stop holding her breath and let all the thoughts forging those awful daily headaches to come gushing out.

'I know what you're probably thinking, I didn't knowingly make a sex tape.'

'It wouldn't have mattered if you had.'

'Well I didn't anyway, for what it's worth.' Which wasn't very much, she'd discovered. 'Nathan, it's silly really, I was getting impatient, so . . .' Laughter bubbled to the surface. 'I shouldn't laugh, it's not really very funny,' she said soberly. 'I thought I'd encourage him to realise what he might miss out on if he didn't hurry up and pop the question, so I *pretend* left him. You know, to shock him into loving me a bit more?' She laughed again. Sarah remained statuesque. 'Anyway, Nathan didn't rush off to the jewellers. There I was, thinking I might be starting the new year with a sparkler like yours. It started with a life-lesson in revenge porn instead.'

'He uploaded a private video? Of the two of you?'

'It was my fault, really. If I'd have just made sure it was deleted. From *everywhere*. Nathan said it was.'

'But it wasn't?'

'Nothing's ever deleted from a computer.' Isobel knew things like that now. 'Nathan turned up one day saying he'd stumbled across *our* video on one of those roasting websites.'

'Roasting?'

'When you get publicly pulled apart.'

'Publicly shamed?' Isobel nodded. 'And he said he'd *stumbled* across it? His own deleted video? What, while he was doing his online grocery shop?' *See.* Sarah would've smelled the same lie Isobel had. 'That's a criminal offence. Tell me you had him prosecuted.'

Isobel ran her finger over the crumpled tissue paper encasing each bath bomb. 'Nathan said he didn't upload the video.'

'He would say that, wouldn't he? What did the police say?'

She lay the two bath bombs side by side on the coffee table. 'The police were never involved. I did threaten Nathan with the police when he said he couldn't take the video back down again.'

'And?'

'And he left. The video was removed within the hour.'

'Bastard,' Sarah whispered. 'And you never involved the police?'

'No.'

Sarah's voice climbed a notch. 'Why?'

Isobel twisted each bath bomb in turn; she noticed the tiny birds printed on the tissue-wrapping. Pretty. 'Because I was embarrassed. And because it was partly my fault for not making sure the video was gone.'

'But he'd told you it was gone?'

'I watched him delete it. It was never deliberate, a silly accident we were ever even caught on film. When Nath realised, he was upfront and showed me the footage on our laptop. Then he deleted it and I took the laptop when I moved back home to my parents' house, holding out for that diamond.'

'So how did it get online?'

Isobel's jaw started to ache. She stopped clenching it. 'It doesn't matter now. The bottom line is, I should have been more careful. Instead of just hoping it would all be fine.'

Sarah slumped into the sofa. 'Isobel, that's one of the most atrocious things I've ever heard. I thought my ex-husband was bad. I'm so sorry. Patrick leaving us was painful, really painful for Will, but never, not even at my lowest, could I have done something like that to hurt him back. How could Nathan put your name and address online too? He must've understood the dangers of doing something like that!'

'Oh, that wasn't Nathan.'

Sarah frowned. 'But you said . . .'

'Nathan didn't post my contact details under the video. Or forward a hyperlink to everyone who knows me and my family.' Sarah gasped. 'That was the handiwork of a complete stranger.'

'*What?* But how would a stranger know those things?'

Because he put the effort in. 'Half the work was already done for him. My name was already in the caption on the video: *Isobel Yvonne Hedley, too fucking good for anyone, even my dull little boyfriend.*' Sarah winced as if she were being physically poked with each word. 'That would've got him my address on the electoral roll, a Google search would've pulled up my social media platforms, work website, and so on. Hey presto, a whole horde of friends, family and colleagues to share my sex vid with. I was so naïve. There I was thinking, *No more video! One threat to call the cops and order is restored!* I had no idea some bastard might've downloaded it first and spent the following six weeks mounting an all-out attack on me.'

Sarah's mouth hung open. 'Who could do something so cruel?'

The million-dollar question. Isobel conjured the faceless, greasy, unkempt loner she always pictured DEEP_DRILLERZ to be. 'I don't know. A total stranger. What does it matter?'

'A stranger? Who you'd never met?'

Isobel nodded.

'Doing all that homework on you? Jesus, that's sinister.'

'Thorough, too. He found everything. Where I worked, who my friends were, where *they* worked even. Then on Valentine's Day last year, when he was ready, he posted the links anywhere he thought they'd cause damage. My work's Twitter feed, the website of my dad's mechanic, our local butcher's review page . . . You name it, if it was related to Isobel Hedley, this guy sent a link.'

Sarah had a look of utter horror on her face. 'But, *why*?' DEEP_DRILLERZ wasn't conforming to Sarah's logic. People hurt each other every day. Husbands and wives. Children in playgrounds. Squabbling siblings. Even random attacks normally came with at least some crossing of paths, some brushing of shoulders. 'Why would a stranger do that? To you? To anyone?'

Because he was messed up? Because he was bored? Because Isobel looked like the wife who'd left him? Or shared a name with the elderly mother he was stuck caring for? Who knew? She'd pickled her brain thinking about it. *Didn't think of the consequences, did you, bitch?*

'Perhaps he did it just because he could. Because he didn't think there would be any consequences.' Or just because he'd felt like teaching someone a lesson.

'It's horrendous. Cleo was so sure you'd come to Fallenbay to fall in love. I'm so sorry.'

Isobel stopped picking. She'd ruined that pretty bath bomb. 'Horrendous things happen every day. People put their families in dinghies trying to reach a better life. Parents lose their children. I just lost my job. And my reputation.'

'It's heart-breaking, Isobel.'

'No it isn't. It's rough, but it's not heart-breaking. My mum used to tell me and my sister, hearts aren't broken by strangers, only the ones you love can do that.'

Sarah didn't look convinced. 'Are you close to your sister? Has she been supportive, I mean?'

'Sophie? Absolutely. I wouldn't be here now if it weren't for Sophie.'

48

Sam was at the table in the sun room, stationed behind a morning newspaper. Cleo scowled at the clock on the microwave and shuffled towards the brewing pot of coffee. There was an ever-so-slight splitting sensation in the top right of her head. 'Harry's left his shin-pads. I can drop them off at the sports centre on my way in unless you're going over that way?'

Sam ruffled his paper. *Still mad then.* 'Harry's not at football.'

'Why not?'

'He's gone and opened up for you instead. Thought you'd appreciate the help seeing as you've just announced to the papers we're holding some big money spinner in two weeks. He's clearing the rest of the storerooms and getting the pastries in while you get your hangover under control.'

Cleo sipped her sweet black coffee. 'What about the league? The other lads won't appreciate him missing matches.'

'That's what I said. He wants to work.'

Wants to work? What a crock. He was saving for something. A fallback in case they didn't buy the drum kit? She picked a piece of toast from the toast rack and pottered into the sun room. The garden needed a spruce, Harry could earn a few pounds at home if he was desperate.

'Did he say what he needs the money for?'

'Nope. Maybe he thought it best to earn it while we can still pay him. Before we start paying tradesmen top whack to get a new function room up and running in two weeks.'

'Sam, if you're going to start up with this again I'm going to need at least one more coffee first.'

He shook his paper again. Cleo pulled a face behind it just before he slapped it down into his lap. 'You know the part really grating with me, Cleo? I'd already said I'd do the work. But you have to go right ahead and pile on the pressure.'

'It's just a bit of plastering, Sam. It would only take you a couple of days.'

'I work, Cleo! For someone else! I haven't got a couple of days. I've got a bossy twenty-five-year-old college prick already breathing down my neck every time I take a whazz, I don't need it, Cleo!'

'Fine, Sam. I didn't mean to say what I said, but it was a really great—'

'I know, I bloody know! A really great sodding opportunity for Coast.'

'Then don't do the work! You're right, you have a normal job. I'll sort out the plastering.'

'Yeah, great, Cleo. So I'll be breaking my back digging footings next week so you can pay my wages straight back out on someone else to do what I can do with my eyes closed, who'll cost more than I'm earning, who won't do as neat a job and who you'll feed up with sticky buns and posh coffees all week. Fucking brilliant.'

Cleo knocked back her coffee. Her throat burned. 'Fine. *I'll* pay them. I have some savings of my own, you know, I'll sort it myself.' *Balls*. Most of those savings had just gone on several brand new outdoor dining sets.

The fridge rattled open behind them. 'Morning.'

'Morning, Eves.'

Sam sat in silence. *That's it, Sam. Give her the silent treatment over a little squiggle on her wrist. Very grown up.* Cleo bit down on her triangle of toast.

Sam did a double-take at Evie's outfit. Cleo followed suit.

Evie hated that top. And those cut-offs, neither riding low over her hips or high along her thighs. They were just cute denim shorts, the sort wholesome young girls wore to jump off jetties into freshwater creeks with their articulate friends on those American shows about sassy kids coming of age. The sort of kids who called their mothers ma'am and never swore or self-harmed or had tattoos.

'Is there any low-fat Greek yoghurt left, Mum?'

'No, I bought normal by mistake.' A complete lie. Cleo had perused the shelves in the supermarket, eyed up the low-fat version Evie had specifically requested, looked into the future and beheld gaunt, bony protrusions where her daughter's sunkissed shoulders once were.

'I'll take it anyway.'

Cleo delighted inwardly. 'What are you up to today, honey?'

Sam shook his paper again. 'Nothing outside of this house, madam.'

Evie sat at the island chopping a banana into a bowl. 'I thought I might sort through my wardrobe. Get rid of a few things, take them to the charity place. The one sending them off to the refugee camps.'

Sam's eyebrows arched. 'Do refugees need ripped jeans and bomber jackets?'

'I think that's a great idea, Eves. I can help you later, if you like?' Evie was wearing clothes Cleo had bought for her; if there was a window of opportunity to swap some of that street-style stuff Evie liked so much for a few more cotton tops and cut-offs, this post-tattoo climbdown was probably her best chance.

Evie smiled at her bowl of yoghurt. She hadn't pouffed up all that lovely glossy hair. She was wearing it in a simple ponytail. And her make-up was very subtle, Cleo had just realised. She hadn't gone crazy with eyebrow pencil. There was a soft pink where she'd used blusher, and she'd given her eyelashes a little help with a light sweep of mascara, but she looked beautiful this morning. Natural. Like little Evie again.

'I know you'll say no, but I just thought I'd let you know in case you think I should. Elodie asked on Friday if I want to meet at hers later, she's got these really great GCSE maths and English study guides and I said I'd ask you guys.'

'You're grounded.'

'Sam, Elodie's on for straight As! It's study!'

'*Study*? She'll come home with her bloody nose pierced!'

'This is Elodie Inman-Holt we're talking about. You know? Goes to orchestra school on weekends, mother has her future as a media-darling all mapped out – the girl who beat her disability to become a classical pianist. I don't think nose rings are on the cards.' Not unless Elodie could play a tune on one.

Sam turned in his chair, glowering at Evie. 'Studying?'

'Yes.'

'At Elodie's house?'

284

'Yes.'

Sam stood and huffed. 'Don't look at me like that, Cleo. Evie's broken my trust. You wanted tough love, this is it.'

Yes she did. She also wanted two As in English and Maths. 'Mr Hildred thinks Evie might benefit from teaming up with Elodie.'

'Fine. But I want to know Juliette's aware of this and I also want you home by six p.m., latest. Understood?' Evie looked at Cleo. Cleo nodded. It was the best she was going to get for today.

'What do you mean, know Juliette's aware?'

'You're going to call her and check it's okay for Evie to spend the afternoon over there.'

Cleo set her mug down. 'I've got to phone Juliette? And do the mumsy thing? After she masterminded that farcical boycott?'

'Only if you want Evie studying with her daughter. Because if Juliette doesn't confirm, Evie's not going.' Sam planted a kiss on Cleo's head, then one on Evie's, before picking up the last of the toast and walking into the lounge.

Was he for real? Ring Juliette to ask if it was alright to deposit their feral little girl at her super-home in hopes of gleaning some of Elodie's academia?

'You aren't going to call Elodie's mum, are you, Mum? Please don't. It's embarrassing. I just won't go. I can meet Elodie in school or something instead.'

'Oh, Evie, calm down.' Cleo leant forwards, peeking through to the living room. Sam was halfway up the stairs already. 'Of course I'm not going to call that bloody woman. I can't stand talking to her, you know that.'

'I can go though? Later on today?'

'Yes, Evie. You can go. But two things. One, don't tell your father I didn't ring that sodding woman. And two, cover up that bloody tattoo before you set one feral foot on Inman-Holt territory.'

49

'Goodness, you really can see all the way out to sea, can't you, darling? And I've never needed to wear sunglasses in a kitchen before. All this vitamin D!'

Max pressed his nose and mouth against the soaring glass panes separating the sleek open-plan interior from the real world outside.

'Really? All this glass? Think of the Windolene, Mum.'

Sarah's mother tutted and marvelled at the glass she would detest having to clean herself. Housewives didn't clean these sorts of windows, though. They employed other housewives to do it for them. Other housewives who needed the money more than they did, who lived in houses with normal-sized windows, like Sarah's home on Milling Street.

'Er, Max, I don't think the estate agents will appreciate your sucker-fish marks, young man,' said Sarah's mother. Max banged on the glass at Will and blew out his cheeks one last time. Will looked up from an artistically placed boulder outside, pulled a headphone out and gave Max a thumbs-up.

'Max, you're leaving marks all over the windows,' snipped Sarah. She sounded irritable. She was spoiling it.

Max's blonde head swooshed around. 'But I thought this was our house now, Mummy?'

'It is!' cheered Sarah's mother. 'They just have a few finishing touches and then you'll be boxing up and moving in.'

'The sale hasn't gone through,' sighed Sarah for the umpteenth time. 'Max, the builders are still using this one as the flagship, the one they show to the other families who are thinking about buying one of the other four.'

'Why?'

'Because this is the best one, Maxy, my boy!' Jon appeared behind Sarah. He squeezed the back of her neck and pecked her head.

'No more sucker-fishing, okay, kiddo?' said Sarah.

'He's fine, Sar, let him enjoy it. It's only a few face prints. Come on, fish face, let's go see that *massive* bedroom of yours again!'

'Yeah!' yelled Max.

Jon hoisted him up on to his shoulders and galloped across the great expanse of kitchen. Sarah watched her mother's eyes follow them, bright with the same reverence she used to reserve for Tim Henman walking out on to court one, or Barry Manilow in concert.

'Mum, I'm just going to find a cloth to clean the glass.'

'Oh, blow the glass, enjoy the view! Look at this wonderful house! Look at this lifestyle you're all going to have!' Her mother set her hand over her chest as if she were about to pledge allegiance to the Corian worktops.

Sarah looked past Max's face prints at the half-finished landscaping outside. The lawns of their monolithic soon-to-be new home graduated to the natural grasses and wildflowers reaching down towards the coastline. Will and his boulder were sat somewhere between the two, neither belonging to the manicured borders nor the rough scrub.

Will laughed heartily at his phone then turned its screen to face the open ocean.

'Darling, why is William waving his phone at the sea?'

'He's Facetiming.'

'Oh. What's Facetiming?'

It had already occurred to Sarah that if Will was exchanging nude photographs, he might be exchanging live footage as well. It had grown like an aneurysm in her brain since leaving Isobel's last night. The implications that Will's teenage behaviour could have on the rest of his life had robbed her of a night's sleep.

'It's like a video call.' That much she knew. Who was he Facetiming? Not a clue.

She watched him through the glass, the angles of his face softening with laughter. His casual skater-park style. He didn't *look* gay. Or did he? Patrick hadn't looked like a man who'd forget his children. Was there even a *look*? All of the boys in Fallenbay seemed to go for either the preppy style or the board-bum thing. Will definitely belonged to the latter tribe, which wasn't to say there weren't any gay surfing or skating kids in Fallenbay, just that Sarah didn't fancy her chances picking one out of a line-up.

But why hasn't he brought any girls home? Wouldn't he have brought at least one home by now? Was Will holding back? *What* was he holding back? Was it her fault?

'I let it change him.'

'What's that, darling?'

Sarah inhaled some of the crisp, clean, cutting-edge air-con Jon had selected from the optional extras. 'Patrick leaving.'

She'd made him grow up too fast. She must've put him off healthy relationships with girls. Thanks to her Will had only ever seen how gut-wrenchingly painful the whole husband and wife thing could turn out. She'd tried her best to keep their family nest a soft, warm place, hadn't ranted about Patrick, hadn't pointed out his failings on those occasions Will had shouted through angry tears, *I wish you'd have gone and Dad had stayed!* She'd tried her best. And still Will had hardened.

'Of course it changed him, darling. It changed you all. But the second I saw you get off that plane I had a feeling you were all going to be better off without him. And I was right. Eventually.'

'You thought that?'

'I did. You are stronger than you think, darling.'

'I don't think Dad shares your confidence.'

'Well, your father doesn't know as much as he suspects.'

'He thinks Will needs more discipline.'

'Do *you* think Will needs more discipline?'

That was a toughie. Cannabis in his pockets, explicit photographs of teenage boys on his phone. Was discipline the issue? She'd had bags of discipline and had grown into an adult who kept secrets just like Will. Pills in the bathroom cupboard, question marks over what she was and was not comfortable with in the bedroom.

'Maybe.' Maybe Will did need more boundaries.

Sarah's mum set an arm around her shoulders. 'Oh, Sarah, Will's absolutely fine. He's just a teenager. A smashing one.'

'How can you and Dad be so different?'

'Opposites attract? Who knows.'

'That's what Cleo says.'

'Oh! How is Cleo, I wouldn't mind her cookie recipe if you could ask? Sorry, darling, I forgot your rotten luck with that nut. Have they still got you on the antibiotics?'

'Yes, still on antibiotics.'

'Aha. No wonder you're out of sorts. Those things play havoc with your system. So tell me, what does Cleo think of this place?'

She wasn't out of sorts. 'Cleo's too busy to be dragged up here to—'

'Cleo would *love* this! Drag her up. You should be showing off.'

'She has enough on, Mum. Cle's been having a few wobbles at home.'

'Children and husbands, by any chance? Believe it or not, darling, deep down we all have the same boring old problems. I wobbled about your father plenty of times. Wobbly marriages are not a new phenomenon.'

'Didn't you ever wonder whether you might have been better off without him?'

'Absolutely not.'

'I've never seen him make you a cup of tea, Mum. Not even once.'

'I know he's far from perfect, darling, but the world's changed since you were a baby. Children need a father, and yours was the only one I had lined up for you. I didn't have a Jon to step into the breach.'

'You say that like Jon was a magic wand.'

'Wasn't he?'

It was exactly what he had been. But now, Sarah didn't know. She couldn't think clearly past the imbalance of one son running around his new bedroom with his new father and the other sitting outside alone on a rock with his phone full of secrets. And it wasn't just the boys. Or the bossy sex. Something else. Or was she just looking for an excuse?

'I'm simply saying . . . families were like loaves of bread back then.'

'Wholesome?'

'No, *uniform*. Geometric. Fewer surprises. Families are made up like tins of Quality Street nowadays, all shapes and flavours.'

'And what if you were raising a child today? In the Quality Street era. Would going it alone be so terrible?'

'With a child? Darling, who on earth would *ever* voluntarily choose that?'

50

Isobel was pegging out the last of the washing on the clothes-line Arthur had fashioned for her at the front of the cottage. He'd spent half an hour tying a length of cord between the downspout of the cottage and the bough of the nearest tree. 'I'm pretty nifty with knots, Arthur, I used to be in the Brownies,' she'd tried, but the more Arthur's gnarled fingers had hampered him, the more determined he'd become to defy his arthritis.

He was using some miracle herbal remedy now; the aching had been unbearable before. Having all this woodland in which to walk Petal was a godsend for him, he'd said. Saved having to manhandle a dog lead with weak, useless hands.

Arthur and Petal had been gone for about ten minutes. Isobel had kept one eye on the woods as soon as they'd trotted off. She jammed the last peg into place and caught a pleasant whiff of flowers. Last night's indulgence with the bath bombs. She'd felt lighter, unburdened, sinking into a slippery, soapy bath after Sarah left.

Movement caught her attention. A red form appeared intermittently through the woods. She set Arthur's peg basket down on the step. The car crawling up the lane honked loudly.

A wild-haired little girl strapped into the back seat frantically waved her arm from the window.

'Aunty Isobelly-button! We've come to see you!'

Ella?

The car swung into the yard. Isobel's brain was struggling to slot her five-year-old niece into Arthur's smallholding. Sophie shut off the engine and hopped out, smoothing the creases from her skinny grey trousers. 'Holey moley, could you have found anywhere more off the beaten track, Is?' Sophie pushed her aviators back through dark bundled-back hair and gave Isobel a *well of course we've come to find you, stupid* look.

She was here! She'd actually come! Isobel launched at her. 'Whoa, go easy, Is. My favourite act was kicked off *Britain's Got Talent* last night, I can't handle much more emotion.' But Sophie was already squeezing back into her.

'I wish you hadn't brought Ella here, Soph,' Isobel whispered. They had things to discuss. Ugly things.

'I know. We kind of come as a pair, though.'

Isobel felt the tears about to rush her. Ella was watching over her mum's shoulder. Poor kid had seen enough of Isobel's tears. No more. 'It's so good to see you. And it's so good to see you too, scrumptious girl!'

'I like your hair yellow, Aunty Isobel.'

'Do I look like Worzel Gummidge?'

'I don't know Worzo Glummidge, Aunty Isobel. I think you look . . . like a mermaid.'

'A mermaid!' Isobel exclaimed. 'Thanks, gorgeous. Now, what are you doing here? You've come all this way!'

'Mummy was sad she missed your birthday. So we're taking

you to the beach but we can't tell Grandad because Mummy stole his car.'

'Borrowed.' Sophie grimaced. 'I told him I was popping out to take Ella clothes shopping. My old banger was never going to get us this far.'

Isobel shared an eskimo kiss with Ella. 'Then we'd better not tell Grandad, had we, Ells-bells?'

'Can we go to the beach, Aunty Isobel?' The beach was as good a place as any. Ella could play while her mum and aunt straightened a few things out.

'That, Ells-Bells, is a blooming brilliant idea.'

51

The tide was coming in.

'Not too close to the water, baby.' Sophie smiled for her daughter before her mouth set to a firm line again. She had always worn her feelings on her face. She was gearing herself up, Isobel knew that look. For now, though, while Soph got her thoughts in order, Isobel would enjoy watching her niece, oblivious to the catastrophe brewing around her.

Ella set down her bucket and spade and dipped her bottom in the well of sea water the tide had just left for her. 'It's cold, Mummy!' she squealed, but she was already trying to find the courage to dip herself again.

Isobel studied Sophie's expression. 'She should get it over with, like ripping off a plaster. Jump straight in and cope with the cold afterwards.'

Sophie remained fixed on Ella from behind her sunglasses.

Go on, Sophie, just rip off the plaster.

The breeze picked up. The smell of barbecue coals began morphing into a sweeter, meatier aroma of things on skewers. Then more mixed scents, charcoal briquettes and sun cream. Isobel took a great lungful of air. 'Smells like the old summers, Soph.'

Sophie didn't answer.

'Can't beat a good caravan holiday,' she tried. Another pause.

'It's nice here, Isobel. '

Isobel gave the surf school instructors a fleeting glance. One was giving a demonstration of hand signals to a fresh class of life-jacketed youngsters. 'This beach is literally littered with surfer hunks and you haven't clocked a single one yet, Soph. Are you going to tell me why you drove all this way instead of just answering my texts?'

She was trying to help Sophie with the edge of a plaster Soph still wasn't ready to pull.

Sophie gritted her teeth and gazed back up the beach. Hobo Bob had been sitting on one of the benches watching the beachgoers when they'd walked down. Isobel had wanted to take Ella further up the beach, but it was even busier towards The Village, too many ears.

Sophie took off her glasses and pinched the bridge of her nose '*Jesus,* this is hard. I'm not even sure—'

'Hello Isobel.' Daniel arrived on the sand beside them. He had a large sun hat on and a smudge of sun cream on his glasses.

'Oh, hello, Daniel.' Isobel's heart was thumping. She needed to hurry Daniel along before Sophie lost her bottle. 'Not joining in surf class today, Daniel?'

'No, I'm helping to make lunch. We're having barbecue chicken.'

Isobel bit her lip and nodded. 'You're making me hungry, Daniel. Don't let it get cold.'

'It's not ready yet, Isobel. Who is this lady?'

Too late. Sophie had put her glasses back on. The shields

were up. 'This is Sophie, my sister. Soph, this is Daniel. Daniel lives next door to Curlew Cottage.'

'Hi, Daniel. Nice to meet you.'

'Hello, Sophie. You look like Isobel but you have different colour hair.'

'I do, you're right,' smiled Sophie. 'Nice Bermuda shorts, buster.'

'My brother gave them to me. They make me look rad.'

'They definitely do,' agreed Isobel.

'Ella?' Sophie glanced around her and clamped a hand visor-like over her eyes. 'Isobel, where is she? Ella! She was right there!'

Isobel's throat tightened. She scanned the shore but Sophie was blocking her view. Hobo Bob hadn't moved from his bench. 'Ella? Ella! There, Sophie!'

Ella looked tiny along the waterline. She was dipping her bucket into the sea, hair falling almost to the floor around her. The tide rushed away again and Ella's balance was tricked.

'Oh my God, her face is in it!' Sophie bolted for the water. Another wave rolled Ella backwards, pulling her further out. Not very deep, unless you were a little girl.

Neither Sophie nor Isobel, following heavy-footed in the sand, reached Ella first. It was the kid skipping over the shallows ahead of them. Ella wasn't in the water any more, he'd already scooped her out, wretching and spluttering. Sophie reached to take her from the surfer's arms and began slapping at Ella's back with jarring, panicked strikes. 'You could've drowned!'

Milo hung back. 'The salt water makes it worse, she

probably hasn't swallowed much, but it kinda burns when it comes back out.'

'Ella, what did I say?' The panic sat high in Sophie's voice. Ella was trying to cry and choke at the same time.

Isobel's lungs were burning too. 'Milo . . . thanks so much. We didn't see her . . .'

Milo was already backing away. 'No worries. I'd better go grab my board.'

'Is she okay?' asked Isobel.

'You shouldn't have gone near the water like that, Ella, you didn't listen, Mummy is very cross with you.'

Ella huddled into her mum, distraught.

'It's okay, Ella. By *cross,* Mummy means scared to death.' Isobel rubbed Ella's cold, wet back. 'I think your mum's forgetting how much *she* forgot to listen to Nanny and Grandad when she was a little girl like you. Aren't you, Soph?'

'Yes, well. Take it from me, Ella, life is a lot easier if you just listen to what Mummy says, okay?'

'Are you alright now, Ells-Bells?' Ella nodded sheepishly. 'Come on then, let's go get a drink, take some of the salty water taste away, shall we? Maybe Daniel will sell us a few from the surf school fridge.'

Daniel had already walked back to the Blue Fin workshop. Some of the kids were in wheelchairs, others sat on the benches, legs withered by the conditions they'd been born with. Isobel led Sophie and Ella up the beach towards them.

'I didn't realise you could go surfing with...'

'Cerebral palsy? Soph, these kids put us to shame. They have all these custom-made boards and things, so the instructors can go out with them.'

'That boy is wandering off again. Do you think we should tell someone?'

'Daniel? He works here, Soph.'

'The boy with Down's? So he's not one of the visitors?'

'No, he helps his brother. Ben's the one in the shades and baseball cap.'

This side of the surf shack, Ben was guarding the barbecue from Daniel and anyone else with seagull-like tendencies. Dan was pointing to Isobel, Sophie and Ella traipsing up the beach. Ben waved a set of barbecue tongs over his head.

They would be there in a minute. And the opportunity would be lost completely. Isobel put her hand on Soph's arm to slow her.

'Why have you come here, Sophie?' She pulled her glasses away from her face so Sophie could see her properly. 'If there's something you need to say to me, say it. Then we can deal with it.' She'd as good as ripped that plaster half off already.

Sophie set Ella on the sand. 'Go on, baby. Pick up your spade, then we're getting our shoes and things on.' Ella ran to an abandoned moat in the sand. 'I've come to talk you into coming home with us.'

'Why? Why today?' Why not yesterday when it was her birthday? The perfect excuse to turn up.

'No reason.'

Ben cupped a hand to his mouth and called down the beach to them, 'Emergency at the Blue Fin Surf Academy, we have too much food, repeat, too much food. Three hungry mouths required for emergency assistance, thank you.'

Sophie was holding back. Isobel couldn't do all the nudging; Sophie had to cross some of the distance.

'Well I need a reason, Sophie. Because I'm not ready to go back to being a non-person again.'

'You're not a non-person.'

'Not here.'

'What, so you're having a holiday romance with this place now?'

'No. But I do like it.'

'You're not here to like it, Isobel. What are you doing?'

'What am *I* doing? Why are *you* here, Sophie? Spit it out!' Sophie's face changed.

Isobel clicked. *You idiot.* She'd gotten ahead of herself. Sophie was here because there'd been a development. Sophie looked away. 'Come on now, Ella. Let's find something to eat.'

The hairs on Isobel's arms stood. 'He bit, didn't he? He took the bait. When? Last night? It was, wasn't it? That's why you wouldn't answer my calls.'

'I wanted to tell you in person. Check you're okay.' They were never supposed to get this far. It became suddenly apparent that Isobel had never really thought they would.

'I'm fine. This was the plan, wasn't it? Are you sure it's him?' She was having an adrenalin rush. *Fight or flight . . .*

'It's him. He hasn't even changed his username, Isobel. The guy's a moron.'

He was a moron. He of all people should know how far into trouble a person's name could carry them. Even a concocted name like DEEP_DRILLERZ.

Right. They were really going to do this then. 'What did he say? Where did he write it? On one of the video sites? How did you spot him?'

'I didn't. There was a notification in my emails.'

'From one of the revenge websites? But the film's already up on those sites. You're not the author, why would you get any sort of alert email?' Sophie watched it dawn on Isobel. 'The notification was from one of our own social media accounts? He's already followed the trail.'

'He's sent messages to both the accounts I set up for you. Facebook *and* Twitter.'

'Saying what?' A new chill ran through her. She imagined his words, typed out onscreen for everyone to see beside the photos Sophie had put on the fake Isobel Hedley pages, of mojito-sipping-Isobel, chalet-girl-Isobel, beach-babe-Isobel.

'Isobel, listen to me for a second. I read something last night, about vigilantism going wrong and—'

'We're not vigilantes, Sophie. We're not even Velma and Daphne on *Scooby Doo*.'

'We don't know what we're poking around in here, Isobel!'

'And?' Isobel jabbed a thumb at herself. 'I was poked first.' Sophie didn't get to choose when enough was enough.

'Isobel, this isn't a schoolyard spat.'

'No, but if it was, if Ella was being picked on by some little monster, bullied, teased, squashed under their heel, what would you tell her? To take it? Would you *bollocks*, Sophie.'

'Ella wouldn't have to stand up to them. I'd go and have the little shit's mother and do to her what her kid was doing to Ella until it stopped.'

'Well I can't do that, Soph! I'm fighting blind here! Waiting for people who've punched me in the dark to crawl out of the shadows so I can have one shitty shot at standing up to them.'

'Them?'

Isobel gritted her teeth. '*Him*.' She shook her head. Sophie wouldn't get it, until she got it. 'Everything about me was attacked. As long as my attacker gets to be anonymous, I don't get to be anything but the idiot left out for the crows. I'm not coming home until something changes, Sophie. Now, what did he say?'

Sophie looked up to the sky and exhaled. '*Hello stranger*.'

'*Hello stranger*? That's it?' *Hello* like they were pals? 'What did you say?' Isobel's heart was thumping in her ribs.

'Nothing. I ignored him.'

'Why? We have to get him to comment on the blog, don't we? Or we won't see his IP address?'

'I ignored him for two reasons, Is. First, I was hoping you'd agree to forget the whole thing. Second, we know the sort of guy he is. He wreaked havoc before, he knows he did. All the responses he got from the kids and parents on your school's Twitter feed, the people who tried defending you on their Facebook pages, all rising to it, arguing with him before finally blocking him . . . he's your typical troll. A narcissistic loser who craves attention. What's the worst thing that could happen to him when he's sending his little messages, leaving his bile everywhere? What's the last thing that dickhead wants?'

'Other than being caught?'

'Yes. What's the last thing he wants, besides being caught?'

'To be ignored?'

'Exactly.'

'So you think he'll try again?'

Sophie was watching Ella like a hawk. 'I think he'll step it up, Isobel. Make himself louder until he feels heard. By you.'

52

Cleo knocked again. 'Harry?' He probably had his head-phones in. She pushed open the door to his bedroom. 'What's all this behind the door? Are you barricading your sister out?' Harry sat up at the head of his bed and wrapped two lean, muscled arms around his knees. 'I'm just going to fetch her from Lady Muck's. Fancy a run out in the car? Get some fresh air?' There was an intercom at Juliette's. She was going to get Harry to press the buzzer and politely ask for entry into Inman-Holt territory. Sod it. It would be on the driver's side, wouldn't it?

Harry's head lolled back against his headboard. 'I've got some revision to do.'

'Why don't you open your blinds, son? It's still sunny outside and you're all cooped up. Are you still feeling a bit off? Maybe you could do with a run to the doctor's? You haven't been yourself since last week.'

'I'm fine. Just need to get this done.' Cleo moved further into his room. She started gathering whites from the laundry bin Harry had propped behind his door for some unhelpful reason. Harry hauled himself off his bed and hovered in front of her.

'I can show myself out thanks, son!' Cleo laughed. 'Let

me just grab a full load for the washer. Harry, why are you hovering, you're like a big bloody moth, what's the matter?'

'Nothing. I just need to get started on my science.'

'I'm going, I'm going.' She did a last scan of his room. 'Any more whites, H? School shirts? Tennis socks?'

Harry's room was fairly orderly as usual. Trophies neatly on display, books stacked, guitars placed lovingly on their stands. 'Harry, have you had a change-around? It looks *sparser* in here for some—'

'Mum, I have to study!' He looked sweaty and pallid again. He pushed the door.

Cleo planted a foot in front of it. 'Harry, where is your TV? Where's your bloody Xbox?'

'Mum, they're . . . one of the lads at school said he'd have a look at them for me.'

'What for?'

'The volume's broken.'

'You only had them at Christmas!'

'I know, I . . . His did the same thing. It's really common. He said he knows what to do.'

'So why didn't you ask him to come over here and do it? Instead of sending hundreds of pounds' worth of gear to a mate's house. Which friend?'

'A friend!'

'Harry! There's no need to shout. What if he gives them to one of *his* friends, huh? Get them back before your father finds out.'

'Okay, I will! *Jesus Christ*, would you just stop moaning all the fucking time!'

Cleo's hand moved quite of its own accord. She'd never

slapped a person in her life. Never even tapped the twins' bottoms.

Harry stood frozen before her. Pale-faced, mouth firm.

'Don't you ever speak to me like that again.' There was a tremble in her voice. Harry had seen videos of his father flooring boxers built like rhinos, the sudden impact of a knockout blow. But never, ever had Harry heard his father use words the same way. It wasn't their way. She looked at him in the doorway, suddenly a stranger, all six foot of him. She moved her foot and left in silence with her bundle of whites.

Cleo made it halfway downstairs before Harry closed his door softly behind her.

53

'No. Now pick one, please. How about . . .' Sarah ran a finger along Max's bookshelf. '*Oh, The Places You'll Go!*'

'No.'

'But it's Doctor Seuss. We love Doctor Seuss.'

'Godzilla.'

'You're not watching Godzilla now, it's bedtime. You have school tomorrow. Now choose before Mummy does. How about *Revolting Rhymes & Dirty Beasts?*'

'Godzilla.'

'Right, that's it. No bedtime story.'

It was obvious, really. Max had been creeping towards this since Sarah had run his bath. The Sunday night build-up. She could've diverted, taken another route. Instead she was making up for not knowing how to speak openly with Will by clamping down on Max.

Max kicked his cowboy and cactus duvet off in protest. Sarah felt her patience begin to fray.

'You seem to think you're the only one who doesn't like Monday mornings, Max. Well you're not. So you'll just have to get on with it like everyone else.'

'I want to watch *Godzilla*!' roared Max. Five minutes ago she'd had her hairdryer on him and they'd pretended to be superheroes, swooshing through the wind. Now he was ramping himself up into one of those screaming frenzies that left him sweaty and damp-headed again.

'Whoa, what's all this?'

Max didn't give Jon a second look. He began thrashing his legs against his mattress. Sarah took a deep breath.

Jon came in off the landing, that post-run alertness about him even though he hadn't been running, he'd been window-cleaning. 'Hey, chief. There's no need for all that, what are we after?'

Sarah gave Jon the *Godzilla, obviously* look. 'I didn't hear you come back in. You've been gone ages. Max, stop that right now. The neighbours will complain.' They were huge windows in fairness, but she'd told him just to clean the bits Max's nostrils had reached, not the whole west facade.

'I had to drive back into town. It was like an initiation task finding somewhere to buy cleaning spray and cloths on a Sunday night.'

'I did say there was nothing at the house. I left the glass spray on the side for you downstairs.'

He thought she was fussing – *So what if it's the show home, Sarah? Who notices what's below eye-level?* – but the housing company had been good enough to leave the keys with them all weekend after Sarah had rain-checked yesterday's look around with the kids to go interrupt a boycott at Cleo's instead. They weren't supposed to leave show home keys with clients overnight. Jon must've gone in and turned the charm on the salesgirls. The least they could do in return was clean up after themselves.

Jon edged into Max's room and kissed Sarah's cheek. 'I

know, walked straight out without it. Trying to get there and back too quickly.'

'Max, I mean it. If you don't stop those silly moaning noises, I'm not going to make a snail garden with you after school tomorrow.'

Max's pursuit of a pet hadn't lessened any since Mrs Upton had laid down the gauntlet for Hornbeam's next mascot. There was an old plastic fish tank in the summerhouse, she'd spotted it while she and Jon had been having frenzied sex in there. While Jon had been whispering a trail of authoritarian obscenities in her ear, Sarah had preoccupied herself thinking up humane solutions for the tribe of snails ruining the hostas her mum had potted by the trampoline.

Jon perched on Max's bed. Max scrambled into his lap.

'That's a good lad, no more tears, okay?'

'I think Max would prefer it if you put him to sleep.'

'Sure, are you okay?' Jon had only been an apprentice for four years and already he was doing a better job of parenting than she was.

'Yep, I might just jump in the shower.'

Sarah got up, pecked Max goodnight and left his room. Will wasn't home, of course. No point going to say hi to him then. She crossed the landing to her room and kicked her slippers rattily over the bed. She didn't want a shower, she wanted a soak. To put her face under water and stay there until her lungs gave up and forced her back to the surface. She grabbed a couple of towels from the dresser on the landing then strode down the hallway into the bathroom. Her phone buzzed in her jeans as she kicked them off on to the bathroom tiles.

HORNBEAM TEXT SERVICE

Mary would be thrilled, having to send out text messages in the middle of her weekly instalment of *Countryfile*.

Due to the anticipated weather system expected to hit Fallenbay coastline around June 3rd, Mr Pethers has taken the decision to bring forward this year's Summer Fair by THREE WEEKS to the next available Saturday in school diary. We understand this is quite the change, however on further discussion, Mr Pethers and the PFA have agreed our marquees will be no match for the tail end of Hurricane Louis and his rampage across the Atlantic.

We hope to see as many friends of Hornbeam pull together, and look forward to seeing you all

THIS SATURDAY!

Parents and Friends, we can do it!

Sarah rattled off a quick text to Cleo.

School Fair changed to this wkend? Did they check this with anyone first? Do you need help getting cupcakes ready in time?

Cleo responded before Sarah could put her phone down.

Er, have you forgotten? Persona non grater over here. Juliette's ousted me for hippy-dippy Lorna and her tofu tuck :(

Sarah smiled.

Persona non grater? Culinary equivalent to someone Juliette's blacklisted?

Grater, grata . . . let's call the whole thing off. Tell me you're not going? I've just had to collect Evie from outside their palace gates. Juliette's obviously shown her the highlife. Evie didn't stop grinning all the way home. I'm not even going to ask her what they got up to in there.

Evie at Juliette's house? Strange?! Have to go to fair :(Am manning drench-a-wench stall. Max will be gutted if we don't go, they're announcing the pet mascot.

You don't have a pet.

No. Maybe he could take Jon, almost has him rolling over for treats. At least one of us appeals!

Who don't you appeal to? Max or Jon?

Max. Is it a loser thing to say it feels like I'm being out-parented? I even forgot the tooth fairy yesterday morning, was having a meltdown because Max was awake early again, but no need! Jon had already sorted it!!! Do blokes remember tooth fairies?

Sarah's phone rang.

'My thumb can't move as quickly as these techno-teens', it's quicker if we just speak. Why on earth do you feel out-parented? You're an excellent mum. Even if you did forget the tooth fairy. Which, by the way, you'll probably burn in hell for.'

Sarah swished away Max's bath toys and pulled the plug.

'I'm being stupid. Ignore me.'

'Please tell me mine isn't the only dysfunctional family in Fallenbay, Sarah, it would really make my day. Evie's come back from the Inman-Holts' like she's been to a bloody health spa. She's glowing. I keep catching her grinning. Even her bloody skin looks happy.'

'Since when did Evie hang out with Elodie?'

'Since your Jon suggested they study together, God love him. Between you and me, Sar, I'm a little bit thrilled. Evie really needs to knuckle down and get through these GCSEs. I think she might be turning a corner. She hasn't said anything all weekend about those horrible little oiks bothering her on Facebook either.'

'That's great, Cle.'

'Yep. Between her pastoral sessions at school and study sessions with Elodie the brainiac, I'm hoping to have a well-rounded, well-educated, well-eyebrowed daughter by the summer hols. Anyway, Evie's had enough airplay lately. Back to your dysfunctional lot. What's up?'

Will's GCSEs had slipped off Sarah's radar. Right now all

she was hoping for by the summer holidays was a son who felt he could confide in her and wasn't doing Class B drugs. She slopped a glug of her best bath creme under the tap and began running a new bath. She let out a long groan. 'Nothing, it's just . . . Will's drifting away from the rest of us, and Max, I try not to overindulge him because he's the baby and it's too easy to, and then he just seems to save all his frustration for when I'm at home, while the sun shines perpetually out of Jon's and Will's arses.'

All that worrying that Max might never know a male role model outside his miserable grandfather and here she was, complaining he had two!

'Sar, that's what kids do! Play parents off! Evie's always creeping around Sam, causes no end of aggro. Is everything okay with you and Jon? I'm not suggesting it means anything daft, but you still haven't looked through those bridal mags I've saved for you.'

Sarah lined up Max's plastic reptiles along the bath's edge. She flicked them into the water one by one. Jon was supportive. Made her feel attractive. Sexy, even. Women all over Fallenbay would jump at the chance to have him whisper into their ear some of the things he'd whispered into hers yesterday in the summerhouse. Jon was a keeper, her mum kept telling her. Sarah could hear him down the hall, right now, reading *The Three Billy Goats Gruff* with actions and excellent voices.

'Everything's fine.'

'Well there you go! Be glad you're not living with Sam. He's hardly speaking to me because of that bloody stunt Evie pulled, and Harry . . .'

'What's up with Harry?'

'Oh, nothing really. I think Ingred dumping him has really knocked him for six. I hear his phone bleep and he looks like he's going to keel over. He has this constant ill look about him. She's obviously still texting him, dragging out his suffering. Cow.'

'Sorry, Cleo. I know you've got your own hassles at the moment.'

'Don't be daft. Look, Max is going to sound off at you, you're his mum. That's what we're here for. To be picked on. So what's happening with Will?'

Sarah opened the loo roll cupboard and felt around for the plastic boat.

'Not a clue. He's never in. When he is he hardly talks.'

'Harry's never *out*! Unless he's earning money at Coast. Which he's absolutely preoccupied with right now. I'm trying not to obsess over an article I read about online gambling. All these betting apps and smartphones, you never know, do you? It's just buttons and numbers. They're just kids! They don't realise the difference between hunting Pokemon and playing roulette.'

Maybe that's where Will disappeared every Saturday. To hunt Pokemon. With *Edward*. 'Please don't give me anything else to worry about, Cleo.'

'Sorry. Just be glad Will's getting his dose of fresh air, that's all I'm saying. How does he look when he's leaving the house?'

'What do you mean?' She popped the pill marked *Sunday* from its pocket and returned the last one to the boat. Pill-free week next week. She could give her conscience a break.

'Does he dress snappy? Shower first? How does he smell?' asked Cleo.

'Um, just, normal clothes, clean . . . aftershave.'

'Oh, Sarah. I have a handful of O-levels. You have a teaching degree. Sharpen up, gorgeous, it's obvious! Will's got a girl! Just pray she's lower maintenance than bloody Ingred. Or our Evie. God help the boy who gets tangled up with her.'

Getting tangled up with Evie would be an easier ride for Will than navigating the choppy waters of homosexuality. If those were the waters he'd found himself in. Snappily dressed and bathed in aftershave. Actually, she didn't even care what waters Will preferred, so long as he didn't drown in them.

'I think you should be glad Evie's headstrong, Cleo. Less chance of her growing up to be someone easily taken advantage of.'

Jon popped his head around the bathroom door. Sarah gobbled her pill, lobbing the toy boat into the bath.

Jon closed the door behind him. She'd been too quick to kick off her jeans. 'I have to shoot, Cle. I'll call you tomorrow.' He moved behind her and rested his arm across her stomach. Sarah patted it amicably, hoping it would be enough. He pressed himself against her.

'Okay, darl'. Ooh, and Sar? Just go straight in for the kill.'

'What do you mean?'

'To redress the popularity balance. Max is five years old, just go buy him something brilliant. Be his favourite parent again. And make sure you lunch in the staff room so you don't miss anything!'

Jon slipped his hand inside Sarah's shirt, his fingers expertly finding their way inside her bra.

'Miss what?' asked Sarah.

'The PFA disciples panicking about the Summer fair rejig! Next weekend – ha!'

Jon was kissing her neck now. One hand holding down her collar while the other fondled on inside her bra.

'Bye, Cleo.'

'Bye!'

Jon spoke at the back of her neck. 'Can I take advantage of you?'

The chance of submerging her face in peace slipped away. 'Hmm?'

'You were saying, just now, about taking advantage?'

'Oh, yes. Evie.'

'What about her?'

Jon nipped at Sarah's ear. 'I was just saying, she's head-strong.' It felt less than comfortable talking about your friend's child while being cupped from behind. She lunged for the cold tap. Her body pulled free of his hand.

'Evie's not *headstrong*. She's unstable.' Jon didn't usually bring work home. That's what school hours and power runs over the bluff were for, he said.

'Evie's unstable?'

He pulled her towards him by the waist. 'She's troubled, Sarah. I've seen it before. Kids like Evie lose their way.'

'*Evie?* She didn't sound lost just now, I could hear her singing.'

'Singing? Was she?' Jon laughed. There was an edge to it. And the grin . . . was he patronising her? He made a reach for her thigh. Sarah made a casual move for Max's bath toys, gathering them, and the boat, stuffing the lot into Max's toy tidy. 'What's the matter?'

'Nothing.'

'Nothing?' Even talking about work hadn't affected him. The change in his breathing still called out sex.

'I'm just . . . not really . . .'

'In the mood? What are you in a mood for?' His tone dipped.

'I'm not in *a* mood. I'm just not in *the* mood.'

It was off-putting trying to have a conversation when one of you had an obvious erection. Jon repositioned himself like a jock in a changing room. 'Fine, Sarah. Something's eating you, you don't want to share it with me, fine.'

Ah. The psychoanalyst voice. *Perfect.*

'I'm just ready for a soak. There's nothing bothering me.' *Liar, liar, pants on fire.*

'Are you sure about that?'

'Yep.'

'Is it the wedding?'

'No . . . it's not the wedding.'

'But it's *something*?'

She refolded her towel. 'Honestly, it's nothing.' She was such a rubbish liar. She used words like *honestly*, and always wanted to touch her face and do all those things Jon had learned to spot in psychobabble school.

'The house? The move?'

'No, the house is beautiful. Stunning.' And far too much just for them.

'Will, then?'

She'd rather own up to the wedding and house move freaking her out than give Will up. She shook her head and tried to look passive.

'Thought so. What's going on with Will?'

'It's not . . . it's nothing to do with Will. It's . . .'

Jon was staring straight through her. He had her blocked in the bathroom, a human lie detector in front of her and a boatload of pills behind her. Bath-time was turning into an episode of *Customs and Excise*. Jon the handsome law protector, Sarah the sweating drugs mule.

'It's clearly upsetting you. Why can't you tell me?'

Jon smelled blood in the water, she had to give him something, anything but Will. 'It's just . . . I . . . I heard a horrible thing recently. That's all.'

'A *horrible thing*?'

She felt the universe striking a mark against her for having only known a thing like this for a matter of hours before using it to her own selfish advantage, but her course was set. She would give him Isobel. The girl passing through. The girl who had come to recover from an attacker who'd managed to put her into a mental health assessment ward, who'd almost pushed her into taking an overdose, who'd almost ended her in every way without ever having come into physical contact with her.

'Yes. A really terrible thing.'

That wasn't a lie. It was terrible. It had bothered her, made her glad she'd never had a daughter of her own. Sarah felt worried for Isobel. She'd made sure first thing this morning that Cleo had Isobel's mobile number in her phone, just in case Isobel ever tried ringing either of them in an emergency.

Jon folded his arms and leant back against the bathroom wall. 'About?' There would be several richly embroidered case studies in this for him. The complexities of the human condition, the fragility of the mind, the tenacity of the heart. Poor Isobel would make for curious discussion, a discussion Sarah didn't want or even hold enough knowledge on. The poor girl had been passed around and dissected enough already. But . . . Isobel wasn't Will. Isobel would move on at some point. It wouldn't affect Isobel for Jon to know this thing privately, but Will's secrets, the boy in the photo, texts through the night, they would be forever pinned to the family corkboard once Sarah stuck them up there for Jon's professional assessment.

'Isobel.'

'Isobel, who I drove home last week?' asked Jon. 'To the cottage up past Acorn Woods? What about her?'

Sarah sat on the bath and sent an apology into the cosmos. 'There was a film . . .'

54

Juliette was like a well-dressed human searchlight, methodically scanning her row of Year 1s for hair-chewing, whispering, signs of dissent.

Mr Pethers crooned the final verse of 'Morning Has Broken' across the assembly hall. He caught Sarah's eye. She put her back into lip-synching at the end of her row of Year 2s. She always struggled with hymns. The melodies were either too low-pitched for her voice, or too high, and she'd spend at least two verses deciding which octave to finally commit to. The too high or the too low.

Mr Pethers closed the singing with a pinch of his hand. Like a sock puppeteer, minus the sock. 'Thank you, children, a wonderfully rousing start to the week.'

Mr Pethers conducted the regional brass band. He and Juliette were united in their shared understanding of music and the desire for Elodie, a former pupil, to eventually make it to concert level. Against all odds.

Sarah's thoughts skipped to Elodie waving over from her table in the Italian last week. Then to Karl cooling things down at Max's football tournament. Will's prickliness. A thread of old memories unearthed themselves from where they'd bored down deep into Sarah's brain. She let herself drift back to Elodie and the barbecue. Elodie and Will.

Juliette's dress had been the talk of the evening. White, floaty, not Juliette's usual style, more like the summer dresses Sarah was wearing to keep cool with a burgeoning baby bump and two fat feet in the sweltering heat.

'White's a brave choice, Jules, with all this mustard and relish,' Patrick had teased.

Elodie ran screaming through the garden, hopping barefoot over the sprinklers in her soaking wet yellow ra-ra skirt. Will, with his too-big front teeth and wet clothes plastered to his skinny body was in hot, giggly pursuit.

'Come on, Milo, stop giggling and shoot straight!' called Juliette. A slightly smaller, slightly slower Milo zoomed past after the others, water pistol at arm's length. A puddle of mud was starting to wear into the grass where the kids' feet had done their worst, brown spray spattering the patio each time they circuited the garden.

'You'll be carrying those muddy brutes into a taxi later, Jules.'

'I won't, Karl will . . . that's if he doesn't drink too much like last time.'

Karl lifted his head from the garden recliner, one hand crooked behind his hat, the other nursing a bottle of Mexican beer. 'Just getting in there before baby Harrison arrives. We'll have to find other barbecue friends soon, Jules. Know anyone else who won't mind our pair wrecking the grass?'

Sarah cut through another couple of limes. She was trying to jazz up a pitcher of alcohol-free fruit punch beside the more disco version Juliette was throwing together with Malibu and Curaçao.

'I keep trying to talk her into one more,' grinned Karl.

Juliette stopped slicing peaches and swished her knife. 'And I keep trying to talk him into having a word with Doctor Snippy.'

'Ouchy,' grimaced Patrick. He stabbed his barbecue fork into something that had fallen on to the hot coals. 'On that note, who's for a sorry-looking sausage? Karl?'

'No need to rub it in, mate. Just because your good lady isn't trying to get you on the chopping block.'

'I might join you soon, mate.'

'What, voluntarily? I've got ten years on you, Paddy, there's life in you two yet!'

'No, no more, mate. I won't have any more. This one wasn't planned, Sarah'll tell you the same. But, you know, you get on with it.'

Sarah had been elated. Growing up an only child was no fun, she wanted more for Will. Laughter and arguments and happy chaos. She'd called Juliette before telling her own mother. Juliette kept her eyes down now, safely on her peaches.

I. Not *we.* Patrick always seemed to prefer being an *I.* *I* would like to travel more. *I* would like to stop with the wedding photography and try something else while *I* am still young enough. *I* won't have any more children.

The kids made another loop around the adults. Karl changed the subject. 'Start drying off, you naughty lot. It'll be getting cool soon. When Paddy opens the summerhouse and lets us all in, you won't be allowed in with those wet bottoms!'

Juliette slapped her arm. 'These awful mozzies! Aren't they horrendous this year?'

'I think we have some of those citronella candles,' said Sarah.

Juliette clasped her hands together. 'Ooh, yes! Let's have candles. I love all these new lanterns too, Sarah. The garden looks gorgeous tonight. So much colour!'

'Thanks, think I overdid it, though. Look at the size of my ankles, I have elephant feet.'

Patrick looked up at the deepening sky. 'There's more colour to come. Who was it who organised those poxy fireworks at the school fair? Bloody dire. Thought I'd show the kids what a real display looks like.'

'You do not have elephant feet, Sarah, you've looked stunning throughout this pregnancy. Tell your wife she has beautiful feet, Patrick. I *hated* being pregnant with Milo, every minute. I was insane!'

'I'm scattier this time too. I found my sunglasses in the fridge last week.'

Juliette batted her hand at the air. 'You are not scatty. It was Sam, wasn't it? On the fireworks? Now *he* was scatty. Sam Roberts.'

Patrick bit into a chicken leg and looked over the dying coals. 'Who's Sam Roberts?'

'He's one of the PFA husbands. You'd know if you ever turned up when the other dads volunteer, Patrick Harrison,' teased Juliette.

'I quite like Sam,' said Sarah. 'He's Cleo's husband . . . you know, Cleo with the twins and the wild hair?'

Patrick nodded. He wasn't a noticer of children or names.

Cleo's wild hair had just pinpointed her in his mind because Patrick was a visual thinker. His vision was professional kudos and artistic acclaim, not barbecues and back gardens. But he had Will now. He'd chosen fatherhood. No one had forced it on him.

Sarah placed a hand over her swollen belly. 'I asked them over tonight, actually, but Cleo's just taken over the lease at the place in the harbour. I think she's a bit pushed.'

Juliette poured herself a large glass of fruity punch. 'Thank goodness, I just don't click with her. She's so . . .'

'Vocal?' Sarah hid her face inside her glass.

'Remind you of anyone, Sarah?' grinned Karl.

Juliette set her glass down. She had a small fleck of mint leaf stuck in her teeth, the shiny eyes of rum already at work. 'I am not vocal! Cleo Roberts and I are nothing alike! Do you know, her daughter put a pile, a *pile* of grass cuttings off the school field in Elodie's lunch box?' Juliette slapped her arm again.

Patrick moved around his barbecue. 'Let me get those candles. Where are they, Sarah?'

'In the summerhouse, I've put the matches in there too.' Patrick had left the matches by the barbecue; Sarah had unlocked the summerhouse and shut them inside, just in case one of the kid's curiosity kicked in.

Patrick set his drink down. 'Do you still have the key?'

Sarah glanced across the garden. Where had she put it? She couldn't remember returning it to the kitchen drawer.

Karl leaned forwards. 'You really do have very lovely ankles, Sarah. Does Patrick give you foot-rubs every night? I'd offer my services but Juliette will become wild with jealousy. I rather liked Jules when she was pregnant.'

'Doesn't make you sound sexy, Karl. Makes you sound like a perv. Now, where are the kids? I need some more ice from inside.'

The bang echoed off the back wall of the house. It was as if it hadn't been in an enclosed space at all. Sarah felt the baby jump inside her. Juliette stood, eyes sharp and focused. Then screaming sliced through the balmy summer air.

Karl was already twisting himself over the sunlounger, leaping over children's garden toys. Patrick beat him to the door of the summerhouse.

Sarah ran too, despite her bulk. She couldn't tell the screams of a young girl from those of a young boy's. Terror peeled away at voices.

'I thought it was a sparkler! I thought it was a sparkler!' screamed Will. The summerhouse smelled of matches. Sulphur. And something sweeter. Something singed, like the marinaded meats Patrick had cooked earlier.

Milo had fallen over. He was screaming too. At Elodie. Elodie and her eyes, white and wild. She began to scream now, hysterical screams filling the air. Juliette grabbed at her, scanning her, trying to understand.

'Where's it coming from?' shouted Patrick. 'I can't see where it's coming from!'

Juliette's white dress was blackeend and bloodied, Elodie screaming and writhing in her mother's arms.

'Her hands! Her hands!' shrieked Karl. 'Call a fucking ambulance . . .'

'Let us pray.'

Sarah blinked. Rows of children in blue and red uniform

bowed their heads. Her eyes went straight to Juliette, then to her lap. She quickly wiped the tear she could feel tracking towards her cheek. She didn't dare blink again, didn't dare close her eyes as Mr Pethers had instructed. She'd felt premenstrual for days; if she started crying for nine-year-old Elodie now, she wouldn't stop.

Sarah looked for Max. Something good to fix her thoughts on before they led her back to the summerhouse.

There he was, in his row, cross-legged, palms flat together, head turned just enough to look for Sarah in her usual spot by the fire exit. His face was wet tears.

What's the matter? she mouthed. Max's chin wobbled. He began weeping soundlessly.

Had she done this? Had Max seen her nearly cry?

It's okay, she mouthed. Assembly was nearly up. She scanned the second row of Max's class for someone who might jolly him. Sebastian Brightman was praying behind him. Seb reached forwards to pat Max's back. He'd noticed Max needed a pal. *Thank you, Seb.* Sarah relaxed. *Tell him, Max, tell him what's wrong*. Max just needed Mrs Upton to notice so she could give him a cuddle and Sarah wouldn't have to step around the children and be Max's teacher-mummy who couldn't leave Year 1 stuff to Year 1 staff.

Sarah gave Max a smile. He turned his head away again as Sebastian drove a pencil into his back.

55

There were definitely worse ways to spend a Monday.

Sophie had thought the cottage basic, but the longer Isobel stayed here the more it started to fit.

'Thanks for the tour of the woods, Daniel. I didn't know there were so many different types of wild mushrooms. You're lucky, living here in all this quiet.' Daniel had knocked on the door and asked if Isobel would like to take Petal for a walk. She'd seen Petal rearing up at Ben just for hugging Daniel, and seeing as Daniel occasionally hugged Isobel she didn't fancy risking it. So Petal had stayed behind.

Daniel pushed his glasses up his nose. 'My mum didn't like it here. She lives with my Aunty Barbara now. They have a garden and no woods so my mum doesn't think about burglars.'

'Burglars?'

Daniel nodded. 'One day we had a burglar. When I was a baby. He came through the woods and got in the house when Mum and me were asleep. Dad got Petal to look after us but Mum wanted to live with Aunty Barbara so now she lives with Aunty Barbara and Petal lives in our house with me and Dad.'

Arthur hadn't included anything about burglars in the cottage ad. 'How old are you, Daniel?'

'I'm seventeen.'

'I don't think you have to worry about burglars any more.' Petal was nuts. Nuts for Daniel anyway.

Daniel began swishing his arms in jerky, assured motions. 'No. Because Ben and me can do karate. We learned it at the cinema in case any bad guys ever come to take our things again.'

Isobel spotted a boy in a school blazer walking off down the lane. Arthur was calling Petal to follow him back inside.

'Who's that, Dan?'

Dan looked up. They could just see the yard and the sides of the cottages through the break in the trees. 'That's Will. He's my friend. He helps my dad sometimes when his arms are aching.'

'Oh.' She thought he looked like Sarah's son.

'Your phone is ringing, Isobel.'

'Huh? Oh . . . no, I don't think it is, Dan, it's in my pocket.' She checked it. No, nothing since Cleo's text this morning: Sarah's passed on your number so I can harangue you if you don't come into Coast enough! Hope okay? Btw, sorry for tattoo fiasco, I'm a shameful drunk, C xx

'It's ringing in the cottage,' said Daniel. 'Shall I show you?'

Isobel could hear it too now. The cottage phone hadn't rung during her stay so far. 'That's okay, Dan, I'll go. Thanks for the walk, I'll see you later.' Isobel skipped up the cottage steps and let herself in. It was indeed the cottage phone, which until then had been like all the other items on the living room bookcase. Something she ignored.

She grabbed the receiver. 'Hello?' The phone was an old affair, white, plastic, no caller display, no display of any kind.

'Hello?' There didn't seem to be any sound either. She turned the base over in her hand and looked for a volume setting. She was about to try another *hello* but thought she heard someone exhale at the other end.

A small rush of adrenalin flooded through her. She held her breath and pressed the receiver to her ear.

She could just say *hello* again. Her nan used to breathe into the handset for a few seconds before talking. Maybe there was a delay.

'Hello, is anyone there?' she tried jovially. The phone went dead.

56

Max drained the last of his neon-blue bubblegum slushy from the Candy Shack and let out a satisfied burp.

'Pardon you, Max.'

'Pardon me.'

Mary in the office had printed off eighty-three *Healthy, Happy, Hooray!* manifestos this afternoon. The school parents would just be discovering them, wide-eyed and indignant, scanning Sarah's list of *healthy, happy tips* to curb the sugar crisis, the obesity crisis, the parents-not-thinking-enough-for-themselves crisis . . . right about the same time Max slurped the last of his slush-puppy.

Sarah studied her little boy, blonde hair falling over big chestnut eyes, neon-blue lips. 'Feeling better now, kiddo?' Max shrugged. 'Do you want to tell me what's been going on with Seb?'

'I did tell you.' Max scratched his forehead. 'You said no one likes Mondays, not just me.'

Is that what she'd been sending him into? Sneaky cruelty in morning assemblies when he couldn't call out?

'I'm sorry, Max. I should've spoken to you more, shouldn't I?' Another shrug. 'You know, Max, sometimes children say mean things. And they hurt our feelings, don't they? And unfortunately, when that happens, quite a lot of the time we have to learn to just do our best to ignore those horrible things, don't we?' Max watched his feet as they walked. Sarah pulled him to a standstill and crouched beside him. 'But no one, not a little boy or a little girl or a grown-up or *anybody*, is ever, *ever* allowed to hurt you, Max. Do you understand?'

'You mean hurt me with a pencil?'

She hadn't lifted his shirt for a look yet. She didn't want to embed it in his mind, she'd catch a look at bath-time. 'That's exactly what I mean. You must, *must,* tell Mrs Upton if that happens again.'

'I did tell Mrs Upton! Seb moved my chair after break and I fell on the floor and it hurt my bottom and he laughed, and I told Mrs Upton because she said, *Max, why are you crying again?*'

Twice in one day? Little sod. 'What did Mrs Upton do?'

'She said, *play nicely.*'

Play nicely? This had been brewing for weeks. And Sarah had done nothing about it.

'Max, I'm going to speak to Mrs Upton. I'm sure we can sort this out so you and Seb get along again, does that sound okay?'

She would just have to speak to the staff in Max's class. Juliette wasn't a monster. Her friendship with Olivia might make things a little sticky, but that might be used to her advantage. Sarah could drop hints about Seb's behaviour, Juliette could pass it all on. Delicately . . . ish.

'Can we go inside today, Mummy?' They'd reached Tails 'n' Scales already. 'Can we look at the crickets?'

'Crickets? Aren't they in the pet food aisle?'

'Seb is bringing his pet cricket to show and tell because he wants to be like Steve Backshall when he's bigger and he says Mr Pethers likes watching Steve Backshall on TV too so Mr Pethers will choose Seb's cricket as the sports day mascot. All the whole class thinks Seb is really brilliant now and everyone is going to vote to have Seb's cricket for the mascot. Can I have a pet cricket, Mummy?'

The idea of a snail haven was crunching underfoot. 'Let's talk about it at home.'

'I think Seb will like me better if I have a cricket.'

They needed a solution. A short, sharp shock of a solution. Something that would stick. *Juliette hates your guts, Sar!* Cleo had already astutely observed. Understandably. But they'd also been good friends once. Juliette wasn't as hard-centred as she looked. She also knew the awfulness of a bully going at your child.

Will's first ever day at high school had fired the starter pistol on a new struggle. He'd come home that afternoon, dropped his school bag in the hallway and kicked it all the way along the floor into the kitchen. *Will's being bullied!* Sarah knew it immediately. Will had hit the radars of bigger, stronger kids. Bigger kids with even bigger fathers to back them up, knowing there was no father at all in Will's background. Sarah had slipped into that cold, panicky paranoia and trodden water in it for weeks. Sometimes he came home with grazes, or just kicked his bag a few times. She'd been so sure Will was being picked on. That he couldn't be the one always throwing the first punch. The pastoral workshops had been a trade, *do this and we won't go down the exclusion route.* Will gelled with the school's new counsellor. The fighting eased off, school bags lasted months, not weeks. Eventually, after a chance whack on the head with a surfboard, Will's counsellor had sat on a beach and shared with Sarah why Will had fought so relentlessly. To stop those boys tormenting someone else. The girl with the ET hand.

It wasn't the same thing. But Juliette would still understand Max's situation, wouldn't she? Bullying was bullying.

Okay. First thing tomorrow she would ask Juliette, mother of the little girl maimed when Will passed a live firework to her in Sarah's summerhouse, to keep an eye on her son for her. To watch over him. To care about him. To keep him safe.

57

More than a week by the sea and Isobel had only just set foot in Cod Almighty; her dad would disown her. Fish and chips was the staple diet of their summer holidays, from *Cod Piece* to *The Chipping Forecast*, Isobel and Sophie had heard it every time. *A good name is essential, girls!* It was hard to imagine how he'd coped with the degradation of 'Isobel Hedley'.

'Salt and vinegar?'

'Plenty please, love.'

Isobel pretended to read the menu on the wall, ready to shuffle forwards in line again once the big chap in front collected his haddock special.

A car door slammed on the street outside, the driver nipping off to find a parking spot up the road as a young girl walked sulkily in through the open door, twenty-pound note clamped in her hand.

Isobel almost didn't recognise Cleo's daughter. Everything looked different, sleeker, simpler. Evie took her place at the end of the queue snaking behind Isobel.

'Hi,' smiled Isobel. Two familiar people in a line-up of strangers. She wouldn't have to keep rereading menus now in a bid to avoid eye-contact with people.

Evie didn't answer. She offered half a smile and also pretended to read the menu over the chip shop counter.

'Your hair looks nice, have you changed it?' It was one of those hollow questions Isobel used to ask her students, something to get their attention right before she asked them to go spit out their chewing gum or turn their phone off.

Another flat smile. Evie squinted at the price list. The woman next in line after Isobel glanced back over her shoulder to see where all that one-sided conversation kept hitting its dead end. Isobel faced the glowing shelf of fried fish and those strange bright orange sausage things Sophie thought looked like half-attempted balloon creatures.

Evie obviously wanted to be left alone, didn't want to talk about her changed image. *Ah.* Was Evie's hair and make-up overhaul down to the comments she'd been subjected to about her appearance? Poor kid. She was probably trying to bend herself around her trolls' spiteful observations the way Isobel had changed her hair, her clothes, to bend herself around DEEP_DRILLERZ's.

She left Evie alone and waited to be served. Another customer stepped into the shop.

'Hello, Evie. Mum not cooking tonight?'

'Er, *no.* But I'm not having anything, I've already eaten. I don't even like chips any more.'

Isobel listened to the jangle of bracelets, Evie repositioning herself for the conversation she didn't want to stretch to with Isobel.

'Always good to hear our young adults are taking good care of themselves,' said the other voice.

'Next?' called the rosy woman behind the counter. Isobel felt hot and flustered just looking at her thick, dark Mediterranean curls peeping from beneath her cook's cap. Isobel listened to another order being placed and waited for the other woman serving to take hers next.

'What about you, Mr Hildred? Fancy something tasty for tea?' asked Evie.

Isobel heard Evie's friend clearing his throat.

'Next?'

Isobel moved down line. 'Hi, just a small fish and chips please. The smallest you do.' Someone touched her elbow. She jerked her arm away.

'Isobel? Hi,' smiled Jon. 'Sorry, I didn't mean to startle you.' He had a pair of black Ray-Bans sitting on his head, his yellow polo shirt deepening an already healthy tan.

'Hi! Sorry, I didn't notice you come in, I was miles away.'

He looked over the glowing display of fried food. 'Sarah's caved. The boys are having takeout. Mondays always wipe her out, and Max is playing up too, I think the idea of a dinner table debate over eating cooked veg was going to be enough to finish them both off.'

'Salt and vinegar, love?'

Isobel glanced back to the counter. 'Just vinegar, thanks.'

Jon nodded at Isobel's chips being swaddled in paper. 'I wish I could go without the salt. I can live without sugar, alcohol, anything but the salt. Always find myself giving in to temptation.'

'Really, Mr H? So you're a salt lover? And there you are at school telling us to take care of our bodies.' Evie glanced at Isobel, who couldn't make out if Evie was trying for cocky or funny. Fallenbay was brimming with teenagers. Isobel had made sure she lived a good thirty-minute drive from St Jude's and its catchment area. Not that it had made much difference. The internet had gone and shrunk the world anyway.

'Six-forty, please, love.' Isobel dug into her purse and paid. She smiled in Jon and Evie's direction as she passed.

'Bye . . . enjoy your takeout.' She had a feeling Evie might not answer so she left her valediction there in the air for anyone who wanted it.

'Isobel? Could I just . . .' Jon followed her outside. She caught another waft of vinegar fumes and a rush of saliva filled her mouth. 'I just, er . . . wanted to say thanks again, for helping out Sarah and the boys last week, after the football incident.'

'Oh, I didn't really do anything.'

Jon looked back into the chip shop window. Evie turned her back to the glass. 'No, you did. Sarah really appreciated you being there to help. I think she's hoping to see more of you actually. You're proving quite popular with my other half.'

The compliment caught her off-guard. Like tripping off a kerb. 'Thanks. I like Sarah, too.'

It was nice of him to follow her out just to say so, although he was going to lose his place in the queue in a minute.

Jon grinned. 'Great. Maybe we'll see more of you then.' He touched her elbow again, the lightest of touches.

'Maybe,' agreed Isobel. She waved her hand and turned for the parking bays where she'd left the car.

He called after her again. 'Hey, you can cross that off your list now then.'

Isobel frowned. Jon imitated scribbling on paper. 'Your "to do" list. At Cleo's? You can go ahead and cross *Friends* off. Sarah and Cleo won't let go now you've made the fold!'

58

Cleo stomped on the bin pedal and let a mound of cold chips slide straight off Harry's plate into the bin.

'Another meal, wasted.'

Sam wiped his mouth with a sheet of kitchen towel. He'd swooped in before Cleo had binned the untouched plate. 'Not all of it. Harry's haddock was nice.' Harry loved fish and chips. They were supposed to coax him out of his room for an evening. 'H didn't go to his basketball game after school. Is he sick?'

Cleo looked for Harry's basketball trainers at the back door where they'd been since she'd got home. 'He missed his game? Are you sure? I just thought he'd beaten me home.'

'I didn't even know he was in the house. I was sitting on the throne and heard someone sneeze in his room. Scared me to death! I went in there with your electric toothbrush, Cle. You can kill a man with an electric toothbrush, y'know.'

'You should've just left the door open, Sam. You could kill a man with a bathroom after *you've* paid a visit.'

She moved the dishes to the side. That was basketball and football Harry had ducked now. Harry, who couldn't walk past the courts without clinging to the metal fencing for a quick look.

'Anyway, I said he was ill last week and you said he was just feeling sorry for himself!' Cleo heard the snap in her voice.

'Cleo. Can't we just have a wayward daughter and a bloody music night to worry about, do we *have* to have another child with a problem?'

'What if he has got a problem?' She didn't believe for a second Harry had got a problem. She just wanted to know what made Sam so blindly sure he hadn't.

'Harry has problems, Cleo. Loads of the buggers. How about . . . exams? Girls? Sister playing up? Are you surprised he stays up in his room? I wouldn't mind staying in mine.'

'He still has to eat, Sam.'

'Eat? I should think the lad's eating like a horse on a fiver a day. How much do school meals cost these days anyway?'

Well done, Harry. Sam was about to start spinning the overspending record again. 'I only give him five pounds a day, Sam, because he's an active boy who needs a proper meal and plenty to drink in this heat. And I've only bumped it to a fiver since Evie started taking salads in.' Evie's dieting was temporary, they'd agreed, prohibited from four p.m. on a Friday onwards when free-food weekend commenced. It was also coming in useful for Cleo's weekly food budgeting. Evie and Harry were practically back to competing for nutrients; it was like having them back in-utero again, only this time Harry was benefiting from Evie's dwindling draw on their shared resources.

'Why are *you* giving him a fiver a day, Cleo?' Sam pointed at himself. 'I was talking about me.'

'*You* give Harry a fiver a day? For lunch?'

'Am I talking another language here? *Yes*, Harry's been having a fiver a day off me.'

'So he's having ten pounds a day? Between us? That's fifty quid a week! No wonder he's not hungry at tea time! What's he bloody well up to, buying bloody Xbox games every week?' He wasn't. Harry's Xbox was still missing in action. A trail of thoughts dominoed in her head. Harry's school trip. Where was the information? Where was the receipt for the cash she'd handed over? Without question.

'Hi.'

Evie walked into the kitchen knocking Cleo's thought's off-track. She hadn't seen that pale blue cotton day dress since their holiday last year. Evie had burnt her shoulders and Cleo had seized her chance to talk her into buying something simple and pretty from the street market, something loose against her sore skin instead of the strappy, tight things Evie had packed.

Evie opened the fridge and helped herself to a carton of coconut milk.

'Darling daughter,' Sam acknowledged grumpily. They should've had Evie tattooed sooner, it had taken Sam years to pull rank.

Evie shot them a *why are you both staring at me?* look and looped back out of the kitchen.

'What are you smiling about?' said Sam.

'Nothing,' smiled Cleo.

'Go on, say it. I can hear your thoughts, Cleo.'

'I don't know what you mean.'

'Sure you don't. You were right, I was wrong. I should've been tougher. Sooner.'

She'd wound Sam up by telling the press about the open-mic

night, but he'd been steadily defrosting since holding her hair back over the toilet while she'd made spewy declarations never to touch a drop of rum ever again. She vaguely remembered saying something equally spewy about only wanting them to have a nice life together, and not meaning to be such an arse about it.

'You were right too, Sam. Taking Evie's phone was a good move. She hasn't even missed it.' And gone with it were all the apps giving her super-quick access to her social networks and all the junk on them. Evie was straightening herself out. *Please let her be straightening herself out.* 'Maybe we should think about taking Harry's phone too, just while he's getting Ingred out of his system. Help him focus on his studies. I know she's still bothering him. I can see it in his face every time he checks his phone.' Cleo was holding Ingred directly responsible for Harry's language yesterday.

'Harry's got a good bunch of pals, Cle. They do him good. Not like Cassie and the fashion crew, Evie's obviously benefiting from a bit of distance there. She looks lovely today. Her clothes and . . . what else has she changed?'

'Oh, *Sam*.' He was nearly there. A man who could pick out the changes in a woman. 'She's changed everything!'

'Hasn't her hair always been like that?'

'No! She's waving it now. They're called soft curls.'

'Well I've noticed the eyebrows are gone, you can give me a point for that.' Sam pulled Cleo into him and pressed a long kiss to her head. 'Bravo, Super-mum. You were right. Tough love. I shouldn't have waited so long.'

'Excellent. You do the discipline from now on then and I'll be favourite parent for a change.'

Sam laughed that deep, growly, undulating laugh. 'Check us out congratulating each other on our awesome parenting skills.'

'I think Pastoral are helping too.'

'Can't argue with that. Evie swatting up on her revision with *Elodie Inman-Holt*? Jon Hildred deserves a Nobel prize for pulling that off. I'm looking forward to seeing her results. I like the idea of my little girl being a doctor someday. She might end up sitting a higher paper.'

Sam was getting swept up. He hadn't seen Evie's arms. The awful angry scratches. Evie had taken to wearing long sleeves over her nearly-tattoo when Sam was home. He didn't know. 'Don't put too much on her, Sam. Just because she's knuckling down. Let's just enjoy it.'

'You're right, love. Let's just enjoy her. I like this new Evie.'

Cleo felt a wave of optimism. She cuddled into her husband. 'I like our new Evie, too.'

59

Max pedalled ahead, taking the last sweeping bend towards Hornbeam Primary. The sky was a positive inky blue, the air a warm pillow, the school ready to inhale a hundred fresh-faced, sun-cream-slathered children.

Sarah's front wheel wobbled where the road became the school path. 'Whoops. Be extra careful while we're on the pavement, Max.' Max's sun hat was sandwiched between his head and cycling helmet so they didn't forget it after de-cobwebbing the bikes in the carport this morning. Jon would've got the bikes out for them last night, but asking carried the risk of being alone together in close quarters again. He'd already walked into the house with the kids' fish and chips, set the boys up to eat by themselves in the kitchen and then followed Sarah upstairs, fishing for another quickie. This time against the landing wall. Only just out of sight of the boys. Is this what her mum had meant? *It's nonsense men reaching their sexual peak at eighteen, darling, your father had a sudden burst in his forties, I think it was his swan song.*

Was Jon just having a sudden burst? Was that what this new thing for frenzied, rushed sex was? Anywhere and everywhere, the riskier the better?

There you go . . . boring boring boring.

'We biked here quick, didn't we, Mum?' declared Max.

'Like rockets, kiddo.' Unpredictable, wobbly ones. The ride seemed to have done the trick though. A few released endorphins and Max's verve for school was renewed. His bike bell tinkled ahead. The sound complemented the morning sun glinting on the ocean beyond the school field. 'Let's pull over here, Max.'

Max clambered off and began marching his bike along the way Jon had shown him so he didn't accidentally bump into anybody. Sarah did the same, scanning faces for Sebastian Brightman's mum, the last person she wanted to bump into. Max headed for the school gates. Two large Hornbeam trees stood sentry either side, parents clustered beneath them like ants seeking out shade. And sticky-sweet morsels of gossip.

Oh boy. Olivia Brightman didn't ditch her riding boots for love nor money. Not even for blazing May mornings. Olivia fussed at Sebastian's backpack while he cradled Chloe Foley's new puppy. Rachel Foley tightened Chloe's plaits, chatting happily with Darcey's mother, the lawyer who made Sarah wonder whether Michelle Obama might have a secret younger sister the world didn't yet know about.

Sarah took a quick deep breath. *Right. Mum mode.*

Oh God, they were going to grill her on the *Healthy, Happy, Hooray!* manifesto, or whether there were political motivations for moving the summer fair to this Saturday, or which family had started the sickness bug sweeping through the juniors.

Mum mode. She'd had a mental practice run on the ride here. *Morning, isn't this weather gorgeous? Anybody have any tips for reviving parched hanging baskets?* No. Too much. And

345

Jon's hanging baskets were picture perfect. *Morning, anyone know when this hurricane is supposed to arrive, you couldn't believe it, could you? The weather's being so kind!*

'Hello, Miss Harrison!' Darcey was wearing pigtails in bobbles with little plastic strawberries on them.

'Morning, Darcey.' Sarah unclipped her bike helmet and waited for the grilling to commence. Darcey's mum smiled over, still chattering away about the law concerning dog foul and the mysteries of it finding its way on to a locked school field.

'Mrs *Harrison*,' Olivia cooed, 'I've been meaning to ask . . .' Wait for it. *Who do you think you are telling us what to feed our children?* 'How are you feeling after that terrible ball to the face? Juliette's husband handled those yobs very well, didn't he? And offering to drive you all home, so kind of him.'

Sarah felt her cheeks get hot. She checked Max. Seb had turned himself so Max was the only child under the tree who couldn't enjoy a look at Chloe's puppy. Olivia, far too busy to notice, still waiting for Sarah's take on Karl's chivalry, eyes shiny at the whiff of scandal.

Metal clattered on metal behind them, a steady bustle starting through the gates Mrs Upton had just opened. Max sunk his hands into his pockets and started kicking at a tree root.

'I'm fine, thank you, Olivia. Mrs Upton, could I just have a quick word?'

Mrs Upton's crucifix chain was tangled in the cord of her school ID badge. The two looked in danger of choking her.

'Ooh, yes. We should. Let's just get these eager beavers out of the way first, shall we?'

Sarah looked for Max again as the masses filtered into

school. Seb was dishing out the contents of the bag his mother had been clutching to her chest.

'Come along, slowcoaches,' called Mrs Upton. Seb caught a kiss from his mother and ran into school. Olivia smiled over again.

'Now it's just the stragglers. What was it you wanted to have a word about, Sarah?'

'Could we pop in your office? It's a little sensitive.'

Max trudged past them. 'Bye, darling. Have a great day. Hey! Can I get a kiss please?' Max kept walking. 'Max?'

He stood still and huffed. 'It's your fault, Mummy.'

Mrs Upton laughed. 'What on earth is mummy's fault?'

Max answered Sarah. 'Seb wouldn't let me have a sweet his dad brought back from his special job in Spain because you are making everyone at school throw their sweets away. I wish you weren't a teacher, Mummy.' He bolted through the school doors before she could call him back.

There were tears. All of a sudden, right behind Sarah's eyes.

'Sarah?' Mrs Upton had put her glasses back on. 'Max will be fine, just fine. Parents on the staff roll will always run into bother with their kids, children are terrible critics. Because Mummy didn't step in, or she didn't step back, ' Mrs Upton leaned in, 'or because she's the person trying to educate the other mummies on healthier diets.'

Sarah wasn't trying to do that at *all*. Mr Pethers was. She was just his human shield.

'Actually, Katherine, that's what I was hoping to talk to you about. Max, when to step in . . .'

'Yes. I was going to call you this morning.' Mrs Upton's enthusiasm dipped. 'There's been a small *incident* in class.'

'I know. Max told me.' Children had broken their coccyxes having chairs whipped out from behind them.

'Excellent. Then we're all up to speed. Juliette and I were hoping to have a sit down with you about it.'

'Really?' They had been watching then. Poor Max. 'That's reassuring, Katherine. Really.'

'Good. It's important we all get our heads together and help Max.'

'It is,' agreed Sarah.

'See how we can help him curb this animosity of his towards Sebastian Brightman.'

60

'Would you like a drink, Sarah? Tea? Coffee?' Katherine Upton was rosy as usual but it all felt very formal.

'No thank you.' Sarah couldn't drink a thing. She was still trying to swallow *Max's* animosity.

Juliette passed on a drink too. She was unnervingly good at sitting still. Sarah couldn't stop fiddling with the strap of her bike helmet in her lap.

Will had spent most of last year's Christmas break binge-watching the beautifully gift-wrapped *Game of Thrones* box set he'd received from a generous school friend. He'd made Sarah watch a scene after she'd wandered in with the hoover one afternoon. One minute and she'd been sucked in, marvelling at the beautiful costumes, a sort of medieval banquet, ornate goblets raised in toast. Next thing she knew, the goblets were tossed, doors bolted, and everyone was murdering each other indiscriminately.

Sarah thought about that scene now, while Juliette sat cold and queen-like on the staff room chair opposite, back straight, hands in her lap. The distinct smell of an ambush in the air.

'We're sorry to catch you on the hop with this, Sarah. We were going to wait until you came in later.'

Sarah swallowed. Juliette knew what was coming next and Sarah didn't.

'No, I'm glad you did,' she lied, 'I'm concerned about Max.'

'So are we.'

Sarah's heart pattered at Juliette's voice. She forced her own into service. 'Go on.' She would wait to tell them about Max's changed feelings towards school. His dwindling confidence. Sarah would let them share their 'concerns' about her little boy, then she would share hers, about not very nice bruises caused by not very nice boys with hidden pencils.

Juliette led. 'The children were asked yesterday to pair up and write a selection of adjectives about their partner.'

Mrs Upton passed Sarah a worksheet.

I can describe my friend ....

Sarah imagined Max writing his name above the dotted line, tongue peeping through his teeth, then swapping sheets with Chloe, or maybe Christian, the little boy whose parents, Alison and Kevin, did absolutely everything, every school concert, every parent-helper stint, side by side. *Siamese parents*, Cleo called them.

Sarah skimmed the page. Beneath the worksheet title was the outline of a child, more like an androgynous gingerbread man, but Sarah could see where this was going.

Mrs Upton tapped her finger on the identical worksheet she was holding in front of her chest. 'Yes, the children were encouraged to modify their worksheets to reflect their partner's physical attributes, then the column down the right is so—'

'The children can *list* those attributes?' finished Sarah. Mrs Upton seemed to think Sarah was in Year 1, too.

'Precisely!' delighted Mrs Upton. Keep this up and Sarah was on for leaving the staff room with a gold star sticker. She noted the extra box at the bottom of the sheet.

My wonderful WOW word for .... *is:* ....!

Juliette rolled her eyes. 'Max was paired with Sebastian.'

'Seb?'

'Yes, Seb. This is Max's worksheet.'

Mrs Upton handed it over. Exhibit B. *I can describe my friend Sabasteeyan*

Max had done a lovely job colouring in Seb's portrait. Sarah read Max's adjective choices. He'd been generous, considering. Seb was the proud owner of a *frendly face, musslee arms* and *fast legs*. Was this about a few spelling mistakes?

My wonderful WOW word for Seb is: Wanker!

She heard a gasp. Blood whooshed to her head. Max had even drawn a smiley after his *wow* word. Wanker. Smiley face. Wanker. Wanker. W.A.N.K.E.R. She couldn't stop looking at it.

'Max . . . Max didn't mean to write *that*!' she laughed self-consciously, wafting the sheet like a used tissue no one wanted to touch. Of course Max didn't know that word! 'This is just some silly mistake.'

Juliette flattened a hand on the coffee table. 'We asked Max if he meant to write that particular word down and he was very firm about it. Adamant, in fact. He wanted Seb to know Max thinks of him as . . .'

'A *wanker*?' sputtered Sarah. Mrs Upton cleared her throat. 'But he's never heard that word!'

Juliette scratched her eyebrow. 'He has heard that word, Sarah. Many times. At home. Max told us himself.'

Sarah's hand had begun to sweat around the straps of her bike helmet. 'Where on earth—'

'From Will, Sarah. Max has heard it from Will.' Juliette's mouth turned hard and beak-like around Will's name.

'Will doesn't use bad language around his brother. Or any of us.' She wanted to scream it, straight down Juliette's ear. William's a good kid, Juliette! He made a mistake! He was *nine years old*.

Juliette's eyes were hard. 'Maybe not intentionally. But *unintentionally* doesn't stop a thing from happening, does it?'

Will had never meant to hurt Elodie. He thought he'd passed her a sparkler. The kids were going to give Sarah and Juliette one each for their cocktails, they were trying to recreate one of the photos in the Inman-Holts' lounge, of a younger Juliette and Karl in St Lucia, garlands around their necks, sharing a strawed coconut.

Mrs Upton tried her calming voice. 'Sarah, it's a tad delicate, but given the dinner ladies have reported one or two cases of *physicality* between the boys, and this new unfortunate development, we think it's a good idea to have Juliette monitor Max for the next week or so, just to note any—'

'You're starting an observation sheet on *Max*?' Her little boy, Maxy, with the long eyelashes and ever-so-slightly-there lisp. Sarah's heart began galloping in her chest.

Mrs Upton winced. 'This is *for* Max, Sarah. So we can head a problem off before it takes root.'

'Seb is the problem and he's already taken root!' There was a note of hysteria in her voice. She was going to sound like one of those mothers who couldn't hear a bad word about their child without firing something back, a ricochet statement. 'Have you seen Max's ribs? Where Sebastian stabbed him with a pencil in assembly yesterday?' She instantly regretted saying *stabbed*. It was too violent, she should've said *prodded*. But it had been more than a prod. A *jab*. Dammit, she should've said *jabbed*.

Mrs Upton took back her evidence, before Sarah could destroy it probably. 'Max needs to tell us if anyone hurts him, Sarah. We can't see *everything*.'

No! You sleep through most assemblies!

'Fine.' She sounded petulant. 'Observe him. Max doesn't like coming to school any more and I'd like to know why.'

Mrs Upton clasped her hands together. 'Then we shall work together.'

Juliette took Max's worksheet from her, slotting it back inside its plastic wallet. Max's wrap sheet. 'Could it be possible that Max's anxieties are stemming from somewhere *other* than school? Max has told us himself of all the transitions around him at the moment. He was worrying about having a new name *and* address to remember soon. Max has a lot going on. Enough to unsettle anyone really, isn't it?' Match point, Juliette. No one was more unsettled about it all than Sarah.

'He's perfectly settled at home, Juliette. He has a lot of attention. Will invests more time in Max than most fathers do.'

Juliette's voice came like a cold pinch. 'I'm glad. I'm glad you feel Will is a positive influence on Max. But we can't have five-year-olds calling other five-year-olds *wankers*.'

61

Isobel was obsessing. Two phone calls did not a pattern make.

She checked the time on Coast's wall clock. Nearly four-thirty.

Two days in a row. Two silent callers. Two hang-ups. She could kick herself for not checking the time of yesterday's. Had it been around the three-thirty, four p.m. mark too? Couldn't have been much earlier, not if Sarah's son had finished school when Isobel and Dan saw him on the lane. Isobel had pretended she wasn't waiting for the phone to ring again today, but she'd been within arm's reach of it when it went, pottering around the living room in slowly decreasing circles.

Today's call was the same as yesterday's. Breathing. No talking. Hang up. Her hand had been clammy on the plastic receiver. She hated that her body still reacted so nervously. As though her physical self couldn't give a toss how far her mental self had come, just to be able to answer those calls. To even be here in Fallenbay.

She didn't like it. Prank calls to the cottage hadn't been part of the plan. But she was staying cool. It wasn't like they were calling *her* phone. Even if it was some loon at the other end, even if they really were making malicious calls, technically they were aimed at the *Arthur Oakes* listed in the phone book. Not Isobel. That hadn't stopped her getting out of the cottage for a while though.

The women at the table next to her fanned themselves with Coast's menus. Cleo had given all of her customers a pitcher of iced water bobbing with lime slices to combat the heat. Isobel poured the last dribble from her pitcher and popped a couple of aspirin from her bag. She had a blinder of a headache today. She reached the counter and studied Cleo's iced-drinks menu on the blackboard wall.

'Hey, Evie, could I get a mango and lime frappé please? Need to knock off this heat.' Evie had been starting her after-school shift when Isobel walked in. She turned her back now without a word. Isobel watched her pick through one of the chilled fruit buckets, first lobbing a few chunks of mango into one of the blenders, next a scoopful of ice. Evie set the lid on.

'So, how are—'

The blender roared to life. The brutal sounds of crunching ice cutting Isobel off. Was Evie deliberately being funny with her? She was only going to ask if the girl's exams had started yet.

Isobel waited patiently, looking about herself for something else to read while Evie maybe was or wasn't blanking her the way she maybe had or hadn't in the chip shop last night.

The blender stopped. Evie slopped its peachy contents into a tall glass and dumped half a lime in the top. It looked like a tortoise stranded in a swamp. She set the glass down on the counter. 'Three-fifty.'

Isobel tried not to smile; teenagers were moody. A common interest usually helped smooth out a frosty start. She held up her arm. 'I saw my sister at the weekend. I asked her where she bought my bracelet.'

Evie's eyes dipped to Isobel's bangle. She drew her mouth into a hard line. 'I don't want one now. Some things look cheaper up close.'

62

It had been over twenty-four hours since Juliette and Mrs Upton had dropped Max's wonderful WOW word in Sarah's lap like an acme bomb. Her ears were still ringing from the blast.

They'd drifted back into Tails 'n' Scales on the way home from school. It might've been the kind lady behind the counter who'd reminded her of her mum, or the way Max had spoken so gently to a box of dried mealworms in case he woke them all up, but Sarah had found herself walking back to the car carrying a goldfish in a bag, a tub of food and a large bag of colourful gravel.

'Max?'

He was laying tummy-down on her bed in his bath towel, nosing through Sarah's jewellery box. He'd wrapped a few bits of costume jewellery around his skinny arms, a bracelet hooked over one ear.

'Yes, Matey?' growled Max.

She sat down on the bed next to him. 'Sorry, Captain. Are you raiding my treasure?' Max nodded. She kissed his head. 'How's it going with Seb? Is he a good shipmate again, or should he walk the plank?' Max shrugged. 'I liked the describing words you used for Seb on your lovely picture of

him. *Fast legs.* That must be why Seb's so good at football.'
Max nodded and tried on another of Sarah's rings. 'What did
Mrs Upton think of your drawing of Seb? Did she like it?'

'Yes. And Mrs Inman-Holt. We had a special talk about
it.' Max's eyes shone with pride. Sarah swallowed the lump
hardening in her throat.

'Lovely. What did they say?'

'It is very neat and tidy colouring,' Max said in a sing-song
voice. 'And I worked hard.'

'They did? Super. What did they say about your *wow*
word?'

'Wanker!' yelped Max.

Sarah clenched her legs. 'Max! That's an unusual word.
Why did you choose that one?'

'Because I want Seb to be my friend.'

Sarah frowned. 'Max, what does that word mean?'

Max stopped fishing through her things and leaned his
head over. The bracelet fell off his ear. 'You know, Mummy.
It means a really neat guy, silly!'

'A *neat guy?* Max, where did you hear that word?'

'You sound like Mrs Inman-Holt, Mummy.'

'Where did you hear it, Max?' The most unsettling word
she'd ever heard from her little boy's mouth.

'Will.'

'Will said that word?'

'Yes. When I was hiding under the trampoline and Jon
drove off. Will said it in the garden. *See ya later, wanker!*'

Her breathing had quickened. 'And you asked Will what
that word meant?' He'd covered his tracks then. Sloppily.

'Yep. I thought Seb will like me more if I writed that he's

a neat guy like Jon. But there was only a small line and we had to say one word.'

'Did I hear ye callin' me name, Cap'n?' Jon walked in, shirt rolled up to his elbows, eyebrow cocked, pirate-style.

Sarah jumped up before Max dropped them all in it. 'Come on, Max, time for pjs, did you brush your teeth yet? That's it, on your feet.'

Max began bouncing. His towel fell to the bed, transforming him from Captain Max to hysterical, naked Max.

'Whoa, champ!' laughed Jon. 'Let's get you those pjs before the neighbours get a fright.'

'I'll get them, come on, Max. Bed.'

'No!'

'Max, come on.'

Jon set his hands on his hips. 'Max? I've just finished cleaning out the old fish tank, we're good to go.'

'Yay! Yay! Yay!' bounced Max.

'I thought you were going to do it tomorrow?' Sarah wasn't complaining. Godzilla had been confined to temporary lodgings in one of her favourite Cath Kidston mixing bowls.

Jon ran a hand over her head. 'Thought I'd do it while he had his bath instead. Are you ready to see Godzilla in his new home then, Max?'

'Yeah!' bounced Max.

Jon walked around the bed. He was wearing Sarah's favourite aftershave. She'd noticed his body becoming more honed lately, his shirts sitting snugly across his chest from all those extra workouts, all those extra runs over the bluff.

I hope he's not having an affair, darling! Her mum had teased. *I've already seen a beautiful hat for the wedding.*

Her mum was closer to the truth than she realised. Jon had met a whopping great house with too much glass and not enough storage, overlooking the ocean. There was no denying he'd fallen quite in love. He literally couldn't keep away from the place. A three-hundred-thousand-pound down-payment could do that, Sarah supposed. Jon's huge deposit was perhaps the reason he didn't give a hoot that the building company were still chasing him for the set of keys he hadn't returned.

'I'll take him to bed, baby, you go grab a glass of wine. Call Cleo back, she wants to ask you a favour, something about the storerooms at Coast. We're good, aren't we, buddy?'

Sarah looked from Jon to Max, so easily a miniature version of him.

'Yeah!' Max emitted a word with each spring on the bed. 'I . . . want . . . Daddy . . . to . . . take . . . me . . . to . . . bed.'

Jon's mouth jerked strangely. He dipped his head and scratched the side of his cheek. Hysterical, naked Max bounced on.

Suddenly, *wanker* wasn't the most unsettling word she'd heard from her little boy's mouth.

63

'I didn't mean *tonight*! I just meant, you know, whenever you're free to help. But before next weekend.' Cleo smiled sheepishly and opened the side door to Coast. Sarah gestured for Isobel to walk in first.

'Tonight's perfect,' said Sarah. 'I needed to get out of the house.'

Isobel followed her through one storeroom into another. Cleo had been scraping paint from small blacked-out windows, shards of view and daylight piercing the room. There wasn't much to see, a corner stacked with chairs, coffee-bean boxes, metal racks. 'And you thought you'd drag poor Isobel along to wade through my crap, too?'

Sarah shrugged, glancing at Isobel. 'Pretty much. Power of three and all that.' Isobel wasn't convinced. Sarah had turned up at the cottage just after the last silent phone call. Some call centre in Asia, Isobel had decided. Absolutely nothing to get paranoid about. She'd been weighing up whether to leave the phone off the hook when Sarah rolled into the drive. Maybe Sarah was checking on Isobel, as she suspected, or maybe she really was just rounding her up to help Cleo clear her storeroom. Either way, Isobel was happy enough to be getting out of her house, too.

'And you don't mind?' Cleo asked.

'Not at all,' smiled Isobel. 'I was a bit bored.' Calling *hello* into a phone did get a bit boring.

'Drinks and biscuits on the side, girls, let's have them now before we get grubby.' Cleo picked up one of the drinks, dunked a biscuit and leant against a metal rack. 'Bored? No wonder. It must get lonely up there at night. Don't you get jittery with all those woods?'

Sarah passed Isobel a drink and they each picked a box to sit on. Isobel took a sip. 'I didn't until Daniel told me why his mum left. An intruder in the house would scare my mum out of her own home. And my dad.' Sophie would take more shifting. She had more fight in her. More of an appetite for conflict.

Sarah straightened. 'Is that why Arthur brought Daniel up on his own? I thought his wife must've died.'

'Sarah, how long have you lived in this town? Mrs Oakes didn't die, she left. And not because of some burglar.' Cleo tried to bite her dunked biscuit but it flopped into her drink. 'I'm not saying she wasn't terrified after the break-in, but she left because . . . she found it difficult.'

Sarah blew on her tea. 'Found what difficult?'

'*Daniel*. Having special needs.'

Sarah's mouth fell open.

Isobel felt the same. 'Poor Daniel. What a terrible shame for him.'

Cleo fished for the soggy biscuit. 'Terrible shame for *her*. Look at everything she's missed out on. I adore that boy. Society could learn a lot about humility from people like Daniel Oakes. He's a bloody smasher. His brother's not too bad either. Don't you think, Isobel?' Cleo winked. 'He's been asking after you, you know.'

'Poor Daniel,' Sarah finally agreed. 'And poor Ben too. I know he's a good bit older than Daniel, but their mother leaving must've been hard on him too. I don't think there's anything Will or Max could ever do to make me want to be apart from them. I can't ever imagine feeling ashamed of them. Not for a terrible accident . . . or . . . or being gay . . . or smoking pot . . . or calling another child an awful word. Shame's for parents like Patrick who always wanted more. Or my father, who always wanted better.' Sarah came back from her thoughts. Cleo was staring at her. Sarah cleared her throat. 'Sorry. I was just saying, love's supposed to be unconditional.'

'I don't think Mrs Oakes was ashamed of Daniel. She was old-fashioned, though. My mother's feeling was she felt responsible for Daniel's condition. His limitations. Better Daniel thinks she left because of a burglar, really. Small mercy for him.'

'I know a guy with Down's, he's at uni now. Gareth hasn't let his limitations get in his way.'

'No, but I'll bet his mum was still offered screening when she was pregnant. And all the choices that go along with it. And so she should've been. But I just wonder how many mothers are told it's not necessarily the end of the world. *Yes, your pregnancy carries a higher risk of Down's Syndrome, but don't panic! There is support! Yours will still be a capable child, who can make their own unique contribution to this world.* I remember thinking when I had the twins, can you imagine, with medical tests advancing the way they do, what if one day every woman finds out for sure they're carrying a

363

baby who has a chromosomal abnormality? Kids like Daniel, and your friend at university . . . they could become *extinct*! Why would anyone want that? I probably can't name five people who can match the character or lust for life that boy's got. If we're going to start ridding the world of sections of people, I can think of other groups to start with. The school momsters, for instance! Who'd want to be ridded of the Daniel Oakes of this world?'

'Ben and Arthur adore him,' said Isobel.

'Oh they do! Everyone dotes on Daniel, even that crazed dog.'

And Daniel was affectionate, too. He called on Isobel most days now, with fresh eggs or milk, or a new book for the cottage. She felt a pang of guilt. Daniel thought she was staying permanently because there was no leaving date in the cottage register. But she was like one of the pirates the bay had fallen to. Here only to plunder, to take what she wanted for herself then leave again. 'He's fond of Will, isn't he, Sarah? Dan was telling me how he enjoys seeing Will up there at the cottage.'

Sarah frowned. 'My Will?'

'Oh to be popular,' trilled Cleo. 'Sam and I had *yet* another blazer tonight. Sorry to interrupt. Sarah, try my cookies.'

Isobel's phone vibrated in her back pocket. Sarah examined a biscuit. 'These don't have nuts in do they, Cleo?'

'No, why?'

'No reason. Sorry, what were you fighting about? Not Evie again?'

'No, not Evie. I applied for a small mortgage extension. To make something beautiful of this place. I forgot to tell him.'

'Oh dear,' said Sarah.

'They're coming to value the house next week. Sam opened the letter. We started rowing, Evie heard us saying we wanted different things, she got upset, next thing we know,' Cleo threw her hands up in the air, 'she says the name-calling's started again on Facebook.'

'I thought Evie was working through all that? I saw her a few days ago, she's looking fantastic. Really *happy*, if anything.'

Evie hadn't been a happy bunny as she'd made Isobel's smoothie earlier. *Cheaper up close.*

'I just don't get it, Sar. I know Eves can be a drama queen, but one minute she's up, the next she's down. And *Facebook*? Sam's taken her phone. She has no laptop in her room either, so where's Facebook coming into it?'

'Maybe she's using her friend's phone?' said Isobel.

'Nope, I don't think so. Evie only really has two friends. Verity she hasn't seen for ages and Cassie keeps ringing the house trying to get hold of her, so I know she's not with Cassie. This is going to sound terrible, I know, but I suspect Evie's hamming this whole trolling thing up.'

Isobel shifted on her box. 'Why?' Her phone buzzed again.

'I just have this feeling.'

'Cle, you need to be sure,' warned Sarah.

'The trolling problem only rears its head when something else is kicking off. Like Sam fighting with me. I'm not saying Evie hasn't had some hassle, I just think tonight, she forgot we've only just confiscated her phone and came up with the Facebook thing as a kind of kneejerk . . .'

'Reaction?' squinted Sarah.

'Or . . . distraction. We used to distract the kids when they hurt themselves. *Look, Harry! A helicopter! Forget your severed leg!'* Cleo repositioned her bum. 'Who knows? Maybe Evie thinks Sam and I are hurting ourselves.'

The storeroom fell quiet.

'Be vigilant, Cleo.'

Cleo followed Sarah's eyes to Isobel. 'Why? What did I miss?' Sarah looked into her mug.

'I had a little run-in with an online troll last year.' Isobel's voice sounded assured, level. She could be talking about the girl down the road. 'Be vigilant. I thought it would go away if I ignored it. It didn't.'

'What happened?'

'Um . . .' She looked up at the tiled ceiling. 'I lost. Just about everything I cared about.' She gave a surprised laugh. 'I sort of tumbled down a big black hole. Without my family, my sister, actually, the outcome could've been very different. So keep the dialogue open with Evie. Even if she is a drama queen, keep your eyes open.'

'The horrible shits,' marvelled Cleo. Evie's problems had just fleshed out.

Isobel set her eyes back on her drink. Cleo nibbled her thumbnail. Sarah slapped her hands on her knees. 'Well, here's something that'll cheer you up, Cleo. Max is on behavioural report at school. Juliette's monitoring him.'

'Why the hell would that cheer me up? On *report*? For what?'

'For calling Sebastian Brightman a wanker.'

Cleo whooped with laughter. Tea sputtered down her T-shirt. Sarah put her hands on her cheeks and shook her head. Cleo's rasping laugh infected them all. Isobel's phone buzzed again and she slipped off her box and dug it from her pocket. Text. Unknown number. Sarah started explaining *wow* words as Isobel swiped open her message.

BLONDE BITCH

64

Sarah was helping Mary in the school office when the last bell went. Mary was having trouble inserting a piece of clip art, a queasy-looking child with a green face and thermometer in their mouth, into the weekly newsletter.

The end-of-day bell sounded again.

'Nearly Friday!' trilled Mary, peering at her computer screen. She clicked *Save* and gave a little clap of delight.

'Nearly Friday,' breathed Sarah. Mrs Upton had promised to let her know the second another incident, of any kind, occurred between Max and Seb. They seemed to have made it through another day, incident-free. 'I'm just going to check Will's meeting Max at the gates.'

'Alrighty, dear. Thanks for the help!'

'No problem.'

Sarah walked the corridor. A few stragglers grappled with their bags and sun hats. 'Bye, Mrs Harrison!' one child called.

'Goodbye, Christian. Have a lovely evening.'

'I'm playing football tonight, Miss Harrison. It's Thursday.'

'Oh yes, I saw you last week. Have a nice time.'

Christian ran off and Sarah followed him through the infants' door on to the smaller playground where Will should be collecting Max. She could see Max crying as soon as she stepped outside. 'Max, what's wrong?' The stern lines of Will's profile made Sarah's neck prickle.

'G-God-zilla's, t-tank. It's too heavy.' Max's words barely broke free between sobs.

'Max, it's okay! I told you this morning, Jon's going to find Godzilla a small plastic tank so we'll be able to drive him in tomorrow for the vote, don't worry!' Max had bounded into school after that very conversation, desperate to share news of his new fishy roommate. He didn't care about Seb's cricket any more, he didn't even care about Chloe's puppy. He had his own candidate for school mascot now. Max had Godzilla!

Will pushed a newsletter into Sarah's arms. She skimmed through it.

Parents and Friends,

To avoid any confusion tomorrow, parents of children bringing in pets to our special show and tell assembly* for the Hornbeam Primary mascot election, please ensure your child brings in the completed permission slip below, AND remembers the entry rules already discussed in class.

In the interests of safety (that of our children and the pets we love), pets taking part must NOT be:

- bigger than the parent handling them (no elephants please!)
- Venomous
- fanged (spiders, snakes, vampire bats, etc)
- encased in anything excessively heavy when carried (fish tanks)

Thank you for your continued support,

Mrs Juliette Inman-Holt.
For and on behalf of Mr Pethers, Headteacher

* All parents welcome. All pets to be accompanied by a parent/
carer at all times. All pets to be cleaned up after <u>by parents</u>.

'She's done it on purpose,' Will raged under his breath.

Other parents were pretending not to listen. 'Will, please.
Max, really, it's all in hand. They don't mean small, plastic,
easy-to-carry fish tanks. It'll be fine.'

'Whatever,' snapped Will.

A huddle of Year 4 mothers were suddenly taking longer
than necessary to straighten their children's hats and handle-
bars for the walk home.

Will jabbed a finger at Max. 'He's missing out. Again. First
he can't go to football in case those dickheads are there—'

'Will!' whispered Sarah. 'Don't say *dickheads* on the playground.'

'Now he can't bring his fish in.'

'Yes he can. Max, don't cry. I'll have a chat with Mrs
Inman-Holt after our meeting's finished. Will, look, you're
right. I don't want you taking Max to football tonight while
I'm stuck here in these intervention meetings. Jon's tied up
and I don't want you running into those men again. Sorry,
but that's the way it is.'

Juliette was walking across the playground with an armful
of papers. She stopped to pop the last of her apple into the

ladybird bin. 'Fine. I'll run into *her* instead then.' Will snatched the sheet from Sarah's hand. He scooped Max up on to his hip.

'Will!' Juliette turned at Sarah's voice. Will slalomed around tractor-wheel planters heaving with the infant children's runner beans and wind-catchers.

Juliette rarely looked surprised. Like she'd just spotted a rogue wave headed her way. 'Yes, can I help you?'

'My brother is bringing his new fish into this school tomorrow. In a tank, or a bucket, or a paper bag if he has to.'

Juliette's features reorganised themselves into a picture of calmness.

'William.' Sarah's tone had absolutely no effect.

'Then I'll look forward to seeing Max's new fish,' said Juliette, calmly. 'But it won't be in a glass tank. There's a health and safety issue. Children get hurt when people are lax with that sort of thing.' Juliette didn't even glance at Sarah before turning for the school doors. She didn't need to.

'If you're that bothered, why only send your letter out now? The night before?' Sarah watched Will's face flex and change with his argument. He wasn't a ranting teen, he was making a clear, concise point. Juliette slowed.

'We'd already made the rules clear to the children. And fish tanks aren't within the rules. I'm sorry.'

Will glared at the sheet in his hand. His voice was low and firm. 'Says no venom here too, but they bent that rule for you, didn't they, Miss?'

Sarah looked at him like an alien being. The mothers weren't even pretending to go home now. 'Will, take Max home please.'

'Not until she admits she's singling him out. Cause he's my brother. Because of what I did to Elodie.'

Juliette half-laughed at the sky. 'Oh, please.'

Sarah suddenly wanted to pull her face off. She slapped her hand down on the ladybird bin. Her engagement ring clattered against the metal capping; it sounded more aggressive than she'd meant it to. 'Will! Home. *Now*. Max, go home with your brother, sweetheart. I'll be back soon, okay?'

Will screwed up Juliette's rules into a ball and lobbed it into the bin. 'Total joke.'

'Will!'

Sarah wasn't sure who will was talking to, her or Juliette, but he made sure they both heard every word as he stormed off. 'Getting paid to look after other people's kids and doesn't know anything about her own.'

65

'Where have you been, Sophie? I've been trying to get hold of you since I got up.'

It was coming. Isobel could feel it creeping back to her. The stifling feeling of powerlessness, the gloopy swell of dark thoughts threatening to break overhead and knock her down, straight back on to her arse again. Sleep had been impossible last night. She'd limped through a couple of hours shifting boxes and sweeping floors for Cleo; her muscles had ached with tiredness, she should've sunk straight into a dreamless, exhausted sleep. But her skin had been too clammy, her mind too restless, the cottage too dark and alien.

Blonde bitch.

She'd bought a new phone before coming to Fallenbay. New phone, new number. No one but Sophie and their parents ever called it; she didn't even get PPI messages. Cleo and Sarah had been accidentally included on that list, but even then Isobel could still count on one hand the people who knew the number.

'Work, Isobel. I have to work, remember? That seven pounds an hour won't earn itself, you know. What's going on? I have, like, ten missed calls from you. Are you okay?'

No. She wasn't okay. She should've known Sophie would drop a bollock.

'Why didn't you warn me?'

Sophie hesitated. 'About . . . ?'

'About putting my mobile number on one of the social media pages? Dangling it like a worm.'

'Of *course* I haven't! Do you think I'm mental?'

'You've put it somewhere, Sophie! I'm getting hate texts again, first one's in! The next fifty en route!'

'What are you talking about? I have no idea what you're saying.'

'*Blonde bitch*. Straight through to my mobile.'

'When?'

'Last night. About seven-thirty, eight o'clock.'

'That's all it said? Nothing else?'

'Yeah, Soph, that's all. I think they forgot to sign off with a kiss. I said I didn't want you to take those pictures of me with Ella before I left. I specifically said no photos of this stupid hair! I hate it! And you've gone and uploaded one. You've posted online how I look now, what were you thinking?' Her voice was pinched, one step from hysterical.

'This isn't a good idea, Isobel. It never was. I think we should back off. I'm coming to get you. I'll leave now, I can be there before nine.'

'You are not.' Sophie did not get to drop the whole thing in the crapper then flounce in like a hero whenever she wanted. 'And don't even think of starting the "*this is no good for your mental health*" crap, Sophie, that ship has already sailed. I'm staying.'

'Isobel, this is important so listen to me. I have *not* put a photo less than a year old of you anywhere. And I have not shared your mobile phone number.'

The fuzzy anxiety Isobel had felt all day was firming up, hardening into something more focused. Like anger. Sophie *never* thought ahead. Never considered the consequences. Never accepted responsibility.

'You know, Sophie, when you've dropped a clanger, the best way to deal with it is to just come out with it. Do you know that?' *Hold your damned hands up.* Isobel closed her eyes and counted to ten. Sophie had never held her hands up in her life.

Isobel tried to shake some of the tension from her shoulders. This was always a part of the plan, to poke around in the muck to see if DEEP_DRILLERZ was still crawling around in it. She couldn't run off the first time one of the other parasites floating around in there with him twitched her way. So what if some random had seen a picture of her with dyed hair and had sent a stupid text to this number? *Blonde bitch.* She'd heard worse. It was fine. Her address wasn't out there. She wasn't even renting under her surname. She could throw this phone away tomorrow if she wanted.

'Isobel, have you told anyone? No one knows why you're in Fallenbay, do they? Have you given your number to anyone?'

That's it, Sophie. Deflect the blame. You put my number online and then look for someone else to pin it on.

Not. Sophie's. Problem.

No one knew why Isobel was really here. Cleo and Sarah

both thought she was here to lick her wounds. 'Of course no one knows. I'm just another face passing through.'

'Isobel, I'm telling you now. I have not compromised your mobile number.'

'Okay, Sophie.' *Whatever you say.*

66

The contents of Cleo's top drawer sat peppered over the surface of her dresser where she'd picked over them like a gull at a rock pool. 'Where have they scuttled off to? Earrings don't have legs.'

The floorboard beneath the carpet creaked in its usual spot, just inside the bedroom door. Sam crossed the floor and slumped on to the end of the bed.

'Where's what scuttled off to? Your Jiminy Cricket? The little voice that used to whisper, *maybe you should check this with your husband first, Cleo?* Is that what you're looking for, darling?'

He started to peel out of the two layers of socks he liked to wear under his workboots. Cleo hated those sweaty, doubled-up socks. Having to pull one from the other, bits of silt and grit flinging in her face before she could sling them in the washer.

Jiminy Cricket. Her conscience wasn't dead and buried . . . she'd just given it an hour off while she'd rung the building society. She opened the drawer to her dresser and swept everything back in with one motion of her arm.

'A pair of earrings. There was a brand new pair of silver studs still in their box, I'd never worn them. I was going to see if Evie would like them.' She wanted to offer Evie's earlobes something else in place of those enormous hoops recently ditched for Evie's new image, before they made a comeback.

'Are you sure you haven't pawned them? To pay for the stack of flyers hidden away downstairs in the utility room? If you wanted to put Coast's latest expenditure somewhere I wouldn't see it, Cleo, you should've tried one of the pubs the other blokes at work get to relax in of an evening. Or the garden chairs on a Saturday afternoon. I'd never have seen your fancy flyers there, too busy grafting somewhere instead. Keeping some money coming *in*.'

She watched him in the reflection of their dresser mirror. His back to her where he sat on the bed. He reached up and rubbed at his neck, new cracks lining his knuckles. His knuckles had always split with his work. It wasn't Sam's boxing days that had seen their bedclothes dotted with blood, it was working for his family. Cleo looked at the back of her husband's body. *And Jiminy Cricket is back in the room.* Sam was right. She was wrong. She'd hit the roof if he arranged a house valuation by himself to borrow money against it. 'I was going to talk to you about the loan, Sam.'

He set his hands on his knees and looked up at the bedroom ceiling. 'Before or after you were going to let my gaffer know he had a few more years graft out of me yet?'

Cleo spun on her seat. 'I wasn't planning on *you* working to pay it off, Sam. Coast will. That's the point.'

'You don't know Coast will. *That's* the point. Do you honestly think I'm going to be giving up work with a twenty-grand loan hanging over us? While my wife bakes, brews and serves every hour God sends?'

'Sam—'

'No, Cle. I don't want to hear it, okay? You do what you think's best, alright? I'll just go sit with the kids.'

'What do you mean, sit with the kids?'

'You're the Captain, Cleo. This family has one pilot and three passengers. So you just keep steering us where you want to go. Until someone gets off.'

One of the kids crossed the landing and started downstairs.

'Son?' called Sam.

Cleo sat quietly. Twenty grand hadn't seemed all that much money, not for what they'd have in return, a beautifully extended eaterie, enviable views right out across the ocean. Sam was different, though. More than just tired of butting heads. For the first time she wondered if applying for this loan might have already cost them a whole lot more than she'd intended.

Harry came quietly to the doorway. 'Hello.' He looked exhausted. Wide-eyed and pale-skinned. He couldn't possibly be getting enough vitamin D.

'Son, have you seen my new DeWalt screwdriver set? Last time I saw it you were taking your bike apart.'

Harry looked around the room. 'No. I put it back in your van.'

'I thought that's where you put it. I need to clear that van out.' Harry went to walk away. 'Hold your horses, H, revision can't be that much fun. Do you know Charlie? Charlie St John? He's our new brickie's lad, must've started in your year.'

'Yeah, I've seen him.'

'He's looking to join a footy club. I told Rich I'd ask you about taking him along with you to training this weekend. Introduce him to the other lads.'

'I can't, I'm busy.'

'Too busy for football?'

Harry shrugged. 'Where's Evie?'

Sam looked at Cleo for the answer. 'Revising, at Elodie's.'

Harry seemed to have no opinion on this unusual pairing. Cleo had been expecting a few wisecracks at Evie's expense, but none had come. He definitely looked ill. She'd ask Sarah more about that bug sweeping through Hornbeam Primary.

'I have to revise too. Night.'

'Harry? I know you've got your first exam next week, and it's great you're applying yourself, but you can't spend every minute studying in that room. Go out, get some sunshine.'

'Your mother's right. You're entitled to a life, son.'

Harry dipped his head. 'Okay. Night.'

67

Curiosity killed the cat. Sarah could hear her mother now. *You shouldn't go poking around in nettle patches unless you're prepared to take a sting, darling.* She sat on the floor in Will's room, back against the cold radiator, toes pressed into his royal blue carpet. She'd listened to the sounds of the street through his open bedroom window. The carport gate opening and clattering shut again. The squeak of Will's bike brakes. The back door. Keys on the kitchen counter. His grown body traipsing upstairs.

Will walked in and froze. His room wasn't ransacked exactly.

'Don't suppose you're in here to dust?'

Sarah straightened her legs along the carpet and pulled her head away from the radiator. Who was this boy, standing in their home? This nearly-man with his father's face and his own ballooning arsenal of secrets? She opened her hand. A plastic money bag like those they used to take to the bank together on a Saturday morning, stuffed with coppers, sat centred on her palm.

'What are we thinking then, Will? Enough weed there for twenty or so spliffs?'

Her reckoning could well be out, her one dalliance with

pot-smoking began and ended in the time it had taken Patrick to sing one chorus of 'Pass the Dutchie'. But Will still looked suitably stunned by his mother's insight. Good.

'It's not mine,' he croaked.

A defence quick and from the hip. Like his dad's. *I didn't mean for this. Sabina's coordinating the exhibition, she has great contacts.* And great boobs and hair.

Sarah opened her other hand. The ten-pound notes she'd found rolled up on Will's wardrobe shelf sat there like a fat cigar.

'Mum, it's not what it looks like.'

'You, Will, are not what *you* look like.'

'What does that mean?' His voice was sluggishly teen-like again. She wanted to yell, *grow up*!

'You look like my son. Who I love more than anything in this world. But I don't know who you are, Will. You were absolutely right, I don't know anything about my own kid.'

'Huh? I never said that to you.'

He had, in Max's playground; it obviously wasn't aimed at Juliette. 'I look at you some days and I don't know who I'm looking at. You don't talk to me any more, you're never home, your phone is going all through the night and people I've never heard of are texting you. And you're so angry, Will. I can feel it. Is it the wedding? You're calm on the outside but there's a tension. Take those men the other night, you can't just—'

Will erupted. 'Those men hurt you!'

Sarah matched him. 'You can't go around doing what the hell you like! Do you know one of the school mothers has made a complaint? She wants you banned from entering on to school property because you intimidated her. Do you understand that? The way those men made me feel on that football pitch, *you* made another woman feel like that while she was collecting a child today!'

'Juliette.'

'No, Will. Not Juliette. Juliette didn't say another word to me.' Which had been a surprise. Sarah and Juliette had done that thing at the intervention meeting where you manage to take part in a conversation with someone without ever addressing them directly. They were both very good at it. 'You shouldn't have spoken to her like that, William. You haven't helped Max.'

Will slung his backpack into the corner of the room. It clattered against his guitar stand. 'Juliette hates me! And I get it. I can take it. But she can't take it out on Max.'

'I agree. Absolutely. But Will, your behaviour at the school today was unacceptable. This, Will!' Sarah held up the pot. 'This is unacceptable.'

'It's not mine. It's not for me.'

'So you're a dealer?'

'No! Not really . . . it's not that simple.'

'Go on then. Fill me in.' Will slumped on to his bed, stilting his elbows on his knees. He rubbed his face as if dabbing cologne. *Eau de Truth*, hopefully.

'I'm not dealing drugs. That's not my money. It's not my weed. I was just trying to help—'

'Help who, a friend? To do what? Score pot? Which friend? Edward?' Will's eyes gave him away. 'Is this Edward's canna-bis? Are you holding it for him?' Will looked away. 'So what's his last name? Is he at your school? Where does he live?'

She stopped herself before she asked what she really wanted

to know. It was there, screaming at the surface of her brain, banging to be let out.

Is Edward the boy who sends you pictures of his erect penis, Will? Have you been sending pictures too?

Sarah's heart thumped in her chest. She sounded neurotic. She sounded like her father. But her father had never had to worry about this stuff when Sarah was growing up; this world with its internet and share-everything culture was a different landscape. It wasn't about keeping your kids safely home any more, it was about keeping the dangers of the world safely out.

She couldn't keep Will safe, that was the reality. She couldn't stop strangers from sexting him. That there was even a name for it should strike fear into the heart of every parent with a phone-wielding child. Gay or not, the thought of Will dropping his guard so catastrophically, literally laying himself bare to the world, leaving himself so open to exactly the kind of exploitation poor Isobel had been through, was so terrifying Sarah could rock in a corner.

'Edward's just a mate,' Will finally said. 'None of this has anything to do with him.'

She couldn't bear it, sitting here, both knowing he was keeping parts of his life – important, intricate, complicated parts of his life – secret from her.

There were so many things she wanted to say. *Remember when we were a team, Will? Remember when I would tell you every night how I would never love anyone as much as I love you and your brother? That will never change for me.*

She knew it. And for Jon and all he was offering her, she was sorry for it.

Will lifted his eyes, waiting for her next move. She had

nothing. He didn't want to tell her about Edward and she wouldn't push. Not yet. Sarah stood with her small cache of money and drugs. 'There's nothing we can't handle if we're honest.' She set them down on his computer desk. 'There is a five-year-old boy in this house I know you love very much. I trust you to do the right thing with this rubbish.'

She walked straight across the landing, past the gallery of photos charting Will's journey towards adulthood and downstairs before she changed her mind.

Jon had beaten her down there, laying casually across the sofa, absorbing a TV programme Sarah couldn't be bothered to look at. Had he heard them upstairs?

The lounge smelled of the bath salts he'd been soaking in while she'd covertly ransacked Will's bedroom. He'd been overdoing the running, legging it over the bluff every other night to swoon over his beautiful house. Sarah spotted the large glass of wine he'd already set down on the mantel for her and went straight for it.

'Everything okay, beautiful?'

'Yep.'

'How's the red?'

'Great.'

She had another glug. Jon aimed the remote. He flicked channel to channel, the shadows of the room reaching and fading, picking out the angles of his jaw, the line of his brow. His undeniable handsomeness. 'I was thinking. If we're serious about the baby thing, shouldn't we look into why it hasn't happened for us yet?'

Fan-fuckety-tastic. She took another sip, propping her elbow on the fireplace. 'Maybe. I think it will happen when the time's right. There's a lot going on at the moment.' She still hadn't heard the flush of the upstairs loo yet. Perhaps Will was planning on smoking it out of the house.

'Why don't we have an early night, test your theory?'

He was on his feet. *Crap.* They'd had sex every night he'd been running for the last week now. The new house was beautiful, but anyone would think it was literally turning Jon on.

His eyes followed her lips to the wine glass. 'Should you be drinking that?'

She couldn't think of a good reason why not. 'Why?'

'Antibiotics?' He slipped the glass from her hand, setting it down on the mantel. His other arm snaked around her waist. She let him move her hair aside and delicately kiss her neck.

'I've finished the course.' She needed to come up with a polite, *not tonight, darling*.

Jon's lips moved along her jaw, chin, finally to her mouth. He kissed her softly, no tongue acrobatics, which, along with jogging to Compass Point, turned him on immensely lately. He whispered against her mouth. 'Finished already? A month's supply?'

'A month of antibiotics? No, only five days.'

He levelled his eyes in front of hers. 'Because even dumb blondes can remember to take meds for five days, hey, beautiful? No need to print the days of the week on a little old course of antibiotics.' The hairs stood on the back of her neck. He set down a spent packet of pills beside her glass. 'I could always hear you in there, clumping around. I just thought you liked checking the loo roll stocks.' His eyes burned.

She tried to think of something to say, something reasonable.

Will appeared in the lounge doorway. Jon's eyes didn't leave Sarah's. 'Your mum and I are just in the middle of something, mate.'

'Sorry. I just checked in on Max . . . we've got a problem.' Will held out a hand revealing a limp orange form. 'Godzilla checked out.'

68

'Morning, Isobel,' Daniel beamed. She opened the front door and blinked into the day. 'Would you like some, we just picked them?' He held out a handful of pink stalks. Isobel took them automatically.

'Thanks, Daniel.' What time was it? Had she slept late? There was a throbbing pain along the base of her skull. Paracetamol. She needed paracetamol, not . . . *rhubarb?*

'It's rhubarb. We grew it. You can make nice things with it.'

Arthur called from his garden, 'Daniel, leave poor Miss Oliver alone. Let the girl wake up.' Arthur held up a hand. Isobel squinted and waved a stalk of rhubarb around the door.

'We're washing the cars today, would you like your car washed, Isobel?'

'Oh, that's okay thanks, Daniel.'

'Please? Dad has a washer, he lets me spray the soap off. And you do have some bird poop on your roof.' He pointed towards the irrefutable evidence. Those ten minutes parked outside the fish and chip shop had cost Isobel a pebble-dashing.

She yawned. 'Okay, Daniel. If your dad doesn't mind. That would be really kind.'

'Okay!'

'Thanks,' Isobel smiled. Daniel brought the same buoyancy to a morning Ella did. Isobel hadn't counted on missing mornings with Ella this much. Would she understand one day? Or would Ella always be on guard, waiting for Isobel to do something crazy again?

If they'd have just been on time. Parallel parking had always been a stretch. And the downpour hadn't helped, everyone making the school run by car, taking all the parking spots. A mother in a 4 × 4 indicated out of a row of vehicles. Isobel's car was half the size so she took her chances. She began shunting and angling but the rain made it tricky to see. Ella simmered with worry, *I'm going to miss register!* Stress levels had climbed. A passing father skipped along the pavement waving a warning. Too late. Her car bumpered the hatchback behind. Her pulse began swooshing with the windscreen wipers. Ella pulled at her door handle, she didn't have time for swapping insurance details.

'Ella! Just wait in your car seat!' Isobel's voice sounded like it didn't belong to her. Pinched and sharp. The hatchback driver left his car. He inspected his bonnet before approaching Isobel's window, tapping the glass. She didn't know him. He could be anyone. *I'm not opening the window.*

He knocked again.

She squinted shut her eyes and braced her arms against the steering wheel while he stared in at her.

'Open up then, love.' He was getting wet. Annoyed.

Her heart galloped. He was a stranger. A strange man. *Little Red Riding Whore, we all know who you are now. EVERYONE knows who you are now.*

Ella's headmistress had talked Isobel into taking her hands

off the car horn. Eventually. She'd escorted them inside school, dosing Isobel with sweet tea until Sophie arrived. No one had asked her to drive Ella anywhere since.

'I can read it if you like, Isobel?' called Daniel.

She hadn't been listening. Daniel lifted her windscreen wipers, retrieving a note from under them. He waved it towards the cottage.

'Don't tell me that's a parking ticket,' she groaned. Parking near Cod Almighty was free after six p.m., she'd checked. She hadn't used her car since.

'It's an envelope,' called Daniel, walking towards the cottage steps. He held it out.

'Thanks, Daniel.'

'I hope it's not a parking ticket, Isobel.'

'Me too. See you later.'

She closed the door behind her and padded into the kitchen. It wasn't a ticket. It wouldn't have sat on her windscreen unnoticed since Tuesday. She'd have spotted it on the drive home. She flicked the kettle on and slid one of the knives from the draining board along the envelope's edge. The note inside was simple and to the point.

Go home slag.

69

Will ducked in through the back door. Sarah slathered another hot croissant with Nutella. It was a wonder there was any Nutella at all; presumably Will had chronic bouts of the munchies these days?

'Will, Mummy let me have chocolate spread for breakfast!' Max whooped. 'Want some?'

Healthy, Happy, Hooray. Pah. It was election day and Sarah was pulling out the stops. Anything to help deliver the news of Godzilla's premature departure.

Jon had also departed prematurely this morning. No goodbyes. Sarah had been nursing a cup of coffee in the bedroom, pondering lost pets and found contraceptives, what her pill had meant to him, when Will had dipped a sleep-fuddled head around the bedroom door, whispering, 'Don't tell Max yet. I'll sort it.'

Will set his keys down on the kitchen counter. 'Any luck?' Sarah asked hopefully.

He shook his head. Sarah's hopes sank. It was a long shot anyway. Will had gone to try the flat above Tails 'n' Scales in the hope they'd take pity on their plight and open up at seven-thirty in the morning.

'Good thing I had a Plan B.' Will pinched his eyes as a yawn took hold. 'Hey, Max, bummer about Godzilla, right?'

I haven't told him yet! mouthed Sarah. Max tore into his croissant and planted his elbows on the tabletop, perplexed.

'Didn't Mum tell you?'

Max's chewing slowed, he shook his head. This was big news, he could tell. Will took a glass from the cupboard and poured himself some milk from the table. 'Fish get homesick all the time. They're taken out of the ocean, then they come to live with cool kids like you and, even though they love it in new houses, they kinda still want to go back to the ocean and surf, y'know? Hang out with their buddies and do all that stuff.'

Max licked the chocolate from his fingers. 'Godzilla will like it at my school today. All my friends will be his friends.'

Will skipped out of the kitchen. He returned from the utility room precariously carrying a Converse shoebox.

Sarah had an ominous feeling. 'Will . . . what's in the box?'

'Mum, chill. Godzilla kinda wanted to go back to the ocean last night, Max. When you fell asleep. He really wanted to go and say hey to his old pals, so he asked his mate, Godzilla II, if he'd come meet your friends with you today instead.'

Shoeboxes didn't hold water. It was going to be a snake. Or a bloody tarantula. Sarah held her breath as Will lifted the lid. Max's redundant croissant fell forgotten to his plate. 'It's a Godzilla! It's a *real* Godzilla!'

'Max, relax! You'll scare him.'

Sarah peered down. 'Is that . . . a *lizard?*'

'Bearded dragon. He likes veg and dandelions,' Will leant in to her ear, 'and he's only on loan, before you freak.'

'Can I hold him? Can I hold him?'

Sarah had stood in the pet shop yesterday convincing herself she was buying Max his first fish as some sort of considered life lesson, nothing to do with her throbbing sense of failure or her popularity diminishing next to Jon's. Godzilla I was going to teach Max responsibility and mindfulness. Godzilla I was already a distant memory.

'Sure, let me show you.' Will reached into the box.

'So . . . is Godzilla II coming to school with us . . . in my car?' Sarah asked tentatively. 'Does he bite?'

'Only Mothra, Mummy. Godzilla II hates Mothra.'

'I'll go empty out the fish tank, Mum. Take him in that. It'll be fine, dead lightweight. Easy.'

'He's a *real* Godzilla!' marvelled Max

'Will, I'm not so sure . . .'

'Mum, roll with it. No venom, no fangs, no stingers. No *heavy* tanks.' Will bit into a croissant. 'No problem.'

70

No sound but the leaves, a woodland doused in summer rain. Isobel listened to the utter resignation of it.

The air had changed. All the sunshiny seaside optimism gone. Someone knew who she was. *Where* she was.

She hadn't even called Sophie after the note. Why bother? Didn't take a genius to guess what she would say. *Get out. Get home. It doesn't matter that you've achieved ab-so-lutely nothing.*

The last few hours had been a haze of packing. It wasn't worth it, this laughable sisterly mission of theirs. They'd messed up. They'd been careless. Was it him? Was that DEEP_DRILLERZ's handwriting downstairs on the scraps of paper shredded into the bin? At the very least they knew he had links to Fallenbay.

Or was it someone else leaving a message on Isobel's car? Had Sophie been more cavalier than Isobel had first thought, that crumb trail of hers leading not only to Isobel's new mobile phone but all the way to Curlew Cottage? To Isobel's car parked outside.

Were they about to start showing up here the way they'd shown up at her parents' home? Creepy loners asking to see the girl in the video, bartering dates and disgusting favours at the front door before her mother could slam it shut?

Isobel stared at the beams above her and listened to the forest leaves beyond the cottage window, trembling beneath the showers.

Go home slag.

Her back prickled. When had the note been left out there? While she was in the cottage? While she was sleeping? Bathing? Walking in the woods with Daniel? Or while she'd been down in the bay, carrying out her flimsy reconnaissance of a town that may or may not still be anything to do with DEEP_DRILLERZ himself. Without a recent IP address still pinpointing him here, she'd never know.

She exhaled, long and slow, and imagined him outside, standing in Arthur's yard with his message. The king of trolls himself. Had he seen her around Fallenbay? Recognised her despite the changes? She pressed her fingers over her temples. No, she was reaching. Any internet weirdo could've left the note, anyone who'd followed Sophie's crumbs. Either way, either weirdo – the one she was fishing for or the ones she wasn't – she couldn't stay here now. The calls to the landline, her mobile phone, the note outside . . . She wasn't anonymous any more. She'd opened herself up, and for what? One crappy *hello stranger* on one of the social networks they couldn't even trace him from? It wasn't enough. Not for all this risk. Not nearly enough bite for her bait.

Her phone buzzed on top of her holdall. She pinched her eyes shut and answered it. So needy. So grateful to be supported. Still so shamefully pathetic.

Sophie's voice was crisp and hurried. 'I can't talk, they're all outside in the car, Dad's beeping me . . . *listen!*'

'Where are you all off to?' Isobel might make the drive home by the time they returned. She could surprise them, sitting on the sofa as they all piled back into the house, marvelling at their tanned blonde visitor. It would be festive. Dad would insist on breaking out one of his special bottles of sloe gin. Mum would ignore the washing up, declaring tomorrow to be the first day of the rest of Isobel's life. Her mum would put in a call to Uncle Keith while Sophie sat in tangible relief at Isobel's safe return, unscathed by the monsters she'd been off in search of. And tomorrow, Isobel would wake up in her parents' spare room and be that girl again. The other Isobel. No career, no home. Just a walking, talking cautionary tale of girls who gave their reputations away.

Petal's barks fractured the air. Isobel glanced towards the window.

'We're going to dinner. That doesn't matter, *listen*. He took it, Isobel . . . He took the fucking bait!'

'What?' She sat bolt upright on the bed.

'He followed one of the links, Is. Dumb-ass followed it straight to the blog and couldn't help himself.'

Her breathing became shallow, her body a stone-like thing weighted to the bed.

Has he commented? Has he left something Sophie can grab on to? She couldn't speak.

'He left a comment, Is! Bold as you like! Straight underneath two blog posts. He's reading them. The horrid little freak is sniffing around.'

'And the IP address?' They couldn't trace anything without

the address. Her stomach rolled. This was where Sophie was going to say she'd gotten it all wrong. How it wasn't as simple as all that.

'We got it. You were right, Is. He's still in Fallenbay. Whoever this prick is, he's still there.'

The first mixed tears of frustration and relief were coming. She felt giddy with them. 'Where? Do you know where?'

Go home slag.

Understanding set in. She might not know where he was, but she knew where he'd been. Here at the cottage. His hands on her windscreen wipers. And God knew where else.

There was a ringing starting in her ears. He could've tried the door handles, the window frames. DEEP_DRILLERZ could be watching the cottage right this second.

'Shit, Dad's beeping again. *Hang on! I'm just getting my purse!*' Sophie yelled. 'Isobel, he left two IP addresses for us. One trace is flagging up the harbour area again, same as before. He's still using Coast's internet.'

Isobel shuddered with the possibility she might have already seen him. He could've followed her home.

'And the other?'

Her heart crawled into her mouth. This was the part on slasher flicks where the person on the phone warns, *He's there, we traced him there, to the house . . . He's inside the house . . .*

She slipped on to the floor beside the bed and huddled there. Not cowering, just keeping her head down while she got it together, her back to the bedside table, eyes sharp on the bedroom door and anyone who might come through it.

'The other IP came up as a kids' p—'

'What? Sophie, you're breaking up.'

'A kids' park.'

'How can an internet address be pinpointed to a park?'

'It's not pinpointing it. That's the problem. The IP tracker only helps if the map pin sticks into a definite building, then you just street view it until you can spot a house number or a shop name or something, figure out the address of the pinpointed building from there. But the pin doesn't always fall directly on to a building, this one's just mis—'

'I can't hear you again!'

'. . . target. Missing its target. Go outside, Is! Get more signal!'

Outside? *Not a chance.* 'What's near the park? On the map?' A house. They needed a house, or even a row of houses. Then they could work out the address, check the electoral register, find out who lived in each one, whose internet was being piggybacked, close the net.

The possibility was solidifying. This might work, this could *actually* work. There was a chance his anonymous, pathetic life was about to be laid bare for the vultures, just like Isobel's had been. Sophie was going to make it happen.

A thought bagged her over the head. Finding DEEP_DRILLERZ was just the first step. She and Sophie still had a lot of ground to cover. More than Sophie realised.

'It's not a residential area, Is. We aren't going to find his home address from this. We're gonna have to wait, see if he comments on the blog again. Hopefully he'll use his home computer this time, but I think we'll be lucky, he seems to like public internet. We've got him at Coast again so we know he's habitual, maybe we could check times . . .'

Sophie was so on it, so dedicated, it was easy to forget sometimes. The part she'd played.

'Coast's a busy coffee shop, Sophie. We need something more solid. What's near to the children's park? On the second IP trace?' Isobel had walked enough of this town, she'd passed parks, she could drive to them now. See exactly what was around them.

'Loads of places. A high school, could be a sports centre. I haven't street viewed it yet, but there were tennis courts and car parking on the map view. Some smaller businesses with smaller car parks. Too much to take a guess at, Is. But at least we know he's a local.'

Isobel knew the park. Sophie had been looking at the high school, and the sports centre occupying the same site. Did the sports centre have wifi? Didn't anyone use their own internet in this town?

Petal had stopped barking. The rain was heavier, noisier, but she had definitely stopped. Isobel got to her feet and looked down on to the half of the yard she could see without opening the window any wider. Arthur's Land Rover wasn't back yet. The cottage felt eerie. Exposed. After hours.

'Isobel, I've got to go, Dad's hanging out of his door. This is good news, right? This is what you wanted? It's what you wanted me to do, right?'

The lines were becoming blurred. 'Yes, Sophie. It's what I wanted you to do.'

'Okay then. Well . . . Sorry I've dropped it on you like I have, but I wanted you to know so you can think on it. I'll call later and we can talk properly. What's the landline number?

I can't cope with crackly mobiles. Or did you take it out of the wall like I told you?'

'There's no point.'

'Why not?'

'Because pulling the phone out of the wall won't solve the problem, Sophie.'

'Why won't it? They were just a few silent calls. People get them all the time.'

'And the text?' It was like leading Sophie on one of their childhood treasure hunts. Waiting for the penny to drop.

'The text could've been meant for any phone number, a slip of the thumb.'

'And if there was a note?'

Sophie's voice changed. 'What kind of note?'

'The kind telling you to *Go home slag*. Left on my car.'

'On your *car*?'

'Yes.'

'Where was the car?'

Isobel's blood was rushing a little faster around her system, her heart fluttering to keep pace. 'Here. Outside the cottage.'

'Get the fuck out of there, right now. I'm not kidding, Isobel, get your shit, get in the car and go. Now! I said this was stupid. I never wanted you to do this. Some of these men are psychos!'

She was right. Absolutely right. 'I am going. I'm ready. I had to clean up, I was just waiting for Arthur, I have the key—'

'Fuck the key! Don't you ever watch the news? There are some real fucking weirdos around. This guy might be *nuts* . . .'

What? Sophie didn't get to do *this*! She didn't get to throw a grenade *and* be the saviour telling everyone to take cover!

'Do you think I don't know that?' snapped Isobel.

'Then get out of there! Get your keys and get in that car . . . or I'm telling Dad.'

Isobel's fury spasmed. It was a childish threat, and a good one. Their dad couldn't know about this thing they'd been doing, his two girls. One secret would hold the door open for the next, too much would trot on out. There would be no turning back for any of them, for Ella.

'I'm going, I'm going.' She heaved her holdall on to her back and staggered downstairs. The rain had called an early twilight. The gloom was thicker down in the hallway, like floodwater rising through the cottage.

'Where are you going, Isobel?'

She had been headed for home. Had been. Now, she might be in his sights, but for the first time DEEP_DRILLERZ was very nearly in hers. She couldn't stay. But she couldn't leave either.

'Hotel. I'll book in somewhere.'

'You're not coming home?'

'No.'

'*Why?* Haven't you had enough? You've achieved something. You're tougher than you were, I get it. Why can't you just leave it alone now?'

She had had enough. Enough to last a lifetime as it went. 'Nothing's changed, Sophie. I came here to change the landscape. Everything is the same.'

'*You've* changed, Isobel.'

'I know.' But the change wasn't meant for her.

'I think . . . I think you should let the police handle it now.' Isobel stood still in the hallway. Sophie hadn't been the one who'd said telling the police would be more harrowing than helpful, their dad had. But Sophie had been riding the no-police campaign bus right alongside him. Now she'd just hopped off. 'I have the transcripts, Isobel. I've kept everything from last time. We've done a lot of the legwork, let's just give it all to the police, okay? Let's do this responsibly now. Safely.'

Isobel was stunned. Sophie ran in the opposite direction to *responsibly*, always had. 'Why are you saying this?' Did Sophie know what she was saying? 'Why now, Soph?' Isobel's heart was thumping.

'Because you're right. Something does need to change. But not like this. He knows where you are. It's gone too far. I couldn't forgive myself if anything happened to you, Is. I love you.'

The rain thrummed against the front door. She wanted to tell Sophie not to cry.

Isobel heard her father's voice. The voice she'd listened to through his chest, back when a cuddle and a fairytale on his lap could fix anything. 'Sophie? What the bleeding heck are you doing? We're all waiting.'

'Coming!' Sophie's voice was light and carefree for him. 'Okay, then, really glad you're moving. Call me when you're all settled, okay, hon?' Sophie was faking a call to a friend. 'Twenty minutes, okay?' she whispered.

'Twenty minutes?'

'Okay, hon. Text me your new address or I'll come find you myself!' Sophie laughed. Jokey-jokey for their father. 'Twenty minutes. Agreed?'

'Okay, Sophie. I'm leaving now. I'll text you within twenty minutes when I know where I'm heading.'

Sophie clicked off. It would be dark soon. Arthur would have to have his key back through the post. Isobel would forgo her goodbyes with Daniel. And Ben. She grabbed her things and pulled open the door, ready to launch herself through the rain. The figure blocking her path jolted in alarm. Rain streaked down Sarah's face.

'Crikey, Isobel, you scared me to death! Next door's dog, it put me on edge. I waited in the car for ages until it stopped barking.' She clocked Isobel's holdall. 'Are you alright? Has something happened? Are you leaving?'

'No . . .' Sophie was right. She was changing. Lies were becoming automatic.

'Great, I wanted to ask you something. I won't stay long.'

Sarah's hair was plastering itself to her head. Isobel wanted to leave now, before it got any darker. 'When I said not leaving, I meant not leaving for home. The water's off.' Another lie. 'I couldn't even offer you a drink.'

'Oh no. Where are you going to go?'

She tried to think of something credible. Sarah was watching her mouth, waiting for an answer. Isobel was taking too long to speak. She pressed her teeth together and accidentally bit the side of her tongue as the paranoia kicked in. 'I think I passed a B&B the other—'

'No need! I still owe you for that lift home. Arthur won't be fixing anything before tomorrow and you have your things packed already. You can stay at mine.'

71

Isobel followed Sarah's lead, shaking out of her wet pumps before walking into the grey-blue kitchen. Copper pans hung uniformly from the ceiling, light bounced off decorative jars and bottles above the units, children's drawings clung to the fridge. She was a wet and bedraggled impostor dripping in the heart of someone else's home. 'Sarah, I'm putting you out, I feel terrible.' The air smelled of popcorn and cinnamon. Isobel's stomach realised it hadn't eaten a thing all day.

Sarah handed her a towel she'd lifted from a stack in the utility room. 'Not at all. It's nice to have another girl here.'

A child's voice echoed through the house. 'Mummy! Come look, we're watching *Deadly 60*. Steve Backshall has got a bearded dragon just like Godzilla II!'

Sarah gave a flat smile. 'Don't be alarmed by our other house guest. Will's borrowed his friend's lizard so Max can feel popular at school. It's in a tank and it won't hurt.' Sarah led them along a long polished hallway to the lounge. Isobel hung back in the doorway with her towel.

'Hey,' said Sarah.

Jon was stretched on the sofa, one arm behind his head, Max and a small lizard in his lap.

'Hi, Mummy.' Max glanced at Isobel then straight back to his nature programme.

Jon looked around Sarah, offering Isobel a homely smile. 'Hello again.'

'Hi,' smiled Isobel. Bedraggled.

'Isobel's water's off. I'm going to make up the spare bed.' Sarah's voice had changed. An old tension hung stubbornly in the air. Cleo said they never argued.

'No water, huh? You look like you've been swimming.'

Isobel could feel the damp spreading across her shoulders. 'Sorry for dripping all over your lovely home. We only dashed from the cars.'

Sarah cleared her throat. 'Is Will home? He'll be drenched.'

Jon repositioned his shoulders and looked back at the TV. 'Nope.'

Sarah gave him a few seconds before turning back to Isobel. 'Let's get a hot drink then I'll show you the spare room. Have you eaten?'

Jon lifted Max from his lap and set him on the cushions. 'I was making a drink anyway.'

'Oh. I'll just nip up now then and make the bed up.'

He stood from the sofa and stretched out. Isobel accidentally caught sight of a tanned, taut stomach where his T-shirt rode up. 'You do that, beautiful.' He patted Sarah on the head then, rubbing her hair into a fluffy mess as if she was a little boy just scored for his team. 'I'll make small talk with Isobel while the kettle boils.' He was just being playful. Of course he was. Isobel waited for Sarah to swat him away, but she didn't. So Isobel looked at her feet instead.

Sarah cleared her throat. 'I'll just be five minutes.' She disappeared up the sweeping wooden stairs.

'Red or white, Isobel?" Jon asked, leading them back through the house. 'Sarah likes a red but we have both open already.'

She'd been holding out for that nice hot cup of tea but Jon was already reaching for a glass. 'Um . . . Either, thanks.'

'Red then,' he smiled. 'Sarah missed dinner. I was going to heat up some chilli for her before I shoot out. Do you like chilli, Isobel?'

'Please don't go to any trouble. I'm already imposing.'

'It's no problem. I'm just going to reheat it.' Jon grinned. He had very good teeth.

'Thanks. I forgot to eat today.'

'Sarah's the same. She gets preoccupied and forgets to take care of herself.' Isobel took her glass. A drink with Sarah might chase away some of the edginess the note on her car had left her with. Or it might soften her up too much. She might end up spilling the whole idiotic story. Sarah might think Isobel was bringing trouble to her and Jon's door.

Jon moved around the kitchen, unhooking pans, splashing oils, chattering away. By the time Sarah walked back in, a small picnic of salads and steaming rice accompanied a fragrant pan of piping hot chilli on the dining table.

'Thanks, I could've got that,' said Sarah.

Jon finished wiping the side down, picked up a set of keys and pecked Sarah abruptly on the head. 'I've gotta run.'

'Where are you going?'

'To have a drink with a bored teenager.'

'Where?'

'Huey's band. We spoke about it. If we're booking Bored Teenagers for the wedding reception, someone needs to hear them play first.'

'That's not tonight, is it?'

Isobel felt herself flush. 'I'm so sorry, I've spoiled your plans. Really, I can book into a—'

'No, it's fine,' smiled Sarah. 'I've seen them on YouTube already, I know they're great. Let's just book them. Huey's your friend anyway, have a drink with him. Catch up. Boys' night.'

Jon nodded. 'I might. See you girls later, don't wait up. Isobel, make sure you lock the bathroom door. Max has a habit of walking in on you.'

'Thanks for the warning.'

He ducked out through the back door. Sarah watched him run across the garden. 'Isobel, did you want to change first?'

'Yes, but I don't think my stomach will let me. This smells amazing. Does he cook for you every night?'

'Only when he's reminding me how perfect he is.' Sarah inspected the bottle Jon had left on the table. 'Sorry. Rocky week. How was yours?'

'Yep. Good.' Psycho stalker aside. Isobel took a sip of wine and felt it tingle over the sore part of her tongue. She caught Sarah looking at her the way she had at the cottage door.

Sarah smiled and dressed both plates with salad. 'Bruxism.'

'Sorry?'

Sarah spooned a mound of chilli next to the salad. 'My ex-husband used to have it too. He'd grind his teeth all night long, I could hear him sometimes from the nursery, while I was feeding Max through the night. And still I never clocked anything was eating him. Do you get many headaches?'

Isobel forked a quarter of cucumber. 'Most mornings, actually.' She let her tongue run over the back of her teeth and questioned the doctor's caffeine theory. The headaches never had really abated, no matter what she cut out.

'Stress is the trigger. I noticed you grinding at the tattooist's. I'll leave you some paracetamol to take up to bed with you. Patrick found taking two as soon as he woke helped. We were always at the dentist, he wore a mouth guard in the end. Guess he got fed up of treating the symptoms instead of the problem. Divorce was probably cheaper than paying Karl, the dentist you met at the football pitch, to repair his broken teeth all the time.' Sarah almost smiled. 'He has beautiful teeth now. American teeth. To go with his American wife and their beautiful American daughter.'

'I'm sorry, Sarah.' Isobel tried to think of something buoyant. 'Hooray for expensive fillings, or you wouldn't have met Jon.'

Sarah stabbed a tomato. 'Definitely.'

'Who knows, you guys might have a little girl of your own one day.'

Sarah nodded at her wine glass. 'Every chance.'

'She'll have two big brothers too, to keep all those horrible boys away.'

Sarah sipped her wine. 'It was actually Will I wanted to talk to you about.'

'Will?'

'When we were clearing Cleo's, you said something about Will going to Arthur's?'

'Yeah, Daniel says he does odd jobs there. Arthur's arthritis is awful. It's good of Will to help. I wouldn't go into that woodland alone, not Arthur's end anyway. Cleo thinks teenagers hang out in Acorn Woods, so I probably wouldn't go in that end by myself either.'

'No. Me neither.'

'What does Will do for Arthur in there? He always comes out of the woods as smart as he goes in.'

'Honestly, Isobel. Nothing would surprise me with Will any more.'

72

Isobel rolled over on a bed that smelled of someone else's laundry detergent and squinted her eyes. Her jaw ached. She needed water, had she brought some to bed? Whose bed was this?

She managed to pick through the items on the bedside table next to her by the landing light seeping underneath the door. Bangle . . . phone . . . She used the light of her phone to remind herself. Clothes draped over the back of the chair. Holdall beside the bed. Sarah's spare room.

A pain shot through the side of her head. *Brux-something?* She hadn't kept up with her routine appointments after the blip outside Ella's school. Dental checks, cervical smears . . . she'd avoided anywhere sterile after her near-miss with the mental assessment ward.

She sat up in the dark, picked up the glass of water and felt around for the paracetamol packet.

Shit. She'd used the downstairs toilet before bed, in case she woke Max or bumped into any half-naked teenagers. They were on the side of the sink right there for Max to find in the morning and gobble like Tic Tacs.

She rubbed her face and sat up. *Just go get them. Do it.*

Don't even think about it. Kids, paracetamol, no amount of sorrys *ever being enough* . . .

The door clicked open nice and quietly. The landing and stair carpet cushioned her bare feet as she crept. She was quick, downstairs, in and out of the loo, tablets in hand. She had one foot on the bottom stair when a quiet hello drifted from the lounge.

Jon was leaning back over the sofa so he could just see her. The lights were off in there, the door barely ajar. He lolled himself over the sofa arm like a tired teenager, getting to his feet before arriving at the doorway, features soft with the alcohol she could smell fighting his expensive aftershave.

'Settled in?' he smiled. He was even more boyish after a night out. Not in the least bit threatening. And still that niggly voice women mentally conversed with on dark walks home or lone taxi rides, that voice you were supposed to take note of, was clearing its throat.

Isobel assessed the situation. Objectively. Her niggly voice was louder than most; she'd been reconditioned to be suspicious of men. Suspicious of everyone. Jon wasn't drunk, he'd just taken the edge off. The social etiquette that might otherwise curtail a meeting like this, hours after midnight in a poorly lit hallway, had been rounded off for him, that was all. But Isobel hadn't been drinking, she'd played at her glass of wine. *You're perfectly in control.*

She told that niggly voice to *shush* and stepped back off the stairs in case she woke anyone above her.

'Hi. Sorry, I left something down here, got it now. Goodnight then,' she whispered.

'Yeah, great thanks.'

He thought she was asking a question. 'That's good,' she replied. She tried again. 'Night then.'

'Nightcap?'

The niggly voice didn't bother. 'Oh, no thanks. That's okay. I don't really—'

'Come on, Isobel. Don't be coy.'

Coy? She wasn't *flirting* with him. Not inviting him in any way.

'Sorry?'

'You say that a lot, don't you? Makes you sound weak.'

The adrenalin was suddenly there. Jon moved towards the bottom of the stairs and looked up at the landing. Isobel's left hand was suddenly in his; he turned it over like he'd caught a thief. For a silly, stupid second she thought he was about to snatch the box of paracetamol back, accuse her of stealing their headache tablets in the dead of night.

He didn't touch the painkillers. He rubbed his thumb over her wrist as if shining a penny. 'You're all the same, aren't you?' Isobel swallowed. She couldn't speak. 'Coy little cock-teasers with your butter-wouldn't-melt faces and bad-girl tattoos.'

She snatched her hand back. 'How dare you.' The words sounded silly and pretend, a seven-year-old telling off one of her teddies, impersonating her grandmother.

Jon's smile was less lazy now, his eyes less benign. 'Don't be shy, I've seen everything you've got to offer already, Isobel.' Her heart was hammering so hard she thought he might hear it. 'Do you know how many times I've watched you, *Isobel Yvonne Hedley*? Rewinding. Freeze-framing.' Jon bit at his lip. 'How is it you've come to find yourself in my neck of the woods, Little Red Riding Whore? Come to look for more trouble?'

'Touch me again and I'll scream this house down.'

He laughed. Laughed her off. Dismissed her. She was just a silly little girl in her pyjamas in his hall. A little woman about to have a heart-attack from too big an adrenalin surge.

'Shout as loud as you like. Shouty little tarts tend to have trouble being heard, Isobel. Even by their friends. You came downstairs to me.' His eyes and his tone held the same message. *Sarah won't believe you.* He looked her over again. *Him*, disgusted by *her*. 'I've got to tell you, Isobel, meeting you in the flesh, I like the blonde. But you were definitely more fun as a dirty brunette.'

73

Sarah, thanks for everything. Early start, didn't want to disturb x

Sarah reread the note Isobel had left on the kitchen shelf with the paracetamol packet while Cleo clattered and banged in the background over the phone.

'Well, what time did she leave then?' asked Cleo.

'I don't know. I didn't wake until Max came in, so before six, I suppose.' Isobel hadn't matched Sarah's wine intake last night. She shook the paracetamol box, checking there were enough for her next hangover dose in one . . . two . . . ugh, three hours' time.

'I don't think a six a.m. start's *that* abnormal, Sar. Take Max . . .'

'I know, but . . . I might be going loopy, but I swear she moved the bed.'

'Which bed?'

'The bed in the spare room.'

'Where the hell did she move the bed?' snorted Cleo.

'Nowhere. I mean, she didn't rearrange my furniture for me. But I think she'd moved the bed over by the door, then moved it back again. But not back exactly where it was. I stripped the bedding and there are dinks in the carpet.'

'Why would she move the bed? Is your Feng Shui out?'

Cleo thought Sarah was loopy too. 'You know what, this is my hangover talking. I'm being stupid.'

'Probably. Hold the phone, This Girl Can is about to walk in. If she *dares* even mention the bloody summer fair on my premises, I won't be held responsible.'

'This Girl Can?'

'Rachel Foley. Happy, smiley, don't-punch-me-in-the-face Rachel. Sam's seen more exercise than that T-shirt has.'

'Easy, tiger. Just be thankful you don't have to do the summer fair this year. I've got an hour to sober up and get down there to erect gazebos.'

'Don't suppose you would hand out some of these flyers for the open-mic night at the fair, would you? I've got hundreds to get rid of, Sam's gone mad. He heard me offering Harry cash to go delivering them door to door.'

'I'll swing through and collect some on my way to the school. Get me a double choc muffin ready, would you, Cle? I'm going to need sugar today, lots and lots of sugar.'

'You're a darling! Will do. Gotta go, Sar, she's smiling right this way.'

'Try smiling back.'

Cleo clicked off. Jon was whistling over the Aga, he and Max had a frying pan each, Jon's congested with bacon and egg, Max's with leftover salad from last night.

'Here you go, Godzilla II.' Max dumped the contents of his play-saucepan into Godzilla II's travel tank.

'And here you go, Mummy,' mimicked Jon, 'because she'll

need her energy today to deal with all those wet sponges, won't she, Max?'

'Yeah! Drench-a-Wench! The people have to put a lady's wig on and then they stick their heads through the hole and *pow*!' Max explained to Godzilla II.

'One egg or two, beautiful?' He did this, went on a charm offensive after she'd messed up. Jon had the big pans out this morning; she'd cocked up big time. Isobel staying over had only deferred it. Sarah had cheated Jon out of fatherhood. He had every right to be pissed off.

'Just one, thanks.'

He hadn't come to bed again last night, even with Isobel taking his new spot in the spare room. There had been sand on the sofa this morning. He must've detoured to the beach on his way home from the gig, trying to straighten his head. Trying to figure out how he'd got himself engaged to a woman who didn't want to bear his children.

'I'm clearing out the summerhouse today while you're at the school fair. Anything you want saving?'

Bugger, the ciggies were still in the chimney pot where she'd lobbed them. 'Nope, thanks.'

Jon set out breakfast and poured her coffee.

'Has anyone seen Will yet this morning?' she asked.

'He's a lazy bones,' said Max.

'Will's a big boy, Max. He goes to bed much later than you do.' There was a note of defence in her voice. Probably for Jon's benefit.

'What time did he come home last night?' Jon asked.

'Not too late.'

'Where did he go? It was pouring.'

'I'm not sure.' To the forest? Sneaking around in Arthur's private woodland with Edward the druggy pervert?

'We need brown sauce. I'll fly to the shop, anybody need anything?'

'Orange juice please, Dad.' Sarah's stomach rolled.

'Sure. Eat your cereal, I'll be back in ten. See if you can finish by then, champ.'

Sarah waited until she heard his engine roar off before slipping off her stool. 'Wait there, Max, I'm just seeing if we've got any more sponges to take to the school fair later.' Jon had already found her secret pill stash, if he found the cigarettes he'd think she was lying about being a non-smoker, too. She slipped on a pair of Jon's shoes and made it across the puddled lawn to the summerhouse. She had a quick scramble around a few obstacles, rolled up her dressing gown sleeve and reached into the chimney pot. She pulled out the rectangular form and examined it, expecting to see a packet of Marlboro Lights, not a phone. She turned the Nokia over in her hand. It was basic, not all singing and dancing like the smartphones they all had now. It didn't look that old but it was missing its battery. One more useless thing to sling before they moved. She lobbed it towards the recycling box by the doorway and took another lucky dip for that cigarette box. A quick feel around and . . . bingo.

74

Rachel stormed across the café towards the counter. 'Cleo! Emergency!'

'Are you alright, Rachel? You look ready to keel over. Juliette and Olivia working you too hard at the summer fair, are they?'

Rachel grappled to catch her breath. 'There's been a hiccup.'

'Oh?' Cleo set a stack of flyers aside for Sarah to collect.

'Lorna's made the wrong cakes. Juliette's going crazy, she thinks Lorna's put something . . .' Rachel pincered her fingers to her lips and imitated smoking '. . . *funny* into the recipe by mistake. They've all got to go in the bin. And now we have no cake stall. A school fair with no cake stall!'

'Golly,' said Cleo flatly. 'This is a quandary. I didn't know Lorna was a pot-head. Would explain a few things, though.'

'Cleo! Lorna is not a *pot-head*.'

'Just likes the occasional doobie, huh?' Rachel looked horrified. Cleo shouldn't tease really. 'Well she's on *something*, that one. So why's Juliette flipped her lid?'

'Lorna's cakes all have nuts and hemp seed in them. Juliette was yelling, "*We have at least two children at this school with a nut allergy! You'll send them into anaphylactic shock!*" '

'At least they'll be too stoned to notice.'

'It's not funny, Cleo.'

'Yes it is, it serves you all right. Now cut to the chase, Rachel. Why are you here when you could be getting your head snapped off with the other PFA disciples?'

Rachel knew she was on the backfoot. Her hands dropped from her hips. 'Could you rustle up some replacements? At cost?'

'How many?'

'Two hundred?'

'How long have I got?'

'Noon.'

'Done.'

Cleo couldn't help herself. Hornbeam always had such lovely summer fairs.

'And could you make them *healthy*, Cleo? Like flax-seedy and oaty? As if Lorna's made them? We're mums against sugar, remember.'

Rachel was starting to push her bloody luck. 'Sure, Rachel.'

'Really?'

'Of course. I'm a friend of Hornbeam.' Just like Juliette said.

'No one can know, Cleo. I know that sounds mean. It's Juliette, you see . . .'

'How will anyone know they're from Coast, Rachel? Now then. A favour for a favour. You are coming to my trial open-mic night next weekend, aren't you? I really need to create a buzz.'

'Oh, Cleo. It's *really* tricky. Juliette might be having a barbecue at hers, to say thanks to the PFA families for all their hard work.'

'I work hard, Rachel. I'm about to spend the next two hours working hard for you. Wouldn't it be nice if you all supported me for once? The way I'm supporting you?'

'I'm really sorry, Cleo, but none of us have seen Juliette's new pool yet. I'll definitely come to your next open-mic night, how's that?'

Rachel looked pleased with her diplomatic efforts.

Cleo smiled. *I like you, Rachel, I really do. But you had your chance.*

75

Isobel had been driving for hours.

Exhaustion had come and gone. She'd sat fully dressed on Sarah's spare room bed all night long, waiting for the door to open. But it hadn't. The sun had come up, birds had begun to sing, and finally Jon's snores from the lounge had signalled it was time to go.

It had all knitted itself together during those long hours in the darkness.

Jon Hildred was a Coast regular. The first IP address Sophie had found had pinned DEEP_DRILLERZ there. The second IP they'd harvested from the fake blog had been inconclusive, the location pin falling within the local park and spitting distance of several buildings, several possible places DEEP_DRILLERZ had gone online. The leisure centre. Horizon Dental Practice. Oakley Finance. And Fallenbay High School.

Isobel pulled up at yet more traffic lights, gazing at the road ahead.

So he'd sat in Cleo's café and berated, hounded and humiliated women over his morning coffee. He'd used the internet at his school to do the same. To wage war on Isobel's world. He'd pulled at bits of her life the way a hateful child pulled the legs and wings off an insect. Isobel had never met a real troll before. She'd expected warts and boils, not Calvin Klein shirts and Ray-Bans.

It was him. Handsome, helpful Jonathan Hildred. The guy with the picture-perfect life. The car, the house, that iridescent future ahead. Lovely family. Beachside home. A good life draped in comfort and class.

Was Jon more of a prize for her now? He had everything she wanted to take from him. Job. Friends. Partner and family. Reputation. All lined up like a row of tender plums waiting to be plucked. All he needed for the full set was the criminal record. Jon hadn't seen that particular item on her, what had he called it again? Her *aspirational list*. He had no idea what Isobel had come here to conquer, or the base camps she'd been planning to obliterate on her way up. Jon thought that list was for Isobel. But it was all for him.

And Sarah?

Isobel couldn't have wished for a nicer partner behind him. That was the point, wasn't it? To make DEEP_DRILLERZ know loss the way Isobel had come to know it. They had a family together, with Max and Will. An enviable, polished bubble. The bubble she'd told Sophie she was going to Fallenbay to burst.

The car behind papped. Isobel checked her rearview mirror then the green light ahead.

They were supposed to be faceless, the casualties. The innocent bystanders of Isobel's troll takedown. But Sarah and the boys weren't faceless. They had lovely faces, like Ella and Isobel's mum and dad.

If she went after Jon now, told the police what she'd found, where he worked, the concerns that would raise . . . there would be no bypassing Sarah and the boys. How would they cope? Will had his GCSEs. Whose stomach would Max clamber on with his popcorn and lizard?

She slammed her hands against the steering wheel. 'You should've listened to Sophie! You were never there to make friends!' Not Cleo. Nor Sarah, whose world would be under attack. It was a giddying prospect, all the devastation she could cause. Then what? Would she just disappear back home, victorious, standing on her summit, staking her flag firmly in the ground while DEEP_DRILLERZ, *Jonathan Hildred*, became acquainted with the Malicious Communications Act? He'd be busy trying to wriggle out of a prosecution for the distribution of sexually explicit images, for breach of privacy, for breach of copyright even. And for defamation, because Isobel wasn't an *HIV-riddled dirt-bag* or anything he'd said she was.

The anger was biting again. Arrogant bastard. *Don't be coy?* Did he think he could be as disgustingly disdainful in real life? In the hallway of his home? Jesus, he was pleased as punch. Happy for the chance to remind her he had the power and she had the reputation.

She pulled up at the junction and made the turn without thinking. She'd been zoned out for miles, a docile pigeon absently flapping home. Every junction the same until the choices had become more complicated. Turn right, turn left? Go home, go back to Fallenbay? Be the victim, be the victor?

Be that Isobel, be this one?

He'd have woken on the sofa this morning, Isobel's car already gone, Curlew Cottage vacated, knowing he'd scared her away. Only Sophie had known Fallenbay was a deliberate choice, now Jon knew it too. *Little Red Riding Whore in my home!* He wasn't stupid. Of course it wasn't a twist of fate. Jon

423

knew why she was here, what she'd come to take back from him. He probably didn't give a shit. She hadn't exactly been Buffy the Vampire Slayer last night. He'd scared her. She'd bolted for home, driving for hours, left turns and rights. That Isobel and this. His words riding gunshot all the way. *Filthy little bitch. Little slag. Little whore. Little Red Riding Whore. Disgusting. Disgusting. Disgusting.* But she wasn't disgusting. He was. He was a disgusting man. A disgusting human being.

She spotted a familiar planter-bed and made the last few turns on autopilot. More of a homing pigeon than a docile one, her subconscious steering her back.

She pulled into the driveway, Petal already barking.

76

'Roll up! Roll up! We've got the Coconut Shy! The Welly Wanging! *Hornbeam's Got Talent* over on the main stage. We've got Drench-a-Wench, we've got our two teams of dads ready for the Barbecue-Off! And many, many more stalls for you all to enjoy. Dig deep, parents and friends, all profits go to funding the new sensory garden, and finally, from me and my assistant here, Hornbeam's first democratically voted school mascot, Godzilla II, we'd like to wish you all a wonderful Hornbeam summer fair!'

'With all that hot air we could've had balloon rides too,' grinned Cleo. 'I thought you said Godzilla was a fish?'

Sarah's wig was itching. 'Long story.' If she kept scratching, Olivia Brightman would start a rumour about nits. Seb would have a field day with Max, fuelled by the bitterness of his cricket losing votes to a pet higher up the food chain.

'Why are some people more popular than others, Cle?' Max . . . Darcey Thurston's parents . . . Jon . . . what was the popularity formula? Luck? Looks? Kindness didn't seem to affect the algorithms.

'Who are we talking?' Cleo followed Sarah's line of sight. Alison and Kevin Brown and Olivia were all laughing, backs arched, at something Heidi Thurston was saying. 'Olivia's popular because she browbeats everyone into agreeing with her. Juliette, because she's so bloody rich and ergo has power over us lesser mortals. The lawyer, what's her name? Halle? Heidi? She's popular because she's intelligent *and* beautiful, and as a lawyer she mentally out-muscles Juliette, which shifts the dynamic again. Have you noticed Juliette is the only momster not pallying up with the lawyer and her husband?'

She hadn't noticed.

'*Power*, Sar. Juliette doesn't want to be toppled. Which is exactly why she's never made up with you. Because you and Jon might steal her and Karl's thunder.'

Wow, mouthed Sarah. 'You got all that in twenty seconds' nosing around the field?'

Cleo shrugged. 'Professional people-watcher. Why do you think Evie has such a hard time getting anything past me?' She scanned the crowds again. 'I like . . . to watch . . . people.'

'So have you really come to help me? Or is there a more sinister motive for that crooked smile?'

'Keep the wig, I like you as a redhead, Sar. You're feistier. To the point.'

'Cleo!' yapped Rachel, nearly galloping over, eyes darting across the school field where hundreds of children were dragging parents and grandparents stall to stall. 'We *agreed*! We were meeting in the car park . . .'

'I know, Rachel, but I like to make sure my cakes are delivered right to the tabletop. They're already over there, look. I even helped Lorna set them out.'

Sarah glanced over towards the candy-stripe gazebo Lorna had affectionately dressed with bunting and ribbon. Cleo leant in to Sarah's wig. 'If Lorna thinks pimping her stall is going to get her out of the bollocking Juliette's going to give her, she has another think com—'

'They are healthy, aren't they, Cleo? Juliette's on her way over. You remembered the oats and seeds, didn't you?' Rachel was as pink as her T-shirt.

'Sorry, Rach, you gave me such short notice and I had so little time to prepare . . . I ran out of *healthy*.'

'Ran out?' Juliette was approaching the display of cupcakes Lorna was hovering behind. 'No matter. Plain is fine, too.' Rachel bit her thumbnail and power-walked towards the others.

'You're still grinning, Cle.'

'I know.'

'So what have you baked up for them?'

'Put it this way, they're not on your *healthy, hippy, hoohah* list.'

A growing band of children encircled Lorna's stall.

'Look, Sar, they're like little sugar-dependent sharklings.'

'Juliette does not look happy, Cleo.'

'I'm quaking in my boots. Oh look, she was right. You really can see "Coast" printed on those cupcake cases from all the way over here. *Fabulous*!'

'Uh-oh, she's coming over.' Sarah busied herself restacking sponges beside the water buckets. Cleo stood square on, battle-ready.

'You know school rules. *No* advertising at the school fair, Cleo Roberts.'

'I know, whatever were Lorna and Rachel thinking?'

'We all know you baked the cakes, Cleo.' Juliette made *baked the cakes* sound like *poisoned the water supply*.

'I'd have a word with your cake stall staff, Juliette. If you don't like what Lorna and Rachel have sourced for you, you'd better go and shut the stall down.' Cleo nodded at the rows of children and mothers in floaty summer dresses, three deep at the stall. 'Or, you could just rake in the profits for the school's sensory garden.' Juliette glowered over her clipboard. 'Smile, Juliette. We're all friends of Hornbeam here.'

'Mrs Harrison? Mrs Harrison?' Olivia Brightman was striding over in her riding boots and Joules polo shirt, Sebastian's spindly arm clamped in her hand.

'Oh look!' sang Cleo. 'Olivia wants to drench-a-wench. Juliette? Fancy donning a witch's, sorry, *wench's* wig and popping your face through the stocks?'

Olivia arrived red-faced. 'Tell her, Sebastian. Tell her what he did. Your son has just stolen money from my son.'

Max was watching from the tombola stand. Sarah took a deep breath and beckoned him over.

'How much was it, Seb? Fifty pence?' Seb shrugged. 'Go on, Sebastian. What was it? Fifty pence? We'd like it back.'

'Seb doesn't seem overly confident of the facts, Olivia,' asserted Cleo. This was only going to go one way now. Us and them.

'I was talking to Mrs Harrison, thanks. Why are you even here, Cleo? You don't have children at Hornbeam any more.'

'Neither does Juliette.'

Olivia scowled. Max arrived at Sarah's side. 'Max? Have you taken anything from Seb?' Max stood behind her legs. 'Max, I'd like an answer please.'

'He's not going to admit it, is he?' spat Olivia.

Sarah tried to ease Max out from behind her. He wriggled free. Seb took it upon himself to try yanking Max out instead.

'No!' roared Max. In one smooth motion he lunged, fist outstretched, planting his knuckles square on to Seb's cheek.

'Max! What on earth are you doing?' yelped Sarah.

Seb landed on his bottom. The slapstick villain who'd yanked the wrong boy. Only he wasn't the villain, Max was, fist still clenched, teeth still gritted, standing over Sebastian.

'Oh my God! Did you see that? Did you all see that? He *assaulted* my son!'

'Max?' Sarah crouched and spun Max to face her. 'What on earth?' Max's chest was heaving, his nostrils flared.

'Will told me. Next time Seb tries to hurt me, hit him as hard as I can.'

Olivia scooped Seb up like a wet insect and tried to cradle him, but he was too big; they looked like they were wrestling.

'I didn't take any of Seb's money,' sniffed Max.

'Oh shut up, you little liar,' snapped Olivia.

'Hey!' barked Cleo.

Sarah pulled the wig from her head. 'Don't you speak to my son like that again.'

'He's a thug! Like his brother. What are you doing, *dragging* them up?'

'Olivia,' warned Juliette.

'No, I hope you're writing this down in your notes, Juliette.'

Sarah caught sight of Darcey's mother picking her way towards them. Heidi Thurston had left her husband comforting Darcey. Oh God, Darcey was crying too. Had Max been on the rampage? Who else had he walloped? *Damn it, Max.* She was no match for a barrister.

'Hello, Miss Harrison, I didn't recognise you until you took the wig off.'

Juliette sidestepped, giving Darcey's mum the floor. Olivia smoothed her hair around her face. Anyone would think Amal Clooney had just strolled on to the school field. Heidi Thurston ignored them all. 'Miss Harrison, could we have a quick chat? About Max?'

Olivia straightened up so fast she almost knocked Seb over.

'Sure,' managed Sarah.

'Darcey had some spending money, I shouldn't have given her so much really, that was my mistake.' Sarah braced herself. 'I'm afraid another child has just tried to take it from her and she's very upset.' Olivia gave Sarah a cold smile.

'Oh,' swallowed Sarah. Two pocket-money muggings and a thrown punch. With witnesses. Max was toast.

Heidi crouched next to Max. 'Fortunately, Max was looking after Darcey, weren't you, Max? Thank you for returning her fifty pence piece. Darcey thinks you're a good, true friend.' Heidi straightened up beside Sarah. 'Mitch and I are taking the kids paddle-boarding this afternoon, do you think Max would like to come with us? Say, until seven-thirty-ish? We'll feed him too.'

Olivia's mouth was agape. The other mothers all vied for play dates with the Thurstons but they were always too tied up windsurfing or rock-climbing . . . generally being the ad campaign for clean living.

'Max? Would you like to go paddle-boarding with Darcey and her family?'

He looked up at Darcey's mum. 'Yes please, Mrs Thurston.'

'Call me Heidi. We can have coffee when you collect him, or I could drop him home?'

'Which child stole your daughter's pocket money, Heidi?' Cleo piped up.

Heidi glanced at Seb. 'Do you know, Darcey was too upset to say. But we all know those children, don't we? Whose parents never pull them up on their behaviour, they nearly always have those overbearing mothers who have so much to say about everyone else's offspring, don't they? Yet do so little about their own.' Heidi spoke amiably at Olivia then. 'I see them in court sometimes, the adult versions of the children they were allowed to be. I always wonder what they would have been like as six-year-olds. Whether they could've been steered differently.' Olivia was red in the face again. A collective of PFA mothers in silence was a rare phenomenon. 'Max, would you help me cheer up Darcey? How about we go and buy some of those tasty cupcakes before they're all gone. I've seen some orange ones, orange is Darcey's favourite colour. Do you like orange, Max?'

Max shrugged. 'Is orangutan poo orange?'

Heidi chortled. 'I hope so! That would be brilliant, I love orangutans!'

'Me too. I'm going to be like Steve Backshall when I'm bigger.'

77

Cleo drummed an erratic beat against her steering wheel and slaughtered the second chorus of 'Telephone'.

'Muum!' groaned Evie. 'Those aren't even the lyrics.'

Cleo looked over her sunglasses. 'Don't care. Love Gaga. Love-her-im-age . . .' She bopped side-to-side with each word like a gum-chewing cheerleader. She felt utterly smug today. First the fair, now her discovery of Evie's little secret. They'd cleared up at Coast, Cleo discovering Evie's love note as she'd emptied the apron pockets to bring them home for washing, she'd found Evie's love note.

Problem with phone. Can't call. Will be at usual place later if you can get away xx

Evie's new image was starting to make sense. Cleo held high hopes for some bespectacled, strait-laced boy who Evie would obviously bully but who'd keep encouraging this new, more demure, more studious Evie Roberts. So long as their little Shakespearean meet-ups didn't get in the way of any study sessions with Elodie, of course.

'You've been weird all afternoon, Mother. Just because you bootlegged a few cupcakes into the school fair.'

Cleo smiled angelically. *Juliette: nul points.* She locked her arms out against the wheel. She felt like superwoman today.

'You know the flyers your father said we wouldn't get out in time? I got rid of those at the fair, too. Every last one.' *Cleo: deux points*. She pulled on to the treed road towards their row of detached houses. Long lawns and low-rise dormer roofs made their place look like a squatting armadillo. Maybe she could get Sam to do something about those bushes before Monday's valuation? Soften the lines of the house? She pulled on to the drive. 'Right, no dumping your stuff, Eves, I've had the cleaners in this afternoon.'

'We have cleaners now?'

'Ha! I wish. No, darling, just a one-off before the valuation. Hope they've done a good job, there were mixed reviews on the Fallenbay Pinboard. I've left a test. Three strategically planted sweetcorn kernels. Bet they're still there.' Evie rolled her eyes. 'Brilliant start, they haven't swept the soil off the path. That rain ruined my borders, I specifically asked . . . We'll have to go through the garage, Eves. I'm not treading that into the hall I've just paid to have mopped.'

'Maybe they haven't been. Dad's working. If Harry went out, how would they get in?'

'Harry hasn't been out in weeks, he's been studying. Anyway, they have a key, H dropped his off at their offices on his way home Friday.' Cleo bleeped the garage door. It began to rise as Evie clambered out of the car, readjusted her ponytail and traipsed towards the garage. Cleo checked herself in the mirror. She could totally pull off Gaga. Her thoughts trailed to all those lovely 'friends of Hornbeam' – now 'friends of Coast', too – nibbling on her cupcakes, reading her open-mic night flyers. She was midway through that thought when Evie screamed her name.

She scrambled for the car door handle. *Intruder.* It was her first thought. Sam had a thing about intruders gaining access to houses through their garages. *Garages are funny places, Cle. Not secure enough. Too sheltered from view.* She burst in, looking for a stranger, heart racing. Evie screaming. Staring at the floor. Screaming. Screaming. Screaming.

The information wasn't transmitting from Cleo's eyes to her brain. 'Harry?' Was he asleep? He looked foetal on the cold concrete floor. She saw blood. Evie's eyes on stalks. 'Evie! Call an ambulance, *now*!'

Cleo got to her knees, her ear next to Harry's mouth. He was breathing, but . . . 'Harry? Can you hear me?' The cut to his head was bleeding, but only a little. It was more bump than bleed. Fried eggs, Sam used to call them. The slightest bump and Harry's head would erupt like a fried egg.

'Ambulance, please! My brother . . .'

Evie's voice trailed away into the background. Why was Sam's punchbag on the floor? Plaster dust in Harry's hair? She quickly forgot about both, everything shrinking down to Harry's brown leather belt, looped and fastened securely around his neck.

78

I am not afraid of storms, for I am learning how to sail my ship.

Isobel blew on the cottage guestbook and left it open for the ink to dry. Hers was the only entry. She wasn't sure if it was poignant or pretentious, but she knew she didn't care.

She'd showered, watched the boats in the distance through the bathroom window and thought on the phone call he'd made to the cottage that afternoon. It had been different this time. She hadn't put the handset down on the voiceless caller. This time, she'd imagined Jonathan Hildred at the other end, knowing now that she hadn't left town after all. Was he checking? Isobel had sat, quite calmly. Breathing, quite calmly. DEEP_DRILLERZ wasn't faceless any more, he was not monstrous. He was just a man. An awful man, but just a man.

Telling Sophie she was safely holed away in a hotel in town had bought Isobel some thinking time. Sophie had been given enough chances. She could've intervened. Sophie could've been the difference, those were the terms Isobel had set for herself. She would commit herself to teaching DEEP_DRILLERZ his lesson, unless Sophie learned her lesson first. But Sophie never learned, and that was bad news for Jon.

Jonathan Hildred.

Isobel had rattled it off on her phone keys, firing his name through the search engine. She'd expected one or two photogenic images to pop up, fished from Jon or maybe Sarah's Facebook accounts. Instead, Google delivered a stream of news threads on a *Falsely accused Jonathan Hildred*.

She had scanned the article synopses, scrolled down for more, scanned and scrolled, scrolled and scanned, the same snippets of information peppering her phone screen. *Sixteen-year-old student . . . sexual relationship . . . cocaine discovered . . . record payout . . .* Isobel had picked one and read the crux.

Jonathan Hildred, 36, was today acquitted of engaging in sexual activity with a sixteen-year-old pupil at £29k-a-year Tibbsley House private school in Gloucester. Mr Hildred's legal advisors argued he'd been subjected to a witch-hunt by members of staff following suspension from his teaching post at the private school pending further enquiries into claims made alleging a three-month relationship with an underage pupil.

She'd skimmed through the text impatiently.

. . . courts did not accept girl's testimony . . . claims the student was pursued from sixteenth birthday onwards in bid to incite her into sexual activity . . . nor did court accept Mr Hildred actively engaged a second female pupil with the intent of discrediting his accuser, since expelled from the school for possession of Class A drugs on campus.
In a move heavily criticised as too-little-too-late by Mr

Hildred's counsel . . . board of governors issued an apol-
ogy to Mr Hildred and his family . . . regrettably failed to
conduct a vigorous investigation into the accusations before
prematurely suspending Mr Hildred from his post.

Isobel gave the ink on the guestbook one last blow. She picked
up her phone from the bedside table and reeled off a text to
Sophie.

> Know who he is. Going to expose him.

She just needed to figure out how to limit the fallout for Sarah
and the boys.

79

Sarah was sitting alone in the garden, drinking a post-school-fair beer, thinking it all over. The brittleness of it all. The peaking and troughing of even an unremarkable life like her own. In just twenty-four hours Max had gone from the kid who got prodded with pencils, to Max! Keeper of Godzilla II! Righter of wrongs! Defender of pocket money! And the first child to be invited back to Barrister Thurston's home to play.

Max was not a delinquent in the making, he hadn't ever wanted to call anyone offensive names or steal their money. Heidi Thurston saw those people all grown up, every day, and she didn't see it in Max.

And Will? Sarah sipped from her bottle and drew her feet up from the end of the sunlounger. Will was about to start the exams that would decide his next step in life. The college he may or may not go to, the people he would fall in with. He was on a path of his own.

A squeaking of bicycle brakes sounded over the hedgerow. Will clattered through the carport and into the garden.

'Hey.'

'Hey.' He looked surprised, as if he'd just found a cardiganned escapee in the asylum grounds. Sarah watched the cool condensation trickle down the neck of her bottle. 'Max has solved his bullying issue all by himself. Thought you'd like to know.'

Will hovered behind her. 'Awesome. How?'

'By following his big brother's advice. Almost knocked Sebastian Brightman straight out with a right hook.'

'No *way*?'

'Way.'

'And . . . you're not mad at me?'

It had all been talk in Sarah's parents' house. All verbal rules and sanctions. Everything so measured, so orderly. But Will's heart ruled his head. And in this home, it was allowed.

'No, Will. I'm not mad. Pull up a chair.'

Will looked longingly at the house, then dropped his backpack on to the grass and pulled up a chair anyway.

Sarah didn't say anything. She wasn't even sure she would. They sat awhile in the quietly dying light.

'I was scoring the weed for Arthur Oakes.'

Sarah held the bottle still at her lips. Weren't teenagers supposed to be interrogated first before they caved?

'Arthur Oakes? As in, grey beard, hobbles when he walks?'

'His hands are killing him, Mum. His arthritis is bad and Ben's not always there to help him and Dan.'

Was he serious? 'So . . . this is some sort of door-to-door community initiative the local youth are running now then, is it? Like those American girl guides and their cookies? Only with cannabis and the chance of arrest?' Patrick's all-American daughter was destined to be a cookie-seller. Disney-cute smile and none of the abandonment issues her half-brother had been left with over the Atlantic.

'Arthur caught some of us in his woods a few months ago. Some of the others were sharing a joint.' Will held his hands up. 'I swear I wasn't smoking it. One of the lads told Arthur it was medicinal, good for pain and stuff. His nan uses it. Arthur said he'd leave us alone if he could take some home to try in his pipe.'

'A sixty-year-old man has you drug-running for him? After you and your friends got him hooked on cannabis?' This just got better.

'He didn't ask me, Mum. I offered to get it. It was stupid, but—'

'But *why*? It's illegal! You get an allowance. If you wanted to earn more—'

'I never cared about the money. I didn't want it! But Arthur started coming into the woods more . . .'

'His woods, you mean?'

'Yeah, his woods. But we're not the only kids who go up there, Mum. Some of the other guys, they're real dicks. I didn't want Arthur going up to them on his own in the dark, asking about . . . *weed*. Not with Daniel up there. He tries to befriend everyone, and not everyone's a nice guy.'

'You need to stop,' Sarah said firmly.

'I know. I'm going to tell Arthur. He didn't like me getting it anyway, but—'

'But he let a fifteen-year-old boy embroil himself in pot-dealing anyway? So what do you gain, Will? Out of that arrangement? If it's not about the money, huh? What does Arthur do for you?'

'Just . . . lets us hang out in his woods sometimes. Lets us have a campfire and stuff up there. It's kinda cool. Out of the way.'

'Who?'

'Just me and a couple of the guys.'

'Who?'

'Just . . . *friends.*'

Edward.

'So why the big confession now?'

Will shrugged. 'Thought maybe I should be honest about it. Make sure you know I'm not an idiot who can't be trusted . . . like dad.'

A silence opened up between them. Will bridged it first. 'So, no damsel in distress tonight?'

'Isobel? No. I did offer but I think sharing a house with three boys was worse than no water.' Sarah had tried to get hold of her. She'd left a voicemail the second time.

'Could've been your cooking, Mum.'

'Unlikely. Chef Hildred rustled up a chilli. You missed it.'

'Couldn't have been the cooking then. Not if *Jon* made it.'

They'd never done the *Jon* talk. All those surfing after-noons Will and Jon had enjoyed, bike rides Will had always come home so refreshed and enthused by, Sarah had taken as his endorsement. It was a conclusion she'd happily clung to like a floating log. And when Will's enthusiasm had dipped, when Jon started to look like a permanent fixture, everyone thought Will's standoffishness was all part of the readjustment. A natural transition. *Of course Will wants Jon to move in, he perhaps just doesn't want to be reminded there's a place to fill in the first place.* And so Will didn't necessarily dislike Jonathan. And so Sarah hadn't necessarily asked him.

'Will?'

'Yeah?'

'Do you like Jon?'

Will puffed his cheeks. 'I like that you like him, Mum.'

'That isn't what I asked.'

'But it matters. You deserve to be happy.'

'So does everyone, but that still wasn't what I asked.'

Did everyone deserve happiness? Patrick seemed to be getting more than his fair share, and what about people like Isobel's internet troll? Who only deserved to have his fingers lopped off so he couldn't use another laptop again.

Will pushed his hoody back. Dark hair fell forwards over his eyes. He pushed that away too. He wasn't just his father, there was something of Sarah's mother in Will, too. Something quiet and kind and trapped under glass. Something Sarah should've been more careful with.

'I'm sorry I messed things up with your dad, Will. I know Jon can never replace him.'

'Replace him? Why would you think I'd ever want you to *replace* that idiot?'

Idiot? Will idolised Patrick. 'Well, because your dad . . . he wasn't always . . .'

'An idiot? A selfish dickhead who ran off as soon as he sniffed something better?'

'Will, it was never about you. He never ran anywhere from you or Max.'

Will bristled. 'Yes he did. He left all of us and never looked back. Never saw Max learn to ride his bike, never saw the

442

photography competition I won without his stupid help, never saw you crying every night, getting skinny.'

'Oh, Will... I had a new baby, things are always fraught.' But Will wasn't a little boy any more. It was easier to play everything down back then.

'I used to wait for you, Mum. To come back out of the summerhouse. You went in there every night after we went to bed. You were so sad, I was worried you were going to do something. I wouldn't go to sleep until I saw you walk back across the lawn.' The muscles around Will's mouth twitched between sentences. The ramifications of his vigils began to set in.

'You waited up?' She'd spent hours in there some nights. Sitting in the dark with the baby monitor, sure the boys were soundly sleeping.

Oh God. She remembered. Will had looked so ragged. Dark circles under his eyes. She'd thought it was grief and had spoken to the school. Jon had been brought on board to help him through the loss of his father when all Will had really needed was a good night's sleep and a mother he didn't have to babysit.

'Will, I'm so sorry. I didn't kn—'

'Don't get upset, Mum. It's not your fault. It was never your fault. Screw him. It's Patrick's loss. Not ours.'

Sarah looked out across the garden, Jon's carefully choreographed planting trying to stand against the boys' discarded scooters, skate ramps, football nets. *What the hell was she doing?*

'Max clicked with Jon from that first day on the beach, do you remember? All this, *moving forward,* seemed easier

443

with Max being so vocal and I guess you being so quiet. It was easy to tell myself it was the best thing all round. But I never asked you, Will. How you felt. About any of this, the house, the wedding . . . '

'Mum, it's fine. Jon's a popular bloke. It's good Max likes him.'

'But not so popular with you?'

Will looked up through his fringe. 'It doesn't matter what I think.'

'It absolutely matters, Will.'

'No, I get it now, Mum. Stuff has happened this year and I get it now. You can't help who makes you feel . . . like you'll never go looking for anyone else.'

But I don't love Jon. She didn't. She was a fraud. She'd tried to but it had just never quite happened. She'd tried to make herself feel it; everyday she'd run through the package – funny, supportive, gorgeous, chivalrous – the list was extensive, like an impressive spec-sheet for a top-of-the-range washing machine. But the butterflies had never come. Whereas Will . . .

'You sound like you've been bitten, Will.' Her heart ramped up a little. All the hours he spent God knows where. The texts. The sexts. The late-night calls from Edward. Her father would disown him, of course. A potentially, possibly gay grandson? Will would be dead to him. Conditional love.

'If you've met someone, Will, you know there isn't any reason in the world you couldn't tell me about them, right?'

Will had picked a tree at the end of the garden to stare at. 'Even if they were someone you wouldn't ever choose for me?'

This was happening. Her mothering about to be tested.

The outcome branded into Will's mind and heart for the rest of his days.

'How do you know who I would choose, Will? I think we've already established our tastes are different.' She was trying for lighthearted. *You can't stand Jon, tee hee! And I don't know how I feel about your mystery Edward, ha ha ha! But it's all going to be okay, son. Horses for courses.*

'You wouldn't have chosen this, Mum. Everyone's gonna have an opinion but . . .'

'But?'

'But we want to be together.'

Will had struggled with it. It was there as he spoke. Coming out to a parent must be petrifying, Sarah would have had no chance. At Will's age, on the cusp of college, she couldn't even confess her love for the arts. She'd wanted to dance for a living, not teach. She'd never wanted to teach.

'Are they over sixteen?'

'Yes.'

'Then it doesn't matter, Will. You'll know a thing's right when you feel it. Whoever it is you feel it with.'

80

'A YouTube stunt? Is this a joke? He nearly killed himself to get on *You've Been* bloody *Framed*?'

Harry's eyes shone with tears. Despondency. Sam had mistaken that look for something else. Embarrassment or shock, perhaps. Cleo blinked slowly, trying to align her thoughts. She looked over at her little boy, lying like a thrown stick on the hospital gurney. They'd wheeled him into a side room off the A&E department for assessment, administering Harry a white comedy dressing, centred on his forehead. They'd given Cleo a sheet: *After A Head Injury*. The official diagnosis? A nasty bump. Two nurses had tutted amiably. *Boys, boys, boys! Goodness! I'd have half my hours if there were no teenage boys!* The Jamaican nurse had chortled before leaving to share the joke with Sam. The hilarity of their son's teenage tomfoolery gone awry.

Sam's neck was aflame. 'Is someone going to fill me in then? I get home to the Neighbourhood Watch camped out on my lawn. What the hell were you up to, Harry?'

Cleo cleared her throat but she'd lost her volume. 'I couldn't call you. My phone's still in the car.' Harry blinked, dislodging a run of tears. Cleo felt it all rush forwards again. Evie's face crumpled. She put a hand over her mouth but ragged breaths gave her away. She buried her face into Harry's neck. Cleo slipped through the curtain before the sound of Evie's muffled sobs pushed her over. She walked. Sam called after her but she walked. Away from the twins. Away from the terrible knowledge they shared. Cleo walked on, straight through the corridor, through A&E, past other people with concussed children, other mothers holding *After A Head Injury* pamphlets, readying their *He's such a klutz!* anecdotes for Monday's teachers.

She walked out of A&E into the cool evening air.

'Cleo! Jesus Christ, would you wait? What the hell is going on?' Sam reached her before she made the ambulance station. Her legs had lost their way. Mothers were not supposed to be lost. Mothers were supposed to navigate. 'Cle?' She should have seen it. She should have been watching.

She was already crying. Each time she pictured him, foetal, face pale, her chest hurt. Everything hurt. Her voice broke. 'I thought he was just looking run-down . . . but he was rock bottom. Waiting for someone to notice. But I didn't notice. I was too busy thinking about cupcakes. And Evie's new hair.'

Sam held her by the shoulders. 'I'm not following. Notice what? Harry larking about in the garage? I told him not to use the bloody punchbag, daft lad. Why are you so upset?'

She shook her head. 'You said you'd mended the fixing, Sam.'

'So it's my fault Harry's knocked a hole in the ceiling then? Might've bloody known.'

'You don't understand!'

'I understand someone has an accident in that house while I'm out and it's still my bloody fault!'

More tears spilled over her cheeks. Something registered in Sam's expression. 'You don't understand. Harry wasn't punching that bag, Sam. He thought it would hold.'

'What the bloody hell was he doing to it then? Swinging from it?'

She sobbed into her hands. 'He wasn't larking about. It wasn't an accident.'

Sam was sizing her up. Back in the ring, preparing for a fist out of nowhere. 'I heard the doc, he said *accident*. I heard him. Harry was messing around.'

It was the story Harry had given in the ambulance, before Cleo or Evie had been able to offer the paramedics another version. He was messing around, the punchbag fell from its fixing, he'd hit his forehead on a box of tiles. He hadn't been unconscious. Cleo had never roused him before the ambulance arrived, he'd been fine all along. Just a bad bump. It was the version Sam had heard, the version no one had disputed. The fried egg on Harry's forehead as proof.

'I took the belt from his neck before the paramedic came, Sam. Our little baby boy, he did it on purpose.' Something awful seeped into Sam's features. 'He thought you'd mended the fixing. He thought it would take his weight. He thought the cleaners would find him, they were supposed to be there! But they didn't show.'

'*What?*'

'He didn't want any of us to find him but we did. We found him on the floor and the doctors don't know because . . .' she was suffocating, tension crushing against her chest, '. . . because Harry lied to them and we let him, because if they know what he tried to do to himself they might try to take our boy away, Sam. They'll put him on a psychiatric ward.'

81

'Congratulations.'

Isobel stopped gawking at the 'Closed For Refurb' sign on Coast's door. Ben Oakes was looking at her, straightfaced and dressed for another day in the Fallenbay sunshine.

'Sorry?'

'You should be. Sweeping a man clean off his feet like that.'

'Umm . . .' she smiled self-consciously.

Ben grinned at the floor. 'My brother tells me he's planning on marrying you one day, Isobel Oliver. He's waiting until he turns eighteen then he's going to pop the question. Which gives you roughly eight months to prove you're worthy.'

Isobel sunk her hands into her pockets. 'I can save you the time. I'm not worthy.'

'Yeah, neither are the rest of us, but let's not burst Dan's bubble.'

Isobel smiled. 'No, I don't want to do that.'

'Good. Because if any Brad Pitts are due to turn up during the rest of your holiday in Fallenbay, Daniel's gonna take that quite hard, you know?'

She was being invited. She didn't know what to, but it felt like an act of defiance, allowing herself to be interested. 'No, sadly, no Brad Pitts are expected to arrive anytime soon.'

'That's too bad,' said Ben.

'Sure is.'

She'd closed Ben down on every other politeness he'd extended her. Now she was sticking two fingers up at Jonathan Hildred, because he didn't get to decide who she was wary of any more.

Sophie thought Isobel should still be wary of everyone and their dog. Soph's nerves had frayed as Isobel had filled her in. How close she'd been to Jon, the way he'd said her full name, handling it like a loaded weapon. How she'd moved Sarah's bed behind the spare room door. How she'd waited hours for the sun to come up before her nerves held long enough for her to tiptoe downstairs past the lounge, her huge holdall biting into her shoulder while she'd fumbled anxiously at the front door. Sophie had listened in complete silence while Isobel tried to make light of her heart nearly exploding from her ribs when she'd finally made it to her car outside Sarah's garage.

Ben cleared his throat. What had they been talking about?

'Any idea when Cleo's reopening?' Isobel asked brightly.

'Not a clue. But you know, there is a better breakfast in Fallenbay.' He held up his brown paper bag for her. She recognised the branding from her apple haul.

'They serve breakfast at The Organic Pantry?'

'Nope, they just supply the vitamin C. So are you coming?'

'Coming where?'

'For breakfast?' He rubbed his free hand over his head. 'It's off the beaten path but you've got your kicks on already, I've got sun cream, we're basically good to go.' Isobel hesitated. Breakfast alone together was a jump. 'We're as good

450

as in-laws, Isobel. Daniel said so. So you're gonna have to have breakfast with me eventually. Plus, it's kinda my job.'

'What is?'

'To vet you. I can't just let Danny go around falling for anyone. I'm his big brother, Isobel Oliver, I'm obliged to check you out.'

82

Sarah was making an effort. And Jon's favourite fresh pasta.

The kitchen calendar was staring at her. She counted back the days of the month, then forwards again. *Five on antibiotics, 1 . . . 2 . . . So birth control finished on Monday . . .* She hadn't miscounted, today was definitely the last day of her pill-free week.

Her shirt felt prickly against her back. *Don't panic . . .*

'Will? Where's the iPad?' Yes. Maybe she would find her period somewhere on the iPad.

'Jon took it upstairs.'

Of course he had. *Again.* To watch porn, probably. He hadn't been near her since pill-gate. Will slid his phone along the worktop. Was he finally dropping his guard a little? 'Oh. Thanks. I just wanted to check this recipe . . .' She speed-Googled *Effect of antibiotics on contraceptive pill,* skim-reading while bathing Jon's pumpkin and sage raviolis.

No effect . . . wary of vomiting . . . extra protection advisable . . .

Her antibiotics hadn't made her vomit. So where was her period?

'What's up with the Roberts?' asked Will.

'Who knows? Cleo was supposed to show me how to make these things but she stood me up.'

Sarah had arrived bang on time at Cleo's last night. All the curtains had been drawn. At seven-thirty on a Sunday evening. She'd shuffled off home and YouTubed it instead before Jon had taken the iPad upstairs again.

Sarah held her pasta spoon thingy up. 'Wait, what do you mean what's up with *them*?'

Will shrugged. 'Evie and Harry were off today. Everyone's saying they've freaked about exams.'

'Off school? *Today*? But . . . *exams*!' Were they held hostage? Sarah quickly reconsidered the drawn curtains, her unreturned calls.

'It was History today, Evie and Harry are both Geography, I think. So their first exam's tomorrow. Charlie reckons they had today off to build up their sickness story, so it doesn't look suspect when they don't show tomorrow.'

'Charlie's the new kid?'

'Uh-uh.'

'Well Charlie probably shouldn't make assumptions about students he doesn't know that well yet.' The twins would have to be dead or dying for Cleo to keep them off this week. She delved back into Will's phone and dialled Cleo's number.

It rang out again. The answer machine was off. Had something happened?

A bleep sounded in her ear. Will had a Snapchat waiting for him. Sarah placed Cleo's potential hostage situation momentarily on hold. 'Ooh, what's a Snapchat?' Sarah asked innocently, swiping it open before Will could intervene.

'No, don't!' shouted Will.

The same teenage boy flashed up, holding himself provocatively for the camera. It was the same picture as before, but this time less of the image had been censored. Sarah could see the bottom of the boy's face now, his mouth fixed in concentration. *Two hours to go!* read the caption, but the countdown on the image had already begun.

'What the hell is this?'

Will didn't even bother to look, so she did again before the last few seconds of viewing time were up.

Her breath snatched. There wasn't just more of the boy in this picture, there was more background too. On the wall behind the naked teen's shoulders, a framed poster of Russell Winter from the 2002 Boardmasters surf festival. Except it wasn't a poster, it was one of Patrick's first ever sports shots. He'd been cheeky, offering Winter's girlfriend one of two blown-up prints for free if she'd get Winter to sign the other for Patrick. He'd left it behind when his new horizons had beckoned, and Will had sold it for a penny at their garage sale when Jon had first moved in.

Sarah slumped on to a stool, blood pumping. Will had sold that print to Harry Roberts.

'Mum, it's not what you think.'

How many times had he said that this week? 'What ... are these pictures ... doing on your phone? Do you know who this is?' Were Harry and Will having a *thing*?

'Huh? No! Of course I dunno who it is. Or the sicko who's Snapchatting them. Everyone's been getting them!'

Sarah's runaway panic derailed. 'Everyone's been getting pictures *of naked boys*?' Of naked Harry?

'*Boy*. For about two weeks, stupid lad. I feel sorry for him. He's gotta be getting blackmailed or something. Bet he's bricking it.'

Did Cleo know? Did anyone know it was Harry? 'And you don't know who's in the photo?' Had Will spotted the Winters print in the background?

'No! No one does. Yet.'

'This is what's going on in that school and you haven't mentioned it? A boy being blackmailed?'

'Mum, I swear this has got nothing to do with me.'

'But you know something about it!' Poor Cleo. Poor, poor Harry. It was appalling.

'I don't, honestly. I know as much as you do. Some dude at school took a selfie while he was . . . well, you know . . .' Yes, she did know. They both knew. They could never unsee it.

'And?'

'And he thought he was sending the photo to his girlfriend. That's what I heard anyway.'

'So *she*'s passing these pictures around?'

Cleo said Harry's thing with the exchange student had unravelled. She'd gone home to Finland or wherever. Could kids blackmail by PayPal? Or was Harry supposed to hit the nearest bureau de change with his pocket money? What the hell were the kids of today doing with their time?

'No, not the girl. There might not even be a girl. He probably just got pranked into thinking some fit bird was texting him. What a goombah.'

'So who's the blackmailer?' They needed to go to the police.

Will shrugged. 'Dunno. Some kid.'

'Another pupil?'

'That's just what I heard. Some little twonk in Year Seven probably.'

'Heard from who?'

'Everyone. This isn't a secret, Mum. Everyone's talking about it. There are others.'

'Other photos?'

'Other *goombahs!* Taking dodgy selfies. The school's buzzing about it. Everyone wants to know who the faces hidden in the photos are. They're calling it "Guess Who". Everyone's getting the Snapchats, screenshotting them and passing them around.' Sarah hadn't thought about screenshotting the images on Will's phone before they'd vanished from view. This was half the trouble now, kids had the technological edge.

'If you don't know the person sending these images, William, how have they got your number?'

'Everyone at school knows everyone's numbers and stuff. How do those accident-claim scam lines know your number, Mum?'

Will was right. He was absolutely right. She'd given numbers out willy-nilly a hundred times. 'Well, why didn't you block it?'

Will shrugged. ''Cause it was a *thing* everyone at school was talking about? I don't know!'

'It's not a *thing*, Will. It's serious. Serious bullying, and you and the rest of the school being dragged into it only makes it a ring, do you understand that? You're involved in a bullying ring. That boy is someone's *brother*. Someone's son, Will, do you see that? The boy in that picture is someone's *Max* in a few years' time. That boy is—'

That boy is Harry Roberts.

She stopped herself. Sarah thought about Isobel, about everything that horrible online bastard had done to her. The

way he'd nailed her to the wall and then rounded up spectators to gawp and point at her. What Isobel must've been
willing to give for just one person to break the chain, one
person to hold a sheet up in front of her.

Will didn't need to know that it was Harry in the photo.

'And the countdown? What's that all about?'

'That's just Snapchat. You get ten seconds or whatever to
view the photo.'

'No, I know that. There was writing. *Two hours to go*,
what does that mean?' There had been writing on the first
image Sarah had seen too, something about *Not long to wait*.

Will rubbed his eyes as if explaining all this was exhausting.
'You like *X Factor*, Mum. *Strictly*. All that.'

Sarah slapped the countertop in frustration. 'What do you
mean?'

'It's strung-out entertainment. We've been doing it in Media
Studies. How do you think those shows make so much money?
They drip-feed the tension, build the anticipation. So there's
more time to make money off it. Genius, really. The Snapchat
build-up.' Sarah glared at him across the steaming hob. 'I don't
mean it's good! I just mean, you know, someone's walking
around in new trainers, a new bike probably too, I reckon.
Think about it, Mum. Back in the day, if you'd have given
someone a selfie like that and they'd threatened to show your
face to the rest of your school on the first day of exams . . .
Knowing Grandad, you'd have paid anything they asked not
to get found out.' Sarah swallowed. It didn't bear thinking
about. 'Whoever's sending those Snapchats must be scaring
the crap outta the naked kid. Every day he's counting down
to the big reveal.'

'The first day of exams?' There was a sociopath in William's school.

'Yeah, to give everyone a laugh after a rubbish day. The others are gonna be revealed on different days. See? Strung-out entertainment.' Will had better achieve an A for Media Studies.

'But that's today. Your first exam was today.' Sarah spun from what she was doing and hunted for her keys on the other side of the kitchen. Two hours to go? That's all the warning Cleo and Sam were going to get before Harry was outed as the first Snapchat kid?

'Mum, where are you going?'

'Out.'

'Your things are still boiling, what shall I do?'

'Eat.'

83

Cleo and Sam were in the kitchen, silently moving around one another like nocturnal creatures again. The world felt as if some horrific natural disaster had ripped through, tearing up trees and shifting earth. Everything left damaged. Unsafe.

'You can't come in. It's not a good time. Mum's . . . not well.' It was the tone of Evie's voice that made Cleo glance through the kitchen into the hallway. She could just see Evie's profile in the hallway, eyes saucer-like, slender fingers clamped around the door. They'd brought Harry home and spent the next two days bumbling around making drinks they didn't drink, holding newspapers they didn't read.

'I'm sorry, Evie, but it won't wait.'

'No!' Evie's voice jumped. Cleo could see Sarah in the doorway looking perplexed but resolute. 'Mum's not up to it. Please, not tonight. Don't speak to her tonight. Just don't!' Evie jammed a foot behind the door.

'I'll get rid of her,' Sam said softly.

Cleo felt a pang of guilt, Sam's choice of words too harsh for Sarah.

'Hello, Sarah.' Sam took over. Evie took a reluctant side-step. She looked pale. They all looked pale. 'Cleo's under the weather. A bug. Might be best you don't come in for a few days. Can I give her a message?'

Cleo listened. 'I'm sorry, Sam. But I need to speak to you both. Right now.'

Sarah walked into the lounge, stiff and formidable. Like a school mistress.

'I'm sorry!' blurted Evie. 'I asked her not to come in. I'm sorry.' Sarah's look of determination turned to one of bewilderment. Evie looked panicked. 'I'm sorry, Mum. I'm really sorry. I'm sorry for everything!' She burst into tears, turned and ran upstairs.

Cleo tried to breathe past it but Evie's tears kicked up her own.

'Cleo? I'm sorry, I didn't mean to upset anyone.' Sarah watched Sam walk into the lounge and plant his hands over the fireplace. Would he cry too? 'Cleo? What's happened?'

Sam's shoulders were softly shaking again. Cleo's voice wobbled. 'Don't worry about Evie. She's, er . . . We've had a bit of a rocky weekend and . . .'

'Cleo,' Sam warned.

Sarah's eyes went to him. 'What's happened? Are the kids alright?'

'Not really.' Cleo tried to smile but the tears were already there again. Sam straightened up, pulled at his nose and left the room. 'Harry's, er . . . Harry's having a bit of trouble dealing with a few things. It's all got a bit on top of him.' She was picturing him again, lifting the punchbag from its hooks. Positioning himself. The thoughts that must've been going through his head seconds before Sam's temporary fixings

460

came free under Harry's weight, dropping him against the last of the tiles. His life saved with a sharp smack to the head.

'Oh, Cleo, I just found out. How is he? Is there anything I can do?'

She blinked at Sarah. 'You know? How?' The words formed a hard lump in Cleo's mouth.

'Will. I can't believe it, Cleo. I'm so sorry. Have you gone to the police?'

Will? Christ, Evie, tell the world your brother's suicidal! Is that what Evie was so sorry about? 'It's not a matter for the police.'

'But . . . they can stop it.'

'Stop what?'

'Private photographs being passed around school like football cards.'

'What?' Cleo's head hurt. Sarah's words were getting all jumbled up, they made no sense.

Sam filled the doorway. 'What photographs?'

84

Cotton clouds hung yellow under a warm, softly lit umbrella sky. Isobel drank it all in.

'So we're doing this then?'

She looked at the door-sized piece of fibreglass. The water calm as a millpond. Standing up straight? Didn't look *that* hard. 'Yep. We're doing it.'

Ben's smile widened beneath the shadow of his cap. 'A girl who likes to dive straight in. I can appreciate that. We don't want to practise too much on the sand either. The natives, they kinda don't like too many newbies cluttering up The Village.'

'Uncoordinated tourists not so cool?' she asked.

Ben grinned. 'Not really. But, y'know, a girl like yourself might pull it off . . . maybe.'

Isobel looked at the sand, wetter beneath her feet as they walked towards the shore. A girl like her? She couldn't help it. She liked how it sat in her ears. Last year those words would've meant something else, now they meant something better. Ben twisted his body, moving the paddle-board under his other arm. Isobel kept her eyes on the board. Cool water lapped the sand and their feet.

'Ready then?'

'Sure. Let's do it.' She stepped out into the water after him.

Just the one board between the two of them, just while he showed her the ropes. Her eyes coasted to the lines of his lower back, disappearing into black shorts. She'd shaved her legs before he'd picked her up this morning. It was silly, they were going into the water, but she'd hunted around her bathroom bag for remnants of the make-up she'd left back home. Anything to make her less plain, less unthought about. For over a year there had been nothing about herself that could be called *good* in any way. She'd stopped worrying whether the names were true. She'd accepted them. But something was changing. Cogs were crunching to a halt, the mechanisms of her thoughts grinding slowly into reverse. She wasn't what DEEP_DRILLERZ or his army of strangers said she was. She was a decent girl, about to enjoy the ocean on a beautiful day with a decent guy.

'The water's perfect for this today. If you're up to it, we could make it to the cove we hiked to Monday?'

'Sounds good.'

She had absolutely no idea what she was signing herself up to, but she was doing it anyway. Something had changed since those two minutes in the dark at the bottom of Sarah's stairs. The monster had shrunk. Was Jon wondering why she was still here? She hoped so. He had more to lose than Isobel did. The shift in balance had opened up a tiny space inside her somewhere, making room for other things. For paddle-boarding. For hiking through a hillside and eating oranges for breakfast in a hidden, perfect cove. For a new friend who scrunched his eyes shut when he laughed.

Ben called over his shoulder as they waded out, 'Water nice and warm?'

Her skin was spasming. 'Oh yeah, like a bath. You have goosebumps, too! Don't say it's not freezing.'

He glanced back at her. 'Didn't know you were paying attention . . .'

A forgotten sensation bloomed in her stomach. She watched the muscles affect the back of his head; he was smiling, she knew it. It didn't all have to be about the last year, did it? Couldn't Fallenbay hold some of what her mum had hoped it would for her? A corner to turn. An experience. It had all been pretend, was it still? Was Fallenbay actually becoming that pretty distraction?

She cleared her throat. 'Of course I am, I'm getting a free lesson. I always pay attention in class. Eyes forwards.'

It was true. She had always loved being in class. Sophie was the one who'd struggled with lessons and didn't turn up. Sophie had never turned up.

Ben stopped. The water biting at their waists. The board between them. He looked at her and patted the paddle-board. 'Okay then, Isobel Oliver. Let's see what you've got.'

85

Sarah stared at the bedroom ceiling.

What if he tries again?

She couldn't purge from her head the sound of Sam crying in his garage. She'd only ever seen Sam emotional once before, when he and Cleo had walked towards the x-ray department, finding Sarah and Patrick sitting silently in the corridor. She remembered it vividly. Sam had split his thumb with a hammer. Cleo kept calling him a clumsy oaf.

Patrick didn't breathe a single word. Cleo had rabbited away while Sarah sat quietly, a boy either side of her, William in stunned silence to her right, little Milo huddled in the seat to her left, his head on her lap. Stroking Milo's hair had calmed him, or maybe it had just calmed Sarah.

Karl had emerged from the treatment room they'd taken Elodie into. One look at Will and he just snapped. He'd moved so quickly, Patrick watching like a bystander, Karl yanking Will to his feet by the collar of his singed Hawaiian shirt. Milo had startled in Sarah's lap when she'd lurched from her seat. She'd tried to pull Karl off Will but her arms were too weak and pathetic, her pregnant body too bulky, her need to protect her son not as great as Karl's need to punish him.

Sarah blinked, finding her bedroom ceiling again.

Only Sam had stopped Karl hurting Will. Not Sarah. Not Patrick. Sam. The clumsy oaf with the hammered thumb and the 'poxy' pyrotechnic display at the school. Cleo had understood the context, she was a mother. Juliette and Elodie's absence on the corridor had fired a warning in her head. Karl going ballistic in the hospital, minus wife and daughter, watch and listen. Sam hadn't waited for the back story, he'd only seen a grown man shaking a nine-year-old boy like an old rag. Sam had neutralised Karl without hesitation.

Sam. Who'd listened so quietly while Sarah told them everything she'd learned from Will about the Guess Who game. Who'd taken himself into the garage and cried alone while Cleo told Sarah the terrible thing Harry had done in there. The terrible thing Harry had tried to do.

The shower in the en-suite shut off. Sarah rolled over, staring at the wall instead. Jon came through the door, a cloud of warm fragrance filling the bedroom.

Cleo was ashen when they'd returned from Harry's room, his phone like a grenade in Sam's huge hand. Sam had sent a message of his own, a warning to the sender of Harry's black-mail. Sam was coming to find him. So far, Sam's threat had held. The deadline to expose Harry's face had passed. Will was Sarah's man on the inside, confirming that there hadn't been any more countdown messages, not to Will's phone anyway. The twins had even sat their first exam, a veil of normality draped over the family. But how long could they keep that up?

Jon pulled on a pair of pyjama bottoms and slipped into bed. She was safe. Jon's new enjoyment for frenzied sex in dark corners had been substituted with more runs on the bluff, more movies upstairs on the iPad, more showers. She didn't even need the birth control now, it was all by the by. Jon wasn't interested. Her period still AWOL.

'Did you want the lamp leaving on? I was going to get some sleep.'

'No, thanks.'

'You okay?'

She should be grateful he was even asking. Bar his lost appetite for sex, Jon's mood towards her had fallen back into its stride. He'd told her once, how counselling was knowing the point at which to pull back. Pull back and let them come to you. *Like fishing.* That was the sort of messed-up, ungrateful thing she thought about now, the thanks she gave for him going easy on her after catching her out, lying to him about wanting their baby. The guy couldn't win. 'Yeah. Just tired.' She suddenly wanted to cry into her pillow. For Cleo and Harry and Sam. For being so ungrateful for her own lot. For not making more effort. 'Jon?'

'Yeah.'

'I thought we could take a ride to Hartley Hall this weekend, before the weather turns. Get an idea how they do things, so we can start thinking about seating plans. We could invite your mum and sister along. Caroline was so keen to play a part and—'

'Isn't Cleo's music thing this weekend?'

Cleo wanted to call everything off. 'I forgot about that,' lied Sarah. It was Sam who still wanted to go ahead. Disguise a family in crisis. Sarah thought they needed to go to the governors but Sam had shot her straight down. *What Harry needs is to put this behind him. He's got weeks left at that school then a summer to forget it. He'll never see half of those kids*

467

again. Sam had already started a week of compassionate leave, the fabricated death of an uncle. He would spend it sprucing up Coast for the open-mic night, Cleo maintaining a watchful presence at home. Nothing was to change, the kids would attend school, the gig would go ahead. Normal normal normal.

'No problem. Some other time.' Jon pecked her on the shoulder. 'And don't worry about my mother, or sister. They'll only take over. Okay?'

'Okay.'

Jon flicked off the lamp. Sarah stared into darkness.

Harry Roberts tried to hang himself in the garage on Saturday. It was like a bee in her mouth. She wanted it out of her. But she'd promised. Couldn't Cleo see? Harry had been victimised. They had to tell the school, the *police*. Harry needed support. *What if he tries again . . .*

'How do you help children? When their parents don't want you to help them?'

No attention was to be drawn to Harry, Sam said. None.

Jon rolled on to his back. 'What sort of help?'

'The sort you offer a child . . . being victimised?'

'Is this about Max? Because if horsey woman's kid is still playing up, I'll deal with it. You're too soft.'

'No, nothing like that. Max is fine. It's something at your school, some of the kids are being threatened. One of them has shared—'

'Photos of himself up to no good? On these photo messenger apps?'

Jon knew? 'By up to no good, do you mean . . .'

'Teenage boys, Sarah. I hate to break this to you but they all toss off.'

She felt prudish. Silly. 'The school *knows*?'

'We don't *know*, we haven't seen anything. We've just heard whispers. And giggles.'

'It's not funny. They're kids!'

'I know. We're having an internet-safety seminar before the holidays. It's the parents who need educating, allowing teenagers with raging hormones free reign over unpoliced phones and internet. We can only teach them about protecting themselves. Prevention.'

'And what if it's already moved past that point? What's in place to support those kids? The young people who've already left themselves wide open to exploitation?' The kids despairing in their parents' garages.

'You mean the young people who are breaking the law?'

'No, the *victims*. The teenagers sending photos of themselves to God knows who.'

'Yes . . . the young people *breaking the law*.'

Sarah got up on her elbows. 'How are they breaking the law, they're the victims?'

'There are two parts to this issue, Sarah. Let's start with those unscrupulous souls who get hold of these sorts of images and, say, *blackmail* the teenagers in them, yes?'

'Yes?'

'The bad guys?'

'Yes.'

'Nice and simple. But what about those responsible for making and distributing the images in the first place?'

'I'm not talking about incidences involving perverts with hidden cameras in changing rooms, Jon, I'm talking about kids, teenagers, taking explicit *selfies*. Of *themselves*. No one else is responsible for making and distributing those images.'

Jon sighed. '*They* are responsible, Sarah. The young people, taking explicit selfies, of themselves, are breaking the law, *themselves*.'

'But *they're* the child in the picture. They're the victim!'

'I know. And it doesn't matter. Anyone distributing indecent images of children, even a dumb fifteen-year-old sending a snapshot of his own tallywacker for laughs, is breaking the law. And if they get caught, there's every chance they're going on file.'

'But . . .' *Shit*. She'd told Cleo to involve the police. 'You're telling me a fifteen-year-old who takes a rude photo of himself then sends it to his fifteen-year-old girlfriend is breaking the law?'

'He's making and distributing indecent pictures of a child.'

'So he could be classed as . . .'

'Some would say a paedophile.'

Her heart was palpitating. Will had received those pictures. Where did the law stand on *that*? 'Don't tell me kids are on the sex offenders register because of *sexting*?'

'There are youngsters on the sex offenders register, today, because of sexting. Parents need to wake up.'

86

*Why aren't you answering my calls? It's been a week!
I'm freaking out here! Xxx*

Slightly dramatic, Soph. Isobel put her phone down. She didn't need updates on their social media traps any more, so what else was there to talk about? It wasn't like she hadn't been in touch at all. She'd sent a text a day since her declaration to expose Jon Hildred. She'd shared her paddle-boarding experience – *Ben says I'm a natural ;)* – her disappointment at Coast remaining closed all week, she'd asked after Ella, chit-chatty updates, all with the underlying message Sophie really wanted to hear. *I'm still alive. No one's murdered me in the woods. Let your conscience be clear.*

Ben had not helped things. He'd distracted her and she'd let him. Isobel had spent a week, a whole week, doing normal. No, *fun*. She'd had fun. She'd had the guided tour of the castle grounds with him, Dan too. They'd been over to the cottage, spotted her pile of bashed apples and taken the lot, and Isobel, to go grill them all on Arthur's oil drum barbecue. She'd even petted Petal. She'd broken a sweat, but she'd petted her.

Jon Hildred had been pushed to the back of beach walks and harbour lunches and beers on the cottage porch. Three days had slipped by before she'd realised, there had been no breathy phone calls to the cottage since Saturday. No more texts. No more notes.

Fallenbay was teaching her. There was nothing left for her back home. Things had changed and couldn't be changed back. And she obviously couldn't stay here, which was a shame too. But she knew now that she could start again, and that was her best lesson. She could change her name officially, slip back into education somewhere, work her way through the channels. She really could have her tattoo removed, her hair could be any colour she liked. She could shed her old life like a skin, she didn't have to live with her parents and work for Uncle Keith. She could go abroad, travel. She had no ties, she could be freer than she'd ever been. The Jonathan Hildreds of this world didn't get to define her. She'd stood in his hallway in the centre of his perfect life and faced him. They both had shaky reputations, but only Jon had built himself back up into a fine, upstanding, respectable teacher. Isobel hadn't. He had more to lose than her and they both knew it.

Isobel pottered around the cottage, turning the lamps on before *Britain's Got Talent*. She would go home soon. This week, probably. She wasn't sure. She sipped her tea and considered the opportunity she was about to give away. Cleo's open-mic night would be warming up, Jon and Sarah would be there right now. Ben had asked Isobel to go, the stage would be set. But she'd been thinking about it all day and the only definite outcome of all that thinking was that she wasn't sure how she felt about DEEP_DRILLERZ any more.

She'd woken up at half four this morning, sat bolt upright in bed with a singular, stark thought. Sarah could have told Jon. About the video. They were a couple, couples shared things. Isobel had had him pegged as DEEP_DRILLERZ, but what if . . . What if Sarah had told him about their conversation and Jon had just gone online for a look at Isobel and her ex, cavorting, and he wasn't DEEP_DRILLERZ at all? But there were the IP addresses, tracing to Coast and so close to the high school. The comments he'd made in the hallway. *How is it you've come to find yourself in my neck of the woods, Little Red Riding Whore?* So arrogant. So abrupt. And then, just as abruptly, he'd backed off. In the cold light of day, after he'd made his silent call to the cottage and realised she didn't scare so easily, Jonathan Hildred must've made a balanced risk assessment. Sarah. The boys. Job. Pension. Resurrected concerns about his working with children. Criminal record. It wasn't a tricky decision. The calls had stopped. Isobel had spooked him already. Maybe that was worse for him, knowing what was in her artillery, hanging over him. He might even change his ways, be a good father and husband, turn his back on the vile online Jon Hildred and live up to school counsellor Jon Hildred, the nice guy who'd helped Will through his parents' divorce and Evie Roberts to deal with her Facebook bullies.

Isobel's phone lit up. She shut the call off. Sophie followed it with a text.

Have I done something?

Delete.

I need to speak to you Isobel NOW.

She rang again.

'Sophie, I'm in the bath!' Isobel lied.

'You tell me you're going to confront this guy then you just stop telling me what's going on? What is going on, Isobel? I'm worried sick!'

'Nothing.'

'Nothing? Every day this week I've tried to call you, I've asked you by text what the hell is happening, and you fob me off with what flavour ice-cream you've been eating. What's going on? Are you slipping again, Isobel?'

'No, Sophie, I'm not slipping. I'm just not rolling over any more.'

'Isobel, you aren't making any sense.'

'I'm making perfect sense to me.' She picked up the remote and flicked to the opening credits of *Britain's Got Talent*. 'Sorry, Sophie, I have to go. *Britain's Got Talent*'s just starting, the boy with the pink hair's about to belt out a Bon Jovi number on a kazoo.'

'*Britain's Got Talent*? I thought you were in the bath?' There was a hammering at the front door to the cottage. 'Is that your door? It's half past eight, who's banging on your door like that, Isobel?'

'Ooh, maybe it's the Bogey Man, Sophie.' There was something acidic in her voice.

'Isobel?'

'I'm going Sophie. Bye.'

'Isobel? Don't open the door. It's late!'

She briefly considered Jon. He'd be schmoozing at Cleo's, playing the dutiful fiancé, laughing warmly at everyone's jokes.

'Bye, Sophie.'

She went for the door.

87

'Sarah, Jon, thanks for coming.'

Sarah leaned in for a kiss. There was a cool film of sweat all over Sam's cheek. His complexion shone in the warm orange glow of candlelight from the glass bell jars on every table. 'Sam, this place looks incredible. You've worked so hard.'

'That's an impressive week's work, mate,' Jon agreed. 'Who are you, Noah? Can't believe you didn't open up that view earlier, look at that sunset.'

Sam nodded. This wasn't his scene, hosting, pouring gin cocktails as the people of Fallenbay danced and mingled beneath the paper lanterns strung like wishes over Coast's new music stage.

Jon was already bobbing to the catchy folk-pop. 'They're good, we should book them for the wedding.'

Sarah frowned. 'I thought you'd booked The Bored Teenagers?'

Cleo put a hand on Sarah's back. 'You look beautiful, Sarah. Blue's your colour.' Cleo leant in for a hug. 'Does Jon know?' she whispered.

'No. No one,' Sarah whispered back. She squeezed Cleo's arm. They must be worried sick about Harry. 'You look fantastic too, Cleo. Are the kids here?'

'No, Harry's at home. Sam's mother's come to stay,'

'So he's granny-sitting then?' smiled Jon.

Sam ran a finger around the inside of his snug collar. 'Something like that.'

'Evie not helping out tonight? Surely this is where you wheel out the teenagers, Sam, make them earn their keep?'

'Actually, Jon, we wanted to say thank you for your help with Evie in school. She's settled right down. We appreciate your support, don't we, Cle?' Sam was offering his hand again. Jon took it. 'If you could just . . .' Sam exchanged a look with Cleo, '. . . keep on keeping an eye on her, we'd be grateful.'

'No problem. And don't mention it. She's a bright girl.' Sarah mimicked Jon's passive smile. He'd told her Evie was headed for trouble. That Evie was *troubled*.

'You'd better get back behind the bar, Sam. There's another queue,' nodded Cleo.

Juliette and Karl were right at the front. 'I thought they were throwing a big pool party?' asked Sarah.

'Guess their plans changed. A few PFA mums are here too. I'll catch you later, sorry, it's so busy.'

Sarah watched Cleo disappear behind the counter. She'd lost weight. In a week. They shouldn't be here tonight, they should be at home with the twins, recovering.

'Are you okay?' asked Jon.

'I'm just going to nip to the ladies.'

'Okay, I'll get the drinks.'

'Okay.' Should she be drinking? She could tell Jon her suspicions, fix everything in one fell swoop. Tonight would become celebratory, she might even be too fat to get married next year, they could put it back, they'd have a legitimate reason. She wove through the crowd, all nibbling canapés and calling their orders up to Sam and the other bar staff. *Nearly two weeks late.* Google was wrong, antibiotics did bugger up your birth control. She pushed on the door to the ladies' and found the last of three cubicles. She took one stride inside and felt a small trickle. *You have got to be kidding me.* She made a quick check, closed her eyes and sent a *thank you* up into the cosmos.

Cleo had a tampon dispenser on the vanity wall. Sarah opened the cubicle door. *Sod.* Jon had all the cash. The cubicle next door opened, Olivia Brightman stepped out and almost said *hello* by accident. Olivia rattily set her bag on the side and began washing her hands.

It wasn't a goer. Sarah needed a plan B. She stepped back inside the cubicle and hovered behind the door. *This is ridiculous. You're grown women! You'd think two girls could come together over a tampon.*

She opened the door. 'Olivia?' Olivia's eyes darted to the vanity mirror. 'Don't suppose I could bother you for a little loose change? Just until I can grab Jon? He's only by the bar.' Sarah let her eyes indicate Cleo's machine. 'Caught short.'

Olivia's eyebrows arched. She looked in her purse, counting a couple of coins into her palm. 'Shoot. I only have . . . ah, no, I have enough.'

'Phew,' smiled Sarah.

'Cleo's tapenade toasts have given me terrible indigestion,' said Olivia, slotting coins into the machine.

'Oh? I haven't tried one.'

Olivia yanked on a handle and a small packet fell out of the chute.

'Oh, no, Olivia, you've . . .'

Olivia popped one of the white tabs from inside their packet. She stuck it in her mouth and shook her box of Mighty Mints. 'That's better, chewing really does help. I'll tell Jon to make sure he asks for change at the bar.'

Olivia walked past Sarah's cubicle. Sarah didn't know why, her hand just sort of did it. She flicked the Vs at Olivia's back before she disappeared through the door. Sarah caught movement in the vanity mirror. Elodie Inman-Holt stood in the next cubicle doorway. She was wearing high-waisted, tight black jeans and a stunned look. *Oh God*. Sarah ducked back into the loo. She locked the door and leant her forehead against it.

Teachers couldn't just go around swearing at school mothers' backs! It was puerile and embarrassing. And just generally not on, even at Olivia. *Crap*. Elodie would tell her mother. Mr Pethers would have Sarah on the black bloody cloud. A shadow passed the bottom of Sarah's cubicle.

Elodie's damaged hand peeped through the gap beneath the cubicle. 'Sorry it's not a tampon, Mrs Harrison. It's just a panty-liner. I always keep one for emergencies.'

88

'Evie?'

Cleo's daughter stood on the cottage steps, breathing hard. Had she walked up here? Isobel looked for a car in the yard, but there was only the dappled light of a sunset fighting through woodland.

'Can I come in?' Evie's eyes were wild and watery. She was wringing her hands.

'Sure. Does your mum know you're here?'

Evie's voice broke. 'No.'

'Evie, is everything alright?' Evie shook her head. Isobel thought about the teenagers, coming and going into the woodland. Had something happened to her? 'Evie, are *you* alright?'

Evie hung her head and began weeping on the doorstep. They weren't supposed to do it, hug students. But Isobel wasn't a teacher any more. 'Hey, hey . . . can I call someone?'

Evie shook her head against Isobel's shoulder and wept.

Sophie had burst into Isobel's bedroom once, about the same age as Evie now. Isobel was home from uni for her twenty-first birthday party, a gulf away from Sophie's teen-age problems. Boyfriends doing runners. Pregnancy tests.

Evie cried like a child. Pained, hopeless sobs. She cried

like Sophie. 'It's okay,' Isobel comforted, 'it's okay. Whatever it is, it will be okay.'

Evie pushed herself away. 'Don't be nice to me. I'm a stupid idiot. I'm just a stupid little girl, just like he said.'

Who said? 'Has someone been calling you names online again?' Evie looked bewildered. 'Sorry, your mum . . . she didn't mean to break a confidence, it's just . . . she was concerned you were being treated badly . . . is somebody bothering you again, on Facebook?'

Evie's face crumpled. 'I'm really sorry, I did something bad and it's come back on our family, on Harry, and it's all my fault. Mum and dad are going to hate me when they find out, and I don't know how to tell them and it's all my fault!' She was struggling for breath.

'Evie, it's okay. Just take slow and steady breaths, okay? I'm going to sit you down in here in the lounge. Come on, everything will be okay.'

Isobel led her to one of the sofas. Simon Cowell had just got to his feet, applauding someone for their efforts. Isobel perhaps? It had been a while since she was the calm comforter.

'Harry . . . Harry . . .'

'Evie, breathe.' She passed Evie the tissue box she kept handy for *Britain's Got Talent* ballads.

'Harry tried . . . to hang himself . . . in dad's garage.'

Like a brick to the head. '*What?*'

'Because someone's . . . got a picture . . . of him naked and . . . they were threatening . . . to show it to everyone at school.'

'Is he okay? Is he in hospital?'

Evie shook her head, tears rolled off her cheeks. 'No one knows about it. Mum and Dad are pretending it hasn't happened. But mum is blaming herself because she was busy worrying about me and not Harry and all the while H was having *real* threats and I . . . was making them up.'

Okay. 'Evie, that does not make such a terrible thing your fault, sweetheart. What did you make up?' Why was she even telling Isobel all this? They were hardly pals.

'I wasn't getting trolled. I never was. Mum is going to kick me out, I know she will!'

'You were never getting trolled? On Facebook?' Why the hell had she pretended she was being hounded? Did Evie think it was a joke? 'Why would you say something like that?'

Evie shook her head and wiped her face. 'The first one was real. Gavin Phelps called me a fat cow because I didn't give him one of my Maltesers. And then Mum and Dad, they were so worried, they were, like, a *team* about it and they didn't make me do any jobs and they stopped arguing and . . . I don't know why, but I made up a few Facebook accounts and wrote some stuff on my own wall. And then a couple of lads from school joined in and wrote some horrible things on there too, but mostly it was the things I'd made up, and people started to be really nice to me because they felt sorry for me and...' Evie was weeping again. 'I took Mum's attention away from Harry when he was really being trolled and he needed us. No one helped him and it's my fault!'

Holy shit. Isobel wasn't the only messed up girl in the world.

'They won't kick you out, Evie, your parents love you, that's why they were so worried.' Evie was more fortunate than the poor girl at Hildred's private school. And she

482

reminded Isobel more than ever of Sophie right now. All mashed up because of her own ridiculous ideas.

'I wanted attention, but Harry didn't, he wanted to die . . . my brother wanted to die. I'm a horrible sister. I've done this!'

Isobel leant forward and tucked Evie's hair behind her ear. 'No you haven't. This . . . situation is just bad luck, Evie. Two sets of circumstances, colliding at the worst time. You've made a mistake, everyone has. God knows I have and it was a worse mistake than yours, kid, and I was a lot older when I made it. Should've known better.'

'You're being nice to me again.' Evie burst into more tears. Why had she come up here? Not that Isobel wasn't sort of flattered to be the chosen one, the person Evie trusted with the deepest darkest bits of her breaking soul.

'Well, maybe if everyone was just a bit nicer to one another, the world might be a better place, right?'

Evie looked around the room. Her eyes kept darting to and from Isobel, like she was taking a run-up at a high fence and then thinking better of it. *Jump . . . don't jump . . . no, jump . . .*

'I left the letter. On your car.'

Isobel stood straight up. As if she'd sat on a pin. 'You did *what*?' She looked to the window on to the yard and then back at Evie, shrinking into her seat.

'I left it. I came through the woods so no one would see me. And I made the calls here to your holiday cottage. And sent the texts to your phone after Mum said she had your number. I wrote terrible things. And I'm *really* sorry.'

Isobel had actually stopped breathing. 'You did *what*? What is wrong with you?' This girl, this fifteen-year-old-girl with half a tattoo was DEEP_DRILLERZ? No, but Jon . . .

Go home slag.

Blonde bitch.

And what was that about looking cheap?

Isobel put her hands on her hips and glared. She probably looked like her mother, about to give Sophie a roasting. 'What the hell do you think you were doing, huh? Do you have any idea, *any idea*, what you've done?' Isobel thought that through. Did *she* even know what Evie had done? It hit her like a bolt of lightning. So it hadn't been Jon? He hadn't been harassing her. Or had he?

The IP addresses. The high school. *Evie's* high school. And Coast. 'Are you DEEP_DRILLERZ? Tell me you aren't DEEP_DRILLERZ!' Her neck was pulsating.

'What?' blinked Evie.

'Are you DEEP_DRILLERZ?' shouted Isobel.

Evie jumped. 'No . . . I don't even like surfing!'

'What?' said Isobel.

'What?' mimicked Evie.

'What the hell has surfing got to do with anything?'

Evie looked wide teary eyes at her. 'You said am I a *deep driller*?'

'What the hell's a deep driller?'

Evie looked lost. 'A drilling, a pounding by the waves. If you're a driller, a deep driller, you suck at surfing.'

Isobel pushed her hands through her hair. She couldn't get it straight in her head. 'So . . . you're *not* DEEP_DRILLERZ?'

'Why do you keep saying that, I don't know what you mean!' Evie's voice was climbing. She did not have a clue what Isobel was on about. Evie wasn't DEEP_DRILLERZ, not unless she was Bafta-worthy, and Isobel didn't think she was. But she'd made the calls, the texts, the letter.

Questions fired through Isobel's mind. 'Did you write anything online?' Evie paled. 'Evie, did you go on my blog or Facebook account?' she demanded.

'What blog?'

Had the new IP trace linked to Evie? Or Jon? 'I have a blog. And social network accounts. Did you go on there and write anything? Did you write *Hello stranger*?'

'No, no I didn't. I didn't write anything online, anywhere, I swear.'

'Nothing at all?'

'No. Just the letter. And the texts.'

Blonde bitch. Isobel tried to imagine Evie keying it into her phone.

'Why did you do that, Evie?'

The freedom Isobel had felt this week had come about only from finally knowing who it was she had to look out for. Jonathan Hildred. Evie had just yanked the paperclip off Isobel's neatly compiled stack of evidence and thrown it to the wind. Was Jon Hildred DEEP_DRILLERZ? Had he commented on the blog? Did the IP traces lead back to him, and Evie's silly harassment was just a second run of shitty luck? What had she ever done to Evie?

'*Why did you do that*?' Isobel barked.

'Because . . .' She was crying again. 'I was jealous. I did it because I was jealous.'

'Jealous? *Jealous*? What makes a teenage girl *jealous* of a twenty-eight-year-old with minging hair and a life in a state of total devastation?' She was ranting. 'Come on then, let's hear it! You have no idea the trouble you could've caused. None! Now why, why why why, would you be *jealous* of a failed school teacher with . . .' she began counting her points on her fingers, '. . . no job, no friends, no prospects, chasing shadows in your stupid town?' She was angry, dammit. *Furious* with this silly, stupid little girl.

'Because my boyfriend . . . he wouldn't stop.'

'Wouldn't stop what?'

'Watching your porno.'

89

'Champagne?'

'Yes please.' Sarah tipped her head and threw back her first glass. 'Think I'll have another.' She definitely wasn't pregnant.

'Whoa, hold your horses, Miss Hannigan. Who's gonna look after Little Orphan Annie if you're sloshed?' laughed Jon.

But it wasn't funny. 'I've just done something terrible.'

Jon sipped his drink and looked over the top of his glass at the rest of the room. 'Don't tell me, you forgot to wash your hands in the little girls' room?'

'You're close. I did something filthy with them.'

'Now I'm intrigued. Keep talking like that and I'll have to take you and that blue dress home early.' Jon was softening. Finally, forgiveness on the horizon.

'It's not funny. I'm in deep trouble.'

'Sarah, you've never been in trouble deeper than an ice-cube tray. What's up?'

It sounded so pathetic in her head, she knew it would sound just as pathetic out in the open. 'Olivia Brightman was in the loos. I flashed the Vs at her when she wasn't looking. Both hands.'

Jon put a hand over his mouth, his eyes widened. He looked like an attractive frog. 'It's off.'

'Sorry?'

'It's all off. I can't marry a woman like you.'

'It's not funny. I was *seen*!'

'I don't think you need to worry about being subpoenaed, Sarah, but just in case we need to ice anyone before they reach witness protection, who saw you?'

Sarah winced. 'Elodie came out of the loos and saw me in the mirror.'

'Ah, the old catch-a-villain-in-the-mirror chestnut, huh? Unlucky.'

'I'm serious, Jon. What if she tells Juliette? There are strict rules about personal conduct when you work in school, I don't need to tell you that.'

'You're right, you don't.' Jon was roughly half a million quid better off because his old employers had tried bending their own personal conduct rules. 'Just relax. How old is Elodie? Fifteen? Sixteen?'

'She's sixteen.'

'And no one else was in there with her?'

'No.'

'Don't go handing your resignation in just yet.' He finished his champagne.

'What do you mean?'

'You cheeked a parent, so? What's the worst that could happen?'

'She could tell!' Sarah sounded like a dithering schoolgirl.

'And?'

'And I'll be in the shit again with Mr Pethers Poo Poo Head.'

'Relax. No one's going to take Elodie's word over yours.

A sixteen-year-old girl over a professional family woman? Forget about it.'

'But they wouldn't have to take Elodie's word for it. If she did say anything it's not like I'd deny it. Try to make Elodie look dishonest.'

'With only one teenage girl to dispute you? Okay, Sar, sure you wouldn't.'

Was he serious? 'Of course I wouldn't, Jon.'

'Good job you washed your hands then,' he laughed. 'They'll be nice and clean when you offer them up for cuffing.'

90

'Evie, this is a really bad idea.'

Isobel was skipping to keep up with Evie's pace down the hill.

'No, I need them to hear it from me.'

'Evie, wait. Your folks have enough on their plates, I don't think the middle of their opening night is the best time—'

'What if they call the police?'

'Who?'

'Mum and Dad! Sarah Harrison was telling them to call the police, about Harry. They'll look at his phone, they might look at mine, too. Then they'll know I lied, about being trolled, they'll find out from the police. Mum'll know about the messages I was sending to you!'

'You're getting ahead of yourself, Evie. Stop!' Evie held back for a second. Isobel stood in front of her. The birds still chirped in the trees overhead, small moths were starting to float between the bushes lining the road. 'Do you think I want anyone else knowing about that film? Evie, you're nearly sixteen, I don't have to tell you how embarrassing that's been for me, do I? For my family? I came here to get away from all that.'

'So you're not going to tell Mum? About the messages?'

Isobel raised her hands exasperatedly and let them fall by her side again. 'No. I'm leaving Fallenbay. This week. And I'd really like it if I could say goodbye to your mum without her thinking I'm any of the things that video says I am.' Jon Hildred, whatever he was, had got away with it. She didn't have enough to pin anything on him now Evie had taken the blame for the messages. Without a definitive IP trace straight back to his home computer, all she had on him were the comments he'd made in the hallway and it would be his word against hers.

'But what about the lies I've told her? About being trolled?'

'That's up to you, Evie. But instead of giving your parents anything else to deal with right now, why don't you just go and enjoy a few hours with them at Coast? Learn your lesson and just . . . save your energy, Evie. Concentrate on telling your boyfriend what's what instead.'

Evie wasn't the first girl to fly into a fit of insane jealousy. What were the chances of that, though? *That* video being the one her boyfriend had taken a liking to. Little creep.

'He won't care. He won't listen.'

'So, just stop bothering with him.'

'It's not that easy. I see him all the time at school and . . . he's started flirting with my friend to make me jealous and . . .'

'Sounds like a real catch.' They'd made it to the sand dunes. 'Have you spoken to your friend?'

'She's just denying it. She's started to be funny with me and he's saying I'm imagining it. But he's saying things to me about Cassie behind her back and I think he's doing the same the other way around. We're not speaking any more.'

'So he's playing you and your friend off against each other?

Does that sound like something a nice lad does?' As if encouraging Evie to watch porn with him wasn't enough.

'No. I think he prefers her. She's sixteen already, and I'm not. And I know what's going to happen.'

'What's going to happen?'

'They'll have sex! Because she's over sixteen. He told me we have to wait, he wants to wait until I'm eighteen, but he says he loves me too much. So I made him promise we could try. When I'm sixteen. But she's sixteen already.'

Isobel wanted to put her hands over her ears and hum. Was this what Sophie had needed? Someone to talk it all through with before she'd jumped into bed with that deadbeat who'd bogged off the second Ella's tiny heart had begun to beat?

'Don't you think this is all best left to the school holidays, Evie? When your exams are over?'

'He'll be away in the holidays, he goes away with his family every summer.'

'Then let him! Let him go, Evie. There will be other boys.'

91

Cleo sipped a glass of water and knocked back two pills. She looked shattered.

'How's it all going?' asked Sarah. She still felt breathless. Jon had somehow turned them into Johnny and Baby on the dance floor, draping her over his arms, making her laugh unselfconsciously. People had clapped, Olivia had sneered into her husband's ear, Juliette had taken her drink out on to the terrace.

'The till's full. Everyone's happy. Another hour and then I can go home.'

Sarah leant over the counter and gave Cleo another hug.

'Don't, I'm close enough already, I just want to get Sam and go home to him. Uh-oh, heads up.'

Olivia arrived at the bar. 'He has a lot of energy, doesn't he, Mrs Harrison? Here you are taking a breather and he's straight into another dance with that young twenty-something. People will talk. Two Cosmos please, Cleo.'

There was a whoosh of movement behind them. Jon planted his hands on Sarah's shoulders. He still smelled good for all the frenzied dancing. He'd had more champagne bubbles than he was used to, the colour had gone right to his nose. Like a happy child in the snow.

The decision she'd made hung heavy in Sarah's stomach. No butterflies now didn't mean no butterflies *ever*, did it? *It's been four years.* 'Speak of the Devil,' beamed Olivia. She smiled and patted his hand.

'Olivia!' he said, like an old friend. 'No riding boots tonight? Can I interest you in a dance while I'm still a free man? Sarah knows I'm only marrying her to stop all the idle gossips, y'know. We're going to be the picture of respectability once we're wedded. We're going to eat bulgur wheat and stick to the missionary instead of giving in to our wildest urges, aren't we, darling?'

Olivia's eyes widened. Jon spun her around and took her by the hand. 'Giddy up, Olivia, let's get those tongues wagging again while there's still time.' He made another circuit of the dance floor, Olivia trying to keep up.

Sarah looked over the crowd. It wasn't like she was going to call the wedding off completely, just postpone it. Relationships were about compromise, she was ready for the move, or the marriage, but not both in one hit. The elation she'd felt in the bathroom, knowing she wasn't pregnant, had resonated too loudly. She didn't want what Jon wanted. She was putting on the brakes. He could choose, they were sticking with the wedding or the move. She knew he would choose the house and that was fine. And it wasn't just about taking things slow for the kids, she wanted to take things slow for *her*. She had to stop being swept along in the current all the time; this was her life too and she was in danger of riding the whole thing pillion.

'Here he is,' smiled Cleo.

Will took the space Jon and Olivia had left. He looked like a college hipster, shirt done up to his collar, growing biceps where the short sleeves ended. 'I thought you weren't coming. Is Max okay?'

'He was arguing with Grandad about going to bed when I left. You know he tried to make me change my shirt? Said I looked scruffy.'

'You look fantastic, Will. Who are you here with?'

Will looked over heads Sarah couldn't see over. He rubbed the bristles on his chin. 'Someone . . .'

'Anyone I know?' asked Sarah.

Cleo moved on to another group of customers. Will glanced over to the same spot across the room again. 'Don't freak, okay?'

'Will, why do I always feel like freaking when you say that?'

'Mum, I've been outside for twenty minutes, trying to pluck up the courage to come in and speak to you. I saw you dancing with Jon. You looked good, Mum. Happy. I don't see you laughing like that very much, you used to laugh all the time before Dad left, and then you stopped. I like seeing you laugh.'

There was a lump in her throat. 'I love you so much, Will.'

Will nodded. His face hardened. 'E—, my friend, thinks you guys look good together. Like a couple in a magazine.' Will didn't look convinced but Sarah had already warmed a few degrees towards his friend.

'So . . . can I meet your *friend*?'

Will rubbed his chin again. 'There'll be aggro, Mum.'

More fireworks. Excellent. 'Then we'll deal with it, Will.'

Will nodded. 'Okay. Just a sec.'

She finished the last of the champagne she'd been holding

for Jon. She would not be a conditional parent. Will could be what he wanted to be.

She waited patiently. Two fair-haired girls walked in through the glass doors. Evie's face looked puffy, and her friend . . . *Isobel?* Crikey, Sarah hadn't realised she looked so young. Isobel was always in pretty tops and skirts, hair crazy-blonde around her shoulders. Now she looked like one of Evie's school friends, plain T-shirt, hair piled back into a big blonde nest.

Sarah threw a hand over her head. Isobel and Evie both looked, and looked away.

'Hi, Mrs Harrison.'

Elodie stood beside Will, nearly as tall as him and with the same unsure expression.

'Mum? Say something.'

Sarah blinked at them. Why was Will holding Elodie's hand? The hand he'd passed a lit firework to seven years ago. Elodie gritted her teeth. 'We just thought it would be easier. If you didn't find out from Will's phone or something.'

Sarah was stunned. She'd have been less surprised if Will had introduced her to a six-foot rugby player. 'Elodie? You two . . . How . . . how long?'

Will and Elodie were like a single entity. The way they moved, their expressions. 'Eight months,' they both said.

'Eight months! How have you kept it secret?'

'Arthur let us meet—'

'In his woods? You've been having a love affair in the woods? For eight months?'

Will turned scarlet. 'Not just the woods, Mum.'

Juliette slapped her drink down on the bar next to them.

'So that explains how Milo's surfing's improved so dramatically, having his Saturdays back at The Village instead of going into Dewelsbury with you, Elodie.' Juliette had done something different with her hair, she looked softer. Prettier. And absolutely livid. Elodie shrank into her shoulders. 'Milo said you didn't want him to go with you any more. I thought he just wanted more time on his computer games.'

Sarah held up a placatory hand. 'I don't think this is a disaster, Juliette.'

Karl looked furtively at Sarah. Juliette repositioned herself. 'Not for you maybe. It was a disaster for Elodie, though, wasn't it? The last time they were around each other.'

'Mum,' objected Elodie.

'I'd never hurt her,' said Will. Elodie's hand was still clamped in his. 'Not on purpose.'

'Oh, well, that's alright then, isn't it? If it's not on purpose.'

'Juliette . . .' tried Karl.

Juliette snatched her shoulder back from him. 'She's supposed to be focusing on her offer from the conservatoire, Karl. She's supposed to be keeping herself distraction-free. Not necking some hoodlum in the woods. They don't just accept anyone, you know. She needs As not Bs! Piano at that level is going to be challenging enough after what *he* did.' Juliette swung to face Will. 'What are you trying to do? Finish her chances off completely?'

Sarah got off her stool. 'He's not a hoodlum.'

The crowd started to turn tide-like towards their simmering group of irate faces.

'Did someone say hoodlum? I thought my dance moves were pretty smooth, didn't you, Olive?'

Olivia was sheened with sweat. Two pleasant dimples appeared when she smiled at Jon. It had taken her three minutes to fall in love with him.

'Elodie and William are in love, Jon,' said Karl soberly.

Jon burst into laughter. His face straightened at the sight of everyone else's.

'This *thing* stops now. Right now, tonight. You both have exams, no one has time for this.'

'I love him, Mum.'

'Home, right now, Elodie.'

'Juliette,' tried Sarah. 'Please, can we talk about this, let's go outside on the terrace. Get some air. Cleo will do us some coffees, we can—'

'I do not want my daughter dating your son.'

'Why do you have to be such a bitch to us?' blurted Will. Sarah closed her eyes. 'You pick on my mum at work, you let your mate's kid pick on my brother . . .'

'That'll do, Will,' said Jon.

Will continued anyway, voice shaking. 'I'm not a monster. I make good grades. I'm projected a few As too. Every Saturday I meet Elodie and get the bus into town with her so she's safe. She hasn't missed a single piano class to be with me, and I've got her home every night for curfew. We don't speak at school in case Milo catches on. We can't even go to the beach together! And it sucks, because . . . we love each other.'

Jon straightened. Patrick hadn't stood up for Will, not even when Karl lost control in the hospital. But Jon was going to stand up for him now. Jon pointed at the door. 'Will, home. You're making a scene.' Sarah shot a look at him.

'I'm not going anywhere,' smiled Will.

'You've been telling porkies, Will. You've been saying you're in one place and sneaking off to another. You broke house rules.'

Will's eyes hardened. 'I'm not the only one, *Jon*.'

Elodie tugged Will's arm.

'Home,' repeated Jon.

'You're not my dad.'

Jon stepped into him. Will dropped Elodie's hand. The music was loud. Karl and Juliette wouldn't have caught Jon's words, but Sarah did. 'You won't be pulling this shit when you're living under my roof, son.' He reached for Will's arm and knocked into Elodie.

'You don't touch her!' reared Will.

Cleo returned, balancing a tray of glasses. 'What's going on?'

'I've had enough of this!' declared Juliette. 'Elodie, we're going home.' Karl shook his head and looked at the ceiling. The music thrummed around them.

Sam hovered behind Cleo at the edge of the group. He'd rolled his sleeves up, the forearms Sarah had seen on photos of his boxing days, still taut. 'Look who I found, love.' His hand looked huge on Evie's shoulder.

Sarah blinked and focused on Will again, jaw set, watching Juliette and Karl walking Elodie towards the coats. Jon wasn't bothered at all, casually surveying the crowd for something to do. 'You didn't stand by him.' Will glanced at her as she spoke.

Jon took a drink from Cleo's tray. 'You're such a mother hen, Sarah. Jesus Christ. Loosen up.'

'He's my son. You know he's not a hoodlum.'

'And I'm your boyfriend.' It sounded so trivial, juvenile.

Boyfriend. 'You're making me old before my time with this bullshit.' Olivia was floating nearby. 'Oh, here we go, the eyes, lighten up, Sarah, have a drink.' He leaned forwards, planting a clumsy kiss on her mouth. An arm reached around her, grabbing at her backside like some piece of fruit on a market he was trying to gauge the ripeness of.

'Don't,' she said.

Will bristled. Evie stepped forwards, away from Sam. Jon's eyes went straight to her. 'Yes?'

Will stepped between them. A wall between Evie and Jon. 'Evie, Elodie wants you, she's outside.' Evie didn't flinch. She sidestepped Will.

'Yes?' Jon repeated. 'Oh . . .' He took Sarah's empty glass from her hand and thrust it into Evie's. 'Two champagnes when you're ready.'

Evie was wide-eyed. She held Sarah's empty glass like a flame in a dark room. 'You said you didn't do that any more.'

'Evie, shut up.' Will took Evie by the elbow and marched her through the dancing crowd.

Sarah glared at Jon before she walked for the terrace, too. 'What is the matter with you? There's obviously something wrong with Evie.'

Jon grabbed her arm. 'Don't walk away from me.'

'Let go of my arm.'

'Thought you liked it rough? You did in the summerhouse.'

She snatched her arm free. 'No, *you* did.' There was nothing seductive about having to call your forty-two-year-old partner, *Sir*.

'Everything alright, folks?' asked Sam.

'You boring little cow. Fuck me, can't wait until we're married. Let the misery commence.'

'Whoa, steady on,' tried Sam. 'It's a good misery.'

'I might be boring, Jon, I might not know a good time when I see one, or a good man, but I know I don't need either to be a good woman.'

Jon blinked. His eyes half-vacant. He crackled into drunken laughter. 'I don't even know what that means!'

'It means you get to enjoy extra bedrooms in your new house. We're not moving in with you. We're staying in our home.'

'Did you just swear at her?' Sarah hadn't seen Will come back.

Jon ignored him. 'Because I called you *boring*?'

'No.' She was boring. She knew that. 'Because I don't love you.'

Evie elbowed her way back through the crowd after Will. 'Didn't I ask you for drinks?' snarled Jon.

'You grabbed her bum. You kissed her! You said you didn't love her!'

'Evie, shut up!' demanded Will.

Cleo came in from the other side. 'Hey!'

'Who's upset you, Evie?' asked Sam.

'You said you felt sorry for her. You're a liar!'

Cleo pressed herself in beside Sarah. 'Evie? Why are you saying this to Jon?'

92

'Isobel!'

Isobel spun around on Coast's steps. She hadn't seen Ben in jeans; the shirt and tie threw her completely. 'Hey.'

'Hey yourself. Changed your mind then?'

'Oh, no . . . I was just, delivering a package. Sort of.' Evie was safely inside with her parents. The rest was up to them.

'That's too bad, I heard Brad Pitt's in town, thought you might wanna come say hi.'

'Ah, well, if Brad's in town, hold the door,' she smiled.

Ben came down on to the step above hers. 'You're here now. Could I buy you that drink? Water or . . . whatever?'

She wanted to. Maybe not here but she wanted to. She looked down at herself. 'I can't, not really dressed for it.'

'You look great. Everyone in there will be wearing joggers. And flip-flops.'

She grinned. 'Thanks. But I have to pack.'

Her time here was done. She'd decided on the walk with Evie. She wouldn't be leaving Fallenbay with anyone's head to mount on her wall, no chaos in her wake, no major change to the landscape back home. Just the understanding that everyone was dysfunctional to a degree. Everyone had scars, and not everyone deserved them. That was just the way it was.

'You're leaving then?'

'Tomorrow. First thing.'

'Oh.' Ben nodded at his feet. Nathan used to do something similar when his team lost. 'So, where are you going *now*? Can I walk you anywhere? To your suitcase?' Raised voices pulled their attention to the terrace, lit up with swaying strings of lightbulbs. The girl from the organic grocery shop was huddled by the olive trees, arguing with the dentist who'd helped Sarah at the football, and his wife, Juliette.

Sarah burst from Coast's glass door and strode briskly across the terrace straight past them, blue chiffon flared like ink behind her. Jon a few seconds behind. Isobel stiffened. 'Hey, don't walk away from me!'

Will barged out after them. 'Mum! Evie doesn't know what she's talking about!'

'Listen to your kid, Sarah.' Jon sounded cold, indifferent.

They were all headed this way. Isobel wanted to get off the steps before Jon reached her but her legs wouldn't move.

Sarah breezed straight past them towards the street. She stepped one foot on to the cobbles and twisted awkwardly, leg moving in one direction, shoulders in the other. She stumbled to her knees.

Isobel skipped down the steps after her. 'Sarah, are you okay?' She looked vacant. Not upset, not hurt. Not there.

Sam's voice boomed across the terrace. 'Hey, you! Don't move.'

Isobel could just see over the steps to the party inside, Cleo's red dress like a beacon, Evie's face in her mother's hands, twisted and hysterical.

Sarah was grasping her foot. 'Are you okay?' asked Ben. 'What's going on?'

'I said, don't move, Hildred.'

Jon slowed at the top of the steps like a schoolboy called back by his mother. He looked down at Isobel and Ben, crouched by Sarah.

'Alright mate?' asked Ben.

Jon gave him a thumbs-up. ' 'Ello 'ello, it's Little Red Riding Hood still skipping around Fallenbay. You want to watch that one, mate. Friskier than she looks.'

'*Hildred.*'

Sam was near-running across the terrace. Jon's smile was lazy, his hands upturned. 'Teenage girls, eh, mate? Dream up some stuff. I did speak to Evie about the boundaries of affection in one of our sessions—'

'Have you touched my daughter?'

Evie was trying to pull free from Cleo. *My boyfriend wouldn't stop.* An unpleasant puzzle was piecing itself together in Isobel's head.

'Are you serious, mate? Haven't you seen my fiancée? Alright, she's on her arse in the gutter *now*, but usually she's quite the piece.'

Sam jabbed him at the chest. 'Have you touched my daughter?'

'Watch yourself, big guy. I'm faster than I look.'

'Is that so? One last time. Have you touched my fifteen-year-old daughter, you jumped up little prick?'

Jon giggled. He looked down and laughed at Isobel, too. And Sarah, about to be helped to her feet by Ben. He was still laughing when Sam Roberts cracked his knuckles like a piston straight into his nose.

'Not as fast as you thought, little man.'

'Sam! Whoa!' Ben jolted towards them.

Sam got another punch in first. Isobel had been paintballing once. A cartridge had hit her visor, brilliant red spattering in every direction. Jon's nose reminded her of that now.

Karl Inman-Holt ran across the terrace. He yanked Sam backwards, holding him like one of those alligator wrestlers who had the beast by the tail and no exit plan. Sam was wild, nostrils flared, the opposite of Cleo, shell-shocked beside a pale Evie.

'You're all dysfunctional!' stated Juliette. 'All of you!'

Jon crouched, spitting blood on the timbers. A blue light danced across his face. Coast lit up blue too, along with the other shop façades along the harbour and the rest of the faces on Cleo's terrace.

Jon eyed the police car driving down the high street. He wiped his nose on his sleeve. 'Excellent. I've never been assaulted by a proprietor before, hope your insurance is up to scratch Roberts?'

The police pulled alongside Sarah and Isobel. The female officer got out first.

'Are you alright, my love? How have you ended up down there?'

Sarah smiled for her. 'I'm fine. Heels and cobbles.'

'And what about you, sir, heels and cobbles?' asked the other officer, rounding his car. Jon didn't respond. Karl loosened his grip on Sam while both officers considered Jon's bleeding face. 'Okay, folks. Anyone got anything else to offer?' He glanced behind him and gave Karl a double-take.

'Dr *Driller*, I didn't see you there.' The policeman took his hat off and rubbed his forearm over his head.

'Driller' pierced Isobel's ear like a dart.

Karl fell in line with his wife, the only semblance of stability in a fractured group. 'Chris, how's it going? Life better without the wisdom teeth?'

'Absolutely. Wisdom's overrated,' replied the officer, sombrely. 'Still enjoying the new premises? Nice and close to the squash courts?'

Karl patted his stomach. 'It's good to play the odd lunch hour, Chris, keeps the puddings off.'

Isobel helped Sarah silently to her feet. Cleo hung back on the periphery, staring at Sam. Jon was stemming the flow of blood with his ruined jacket. It was difficult not to watch him, he was like a fly stuck on a web. Waiting. He was in trouble. For trolling Isobel or something else. Evie Roberts. Jon was in trouble for something.

The officer with Karl scratched the back of his neck. 'I was hoping you'd be home actually, Karl, so we could deal with this quietly, but your boy said you were here for the night.' The female officer took the steps to join her colleague on the terrace. 'Dr Inman-Holt, this is Officer Baxter.'

Karl aimed a perfect smile at her. 'Evening, Officer Baxter. Sort what out quietly? You've been to my house?'

Officer Baxter didn't look as uncomfortable as the other officer. 'Karl Inman-Holt?'

'Yes?'

'I'm arresting you under the Malicious Communications Act.'

93

They'd walked in total silence. Birdsong on the lane replaced by the chirping of crickets. The night was a pressing, palpable thing. Ben's footsteps beside Isobel's were quiet, her flip-flops providing the only soundtrack to their existence.

Sam thought the police had come to arrest him. They hadn't.

Trouble hadn't found Jon yet either, but it had laced up its boots. He'd made his bloodied retreat, throwing warnings at Sam as he went, while Juliette erupted a non-stop flow about *legal repercussions* and the *Independent Police Complaints Commission*. The Inman-Holts were on their way now to Dewelsbury police station. The Roberts family had regrouped and followed Sarah and Will towards the beach, leaving Isobel with Ben, and a head full of questions.

Dr Driller, the officer said. What was that, a term of endearment? A light-hearted nickname? It was too close for comfort. It whirred through her thoughts now, right along-side *The Malicious Communications Act*. The Malicious Communications Act! It sounded so paltry. A law to control swearing on buses or hounding exes with late-night drunken calls. But it meant more than that. It meant no one should have to endure the torment Isobel had. And so one question burned brightest, all the way home on her silent walk with Ben. *Who has the dentist been tormenting?*

The air was getting cooler. Her head was beginning to hurt. She couldn't unknot the mess. Hildred . . . Evie . . . the dentist . . . DEEP_DRILLERZ.

Everything Evie had said, about her boyfriend, all of it about Jon. The boyfriend who wouldn't stop watching. It made Isobel's skin crawl. The way he'd acted in Sarah's hallway, touching her wrist like she'd turned up in the muck. A grubby curiosity to pocket. She'd been so certain Jon was DEEP_DRILLERZ, now nothing was clear. Evie had never said when she'd first seen the video on her boyfriend's phone, it hadn't been relevant when Isobel had assumed she was talking about some awful hormonal teenage boy. But Evie wasn't talking about a teenage boy, she was talking about Jon. The game had changed completely.

If Jon had only recently seen the video, he couldn't be DEEP_DRILLERZ. If he'd seen it last year, he was still in the running. But there was no confirmation either way. She couldn't exactly ask Evie, or Sarah. The two people most likely to know roughly when Jonathan Hildred's's preoccupation with Isobel's *porno* had started.

And what's Karl Inman-Holt been up to?

She was grinding her teeth again. Her jaw already ached. She needed a good dentist. Like Juliette's husband, kindly offering to take Sarah across the street to his surgery after the football incident. Isobel remembered the dental practice, the modernist building with the nice lawns and sleek signage. *Horizon* something. A stone's throw from the leisure centre. And the high school. And the children's park Sophie's IP trace had stuck its useless pin into.

Why had the police arrested him? Had Soph gone through with it, had she gone to them with her incriminating dossier on DEEP_DRILLERZ? Was Karl Inman-Holt the destination they'd arrived at after picking over Sophie's breadcrumb trails? Isobel thought about him. Designer glasses. Designer life. Did Karl Inman-Holt like to victimise women?

Think, Isobel, think.

The first IP trace had led straight to Coast. Did Karl even go in there? He had sushi delivered for lunch, fresh every day, Cleo's menu wasn't upmarket enough for the millionaire dentist, those were Cleo's *exact* words. Karl couldn't have been the one using Cleo's wifi to wage a hate campaign then. Could he?

Isobel needed to speak to Sophie. Ask her if she had contacted the police. She'd have warned her, surely? Isobel patted down her empty pockets and remembered shooting out of the cottage after Evie without her keys, phone, anything.

'What did he mean, *Red Riding Hood*?' Ben's voice was like a twig, snapping in the dark.

She looked into the night ahead of them. 'A bad story. You wouldn't want to hear it.' There was no point lying. Not now the world had Google.

'I wouldn't want to hear it . . . or you wouldn't want to tell it?'

More quiet. More crickets. More flip-flops in the dark. 'Both.'

'Oh. I'd say some other time then. But you're leaving.'

'Yes.'

'Damn.'

Yes.

The trees blotted out nearly all the dark blue light from the horizon. It was only the steep incline and the ache in her calves that said they were nearly back at Arthur's.

Ben strode ahead of her and turned so he was scaling the hill backwards, facing her.

'What are you doing?'

'It's easier backwards. Try it.'

'No thanks, I like a struggle. And to see where I'm going.' She thudded into his body. 'You stopped!'

'I thought you liked to see where you were going?' She expected him to move, but he didn't. 'This almost feels like one of those kiss-the-girl-on-a-quiet-lane-before-she-leaves-town-for-good moments.'

Ben was one of the good guys, wasn't he? He might just be more than she could ever have come looking for. Something different. And maybe wonderful. But there was too much background noise here. She would go tomorrow and not look back. There was no sense blurring the lines.

Ben found her hand at her side. She let him. He was close enough that she could hear the change in his breathing. He was waiting. For permission to blow the rules out of the water.

Isobel found his waist. She reached for him, in the dark, and pressed her mouth to his. She let everything else, all thoughts of all things, fall away for those seconds with Ben on the lane, lost in a kiss. Lost, until the sound of Daniel's cries found them through the woods.

94

Ben disappeared into the forest after Daniel and his flashlight.

Isobel closed the cottage door behind her and leant against it. When they did find Petal, she wouldn't be on a lead. *Better to be on this side of the door.* And she should call Sophie now, before Ben and Daniel came back.

Phone. Where had she left it? She'd been talking to Sophie in front of the TV when Evie had turned up. Isobel walked through the hall and noticed the lamp. Small hairs stood to attention along her arms. She hadn't left the landing light on either. It had still been light outside when Evie knocked the door and confessed all. The toilet flushed upstairs, Isobel froze at the bottom. *You idiot.* Jonathan could've gone anywhere. Why hadn't she thought? Because Ben had been with her. And now he wasn't.

Someone was in the bathroom. *You're about to get murdered in your own cottage. They'll find you wearing your bikini bottoms under your joggers because you forgot to put your knickers on the airer last night.* Her mother was always trumpeting the need to wear nice knickers, in case you ever had to have them cut off your lifeless body. The bathroom door opened.

Two gold sandals appeared at the top step. Isobel's murderer liked French manicures.

'Sophie, what the hell!' Isobel planted her hand against the hallway wall and tried to breathe without hyperventilating.

Sophie jumped and threw a hand to her chest. '*Jesus*, don't do that! I bloody called! You left your phone on the fireplace. And you left the goddamn front door unlocked, Isobel! *I* should be shouting *what the hell*! . . . What the hell!'

Sophie came to a halt one step from the bottom of the stairs. They should be hugging by now. Isobel gave the lounge a cursory glance. She checked the bottom of the curtains for Jon's feet, just in case.

'I left in a hurry. Where's Dad's car?'

'I came in mine. It's parked by that Land Rover. The rust helps it blend right in to the mud over there.' Sophie smiled but it didn't make her eyes. She was lucky she hadn't bumped into Petal. 'Are you okay? You look pale.'

The cottage flooded with silence again.

'Have you said anything to the police, Sophie?'

'No, not without the okay from you.' Then Karl's arrest couldn't be anything to do with them. 'Why?'

'It doesn't matter. What's with the sudden drive back to Fallenbay? Did you forget something?' *Did you forget to tell me something?*

Sophie slumped down on to the bottom stair and tucked her hair behind her ears. 'I freaked. Mum was watching *Most Evil* again. I didn't know who was banging on your door, Is, and you just hung up . . . after joking about the Bogey Man. I can't cope with it any more, Isobel, you being here, it's turning me into a nervous wreck.'

'Sorry, Sophie. That must be really awful for you.' There was more than just a note of shittiness in her tone. Sophie caught it but still managed to hold eye contact. Sophie could stare anyone down, no matter what she'd done. 'So, aren't you going to ask? Who was at the door?'

'Who was at the door?'

Isobel set her hands behind her, flat against the hallway wall. 'A troll.'

'What? You mean *him*? That *bastard*?'

'No. I mean *her*.'

Sophie's face crinkled. 'DEEP_DRILLERZ is a *woman*? But the IP traces . . . that *shit* Jon Hildred . . . everything he said to you, everything he knew . . .'

Isobel walked into the lounge and sat down. 'I said *a* troll, Sophie. Not *the* troll.' Not DEEP_DRILLERZ, the head vampire. Sophie got up like a dazed toddler and followed. 'It turns out there are a lot of trolls around, Sophie. Lurking in dark corners. Waiting to spring something horrible on you.'

Sophie blinked and sat down slowly on the other sofa. 'Who was it?'

'Evie.'

'Who?'

'Cleo's daughter.'

'*Coast* Cleo? Her daughter's a troll?'

'Suppose it depends on your definition of troll. Evie left the message on my car, and the texts. She was the one calling and hanging up. She didn't want me here.'

'What the f—'

'Jealousy, Sophie. And immaturity. They're enjoying a long friendship aren't they, those two?'

Sophie missed it. She was preoccupied, rubbing her forehead, trying to patch it all together. 'Why's Cleo's daughter jealous of you? Sorry, I don't mean . . . You're beautiful, Isobel, I just meant . . .'

'Because she's been involved in something she shouldn't have . . . with Hildred.'

The colour seeped from Sophie's face. 'Oh my God.' She looked off into space. 'Oh my *God*. Isn't he her . . .'

'Teacher.' Another fallen teacher.

Sophie swallowed. 'What tripped her off on you, though? I don't understand. Did he say something to her about you? Why was she jealous?'

Isobel's stomach rolled. 'Evie told me she thought her boyfriend was messing around with other girls. So she looked through his phone and found the video of Nathan and me. I'd have called her parents right then if I'd known who she meant.'

'Her *boyfriend*? Sicko. And he just leaves that stuff lying around on his phone? With a fiancée and kids around?'

'He bought a pair of pay-as-you-go phones, so they could contact each other under the radar.' Everything Evie had said earlier tonight had taken on a more sinister tone since Sam had broken Jon's nose. Jon had manipulated Evie. Groomed her. But he hadn't factored on Evie wrestling with her conscience, or walking into Coast and making a scene.

Sophie was staring again, visualising Ella coming into contact with a teacher like Jon Hildred. Isobel would bet. Isobel could read her like a book. Sophie should be worried for Ella. It was too easy for children, and adults, to be manipulated by bad people. 'Evie said her boyfriend wouldn't have sex with her until she turned sixteen. I even told her I thought he was sensible for suggesting it.' Isobel's stomach lurched at that ignorants comment now.

'You didn't know she was talking about a pervert, Isobel. Sixteen? Doesn't the law against teachers perving on school-kids soften once they hit sixteen? Rat. And hate texts? Notes on your car? She's no better.'

Sophie was hopping on to a high horse now? 'Ha! I don't blame Evie for what she did, Sophie. She's a kid. That's what adolescence is for, to figure stuff out. By our age people should have themselves sorted out, and neither you nor I have done so great.' Sophie held her hands up defensively, but it was too late. Isobel's path had already changed. 'When a grown man tells a young girl to watch, and I'm using Evie's words here, a *porno*, telling her she can learn a few tips to make things *really special* when they finally "make love", I'm not surprised Evie felt the way she did towards me.'

Sophie stood. 'You're right. We're going to the police. He needs locking up. For what he did to you, and to Evie . . .'

Isobel's blood pressure was still climbing. The endless crap, all because that video made it online in the first place. 'You want to go to the police, Sophie? Really?'

'Don't you?'

'Sure. You do realise you'll have to give them the full story, though? Not just the end scene.'

Sophie hesitated. 'I don't follow?'

Isobel could feel her eyes burning. 'Sorry, harking back to the days I still had a job there for a sec! Your *story*, Soph, before you go to the police with it. It needs a beginning, middle and end. It's basic English. So, the end is what we know now, about Jon and Evie and that unpleasant stuff, the middle can be about me having a breakdown and almost being committed because of the hate and bile and relentless misery I was subjected to, and the beginning . . .' There were tears now, sliding over Sophie's cheek. Isobel realised she was crying too. She could see the underside of Sophie's wrist, the tattoo Sophie had chosen for their sisterly pact. 'The beginning will be how you found a video of your sister, uploaded it to a hate site, and fed her to the wolves.'

95

'Did you have a lovely evening? I wasn't expecting you back yet. Where's Jon?'

Where was Jon? Sarah's eyes and ears were on high alert. She tried listening to the sounds of the house over Robert Redford whispering a horse back to life on the lounge TV and her father snoring in the armchair.

'He's coming,' Sarah said automatically. He would come.

She threw her shoes under the stairs; scandal was a marvellous analgesic, she hadn't felt her ankle at all during the ride home. Will piled into the lounge after her. He'd been straight up to check Max . . . did he think Jon might take him?

'He's sleeping.' Sarah looked at her eldest son now and felt instantly reassured.

'Of course Max is sleeping, darling, is everything alright?'

Will and Elodie had seen Jon alone in Arthur's woods. Will had chosen not to mention it, to avoid upsetting Sarah or Max.

Sarah pecked her mother on the cheek. 'Let's get you off home, is Dad ready? Shall I get your coats?'

'Well . . . shall I put the kettle on first?' Her mother had never had a social life, she liked to nourish herself with the finer details of other people's. A whole marriage-worth of social enrichment, by proxy.

Will fidgeted, watching the back door. Jon would come. He thought there was fifty thousand pounds of his cash sitting in the cellar.

Evie had told them everything on the beach. Her chance meeting with Jon in Acorn Woods after Verity had stood her up to meet a boy in McDonalds. Jon had been taking Mr Fogharty for a shit in the forest when the dog had scrambled up Evie, scratching her arms. Jon had nobly administered some of the antiseptic cream he kept in the car for Max's nettle stings.

Evie shared the hints Jon liked to drop at after-school cardio club, the route he ran over the bluff, the times he would be there, the beautifying benefits of a good run on the body. He'd been meeting her in the woods, sometimes at Compass Point. She'd been around the perimeter and inside the garages, never inside the house, oh no, Jon wasn't stupid. Showing Evie the colossal en-suites or the natural stone surfaces would be like flashing her a birthmarked penis, facts she could positively ID him by, corroborate any tales she might tell.

It was Jon's idea that Evie keep her secret phone at her friend's . . . Cassie or Carrie? Sarah hadn't been concentrating. Only Cassie or Carrie wasn't Evie's friend any more because she liked Mr Hildred too, so there was little chance of Evie having the phone back to prove anything. And the big one. Sex. Evie said they hadn't yet. They'd *only* kissed. Evie swore it. Perhaps she was just doing her distraught father a kindness. For all of them, Sarah hoped it was the truth.

Cleo had cried. Sam too. Sarah hadn't told any of them about the Nokia she'd found in the chimney pot in the summerhouse. Or how Jon had come home from all those runs, horny and hyped. That Evie had been his warm-up and Sarah his workout. His doll. Sarah had been Jon's blow-up underage Evie.

'Oh, here he is now. Jon'll have a cup of tea.'

Sarah heard the back door slam too. He'd sobered. She could tell by the surety of his footsteps coming through the house. He glared at her when he passed the lounge doorway, as if all this was her fault. It was her fault. She'd been so willing to be the sheep again, she'd traded one unpleasant shepherd for another and called it progress.

'Jon?' Sarah's mother came into the hall after her and watched Jon let himself down into the cellar. 'Good Lord, Jonathan, what happened to your face?'

Sarah hadn't moved the cellar keys. She'd moved the phone. It was all she needed.

'Take Gran into the lounge please, Will.'

Sarah waited at the top of the cellar steps. Jon moved back into view at the bottom. He would deny it all. He knew Evie had no proof. He'd been so confident on the terrace. *Evie's been sending herself hate-mail online, did you tell your folks that, Evie? All verifiable if anyone wants to call in the police.* Cleo and Sam were crap parents, it was all down in Jon's notes. They argued so much their daughter had faked her own bullying. *And you're honestly listening to her now?*

Jon looked up at her. 'It had better all be there, Sarah.' Even now, he was so sure of himself.

She cleared her throat. 'Of course it isn't. You told me to put some aside for the wedding.' He disappeared into the cellar. Undoing locks, unzipping satchels. She listened. He'd told her to put just fifteen thousand into an ISA, so it didn't bump the allowance threshold. After the first nervy trip taking it all into the bank, Sarah had taken another fifteen thousand for both Max and Will's dormant ISAs, not for the boys, for safekeeping. Things happened. Kids played with fireworks. Houses caught fire. Savings went up in smoke. She was being sensible. Boring. Of course it was still Jon's money.

'There's only . . . *five* grand in here. Where the fuck's the rest?' She'd never seen him in shock. It was a curious thing, like seeing one of Max's transformer toys morphing. A sweaty nuclear weapon emerging from a reliable family car.

He slammed his hand against the wall. 'I'm taking what's mine with me, Sarah.'

'Then make sure you don't forget the chimney pot before you leave.'

Jon charged up the first few cellar steps. She jumped but she wasn't frightened exactly. 'Where is it?' he growled.

'The money? Or the Nokia?' She'd overheard Jon asking Max if he'd seen Will messing around in the summerhouse and had kept out of it. In case Will had broken something critical, like Jon's redundant treadmill. 'You weren't clearing out the summerhouse while Max and I were at the school fair last weekend, you were looking for your secret phone.'

The smugness was leaching away. He stared vacantly at his satchel and what must look like pocket-change now. Five grand wasn't going to help. Three hundred thousand of his money was tied up in the house. He didn't have enough to pay the rest now Sarah wasn't selling.

'I never understood why you chose me.' Not until she

thought someone might be grooming Will and started reading up on all the ways a person might manipulate another to serve their own purposes. 'But I understand now.'

'What?'

'You thought I was vulnerable, Jon. You counselled my little boy after his father left, you knew where the holes were. You thought you could slide in and mould us into a nice respectable façade to hide yourself behind. You groomed me then, and you groomed me again when you planted seeds of doubt about Evie, about her state of mind. Laying the foundations in case one day she spoke up.'

'Sarah, please . . . It was a slip-up. Nothing happened, I swear.'

He was bluffing again. He knew she couldn't possibly know what was on that phone, he'd kept the battery separate. 'You can't have the phone back, Jon. But you can have the five grand.'

Sarah couldn't see what was on that phone, but the police would. He knew that.

'Please, Sar . . . She threw herself at me. They all do. The fucking mothers do, too.'

'Did Lucy Timmons? *Poor Lucy Timmons*, who you were only trying to help at Tibbsley House? Was it you who discredited her? Or did you get her friend to put the cocaine in her dorm room? No one listens to a druggy, do they, Jon?'

'You know what they'll do to me.'

'You should have thought about that before. Maybe you'll think about it now. Because if you ever work with anyone under eighteen again, I'll take the phone to the police myself.'

96

Sophie's head was in her hands. 'You knew all the time. And you didn't say anything.'

'Not all the time.' Isobel's tears had already stopped. A numbness taking the place of all those other emotions she'd been feeling. It had been after Sophie had first told her how they might be able to identify DEEP_DRILLERZ. The bad guy. When Sophie had shown Isobel that first screen grab of his IP address and Isobel had found a renewed hope, a way forwards. Sophie handing it all to her like a ripe peach.

Sophie peered up beneath parted hands. A new vein was sitting proud on her forehead. 'When did you find out?'

'When you were trying to find a better job. You'd used my laptop to write your CV so I proofread that first. It was perfect. But I still had a whole day left to kill moping around Mum's. You said there wasn't anything around worth applying for, I thought I'd look for you, but I couldn't remember which recruitment sites you said you'd registered with so I pulled them up from the history list on my laptop.' Sophie set her head back in her hands. 'I don't know why I even looked back that far, months and months, but I saw it. PegOr2.com on New Year's Eve. While I was out partying with your mates.'

Sophie's skin had gone a funny colour. 'I was pissed off, Is.

And I had no right. I can't believe I was even thinking . . . I was *so* jealous when you guys all left, because I had Ella and . . . Mum and dad were banging on and on about how you needed the bigger bedroom because your job was a *proper* job and loads more important than mine, and your needs were greater and—'

'Let me stop you there, Sophie. Don't give me a bed of reasons to lay it down on, okay? Just give it to me. You did it because you wanted to knock me down a peg or two. End of.'

Sophie swallowed. She pushed the hair from her eyes. 'It was an accident.'

Isobel laughed then. A bitter, sharp sound. 'Everything you ever *do* is an accident, Sophie! You're the most accident-prone person in the world. Accidentally joyriding in Dad's car . . . accidentally getting pissed in Home Ec . . . accidentally getting pregnant . . .'

'Do you think I don't know that! That I'm one huge fuck-up next to you, Isobel? Jesus, do you think Mum and Dad don't remind me *all* the time? I know exactly how this sounds, and it's still spiteful and ugly and shameful, but I swear, on Ella's life, it was an accident! I was just messing around. Bored. Fed up! I found the film in Nathan's desktop file on your laptop. One second I was laughing at his workout selfies and the next . . . it was just there. Proof that you weren't the golden child. Mum and Dad were clucking around you for breaking up with Nath, and you were upstairs telling me it was a game plan to make him propose!'

The numbness was wearing off. She wanted to cry, throw Sophie out, scream in her face . . . all of the above. 'How could you do that to me?'

Sophie's shoulders slumped. 'It was an accident, Is.'

'*Look at me, Isobel Yvonne Hedley . . .*'

'I know! I know I wrote that, I typed it all out, but I was *never* going to upload it, and then, I don't know what happened, you came home early because you were too pissed and I shut the laptop before you could see anything, but my hairband . . . I'd taken it out and it must've been on the keys and when I slammed the laptop shut, the button—'

'You expect me to believe anything you say? Ever?'

'No. But it's the truth. And I'm so sorry, Isobel. For everything this brought back on you. I deserve whatever you want to do.'

'Are you for real, Sophie? You think there's anything that can fix this now? You couldn't even hold your hands up! I've been here for *weeks*, waiting for you to grow a pair and say something. Anything!'

'What? But . . . you came to find *him*.'

'No. I came to find you. You came up with the stupid plan, you were trying to make yourself feel better by doing something, purging yourself. Yes, I did think about it at first, I wanted to know who he was, I obsessed about it. But then I found out the truth about my own *sister* and everything changed! You messed up! I just wanted to give you a reason to get off your arse and do something about it. To own up, because you didn't want to own up when I was at home all safe and snug in my new shit life. You were coping with your conscience just fine, so long as there weren't too many crazies turning up on the doorstep. Do you think *sorry* is ever going to be enough now?'

'You scammed me?'

'You are *kidding*? Y'know what, sod this, I'm going to pack.'

Sophie was indignant. 'I thought we were baiting him, but . . . you were baiting *me*?'

She was actually pissed off! With Isobel! *Good*. 'Suck it up, Sophie. People aren't always what they seem. Be glad you get to hide your mistakes, I have to walk around with mine hanging around my neck like the Scarlet Letter. It might as well be written on my face – *Isobel Hedley, internet whore*.' She pulled off her bangle and threw it across the floor, held out her wrist. '*I'm marked*! By my own sister!'

'Isobel, I said I'm sorry! *Please* believe me.'

'I do believe you, Sophie. Of course you're sorry. But there are still consequences and you never learn. You think Mum and Dad were rough on you, but they totally *mollycoddled* you! I had to study hard, be home on time, eat my greens. You got to play around. You're spoilt, Sophie. You let me blame Nathan! He swore it wasn't him but I wouldn't hear it. Maybe we could've salvaged something but you never gave us the chance. He was splashed all over the internet too. Dad wanted to kill him and you knew!'

Sophie was weeping again. 'I know, Isobel, I'm—'

Isobel took the first few stairs. 'Let me guess, sorry?'

'Isobel, please don't go upstairs, talk to me.'

'I can't even look at you, Sophie. I'm ashamed of you. I'm finally ashamed of something else more than I've been ashamed of myself.'

The door knocked. It would be Ben. Or Dan with a progress report on Petal's whereabouts. Sophie moved to the door.

'Don't! Don't answer my door. Don't you touch any part of my life ever again.'

'I'm going, Isobel. I won't bother you any more.'

Sophie opened the door. Jon stood in the doorway, fox-like and pale, the beginnings of two black eyes like blotting ink either side of his bruised nose.

97

It had always bothered at Isobel, sitting with Sophie on their father's lap listening to him read, how Grandmama and Little Red Riding Hood would have handled the old wolf situation if they'd both been in the cottage when he'd first arrived. Would they have banded together? Would the wolf still have bothered hiding who he was? Would the outcome have been better, or worse, for any of them?

Jon's foot was almost inside the door. He looked at Sophie in the hall, then Isobel hesitant on the stairs. 'Hello, Isobel. Been making more friends, have we?' Sophie's stance betrayed the fact she already knew the stranger at the door wasn't welcome. Jon's eyes brightened. 'Obviously not going to introduce us then,' he smiled. Sophie kept her eyes fixed ahead. Jon moved forwards into the doorway. Sophie blocked him. 'Friendly bunch, aren't you?'

Isobel stepped down into the hall. 'It's okay, Soph, I've got it.' It wasn't okay. But it was less okay Sophie standing so close to him.

She should've known Sophie wouldn't fall back, so they stood shoulder to shoulder. 'What do you want?' Isobel sounded weak. A weak little woman.

Jon grinned, but it was all menace. 'I want to know what you said to Evie Roberts before you walked her into Coast tonight and watched her blow my marriage apart.'

Sophie tensed beside her. She knew for sure who she was looking at now.

Isobel straightened her back. She felt braver with her sister here. 'You blew your own marriage apart, Jon, before it had even started. Sarah would've figured you out at some point.'

Without warning Jon stepped forwards into the cottage. Isobel froze then, all bravery fleeing her. Sophie lunged her whole body forwards, blocking him. 'No you don't.' She caught Jon off-balance, with the help of gravity and two stone steps. He fell backwards, landing gracelessly at the bottom. A second or two and he was scrambling back to his feet. The tension jumped a few notches.

He looked straight past Sophie at Isobel in the doorway. 'You stupid tart. You don't get to stir my shit up for free. You think you've had a bad time from all those nasty boys online?' He was rubbing his knuckles by his eye, pretending to cry. 'You wait until I've had a play with your little movie, see if I can better the efforts of your online friend Sarah was telling me about. I'm not some numpty with a laptop trolling bints like you for kicks, I can be pretty creative with the old video editing if I want to be. By the time I've added a few new features, you'll wish you'd kept your knickers on, darlin'.'

Sophie was rigid. But her anger was futile. She knew she couldn't fix this.

Isobel thought of Karl Inman-Holt. Where he might be, right now. What malicious communications the police had arrested him for. *Dr Driller*. DEEP_DRILLERZ. Far too close for comfort. She held Jon's gaze. Here she was, finally facing the monster, and he was the wrong monster. She tried to keep her voice steady. 'Go right ahead, Jon. Do what you think's best. And I'll do the same.'

'What can you do?' She amused him.

Send a friendly email to the head of that posh school you used to work at, before the rumours about you sleeping with the students started circling.'

He shrugged. 'Who's going to listen to you? You're a stupid tart.'

'And Evie?' She was bluffing. She didn't exactly have Evie in her hand.

He was grinning now. 'Another stupid tart.'

Isobel nodded at the floor. She tried to ignore the tremble fighting into her voice. 'The thing is, Jon, you cost Tibbsley House a *lot* of money. They won't care who's offering them a chance of recouping their cash, or their credibility . . . they'll only care that they're getting the chance.' He didn't like that. Strangers knowing personal things about him. Details of his murky history. Isobel had to agree, it sucked. 'I'm not the only sleaze story floating around on the web for everyone to look at, Jon. Rubbish, isn't it?'

He snatched up his keys and patted some of the dust from himself. 'Whatever. The difference darlin', is what people really think. Quietly, even blokes like Sam Roberts are thinking, *Fair play, Hildred can pick up a bit of skirt in her teens*. But you know what people are really thinking of girls like you, Isobel? Even with your boohoo stories? They're thinking . . . *stupid tart*.'

Sophie's eyes darted from Jon to Isobel again. Jon had just nailed it. It didn't matter what Isobel went on to achieve, there would always be someone encapsulating her now as nothing more than a *stupid tart*.

Jon turned for his car. He crossed the track looking over towards the forest, men's voices and a few barks breaking through the distant woods.

'Who's that by his car?' asked Sophie.

Daniel's glasses caught the light from the cottage. 'Excuse me, big guy,' said Jon. Daniel stood unmoving in front of Jon's driver door, fists on his hips, chin lowered. Combatant.

'Not until you say sorry to Isobel,' Daniel said firmly.

'Daniel, it's okay,' called Isobel. 'Come over here, have a drink with us.' She wanted Daniel away from Jon Hildred, too.

Daniel pushed Jon the way Sam Roberts had, only more softly. 'No. We are not mean to girls. We look after them.'

Jon shouldered past him. 'Move out of my way, blockhead.'

'That's it,' snarled Sophie. She grabbed a rock the size of her fist and marched towards them.

'Sophie!'

'I will do kung fu on you now,' warned Daniel. He grabbed Jon's sleeve.

'Get off me,' growled Jon.

Sophie got within hurling distance and sent her stone straight through Jon's windscreen.

'Sophie, what are you doing? Daniel! Stop it!'

Jon shoved him again, harder this time. Daniel called out.

Isobel didn't even see her. She heard Ben and Arthur call the warning, but Petal gave none. She swept in low from the trees, slipping straight between Isobel and Sophie like black water. Jon didn't stand a chance.

98

'You still haven't touched your pastry.'

Sarah looked at the breakfast basket Cleo had tenderly prepared for them. 'Neither have you.'

They were both more than happy to keep out of the way of passing eyes for a while, and breakfast on Wednesdays seemed even more essential to their friendship now than it ever had. Cleo looked about them at the secret beach. She hadn't been to Mooner's Cove for years.

They both sipped from their flask cups and watched the wind whip up the surf. 'Why haven't we ever taken breakfast here before, Cle?'

'Because it's nearly an hour's hike, a squeeze through a hillside and it's bloody freezing. I have wet sand in my coffee.'

Hurricane Louis was drawing his dying breaths somewhere over the Atlantic. The Village tribes had delighted at three solid days of competition-standard surf. There was something hypnotic about watching them out there, tormenting the ocean. Even Harry had been out this week. Cleo had sent up two prayers. The first, that Harry was remembering how happy and full his life was; the second, that he didn't get crushed against the rocks before he'd sat all his GCSEs.

'It's also very beautiful, Cle.'

Cleo nodded to herself. 'It really is. Sam and I used to come out here skinny dipping.' Many moons ago. She'd done a lot of thinking since the open-mic night. She could pick any year in the last twenty-five, all the highs and lows of life, and there had been only one constant. One fixed mark. *Sam.* That she'd even compared him to Jon Hildred made her skin itch. She *hated* that man. For Evie. For Sarah. But most of all, for making Cleo like *his* version of her own little girl. 'I really am sorry, Sarah.'

'Cleo, please don't. It's done with. Evie's okay, and she wants to put it all behind her, that's the main thing.'

Cleo had been thinking about this too. It was the main thing, wasn't it? Or did she and Sam have a duty to report Jon? For the young girls who might go after Evie, or perhaps the ones who had gone before.

'Cle?'

'Hmm?'

'Evie does still want to put it behind her, doesn't she? Because if that's changed, you know I'll speak to the police, offer them what little I know.'

And there was Sarah too. Were they cheating her out of a revenge blow? The gossips had already started, listing all the ways Sarah must've been lacking to lose an essentially great guy like Jon Hildred.

'Evie doesn't want to go through any sort of hideous *formal* channel. We both know how some of those girls are treated,

Sar, they'll tear her apart once they know she made up the trolling.'

Sarah breathed deep and steady. 'You're sure? He's being discharged from hospital soon. He won't hang around.'

'Discharged? That's a shame.' Sarah had already outlined Jon's injuries for her. If Arthur's dog had just aimed a bit higher, it would have been Jon's grotty little groin area the surgeons would have had to repair. As it was, Petal had left Jon Hildred with an upper-leg reminder, every time he dropped his shorts, of what happens when girls bite back. 'They'd better not put that dog down.'

'Jon won't press it. He won't press anything while he thinks I have the other phone. He knows I'm usually rubbish at getting the recycling out on time. It was bad luck really, that I slung it out with Max's broken toys. So long as Jon thinks I still have it, he'll be desperate to jump ship.'

'Like a rat?'

'Like a big rat. So now's the time if you want to get anyone else involved, Cleo. Before he disappears.'

Jon couldn't disappear. Not really. The world was becoming a smaller place. You only had to own something with a microchip and you were on the map. Cleo had thought about changing the stores to an internet café once. Coast could go live! The thought made her shudder now.

'No. We've spoken about it and we don't. But thank you, Sarah. You've been incredible, given everything. Are you sure you and the boys are okay? Really?'

'I know you think I'm putting a brave face on. But honestly, we're good. Max was the concern, but now Elodie's said Godzilla II can live in his bedroom for good, I think the rest of us could keel over tomorrow and he wouldn't notice until he was hungry.'

'I still can't believe Juliette allowed a lizard called Godzilla II in her house.'

'She didn't, she let a bearded dragon called Rachmaninoff in there. Godzilla II is his political name.'

Cleo blew over her sandy coffee. She'd been checking back to the lone figure further down on the beach since they'd got there. At first she'd thought she was watching a cautious girlfriend, anxiously spectating the surf. But the wind had just blown her hood back and Cleo recognised the Chloe sunglasses that had made her sick with envy at the school fair.

Sarah was studying the same distant profile. 'Is that Juliette?'

Cleo looked back out to the grey horizon. Sarah was picking over her words before serving them. 'I know what he did to Harry was horrendous, Cle. But it must be horrendous for her, too.'

'How could they not have known, Sarah? How could Karl and Juliette have been so blindsided? He'd been doing it to people for over a *year*.'

Sarah was looking back out to the ocean. She wouldn't say it. She didn't need to, Cleo was already thinking it anyway. None of them had known what their children were getting up to.

'I don't think anyone was more shell-shocked than Karl and Juliette, Cleo.'

'I know.' Sarah was right. But if parents could fall out indefinitely over nit outbreaks, wasn't it reasonable to feel like this? Knowing your own child had been driven to a suicide attempt by someone else's?

The police had seized Karl's computer equipment after his arrest. He'd given it willingly. He had no idea what was to come, of course. Milo had built himself quite the portfolio. He'd harassed a gay policeman, a couple of teachers, even Fallenbay's own Paralympian. And those were just for fun. Milo's bread and butter had been blackmailing a selection of pupils at the high school, but one of those kid's parents was a lot sharper than Sam and Cleo had been, they'd had the police on it weeks ago.

'Two others . . . tried to . . . do what Harry did.' Cleo cleared her throat. 'Sorry, it still catches me off-guard.'

'It's okay, Cleo.'

'No it's not. Harry could've died, Sarah. I could've lost my son.'

They let the quiet sit down with them awhile. Cleo held her cup to her face and watched Juliette in the distance over the rim. Disliking Juliette had always come so naturally, now she was losing sight of the rage she'd thought would carry her through. Cleo hadn't lost Harry. Harry would bounce back, she was sure. He would get back to regular surfing and basketball and arguing with his sister. But Milo? Milo would never bounce back from what he'd done. Take Hobo Bob, one spiteful rumour started by his ex-wife and that was it, doomed to scour bins for food. Milo would never go back to school here. He'd never get a nice girlfriend here, be welcomed into another family here. And the courts hadn't even dealt with him yet. Cleo hadn't lost a son. Juliette had.

She picked a few things from the basket and got to her feet.

Milo wouldn't be surfing anytime soon. Juliette wasn't anxiously watching anyone. She'd come to Mooner's to hide. From that perfect life Cleo had so lusted after.

'Where are you going?'

'To see a mother about a hot flask.'

99

August

'Are we all set? Bucket? Spade? Mermaid's tail?' Ella's head bobbed up and down beneath her sunhat. 'Rightio, I'll go get Sam to box us up a few of those apple cakes while you guys finish your milkshakes. Soph?' Isobel jabbed a finger at her. 'You're buying the next box of cakes.'

Sophie was going back to school. She would be a poor student come September, getting her to buy a round was a now or never scenario.

'Deal,' Sophie managed around a mouthful. 'Grab a few more of the flapjacks, too. They're so good.'

Isobel reached the counter. 'Hey, Sam, we need loading up with treats for the beach.'

'No problem, Robert here will take your order.'

'Hi Robert.'

'Hello again, Miss.' Isobel tried to place his face. 'What would you like?'

Isobel glanced at her family gathering themselves, then back to Cleo's cake display.

'Better take two of everything please, Robert.'

Sam nodded at the sign behind them. *Welcome to Coast. DISCONNECT YOUR DEVICES. Thank you.* 'We've had to hire. Cleo hit a central artery when she banned internet and gadgets from the place. Digital detox, she calls it. We're ahead of the game, the tourists love it.'

'Who knew people still liked conversation so much?' smiled Isobel. *And views*. That beautiful broad view of the horizon.

'Thought I'd seize the chance to hire in a bloke, even up the keel, didn't I, Bob? Sorry, *Robert*.'

Robert smiled a thank-you. 'How is working with Cleo, Sam?' grinned Isobel.

'Harder graft than building houses, but I'm glad I jacked it all in to be picked on by my lovely lady every day. I'd complain she keeps slipping off for brunch with her pals over there, but it gives my ears a break' he winked. Isobel had already waved to Sarah and Cleo, sitting in the corner with Juliette. Maybe she would've gone over but the conversation playing out had seen their frothy coffees sit unnoticed on the table.

Isobel wasn't the only one to notice the birth of a new alliance. The three women at the next table were glancing that way too. *She's lost so much weight, though, Olivia. It's the stress. I heard Juliette's on the brink of a breakdown, just waiting for Milo's next victim to come forward.*

Isobel tuned them out, stealing another look for Ben through the harbourside window.

'Robert here's taken over your place, Isobel. Curlew Cottage. Did Ben say? Arthur's given up the holiday-let game, says Petal is a lawsuit waiting to happen.'

'He did mention it.'

Ben said Arthur had found a decent chap to help out around the place. Bed and board in exchange for the chores his arthritis couldn't manage, and company Petal could rub along with. Curlew Cottage was no longer available, Ben had pointed out, so Isobel would just have to use his place when she visited Fallenbay from now on. It was only small, cosy, but it had excellent views of the ocean. Isobel had enjoyed those views every weekend for the last month.

'Petal likes me,' said Sam's new apprentice. 'Or she wouldn't have led me back all the way to Arthur's house. I only went looking in those woods for a mushroom supper, somehow found myself a home and work.' Robert shook his head and smiled. 'Lucky for me they're more intuitive than people.'

Isobel studied his face. Hobo Bob was a different man, with just a shave and an opportunity. She'd never spoken to him before, he'd held back near the woods that night while Ben and Arthur had prised Petal off Jon's thigh. Arthur had taken Hobo Bob inside for a hot drink after the ambulance had left and the police had taken everyone's statements.

A kid had thrown a stone, maybe from the woods, no one had seen. There were always teenagers hanging around in Arthur's woods. Jon's car window had smashed. Petal had spooked. Who knew why animals, or people, behaved the way they sometimes did.

Ben hadn't pressed her, but Isobel had told him the whole sorry story watching the sun melt into the Atlantic one night. It was a lot to take in. She'd left Jon out of it, for Evie's sake. But there was still enough there to scare any normal person away. Ben had listened, Isobel trying to size up whether she thought he would look for the footage or not. He'd shrugged it off with, *If you can do all that balancing on a chopping board, we should get you into training for next year's Boardmasters.*

And in Ben's unruffledness the video had suddenly become smaller. Less than it had been.

As promised, he'd dragged her out on to the ocean, stirring instincts she'd thought long lost in her old life, back in those precious, less-careful chalet-girl days. Her surfing game was really coming on.

'There you go, Miss.' Robert passed Isobel a box of cakes. She was as guilty as the next person for accepting rumour as truth.

'Thank you, Robert. I hope you enjoy Curlew Cottage.'

'Come *on*, Nanny and Grandad! We're going to the beach to meet Aunty Isobelly-button's new boyfriend!' Ella was pulling Sophie to her feet. Isobel's mum swung around from the window and smiled brightly while she fiddled with her necklace, her dad gleefully pocketing spare packets of sugar left over from his tea. There had been a nervous excitement from both of them on the way down here; Isobel couldn't decide if it was all about Ben, or their first family trip to the seaside since Isobel and Sophie were still in matching roller boots.

Someone touched her elbow. 'Isobel?'

Milo's mother had lost weight, the gossips were right. Her eyes were larger than Isobel remembered. Less sure. 'I don't think I've introduced myself before. I'm Juliette. I'm . . .'

'I know,' smiled Isobel. She shook the hand Juliette was tentatively offering.

Juliette checked over her shoulder. Cleo and Sarah were pretending, unconvincingly, not to watch from their table. Nobody had wanted Milo to be the monster. Not Cleo, whose son had been caught out by Milo's game. Not Sarah, who'd missed Milo ever since he'd last played in her garden sprinklers. And not Juliette, who loved Milo most.

Isobel had caught the whispers, the inexhaustible theories of the locals. Milo was a troubled young boy. Or he was evil. Or struggling with his own sexuality. Or stifled by over-achieving parents. Or spoilt. Or rebelling. Or just mucking about. Or the victim of a dangerously digital era. Or . . . he was just a kid, who didn't think of the consequences.

Juliette set her chin against her chest and took a deep breath. 'My son . . . he . . .' She cleared her throat. 'I've seen some of the things . . . on his computer . . .'

Juliette stalled. Isobel's heart was galloping. She'd heard it all from the school mothers at the next table. Juliette was playing a waiting game. While the police contacted all those people Milo had persecuted, asking if they wanted to press charges.

'Your hair. You're brunette again.' Juliette had seen. She knew. And she must be terrified, asking herself this very second why it was that Isobel, a woman on her little boy's online hitlist had come to be in his hometown, just when the police were unpicking his online behaviour.

Juliette tried again, her voice barely above a whisper. 'If you need anything, Karl and I . . . we won't obstruct you in any way—'

'I'm just here on holiday, Juliette.'

Juliette swayed. 'Holiday?'

'Just a holiday. To spend time with family . . . and new friends. Nothing more.'

'Juliette!' Cleo was pointing down at the lunch Sam was laying out for them. Sophie had stopped scoffing flapjacks, pretending like the table of school mothers that she wasn't also hypothesising about the basis of Juliette and Isobel's conversation.

'Your lunch is ready, Juliette. Tell the girls I'll catch up with them later.'

Juliette nodded. 'Will you be here for long?' Isobel didn't blame her for asking.

Ben stepped up on to the terrace. For the first time he looked nervous. Soph pointed him out to their mum.

'I'm not sure.'

Juliette's chin wobbled. 'Sarah and Cleo said you were a nice girl, Isobel. Decent. Perhaps we could all have lunch together one day.'

'I'd like that, Juliette.'

100

September

'Thanks for coming with me, girls. I've been having visions of swerving to miss a squirrel or something, four hundred fifty-pound notes fluttering across the dual carriageway.'

Sarah expertly parallel parked the Volvo alongside a row of unloved terraces. Cleo leant over to Isobel in the back seat. 'I think we should just bundle Sarah into a layby and the three of us head to Monaco for a month. Twenty grand . . . that would buy us a lot of cocktails on the beach.'

Juliette pushed her glasses through her hair. She still looked gaunt, the way Isobel would expect any mother to look if their child had just been placed on the sex offenders' register. But she was trying. Trying to face her new life as best she could. 'Thanks again for asking me along, Sarah. I needed to get out of Fallenbay. Are you sure it's number seventeen? I didn't see her go in.'

Cleo pulled herself forwards by Juliette's headrest. 'I think I saw her go up those steps. There was definitely a woman walking a girl up there when we drove around the corner. She must've taken a short-cut through the park.'

They all looked through the car windows at the block of flats across the street. Isobel stretched her legs as best she could beside Cleo and Juliette's handbags. They'd been driving for three hours, and following a woman and her child about town for another two.

'This is what the electoral register says.' Isobel had become an oracle on online data. All the places a person's names and addresses might turn up.

'I don't think the people around here are voters. Can't you contact her on Facebook instead, Sarah?'

Sarah glanced over from the driver's seat. 'That sounded very snobby, Cleo.'

'Sorry. My new handbag's gone straight to my head. I can't believe you were going to chuck a Fendi, Juliette.'

Sarah got back to scoping the flats. 'She's not on Facebook. She's not anywhere.'

They were all thinking it. *Very wise.*

Juliette opened her door. 'Come on, let's go do something good.'

Cleo reached for Sarah's shoulder. 'It's a lot of money, Sarah. I know you're only giving her half of it now, but how do you know she won't just go and . . . spend it all on drugs?'

'We've been stalking her all day, Cle. She works hard, drops her daughter at school in impeccable uniform, she wouldn't let her go in until she'd kissed her like a mazillion times.'

Juliette smiled. *Mazillion* was one of Elodie's words. Isobel had heard her using it at Sarah's house.

'But what if she's with some deadbeat?'

Juliette ducked back into the car. 'The electoral register says she's never lived with anyone since the young mothers' unit. She grows runner beans on that little balconette, Cleo.'

'Yes, I did spot the beans. I spotted the little girl too. Did anyone else see?' They'd all seen. Jonathan Hildred's genes weren't as weak as his moral compass. Cleo's expression hardened. 'Why do you think she didn't tell the police? She had living proof of what he was getting up to. That little girl was conceived while her mother was still in school.'

Sarah still had her hands braced on the steering wheel.

'She was expelled. Disowned by her parents. Ignored in court,' said Isobel. 'Maybe she didn't have any more fight left in her.' Poor kid. Twenty grand seemed paltry now.

Sarah unclicked her belt. 'I don't know what she'll do with the money. I just know I don't want to spend it, and that little girl deserves at least some support from her father. Even if he doesn't know he's providing it.'

Cleo opened her door. 'Alright, alright. Come on then, Robin Hoods. You know, if you wanted a financial cause to support, Sarah, Evie's eyebrows are back and bigger than ever. They're going to cost me a bloody *fortune* in kohl.'

ACKNOWLEDGMENTS

Four books on, that I'm able to call writing stories 'my job' is beyond all hopes I held for myself. Here are some of the many people I'm grateful to for the opportunities and experiences that keep finding me…

HarperCollins, I'm so proud to be published by you. Thank you for asking which direction I'd like to take my writing in, and then letting me loose in this new landscape. Special mention to my editor Anna Baggaley for patiently battling through hideously engorged word counts before gently suggesting where this story needed to shed a few stubborn pounds.

To Maddy and the team at The Madeleine Milburn Literary, TV & Film Agency, thank you guys for being in my corner. A bit like Mickey on Rocky I, II and III, but better-looking and not at all shouty.

A very special thank you to Sophie Hedley and Jonathan Hildred (who despite their namesakes in this book are thoroughly good eggs) for bidding to 'appear' in this novel and for giving so generously to an excellent cause in CLIC Sargent's 'Get In Character' charity auction. Rather sportingly you were both open to appearing as colourful characters… hope I've delivered. On that note, Real Life Sophie Hedley – thanks for hanging on for this book, and for being so much more affable than the other Sophie. Phew! And Real Life Jon Hildred – don't get any ideas about letting your behavioural standards slip in any way after reading this book. I've met your lovely wife, I doubt she'd stand for it.

To my family, who I owe more thanks than anyone. This last year, the world changed and somehow we've hung on tight. We're luckier than we know, despite the days it aches beyond words.

And finally.

To Mena. Our gentle-hearted girl. This book gave me somewhere to be when thinking about you was too painful. If you hadn't have been so brave, none of us would've been able to function, let alone write stories of other families in crisis. For being so tough, so beautiful, and for being my little sister – thank you. I miss you. I love you.

ONE PLACE. MANY STORIES

Bold, innovative and
empowering publishing.

FOLLOW US ON:

@HQStories